A ROOKIE MISTAKE

LAURA CARTER

Boldwood

First published in Great Britain in 2025 by Boldwood Books Ltd.

Copyright © Laura Carter, 2025

Cover Design by Rachel Lawston

Cover Images: Rachel Lawston

The moral right of Laura Carter to be identified as the author of this work has been asserted in accordance with the Copyright, Designs and Patents Act 1988.

A CIP catalogue record for this book is available from the British Library.

Paperback ISBN 978-1-83678-776-1

Large Print ISBN 978-1-83678-777-8

Hardback ISBN 978-1-83678-775-4

Trade Paperback ISBN 978-1-80656-020-2

Ebook ISBN 978-1-83678-778-5

Kindle ISBN 978-1-83678-779-2

Audio CD ISBN 978-1-83678-770-9

MP3 CD ISBN 978-1-83678-771-6

Digital audio download ISBN 978-1-83678-774-7

This book is printed on certified sustainable paper. Boldwood Books is dedicated to putting sustainability at the heart of our business. For more information please visit https://www.boldwoodbooks.com/about-us/sustainability/

Boldwood Books Ltd, 23 Bowerdean Street, London, SW6 3TN

www.boldwoodbooks.com

To everyone who powers through in the face of adversity – you're incredible, but it's okay to ask for help.

1

JANUARY

Sas
Wild Card Weekend

The Alamo Stadium is sold out and the atmosphere is electric. It's the final quarter and there are twenty-nine seconds left in the game. The San Antonio Bears are trailing by four and they're on their third down, eight yards out from the end zone.

I'm sitting with my dad, Harris, in the padded seats behind the Bears players and staff on the sideline. Strictly speaking, we're here in a professional capacity, but we would have got tickets to one of the Wild Card Weekend games anyway; we just happen to be here for the Bears versus the Pittsburgh Pythons.

We're a sports family.

As the offense takes position at the line of scrimmage, Dad puts a hand on my knee in a silent plea for me to stop bouncing my legs. I can't help it. I'm invested and I'm rooting for the Bears.

The ref signals start of play and the center snaps the ball to the Bears' quarterback, Tommy Thieriot. There's a load of jostling. The defense does *not* want Tommy to get this pass off.

The offense can't get free, and the game clock is counting down. Tommy's searching for the pass and as soon as I see our client, wide receiver Colton

Quinn, break free, I rise from my seat. Hands locked together, I bite down on my knuckle as Quinn blazes into the end zone.

The ball seems to travel a yard a minute in Quinn's direction. The Pythons' cornerback closes in but it doesn't stop Quinn from catching the ball and getting his feet down on the turf.

Colton's teammates swarm him as my dad grabs me by the shoulders of my Bears hoodie and shakes me as fiercely as the yell of delight that comes from the bottom of his lungs.

It's a good thing the stadium roof is open tonight, otherwise the roar of the Texas home crowd would have blown the top right off.

* * *

It's a while after the game, once the celebrations have subsided, that Dad and I make our way through the tunnels toward the home dressing room. We're stopped a couple times by other sports agents Dad knows. He's been in the business almost three decades, since injury put an end to his own pro-football career before it really got started.

Coach Roy is stepping into the corridor from the dressing room and spots us. 'How're y'all doing?'

'How are *we* doing?' Dad asks. 'You just got through to the divisional play-offs, Glen. How're *you* feeling?'

'Like we've got three games to go,' he says, referring to the Big Game in February.

'I hear that,' Dad tells him.

'Congratulations, Glen,' I tell him, moving in for a hug and pretending like his stress-sweaty back doesn't bother me at all.

We're here as friends – more accurately, best friend and goddaughter – so naturally, we have a few minutes of spilling the tea before Glen says, 'I'm fixin' to go to dinner with Millie. Join us?'

Millie being Glen's wife, my godmother.

'We'd love to but we're flying back to New York tonight,' Dad says. 'Next time.'

'You know it.'

But we're not only here to tell a friend he did a great job. So, as Glen leaves us, Dad calls, 'And Glen, I'll be in touch about Quinn's contract extension. Better get your wallet open.'

'We'll talk,' Glen tells him, still walking away.

Dad turns to me and winks. We both know Colton Quinn's rookie contract will be extended and we know he deserves a salary increase. 'Let's speak to the guys.'

As we enter the dressing room, it's clear the players are pumped. Deservedly so. A voice I recognize well calls out, 'Lady present!'

I know it's Tanner Pace before he scoops me up from behind and spins me around. 'Firecracker! It's been a beat.'

Pace has been on the agency's books since he was drafted to the pros twelve years ago. Dad negotiated his rookie contract, and he's stuck with him ever since. At thirty-three, he's one of the highest-paid tight ends in the league.

'Put me down, caveman,' I tell him and congratulate him on the win when he does. Looking up, obviously, because even though I'm taller than average, Pace is a bearded giant.

'They finally let you out of the library, huh?' he asks, folding thick arms across his sweaty jersey. He hasn't showered yet.

'Yup. No more studying and no more internships. I'm a fully-fledged associate at the agency now.'

'Nice work.' He offers me his fist, which I meet with my own.

'You guys crushed it out there,' I tell him. 'That catch you made on the fifteen-yard line at the end of the second quarter changed the game.'

'All right, all right, don't blow too much smoke up his ass.' Max, another of the agency's clients, comes over.

It seems unlikely but we have three players on the roster for the Bears. Pace, Max and Quinn. The latter being the only man of the trio I haven't yet met in person.

'Colton, my man. Get over here,' Dad calls, waving over all six feet four inches of bare-chested, tanned and chiseled split end. I'm both thankful for and devastated that there's a towel wrapped around his waist.

For a *nano*second, I want to follow the drips of water running between two firm pecs and more abs than my mind can compute right down under—

Dad shakes Quinn's hand, commends him, then says, 'This is my daughter, Kansas.'

I thrust out a hand before Dad has a chance to undermine me profession-ally any more. 'I'm Sas.' I give Dad the side-eye treatment. I don't want him to refer to me as his daughter and I certainly don't want to be introduced by my full name. Not when I was named after the place I was conceived. That's a story that never needs to be heard.

Colton's eyes narrow as he appraises me. He looks at me the way most players look at a woman they don't realize has been around pro-sportsmen all her life: as if he's waiting for me to fangirl. Fall at his feet and beg him to screw me.

The truth is, Colton is talented. Really talented. His stats say he's the fastest player in the league. His trophies say he was the best rookie in his first year of the pros. His college accolades tell me it's a wonder he even bothered to stick it four years to finish his course, when he could have been drafted after three.

The guy's impressive, undoubtedly. And, yeah, okay, he's hot. Objectively so. Disarmingly so. What tall, broad, athletic man with shower-wet and kind of intentionally messed-up, tousled dark hair isn't?

But when it comes to the footballer aura that renders women stupid, I'm immune. I'm like a gynecologist to a vagina. Completely desensitized – that teensy blip just now aside.

I've been burned enough times by falling for the sports guys in college. There wasn't one special guy I dated, it was all of them. They're in it for a good time, not monogamy.

I look him directly in his searching dark eyes and tell him, 'Though I am his daughter, I'm also an associate at the agency. I'll be supporting Harris with your contract negotiations and endorsement deals going forward.'

The immediate shift-change in the way he's scrutinizing me tells me I was dead on with my initial assessment.

But whether Colton Quinn is a fuck boy or not doesn't concern me, so long as he's playing like he did tonight.

I do, though, suddenly wish that I was wearing one of my work suits and a pair of don't-mess-with-me heels, rather than my Bears hoodie and jeans. Maybe I need to work on my first impression, too.

COLTON QUINN LOSES POSSESSION AND COSTS BEARS A PLACE IN THE CHAMPIONSHIP PLAYOFF ROUND

JANUARY 17
WRITTEN BY STEPHEN JACKSON

After helping the San Antonio Bears turn around their dire start to the season, Colton Quinn literally threw it all away.

COLTON QUINN FINED BY LEAGUE IN DIVISIONAL PLAYOFF GAME FOR WEARING UNSANCTIONED ARMBAND

JANUARY 20
WRITTEN BY ROBERT RAY

To add insult to injury, after fumbling the biggest catch of his career in the divisional championship playoff game, Colton Quinn has been fined for wearing a black armband over his Bears jersey on Sunday. Quinn has refused to comment on the meaning of the band.

BEARS CHEERLEADER KICKED OFF SQUAD FOR FRATERNIZING WITH PLAYER

FEBRUARY 27
WRITTEN BY LEONIE RIVERS

Bears cheerleader Molly Smith has had her contract with the squad terminated after breaking the no fraternization clause. Though not confirmed, the player is rumored to be Colton Quinn, wide receiver for the Bears.

SAN ANTONIO WIDE RECEIVER COLTON QUINN IN PUNCH UP WITH ST LOUIS QUARTERBACK

MARCH 5
WRITTEN BY STEPHEN JACKSON

Fans are asking, what's happening with Colton Quinn? The notoriously private wide receiver, who was awarded Rookie of the Year in his first pro-season, has gone completely off the rails. His latest in a string of unprofessional antics is an off-field assault on St Louis quarterback, Auston Rogers.

2

MARCH

Sas

Off-Season Negotiations

Texas is warming up as spring arrives. Dad and I swung by our hotel right after the long drive from Austin airport to ditch our overnight bags and heavy jackets – they'd been necessary when we got on the plane in New York.

My room is on the eighth floor, with a panoramic view of both San Antonio city and the river walk. Down below, people are lunching or taking coffee under the shade of multicolored parasols, fending off the afternoon sun as they caffeinate. Speaking of which, I'd like to caffeinate myself. We had a disgustingly early start to catch a red-eye south.

Our executive car is waiting for us at the main entrance and a white shirt, cream pants kind of concierge opens the rear doors of the Chevy for Dad and me to slip inside. Before I do, I pause to inhale the strong scent of...?

'Grape soda?' the concierge asks me as I sniff the air.

'Yes, actually.'

He points to several trees with purple blooms nearby. 'It's the smell of the Mountain Laurels in bloom,' he tells me.

Being from the city, the scents I'm used to vary from the unbearable and indistinct street stench to smells of scrumptious foods from the boundless choice of eateries. This scent is one I only get when I spritz myself with perfume.

Dad reminds the driver that we're headed to the state-of-the-art training facility of the San Antonio Bears. Then he tells me, 'You let me do the talking with Monte. You're here to observe and learn.'

He tugs the cuffs of his shirt so they're exposed beneath his suit jacket by the same amount on each wrist, which means he misses me casting my gaze to the heavens and asking whoever is up there to give me strength.

'This isn't my first rodeo, Dad.'

He glances my way now. 'You're in your first year at the agency, Kansas. You're a rookie.'

'I've interned at the agency every summer for the last six years.'

'Interning isn't the same as turning pro.'

'Fine. Then I've been around you, *learning*, for twenty-five years.'

He gives a short laugh. 'You were negotiating sports contracts when you were in diapers?'

Not far off. With one pro-hockey-playing brother and one on the cusp of being drafted, I've been around contract speak both at home and in formal training.

'The point is, I'm here to help. I know the industry and I'm an attorney now. I understand how to negotiate contracts. If I didn't, I wouldn't be here.'

'Sas, you're here because you've been chewing my ear off about getting out in the wild since I took Patrick to lunch with Jason Evans.'

Jason Evans is a veteran running back for the New York Ravens. Patrick is an asshat at the agency. He's two years more qualified than me, wears his pants too tight and his black hair greased like he's stepped right out of the fifties. More importantly, his head is so far up my dad's ass that it's impossible to tell which pair of legs belongs to which man.

The worst part is, Patrick's slime and slippery actually works. Most of the senior agents – including Dad, co-founder and most senior agent left in the business – take Patrick along to big meetings. And boy does Patrick like to tell me about it.

So, yes, I pushed to be brought on this trip to Texas, but it also makes solid business sense. I've known Pace and Max since I was a teenager. I've been rooting for them for years. They've been to our house for dinner. We've played touch rugby together – *not* a euphemism – every off-season. I've kicked their butts at ice hockey multiple times and given them a damn good run for their money on a golf course, too. They're as much family friends as they are clients these days.

Colton Quinn will become another member of the gang soon enough. And it's Colton who is the primary reason for our trip. With one year left on his four-year rookie contract, it's time to open negotiations for an extension. We're in the short window permitted by the league for agents to broker deals each year.

And I'm pretty sure the reason Dad is being crabbier than usual is because he knows this might not go well.

'Regardless of why you brought me along, you and I both know that I can add value,' I tell him. 'I've known Glen forever and Monte for, what, five years now, since he took over the GM role? They like me. I can be good cop. Or bad cop. The Jekyll to your Hyde. Mike Ross to your Harvey Specter.'

Dad sighs. 'Like I said, let me do the talking.'

'You got it, Harvey.'

That even gets a chuckle from the driver, forcing me to turn my smirk to the window. I see a sign for the Bears' training facility as we pull off the highway.

* * *

'That's barely more money per year than under his existing contract,' Dad says, calm and collected, whereas *I* have wedged my hands between my crossed legs to stop me from throwing up my arms in outrage.

We're sitting in leather chairs around Monte's desk, which isn't fancy at all. He's pushed his three screens to one side, in order that he can see Dad and me sitting opposite.

Coach Roy is standing, sort of hovering uncomfortably, hands in his pockets. Behind him is a whiteboard full of cards with players' stats on them. Each card has been positioned with the players to leave gaps where the team is lacking quality and might need to make acquisitions.

Colton Quinn's card is up there as split end.

I've seen my dad in these kinds of meetings before and his tone is always the same, no matter the money on offer. Me? I'd want to let the GM know that my guy deserves an increase. Colton is a starting receiver. He has been since his predecessor got injured two games into Colton's rookie season and never made it back to his position.

'He didn't end the season well,' Monte says matter of factly.

Monte's background is mathematics. He's a number cruncher, as opposed to an ex-scout or player. Dad's always said that's what makes him difficult to negotiate with. He's all about...

'There's a salary cap to consider, Harris, and we're weeks away from the draft.'

Dad and I both know there are ways around the salary cap when a general manager really wants to keep a player.

'That's hardly a consideration, Monte, and you know it. One fumbled catch doesn't ruin a player. Quinn was on fire last season. His stats speak for themselves.'

Monte shrugs and I have to squeeze my thighs harder to keep my hands in place. I don't even know Colton, but I do know that the marginal increase in salary that's currently on offer is an insult.

'The offer's the offer,' Monte says, either truly impassive or really good at faking it. 'It's more than a dropped catch. Since I was brought in, I've been trying to clean up the Bears' reputation.' He holds up a hand, four fingers spread wide. Then he bends one and says, 'The worst game of his professional career in the divisional play-offs.' He bends another finger. 'Fined by the league for a uniform violation.'

'Everyone gets fined by the league for a uniform violation at some point,' I say, unable to help myself and receiving a death stare from Dad.

Monte drops another finger, this time looking at me as he says, 'Fraternizing with a member of the cheer squad and losing the girl her spot. Not a great look for any man in this day and age.'

I'll concede that. Though... 'Arguably, it's the cheer squad rules that are a load of—'

'Kansas,' Dad warns.

I'm shaking my head as Monte bends another finger and says, 'Saving the best until last. He put Auston Rogers in the hospital.'

'He got five stitches in his cheek. That's nothing for a pro-baller,' I counter, though I do agree, off-field violence is a bad look for anyone, especially when...

'With no apology or explanation.' Monte's composure is waning.

Oops, I think I got to him. *Sorry, not sorry.*

He speaks to Dad now as he says, 'How can we put a spin on anything if the kid won't tell us why he went Rocky Balboa?'

Dad nods. 'It's not been his finest off-season, I agree. But we all know Quinn isn't a loose cannon. He's one of the most level kids I know. All this is out of character.'

Monte rises from his seat. 'The problem, Harris, is that I have no promise it'll stop. What if this is it? My starting receiver might be a bust come September. So that's my final offer. Put it to him.'

Dad rises, much taller and broader than Monte. He holds out his hand, closing the meeting. 'I'll put it to him, but you know I can't advise him to take it. You want to keep Quinn, Monte. Any offense will be lucky to have him, and with this offer, I'll recommend he waits to be a free agent next year.'

If this negotiation window closes and we don't make a deal, Colton will have to wait until this time next year to renegotiate with the Bears or look for another club.

Monte shakes Dad's hand. 'Then that will tell me how much he wants to be a Bear.'

'I'll show you out,' Glen says, walking Dad and me into the empty corridor.

When it's just two old friends and a godchild, my heels loud against the wood and echoing in the emptiness, the training field similarly deserted through the wall of windows, Dad finally speaks.

'Come on, Glen, you know Quinn's worth more than this. I don't even want to put the figures to him.'

We reach the elevators and stop, Glen pressing the button to call our ride.

'My hands are tied, Harris.' He shrugs, genuinely remorseful, I think. 'I've got confidence in his ball skills. I've watched him since his freshman year at college. The difficulty is, I don't know where his head's at right now. He's never been a talker but now he's shut like a clam.'

I physically recoil at the imagery as a ping announces the arrival of the elevator.

Dad and I step inside and turn back to face Glen. 'You and I both know that this game is 15 percent physical and 85 percent mental, Harris. Put together his antics on and off the field and he's making it hard for me to defend him. I don't need any more guys drawing the negative attention of the league when I've got show-boaters like Daniels and Kubiak racking up fines like chips in a casino.'

'He's off-sided the media, I'll give you that,' Dad concedes. 'But the league doesn't care about one fine. As for on-field, he's had a blip, nothing more.'

Glen shrugs again. 'Monte's a stickler, you know that.'

'He'll lose out if Quinn walks next year,' Dad says. 'I'll let you know his decision.'

'All right now.' Glen reaches inside the doors and presses the button for the ground floor, then steps out. 'Y'all have a good day. When this business is over, you still need to come to Millie and me for dinner.'

3

MARCH

Colton
Zero Shits Given

I know the update about my contract extension isn't great. I thought as much when my agent told me he'd handle the first meeting with Coach Roy and our GM. When it's great news, they get the player in the room to share it.

My doubts were confirmed when Harris called me and told me he was taking me for steak.

After tossing the keys for my Maserati to the hotel valet, I'm welcomed by name and escorted through San Antonio's most notable luxury hotel to the rooftop. The place is a renovation of an old brewhouse, done by some fancy architect. It has Mexican Talavera patterned tiling on the floors. The old brewhouse metal tanks, pink mortar and masonry have been retained, and there's a heavy dose of southern Texas everywhere. From countless statues of longhorns, and ornaments of lone stars, to the smell of pecan pie wafting out of the lobby café. Pie that I know is damn good.

The hotel's an oasis in the Savannah, or tranquility in the city. It's also one of few places where I don't get asked for autographs. Not because people don't recognize me – it's hard to miss a guy my size – but because it's the kind of place where people respect privacy.

None of this is the reason I suggested the hotel for my late lunch with Harris today.

The sole reason I come here *ever* is for the Tomahawk steak. It's the best in Bexar County.

Scratch that. It's the best in Texas State. And I should know. I'm homegrown.

As soon as the elevator doors open, I'm assaulted by the smell of grilled beef and I'm literally salivating. I'm ravenous, despite the feeling of trepidation I have coming into this meeting. I'm always ravenous. I'm not one of those guys whose mood affects his appetite. My appetite is fierce and relentless. My temperament – off the field – is generally the exact opposite.

The sun is welcome and beating down on the rustic wood tables around the rooftop. It feels like spring has arrived, which usually means months of feeling discombobulated and eager to get back to playing ball. This year, it might be necessary respite. My body feels as heavy as it ever has.

Slipping on my shades from the pocket of my shirt, I follow a member of restaurant staff to a table at the front of the rooftop, noticing Harris sitting beneath a sunshade. He's wearing slacks and a tailored shirt, smarter than me in jeans, boots and a casual shirt, cuffs rolled up my forearms.

Sitting next to him is... an undeniably attractive woman. Legs crossed, shades on as she looks out to the view across the city and the river walk. Waves of caramel blonde hair fall across her shoulder and her finger draws lazy circles around the rim of a wine glass, condensed from the chilled beverage inside.

It takes me a beat to realize that the woman wearing a tailored dress – sophisticated in a way that's as hot as it is intimidating – is Harris's daughter, Sas.

'Colton. Good to see you,' Harris says, standing when he clocks me and offering his hand, which I shake.

'You too.' I speak to him, but I can't help my attention drifting to Sas.

When she stands, I try not to gawp, but even monks would have to appreciate the shape of this woman. I'm not helped by the smell of absolute seduction that engulfs me as she leans forward to offer me the same greeting Harris did.

'Colton,' she says in a manner that makes me wonder if she can sense my inappropriate ogling from behind my Tom Fords.

'Sas.' I don't know why I give her the same severe response. Calling her raise, maybe.

We chat about the mundane, intermittently being interrupted by wait staff until we've ordered – me the Tomahawk and a beer – Harris and Sas, lobster thermidor.

In a bid to get the sack over with before it ruins my steak, I'm the one to move us on to, 'How did the meeting with Monte and Coach go?'

I'm braced for it, so when Harris tells me, 'Not as well as I'd have liked,' I don't react. Internally, I'm prepared for it, so externally, there's nothing to show.

That's the mantra of my life. Be prepared. Plan one step ahead. Control the controllables. In this case, that's my reaction to the news that the Bears *will* extend my contract, *but* their offer is one that tells me they aren't impressed.

'It's not great,' Harris tells me. 'It's well below average for wide receivers in the league and Monte is telling me that's the final offer.'

I take off my shades and rest back in my seat, taking a drink as I consider the state of play. It's not as if I don't earn good money. Insane money. But the offer is a reflection of how the GM and Head Coach see me. A below-par offer says they aren't confident in either my game or my attitude. Both, probably, given the last couple months.

'What are my options?' I ask Harris.

Sas inhales, as if she wants to speak, but Harris gets in first. I'm still watching her, noticing the way she looks like she wants to tackle her dad for shooting her down as he talks.

'We can play around with the figures. Take a hit on the first year and try to build in an increase based on performance.'

'Which requires you to actually perform,' Sas cuts in, abruptly dragging my attention back to her. *Did she just mouth off at me?*

I'm shocked enough to make my lips twitch in disbelief.

'Or we turn it down,' Harris continues. 'Threaten to walk as a free agent next year.'

'The risk being, they might let you walk. And, or, they think you're not committed to the Bears,' Sas adds.

I can tell Harris is boring holes in her from behind his tinted lenses and, despite the severity of the discussion, I'm silently amused by their dynamic. Kind of reminds me of my mama and my sister.

And that thought alone thrusts me into a darker place than any discussion about money. It reminds me what's important.

'Accept it,' I tell them. 'I'm a Bear. This is my hometown. I don't want to play anywhere else.'

Harris's eyebrows rise, then pinch together, then his mouth sort of falls slack. He clears his throat, swallows and fiddles with his fork. I couldn't easily write his reaction but in summary, it's a negative one. Kind of like watching someone react to a bear taking a dump in their mouth.

Yet Sas, she leans into her seat, taking her glass of wine with her and watching me over the rim as she sips. It's her response that somehow knocks me off balance.

I'm a little fixated, honestly. Thrown, I guess, by her unexpected calmness – that's not what I've seen of her in our two brief encounters – and from the way she's triaging me. I hope my polarized lenses are thicker than hers because I can't tear my gaze away, despite listening to Harris speak.

'I don't advise it, Colton,' he says. 'The annual average isn't good enough for someone of your pedigree. You've had an interesting off-season, granted, but it doesn't change the fact that you're an outstanding player and you'll only get better with experience at pro-level.'

Naturally, that's nice to hear, but I can't help feeling like he's just being an agent, beefing up my ego with the end goal of lining both our pockets. The game has changed for me. I need to stay in San Antonio, or at least the state. This isn't just about playing for the team I dreamt of as a kid anymore.

I guess he can tell I'm not convinced by his authenticity because he goes on. 'It's not a good look for your future. It lowers your value and the value of wide receivers in the league. Not to mention the negative message it sends to sponsors, and the damage to endorsement earnings potential.'

I fight back a scoff. I've done enough damage in that respect recently.

Sas still hasn't shifted in her seat or changed her expression. She's as restrained as I've seen her. It's intriguing. So much so, I haven't responded to Harris.

My agent does what people tend to do in a silent void: he fills it. 'I know this is a blow and it was unexpected, but I really think you should sleep on it, Colton.'

Finally, she reacts. I watch the sides of her eyes crease at the word 'unexpected'.

'What do you think?' I find myself asking her.

She places her glass down on the table and angles her body my way, elbow resting on the back of her chair, fingers entwined. Damn she's confident.

'It's not *that* unexpected, surely?' she says.

I cock my head to one side – *tell me more.*

'I mean, the fine from the league, who gives a—?' She rolls a shoulder in place of an expletive. 'Having a hand in a woman losing her job? Not a great look for endorsements of certain brands but, hey, it takes two to tango. She knew she had a no fraternization clause. As for fighting off the pitch, maybe you'll explain that away one day but sure, it's not the image the team wants to project.'

I cough, choking on her brazenness. She's laying me out here.

'Kansas,' Harris warns.

I hold up a hand and shake my head – *no, please, let your junior associate continue to flay your client to his face.*

She shrugs. *Shrugs.* Zero shits given. 'The fact is, what people care about is whether you're playing well. Ballers can get away with almost anything short of criminal, so long as they're playing well.' She leans forward now, elbows on the table, bracing to really stick it to me and, for some unfathomable reason, I'm here for it.

'It wasn't just the dropped catch in the divisional play-offs.' Now I'm leaning forward, meeting her posture across the table. 'You started out last season as if your entire body was doused in Stickum. Everything stuck to you. You ended it like Teflon.'

'Teflon?' I ask, one eyebrow raised behind my shades.

She nods. 'Teflon. Nothing stuck.'

That would actually be funny, if it wasn't aimed at me and my game.

'You got lucky in the game against the Raiders. If you hadn't caught that Hail Mary, I think you would have ended the game in negative yardage.'

'But I did catch it,' I say, giving the impression of self-assurance, while she's cutting me down at the knees.

'And against the Steelers. With a positive spin, the defense was man-marking you. Through a different lens, you weren't making good runs.'

All right, I'll bite. 'What are you, a broadcaster for ESPN?'

One side of her plump lips curves up. It's as sexy as it is passive-aggressive and in this moment, I decide I don't like this woman.

As we stare at each other, a plate with a large, delectable-smelling steak is placed between us.

'For what it's worth,' Sas says, unfolding her napkin and placing it across her lap, 'I think you're a hell of a player. I agree with Dad; you shouldn't accept the offer on the table.' She forks a chunk out of her lobster and I smell the sickly-sweet combination of buttery garlic from her dish. 'I think something got in your head toward the end of the season.'

Her words are like a dagger striking me and I jut out my chin as I eye her. My reaction gives away my hand. It's the confirmation she's looking for and that I don't want to give. My private life is just that. Private. Compartmentalized from the game.

'If we turn it down, maybe they take the bait and raise the offer. We all know the salary caps can be messed with. But don't be surprised if they wait, that's all I'm saying.'

I watch her wrap her mouth around the food on her fork and think how in the good Lord's name can that move wake up everything below my waistline. Until she speaks again. 'If you can get your head straight and start next season the way we all know you can play, you'll get an even better offer than if they improve on their position sooner.'

'And there's always the very real possibility that another team gives you a real good offer,' Harris adds, lifting vegetables out of a side dish and onto his plate.

'I'm staying with the Bears,' I tell him. Then I do what I do best: I bury the conversation. Box it somewhere in my brain for a later date, because I just want to enjoy my meat.

* * *

Harris picks up the tab, which I feel bad about. Yeah, I'm his client and he's more than capable of picking up a lunch tab, but I'm always mindful of how much I earn. And how much I eat.

We ride down to the ground floor in the elevator together and that sweet perfume Sas is wearing envelopes me again. Only now, I'm thinking a delicate flower is enormously misplaced on this woman. She's brutal. Kind of prickly. And no shrinking violet.

Harris and I shake hands while we wait for the valet to bring around my car. Sas goes in for an overfamiliar hug and kiss on the cheek – evidently one of those people who fire out their piece and move on with no grudges held. She's a big personality but she feels neat as a wrapped parcel in my arms.

Harris and Sas are staying in a hotel nearby and walking back. 'Let us know,' Harris says as I head to my ride. 'Trust me,' he calls after me.

The thing is, it's hard to have complete trust in him, despite all the great things he's done for me, when I don't feel like he's being 100 percent truthful. Ironically, I would trust the woman to his side, who seems to have no time for bull. Probably makes her a terrible businesswoman, given most sports guys have a chip of arrogance on their shoulders and don't like being told they're underperforming by anyone. But I respect her honesty. I've got no time for crap either.

Inside my car, I check my phone and wind down the windows, which means I hear as Sas tells her dad, 'Don't look at me like that. He asked for my opinion.'

I lean closer to the open window as they're walking behind. 'You have a lot to learn, Kansas.'

'About lying?'

'About tact. Agency is about building relationships and making connections, not off-siding your clients the first time you meet them.'

'It's the second time I've met him and all I did was lay out the home truths exactly as he knows them himself.'

'Yeah, well if you and your home truths lose me a client, I'll freeze your salary for the next decade.'

'Dad, this isn't like the time I dressed as a slut for Halloween and you cut my allowance.'

I chuckle. Probably the first time I've laughed in months.

'No, it isn't. This is real life and real work, Kansas. You aren't a student anymore.'

'I'll make you a deal,' she teases.

'No,' Harris replies bluntly.

'Hear me out. If Colton drops you or if he takes the deal on the table, I'll quit and leave you to your old-hat ways. I'll go get a job as an attorney in a corporate law firm and give you the satisfaction of seeing your only daughter miserable day in, day out. But if he changes his mind and holds out for a better deal, you give me my own client.'

'No chance. You're a rookie.'

I can see them now in my wing mirror and though their tones sound unfriendly, their body language is something I recognize in my own family – me and my old man, me and my sister in times gone by: it's playful.

'What if I win the client myself?'

Harris stops and turns to her. After a pause, he holds out his hand. 'Deal. If Colton stays with us, and gets a great deal, *and* you bring in a client, you can keep him. Or her.'

Sas straightens her back. 'Just you wait.'

That chick is feisty. Like, tell me a girl's from the city without telling me the girl's from the city.

4

AUGUST

Sas

Pre-Season Training Camp

Unlike other teams in the league that go on a road trip for it, the Bears' pre-season training camp takes place in their own state-of-the-art training facility right here in San Antonio. So I'm back at the scene of the disaster for the first time since Dad and I convinced Colton Quinn to walk away from an offer to extend his contract. Of course, we hoped the Bears would improve their offer, rather than risk free agency at the end of this season, but it seems they're playing hard ball with us. The window has closed and the League's rules dictate that no one can even whisper about a deal now until next spring.

To add real insult to injury, we managed to negotiate hefty extensions for both Max and Pace.

It's no surprise then that when the guys break from running drills for a drink, Pace makes a beeline for me, where I'm standing at the edge of the training field, right by the entrance to the indoor gym.

'Hey, girlie!' he says, leaning across the low barrier between us for a hug. I'm acutely aware of phones being raised around us – most likely filming Pace but there's always potential for a girlfriend story to land on social media. That, coupled with the fact his new-season, state-flag-colors jersey is absolutely saturated with sweat, makes me pass up the PDA.

'How about a fist pump?' I offer instead.

Chuckling, he takes off his glove and we knock knuckles. 'Not in for a sweaty guy, firecracker?'

'Not one that's like an older brother to me.' I lean into him and whisper, 'That's incest, even in Texas.'

His deep, throaty laughter makes me smile.

'Anyway, I'm here in a business capacity.'

'I can see that,' he says. And I guess it is obvious, since I'm the only person at the ground wearing tailored clothing: a button-down vest and wide-legged cream pants to match. 'Oh, that's right, you're a swish attorney now. Should I call you ma'am?'

'If I said yes, would you?'

He scrunches his nose. 'Nah, I prefer firecracker.'

The Bears' center makes his way over to the crowd nearby and offers to sign autographs, which distracts fans around Pace and me long enough that I can ask... 'Speaking of firecrackers. How's Colton doing?'

He shrugs. 'Hell would I know?'

'Because you're the offensive captain and he's one of your guys.'

He adjusts his giant frame so that we're both watching the squad – now making their way back onto the field to continue training. I don't know how they're doing it in the late-morning heat. It must be ninety degrees out and it's as humid as a thermal bath.

He leans on the barrier, one ankle crossed over the other, helmet in hand. 'Quinn's not really anyone's guy. He only speaks one language and that's football. Three years in and I'm not sure any of us really *know* him. He keeps his cards close to his chest.'

That doesn't at all surprise me. 'He looks in good shape,' I respond, not wanting to be negative about my client. Whether he's a talker or not, he's the agency's guy. He's Dad's guy. And that means I've got his back, too.

Truthfully, *good shape* is the understatement of the millennium. A woman could grill a steak on that behind, it's so hot. Objectively speaking.

'Just about the only one of us that hasn't developed a dad bod in the off-season.' As I scoff, Pace slaps the barrier between us. 'I've gotta get back to it. We should do dinner while you're down here.'

'Sounds good.'

I watch him head back over to the group, the offensive coordinator shooting daggers at him as he saunters, rather than jogs, back to his team. As I do, I register two eyes that I know to be wide and cocoa brown fixed on me. I'm no stranger to fit men in football uniform but some wear it, some wear it well, and Colton Quinn—

I clear my throat, glancing around me because I would like to state for the record that I do not, I *will* not, mix business with pleasure. Because I'm a serious attorney. A professional. One day, I'll be a fully-fledged sports agent.

Moreover... because my dad would kill me for crossing that hard line.

When I look back to Colton, he pulls on his helmet and falls into step running the route tree.

It's early in the pre-season but watching him, I feel like his physical shape is looking a lot better than his game. I'm not a pro-baller but I've been around the sport enough to know that he isn't moving well. He looks quick and he's handling the ball fine. But the way he's moving is off.

I watched Colton play college ball a few times. I saw him play in his rookie year in the pros, before he'd even settled into his groove, and watching him was like reading poetry. The way his hands and feet, his whole body, move in rhythm. He started last season that way.

But the man I'm watching now looks sort of clunky. Not at all like he's in a contract extension year and seeking a great offer to stay with the Bears. Not as if my shot at getting my own client hangs in the balance.

The guys are loosely running plays. Between Tommy Thieriot throwing a bullet pass to Colton and him catching it then turning to run, something happens. Trent Daniels, cornerback, gets in Colton's face. He's pushing Colton's chest, knocking him backward, off balance but still standing. And Colton... doesn't react.

As the crowd's interest is piqued and phones are held up to record the incident, I take the risky move of climbing over the barrier in cream pants, making my way closer to the team.

Even yards away, it's not clear what's happening, other than Trent is throwing a heap of expletives Colton's way and none of his teammates are doing anything to stop it.

'Glen!' I shout, nearing Coach Roy, who does a double take. Then, realizing that yes, I have jumped the barrier and I *am* inviting myself into his practice, he scowls at me. 'Aren't you going to wade in?' I ask my godfather.

'Aren't *you* supposed to be standing back there in the crowd?' he retorts, clipboard in hand. Then he checks his watch and shouts to the players. 'That's time. Break for lunch.'

The players file past, Colton taking off his helmet and falling into step. Trent is still in his face being a dick as they walk.

Why isn't Colton pushing back? Why is he taking this shit?

Well, he's my guy and I'll have his back if no one else will. It's like watching *Mean Girls* meets *The Waterboy*. I'm grateful for my wedge heels as I stride onto the turf toward Colton and Trent. Only now does Colton raise his eyes from his feet, meeting mine.

Still stomping in his direction, I open my mouth to give Trent a piece of my mind when one big arm hooks around my waist and spins me off the field, away from the team.

'Easy, firecracker,' Pace tells me, setting me down. 'This isn't your party.'

'But Quinn *is* my client, which means I'm invited.'

Colton has now followed us over to the tarmac. 'What are you doing?' he asks calmly, as if he didn't just have that showdown.

'What you should be doing for yourself. Are you going to just take that from him?'

Pace glances between us, then heads inside the facility. When we're alone, I suddenly feel... exposed under Colton's scrutiny. He drags a hand through his thick, wet hair and I can't help thinking, *I bet that feels nice.* It's the kind of length a woman could take hold of.

I watch a trickle of sweat roll from his temple, down his sculpted face, and I'm unexpectedly thrust into a moment of pure indulgence, imagining his hot body hovering above mine.

Thank God he speaks, at last, and puts paid to my moment of semi-lucidity. 'I'm not in for drawing any more negative attention to myself and I'm for sure not in for fighting with my teammates.'

Nope, actually, that slow southern drawl is *not* helping pull my mind back from the gutter at all. Smooth and deep. Panty-melting, some might say.

Not me.

Strictly. No. Athletes. No clients.

'You've got to ask yourself sometimes what it is that people want,' he says, brown eyes piercing mine in a way that makes me thankful for the protection of my Gucci shades. I'm fast learning that UV protection a million may be necessary around this man. 'If they want fire, don't give them fuel.'

Basically, Ironman just erupted in his face and Colton is cool as ice, while it was red rag to a bull for me. And I'm wondering which version of him is real. This one. So laid back he's practically horizontal. Or...

'This from the guy who put Auston Rogers in hospital?'

Now, his composure wanes. 'That was different.' He stalks off in the direction of the facility, calling back without turning to me, 'And no, I don't want to talk about it. You do more than enough talking for us both.'

His words ought to be hostile but his tone isn't at all. It's nonchalant. I totter after him, as best I can on the spongy surface. 'Do you intend to be passive-aggressive or is that a little side dish with the main of silent and brooding?'

He shakes his head but keeps moving, long strides forcing me to jog in my wedges. It's not a good look for me. I feel more *Legally Blonde* than *Jerry Maguire*.

'What do you even mean by I talk enough for us both?' I tug on his arm when I reach him, planting myself as firmly as I can and forcing him to turn and face me.

Forcing may be a stretch. I know for a fact that Colton is almost two-hundred pounds, so I'm relying on him choosing to stop and speak with me.

Thankfully, or unfortunately, he does. Sort of. He stands at full height, broad frame even wider in his protective pads, and crosses his arms over his torso. His indigo helmet that's probably the size of two of my heads held in one hand.

'I'm on your side, Colton. I might not be your lead agent but I am working for you. And if I see another player giving you shit, I'm going to call him out on it. I'd call anyone out who tries to put someone else down to make themselves feel good. I hate bullies.'

It's barely a reaction but I see the corners of his eyes crease ever so slightly. 'What if it was justified?'

'It's never justified to try to publicly bring someone down. He can speak to you privately if he has a problem.'

'I appreciate your attempt at world peace and all, but this is football. Guys shit talk all the time.'

'Not to their own teammates and not unless it has a purpose, like firing them up in a game.'

He sighs and unfolds his arms. 'Fine. But honestly, he's only saying what the other guys are thinking.'

'And what's that?' I look up to him. He's a neck-breaker. A long, decadently sculpted neck-breaker.

'That the team's reputation was just getting back on track and everything I did in the off-season is threatening that, which means it's threatening their endorsement deals.'

'What a load of crap,' I say, planting a hand on my hip. 'So long as they're playing, and playing well, sponsors will be interested.'

I can tell he doesn't agree and despite this guy who, by definition of being a pro-athlete, is confident, arrogant even, I see something in his expression that's much less certain.

'You really are a firecracker, aren't you?'

I smile at his use of Pace's nickname for me. 'Don't let Harris hear you say that. I've promised to be strait-laced and professional down here.'

The sound he makes is barely a laugh but the way it twists his lips at one side suits him. 'You've made a great start.'

He stares at me, and I stare back at him, neither of us speaking, which is completely unlike me and, honestly, a little awkward. Why *are* we staring at each other?

'I'm gonna grab lunch,' he tells me, gesturing with his helmet in the direction his teammates went.

I step aside but as he's walking away, I say, 'You didn't answer me. What do you mean, I talk enough for us both?'

He turns, watching me as he moves backward. 'You talked me into turning down Monte's offer.' He holds his hands out from his sides. 'Now, I have no offer, and half the roster is pissed with me.'

Again, his tone is unemotional, while his words should be angry. Maybe it's this combination that's discombobulated me into silence. What I should say is, *All you've got to do is play well this season and the money will follow.*

But to get everyone back onside and silence his critics, he needs to rebuild his off-field reputation, too. It's a showman's league, after all.

'I was going to ask if you want to come to dinner with me,' I say, walking toward him when he stops. 'I feel as if we got off on the wrong foot, and you're my client, so let me treat you to another caveman-style meal and enjoy the sight of you sucking marrow from cow bones.'

Unexpectedly, he gives me the kind of lazy, lopsided smirk that's befitting of his southern drawl. 'Caveman?'

I shrug, too busy dining out on his slightly better humor, which happens to be disastrously fine on him, to think of a cunning retort.

Too quickly, it's gone. 'I can't,' he tells me. 'I've got a long drive after practice tonight.'

'Oh. Okay.' I guess I should have planned ahead. Dad would have done.

'Maybe you could use the time to figure out how to get me a new contract.'

I truly can't tell if that's a joke or a bitterly resentful remark.

He turns away.

'Train hard and get in the end zone, that's how,' I call after him.

I watch him shake his head with the distinct feeling that I'm not doing well at precisely the thing Dad sent me down here to do, build a relationship with Colton Quinn.

5

AUGUST

Colton
The Ranch

When I step inside the training facility, Pace has hung back from the rest of the squad, clearly waiting for me. He's leaning against the Bears-logo-emblazoned wall, still kitted up.

'The first time she went in to bat for me, she was fifteen,' he tells me, and I know he's talking about Sas. 'She squared up to Quinnen Jones after a game.'

'Quinnen Jones, Cincinnati's old defensive tackle?'

He chuckles. 'All three hundred ten pounds of 'im.'

Pace is a loudmouth and showy, but he's a hell of a baller, so it's his prerogative. I know plenty guys like him. On the right day, catch me in the right mood, I might laugh at his show-pony banter. But generally, Pace isn't my kind of guy, off the field.

So, the fact we're having a one-on-one that isn't directly about football feels out of the ordinary.

I shake my head. 'She's crazy.'

'She can be,' he says. 'But she's smart, competitive and fiercely loyal. So do yourself a favor and get to know her. Trust her.' Striding down the empty corridor in the direction of the showers, he calls, 'Her old man's the same, just a tamer version. You're one of the pack now.'

I'm left thinking, *If Pace likes her, I can guarantee she's not my kind of woman.*

* * *

The beauty of training camp being so close to home for most of the squad is that we don't have to stay over for the duration. The family guys filter off first after we're done in the gym and a few of the single guys are meeting up to have a *Grand Theft Auto* session.

I turn down the invitation because, like I told Sas, I've somewhere to be.

We're ten days into training camp and for the tenth day straight, I climb into my Range Rover to take the two-hour drive northwest. When my phone pairs and my country music plays through the speakers, I shut it down. I've heard enough noise today. Instead, I enjoy the silence as my surroundings switch from traffic to the rugged gold and green landscape of the country, until eventually, I turn up the driveway to Sunshine Ranch.

Sunshine Ranch has been developed in recent years – we've acquired a herd of longhorns, increased our horse count to ten, and built out some of the activity zones, like the pool and the campfires.

But it'll always be home. It will always be the place I grew up with my parents, Annie and our fosters from time to time. The heat of the day is still fierce despite the sun falling west from the sky.

At the sound of my wheels on the gravel, Bear, Mama's collie, comes rushing up to me, tail wagging.

'Hey boy,' I say, crouching to hold out my fist and receiving a paw tap in return. 'Where is everyone, huh?'

Bear barks in the direction of the porch and I swing my legs, one then the other, over the white picket fence, Bear hot on my heels. Sure enough, my old man is resting in a rocking chair out front of the house. Eyes closed, foot tapping as he swings forward and back, mug of coffee in hand.

'How're y'all doin', Pa?'

He opens his eyes and stills his chair. 'Same as when you left this mornin', son. Your mama's already in bed for the night and your sister's nauseous.'

'She's watching reruns of *Gilmore Girls*, again?' I ask, coming to sit in a matching chair to his, Bear lying down on the wood deck between us.

'I'm starting to think this mornin' sickness is just an excuse to get hold of the TV controller.'

I scoff. 'Maybe keep that to yourself.'

We fall quiet – one of the things I love most about my daddy – and slip into a synchronized rocking rhythm, looking out across the corral where four of our ten horses are grazing, daring now to come out of the cool shade of their stalls to stretch their legs.

One of them is mine. Tall and broad, with a thick mane and white socks that come up to his knees. He's an old boy now, twelve years old. Mama said on the day we got him, he reminded her of me, and she called him Luke. My middle name. An intentionally biblical name.

Up until this off-season, I forgot how much I love to ride. Taking off into the surrounding land on Luke feels like getting away from the noise of the world.

I forgot because I wasn't here. I was caught up in the mayhem. In football.

So much so, I missed things much bigger that were happening here at home, where I should've been.

'How was training?' Daddy asks, like he does every day, but the enthusiasm he had for the game, *my* game, feels like it's waning of late. Understandable. More than.

Some things, it turns out, are bigger than sports.

'Great,' I lie. 'Looking forward to the first pre-season game this weekend.' I honestly don't know whether I'll start. Given how I ended last season and how I've been dragging my heels at camp. Sometimes, a starting vet will get a fitness run out in a pre-season game but there's no need to see how they play; they've already proven themselves. In my case, Coach might want to put me in with the rookies and back-up squad, to fight for a spot on the active roster.

My starting position for the Bears is far from a given this year. The way contract negotiations (or lack of) have gone so far, I know I'm not flavor of the month.

Daddy nods. 'D'you want coffee?'

'I'm good.'

He leans down to the porch, picks up his dusty old cowboy hat and sets it on his head as he stands. 'Then let's get to work.'

That's what we do – mucking out the stalls in the barn, feeding the hens, and making a start on building a fence for a new corral.

Against mine, my sister's and Daddy's better judgment, Mama wants to keep Sunshine Ranch running as normal once the summer break is through.

Normal means offering long weekends of respite to families caring for sick kids. To give their siblings a break, their parents support and, sometimes, to bring the sick kids themselves a chance to be free of their routine for a few days.

If that's what Mama wants, that's what I'll give her.

6

AUGUST

Sas

A Fake Proposition

'I'm so happy this worked out,' I tell Blake.

I know her from back home in New York. We met in college, when I was a junior and she was a senior. We both turned up to the same Halloween party dressed as a slutty corpse bride and have been forever bound by the experience.

We also have our agencies in common. Blake decided to go straight into the business of talent agency and I opted to go to law school first. So, Blake's been at this for a few years now and has her own clients.

'Me too,' she says, accepting a leatherbound menu from a waiter. We've chosen a Tex-Mex in San Antonio. 'Imagine if we'd actually tried to be in the same city at the same time. It'd never have worked out.'

'So true.' Though this restaurant doesn't feel so much city, more country ranch. There are saddles for horseback riding hanging from the ceiling. Longhorns decorate pretty much every available surface. Cowboy hats and lassoes are nailed to the walls. And it's a low-light place, which somehow makes it feel more Mex than Tex.

It's not really my vibe. I prefer the slickness of a New York bar, but when in cowboy country...

'I'll take a margarita to start and a burrito bowl for main,' Blake says, barely paying a cursory glance to the menu.

She still looks like the girl from New York – blonde, immaculately styled waves of hair, a long, sleeveless blazer-heels combo, but there's something more *south* about her now. A tan. A slower pace when she speaks. The ease with which she orders a burrito bowl.

I order the same and ask her, 'How's the south treating you?'

She shrugs. 'I miss New York, but life is here now, you know? Work is going well, though I'm on the road a lot to see clients. And Rod is here, so it's where I need to be right now.'

Her boyfriend Rod is a country artist – also on the road a lot – but born and raised in Austin.

'I love that you guys are figuring it all out, what with schedules and busy lives of your own.'

She smiles in a way that shows how into their relationship she is. Then, she flips a switch. 'Can I cut to the chase, Sas? Then we can focus on the tequila?'

I chuckle. There's the city student I know and love.

'I've got a client, Megan Frost.'

'From the teen musical show – what was that, again?' I slap the table, too loudly. 'Oh! *To Be Seventeen.*'

'You got it. Did you ever see it?'

I shake my head. It was a few years late for me. I'd already moved on to my college-drama era, in real life.

'So Megan played, like, an Ariana Grande in *Victoria* type character, right. Or a Vanessa Hudgens in *High School Musical*. All the singing and dancing. Fast forward five years and she's struggling to transition into an adult role. The peppy high school reputation is haunting her.'

I know my confusion is written all over my face, even as our drinks are placed on the table and I sip from the salt-rimmed glass, the sourness hitting me behind my molars.

'I heard that you're in town to see the Bears guys. Oh, shoot, I should have started with congratulations on the role at the agency.' She raises her glass to chink it against mine.

'Go on,' I tell her.

'Well, I was thinking, if you could maybe get Megan some airtime with one of the players, that would really help her rep.'

'How do you mean, exactly?'

Blake holds up one finger as she takes a drink. 'Glad you asked.' She sets down her glass. 'She's got an audition coming up for a new show – kind of *Dallas* meets *Reacher*.'

'That's quite a combo. You have my attention,' I tell her, leaning back into my seat, starting to see where Blake's heading with this.

'The script is great and the cast is even better. It could be a huge adult breakout for Megan.'

'But...?' I raise an eyebrow.

'But the casting director thinks Megan's too much of a sweetheart for the role. She was also a little dubious about her Texan accent. So...' She picks up her cocktail again, wetting her mouth, signature finger in the air again. 'If she could be seen with one of your guys – you know, a real burly-man type – I think it would change perceptions. And if your man could help her out with the accent, that's a bonus. Her nondescript southern with a side of Illinois twang is not going to cut it.'

A short laugh escapes me. 'Are you proposing a fake relationship?'

Blake leans her head to one side, lips pursed. 'Or a real one. Either way.'

'I don't know, Blake. That doesn't feel good to me. I'm all about authenticity and, honestly, I don't know that I have a match for you anyway.'

Blake rolls her eyes the way I've seen her do to any number of uppity sorority girls before. 'This is the entertainment industry, Sas. It happens all the time.'

'Not in sports.'

'What? You don't think footballers are in the entertainment industry?'

'You have a point.' The whole reason they're paid ludicrous sums is because the league makes so much in television and merchandise deals.

'I know.' She leans forward on the table. 'Now, correct me if I'm wrong but I think your agency represents Max Kingsman, Tanner Pace and Colton Quinn, right?'

I nod. 'But... even if I did pay this any credence... Max has an on-off girlfriend. And how old is Megan?'

'Twenty.'

I shake my head. 'Pace is too big a character for a sweet girl and there'd be a question mark over the age gap. It could be too ick.'

Blake holds her hands out as I take a sip of margarita. 'Colton Quinn it is, then.'

I almost choke on my drink. 'Absolutely not going to happen, trust me.'

'Megan's a catch. It wouldn't be a hardship.'

'He's a robot, Blake. He doesn't speak. Never smiles. And, I don't know, there's something—' I stop myself short of sharing too much information about my client. If there's something going on in Colton's personal life right now, as I suspect there is, he's chosen not to disclose it and I need to respect that. 'I truly don't think I could convince him to hang out with someone, let alone fake date them.'

'Wasn't the hot, moody sports guy your forte in college?'

Now I do spurt my drink. 'I learned the same lesson every time. Plus, while objectively aesthetically pleasing, Colton is no longer in the college of brooding jock; he's graduated from it. I've seen happier stone walls.'

Not to mention, I'm fairly certain he can't stand me. For sure, he thinks I talk too much. I mean, by comparison to him, *everyone* talks too much.

'Think about it?' Blake asks, sickly sweetly, with those wide puppy-dog eyes that used to convince me to do just one more shot *every* time in college.

'I'll think about it. But I'm probably seventy-thirty against this as an idea.'

It's unprofessional. Dad would hate it.

But if Megan is America's sweetheart...

And Colton's reputation needs cleaning up...

* * *

'No,' Colton tells me. It's emphatic yet as cool as the way he's leaning back against the door of his Range Rover, Tom Fords over his eyes, all freshly showered after training and smelling—

His heady concoction of pine and spice is not the point here.

Nor is that giant buckle on his belt that's drawing my attention to exactly where his... checked shirt is tucked in.

'That's all you're going to give me?' I counter. 'Just *no*?'

The way the muscle in his chiseled cheeks twitches makes me feel like the kind of girl I always tried not to be in school – the one not smart enough to realize why she's standing in the principal's office and why he's evidently losing his patience with me.

'I don't do lies. I don't do girlfriends.'

Admittedly, I didn't like this idea myself at first. I'm still not entirely convinced by it. But the way he's so damn strait-laced about everything is getting my hackles up.

Knowing it's unprofessional, even as my voice box works and my tongue starts moving around, I tell him, 'So you *are* a typical jock slut.'

He leans his head to one side and clears his throat. Confirmation.

God, I'll bet he has his pick of women.

'D'you speak to all your clients this way?'

Fair point.

I relent, taking a step back from him and a deep breath. 'Sorry, you're right. That's a prejudice from my past and the product of having two hockey-playing brothers. I recognize a fuck boy.'

His mouth opens fleetingly, with shock, I think. Then that lopsided grin – ever so slight – is back and I can't help the buzz it gives me to make the unsmiling man falter.

'Look, I want to help you out here, Sas. For whatever reason, I want you to get your own client.'

I feel my eyes narrow on him.

'Yeah, I heard your deal with your daddy. If I get a better deal and extend my contract, you get a client. Win-win, right? But for one thing, I don't like my personal life being anybody else's business, to the extent I can keep it that way. For another, I have a lot of stuff going—'

He cuts himself short of, I think, giving me some tiny insight to better understand him. The reason Dad sent me down here: to get on his wave-length and make a connection.

But it's gone with the warm breeze that blows my hair into my lip gloss.

Catching me completely off guard, Colton reaches out and runs a finger down the rogue strands, gently moving my hair from my lips. It's a subtle move but one that redirects my train of thought and leaves goosebumps on my skin in its wake.

Na-ah, lady. We are NOT going there.

Brooding is no longer my thing.

I'm a woman now. A grown-up with a real job. Speaking of which...

'Would you just think about it? You could not *lie* but rather withhold the truth. You're a pro at not talking.'

I know he's focused on me from behind those shades. Glaring at me, probably. 'Give me one good reason why I should even consider doing this.'

Though his words would look like they should have bite on paper, that southern drawl and Colton's typically neutral attitude means they sound easy-breezy.

'Fine. Because, news flash, bad boys aren't trending in this day and age. Parents don't want to put the name of the ball player who beats the crap out of people and disrespects women on the back of their kids' shirts.'

He rears at my words, and I think, finally, the message might be getting through. Sometimes, you've got to pull the Band-Aid.

'Monte and Coach Roy are pissed with you because they've been working hard on cleaning up the rep of this team. Your teammates are pissed with you because until the rep of this team *is* cleaned up, they think all your endorsement deals could suffer. To date, you've refused to respond to press criticism of you. Which offsides the media even more. So, unless you come up with some really great explanation as to why you've fucked up over and over again—'

'You literally forget to take a breath when you're talking. Have you noticed that?'

Nothing fazes him. *Nothing.* He's just so damned... sultry and, yeah, brooding, and yeah, I hate myself for finding it hot as hell.

'No, actually, I haven't noticed. And *you* shouldn't be watching my chest so closely.'

I regret the words as soon as they leave my mouth. They sound unethical at best and flirtatious at worst. It's moments like these that I have to stop. I'm a sports agent now – or one in the making. I put this blip down to the months I spent cooped up studying without human interaction and not enough s—

Ahem... No excuses.

The problem is, watching Colton's lips turn into that devilishly sexy smirk is almost worth the faux pas. Even if he is mocking me.

He smiles. The slightest bit of personality on display.

And I really shouldn't be as buzzed about it as I am.

He zaps his car and opens the driver's side door. Hand braced on the door frame, he says, 'What happened to if I play well enough, nothing else will matter?'

His hands are so... big... and I *know* they handle equipment well.

I look from that big paw to his sun-kissed face and tell him, 'The fact Coach is making you play in the first pre-season game with the rookies isn't a good sign, Colton.'

With that, he turns away from me. Right before he pulls his door shut, I hear him say, 'Tell me something I don't know.'

7

AUGUST

Colton
Life Isn't a Game

'What exactly does that mean? In layman's terms?' I ask.

I'm sitting with Annie and my mama and daddy in the lounge at the ranch. It's eerily quiet. Not even the dog is moving. And in the absence of sound, I'm terrified. Because I've asked the question but I already know the answer.

From her spot on the sofa, Mama reaches out and places her hand on my knee. It's unwelcome. I'm barely holding it together inside and her touch could be the thing that tips me over the edge.

I don't want that because I'm here to be strong. For her. For them. The way they always have been for me.

I was given everything I needed as a kid. All the support available. Even with my younger sister and a bunch of foster kids around, Mama always prioritized me. My football.

Now, I need to return the favor because there's nothing bigger in the world to me than the people in this room and I feel as if it's taken a terminal cancer diagnosis for me to see the most pertinent things. *Life isn't a game.*

'It means the cancer is too aggressive, darlin',' Mama responds. 'Conventional treatments aren't working.'

I can't look at her, so I stare at the mug of coffee between my hands. 'Conventional, like there's an unconventional option?'

I feel and hear her intake and release of breath. In my peripheral vision, I catch her looking at Daddy. I'm still too chicken to glance up.

'There's a new trial.' Now, I do look at her, sharply. 'But...' She sighs. 'It's not got a good chance of working on me and... I want to enjoy the time I've got left. I want to be here and present. I want to see my first grandchild born.'

My sister whimpers and I know she's thinking what I am – if Mama is left untreated, there's every chance she won't see Annie's baby born.

'Now, listen, I don't want to make this the news of the town, okay?' Mama says, though I'm listening to her over ringing in my ears. 'I want Sunshine Ranch open as usual come September. I want to throw the best spring party for the kids and their families that we've ever thrown next year. And I want to be allowed my dignity for as long as possible.'

Fuck.

Emptying my lungs, I set my mug down on the big oak coffee table that Mama upcycled herself. Sitting on it is a picture she had framed a couple years ago, of the four of us surrounded by a group of Sunshine Ranch regulars.

The room suddenly feels excruciatingly small. I lean down and kiss Mama on the scalp, letting my lips linger there, against the smell of her citrus shampoo, and tell them all, 'I'm gonna finish chopping the wood.'

That's what I do. I cover my stinging eyes with shades, my head with a cowboy hat, and I head out to the land, slamming an axe into a tree trunk over and over, until my body is aching and there's a stack of logs ready for campfires this season. And I stare at them. Or through them. Regretting every moment I haven't spent with my mama over the years because I've been so obsessed with playing ball.

'Whatcha doin' out here, lumberjack?'

Annie. Her eyes are red and puffy in a way that I can't stand to see. Her baby bump is certainly noticeable these days. It's still wild that my kid sister is having a child of her own.

Training my focus back on the pile of logs, I set down the axe and stick my hands in the pockets of my jeans, suddenly not knowing what to do with them.

'Choppin' wood.'

She scoffs. 'Okay. Good talk. I'll be seein' you, then.'

I chuckle, despite the heaviness of the sound. 'There's not much to say,' I tell her.

She comes to sit on a trunk and pats the space next to her. I take her up on the offer.

'How're you feeling?' I ask.

She nods. 'Nothing I can complain about.'

Nothing compares to what Mama's going through right now.

'How're you feeling?' she asks. It's a loaded question but I choose to ignore it.

'All good.'

'Sure, Colt. All good. Always *all* good.'

I shrug. 'What do you want me to say, Annie?'

That I wish I could do something to help? That I wish I could convince Mama to try a new treatment and that I'd do anything to make it work for her?

'I'd just like you to admit that you're hurting. We all are.'

My nostrils flare with my next inhalation.

Neither one of us speaks for a long minute, until she tells me, 'I felt the baby kick this week.'

I look to her now and smile. 'You got yourself a baller in there, huh?'

'Like his uncle,' Annie says. Then placing her hands on her bump, she adds, 'And his daddy.'

I feel every muscle in my body stiffen. *His daddy, who isn't around.*

'You don't need him, Annie. You've got this.'

She forces a smile that doesn't fully reach her cheeks and rocks into my shoulder. 'I've got you.'

Yeah. She has. And I'm going to be around for this kid where my old friend has chosen not to be.

I'll be around in the state. On the ranch. Nearby. If I'm not training or playing, I'll be here. As much as I ought to have been around to stop her being in this position in the first place.

'I'll be chief sitter while you're finishing up your last year of college.'

'Colton,' she warns.

'You promised me you'd take your time to think about deferring before you quit, Annie.'

I won't let her ruin her future because she got knocked up by the guy I

introduced her to. By the man who's too fucking cowardly to accept respon-
sibility.

* * *

Less than twenty-four hours later, I'm suited up and sitting on the bench for
the first pre-season game of the season. Thankfully, I'm not starting because
my head and my heart aren't in it. It also means Coach Roy might be showing
a little faith in me.

In the fourth quarter, he lets me stretch my legs. I'm not tested, though I
feel slow. Laggy. I don't add anything to the game.

I cling on to the fact that Coach didn't start me with the rookies, but that
alone isn't enough to get everyone back onside. To reset the narrative of my
off-season (in more ways than one) and guarantee I'll be playing for the Bears
in years to come.

At the end of the game, I'm walking through the tunnel when I spot Sas in
the crowd, sporting the new season's Bears jersey and cap, hanging over the
edge to fist pump Max and Pace, who also got nothing more than a run out
today.

So, when I get to her, I reach up and take hold of her hand, encouraging
her to lean into me.

'You win,' I tell her. 'I'll do whatever you need me to do. Set this thing up
with Megan Frost.'

Because I need to stay here.

For my mama.

For my sister.

For the ranch.

And to make sure I'm playing with a team of guys who *want* me on their
side.

Sas pulls back from me, allowing me to see her surprise. Before it melts
into something else. With wide, pink lips, high cheeks and sparkling, dark-
sapphire eyes. Something I like. Something I'd like to disappear into.

But the problem is: I need another distraction like an alcoholic needs one
more glass of whiskey.

8

AUGUST

Sas

How is This Going to Work Exactly?

Colton picked me up from my hotel, so I'm sitting in his Maserati transfixed by the way he handles his steering wheel. One hand, not even gripping the wheel, yet completely in control. Turns out he drives like he's doused in Stickum, too.

I wonder what else he handles—

'Sorry, what was that?' I ask, rattling my head, trying to knock some sensibility back into my treasonous brain.

'I asked, how is this going to work exactly?'

'*This*. This. Right. With Megan?'

He looks at me like *duh*. An arrogant expression but one that's easy to forgive, since we're heading to the Japanese Tea Gardens to meet Blake and Megan. A meet-cute, or first fake date, that Blake and I set up.

I grab my takeout coffee from the center console, now sufficiently lucid to hear a slow southern twang in the voice of the singer coming through the speakers, singing about neon signs, whiskey and taillights – naturally. 'I guess I'll introduce you to Blake and we'll meet Megan, officially. Then you two can walk, talk, eat, whatever.'

He side-eyes me and I notice his jaw tense, the muscle in his cheek tightening in an unfathomably hot way. He still isn't cool with this but we both understand why we're here. It's an arrangement that stands to benefit both Megan and Colton.

'Harris called me last night,' Colton says.

I swallow my coffee. 'Dad? Why?'

He glances my way then focuses back on the road ahead, as I try not to focus on the way his forearms flex where they're exposed by the rolled-back sleeves of his white shirt.

Note to ovulating self: never let Colton Quinn drive you anywhere ever again. Period.

'Under the guise of asking about the pre-season game,' he tells me.

'Guise?'

He nods. 'You told him about this... arrangement, right?'

I did. Once I had, I immediately wished I hadn't. I guess I'm still not sure if this is the right call and I wanted Dad to be a sounding board. By the time I'd given him the rationale, he decided to leave the final judgment to me. Or so I thought.

'He told me I shouldn't feel pressured into it by you.'

Traitor. 'You're a big boy, Colton. I doubt I could pressure you into something you were vehemently against.'

He glances my way again and I try to hide from my expression how pissed I am at Dad for going behind my back. 'I told you to set it up, didn't I?'

He did. It was his change of heart that made me set it up. But I feel bad if I *did* apply pressure. More pressure is the last thing he needs right now.

'Well, that's what I told Harris, too.'

He had my back.

'How did he respond to that?' I ask, feigning disinterest because I *am* interested to know how Dad is portraying me to our clients. As his naïve daughter, or as a professional?

'He told me that if I play well enough, the world will forget the bad shit quickly. Verbatim, he told me it's a risk but that I don't need to lie or lean into anything I'm uncomfortable with.'

I feel my cheeks heat. I don't know if the flush is more embarrassment or rage, but I know my skin is pinkening.

He couldn't keep his nose out, could he? I've always been the daughter, the sibling, who couldn't quite figure things out for myself.

Well, his little dip into my business has had the opposite effect anyway, because Colton is onboard, and me? I'm more determined than ever to prove him wrong.

'Thank you, for telling me,' I say.

He shrugs. 'Like I said, despite what we're about to go set up, I'm a straight-up kind of guy. I want to be level with you.'

Okay, so he's still a hot jock and he's still hugely crabby, but I respect that he told me. It feels a small step closer to us being a team.

This fake relationship is going to work. He'll see.

When he does, things will be better for him, and Dad will owe *me* a client of my own.

We pull into the parking lot of the gardens and I make sure to avert my eyes while Colton uses the heel of his hand to swing us backward into a bay.

I check my phone and see that Blake and Megan are waiting for us inside. 'By a stone arch bridge, overlooking a koi pond, apparently,' I tell Colton.

He nods. 'I know the one.'

I expect him to look nervous – this is a first date, after all – but in true Colton Quinn fashion, he zaps the car locked and heads to the entrance, making me run-walk to keep up with his Avenger-worthy strides.

Something tells me this man does nothing by halves.

He pays our entry – despite my offer – and signs a postcard for the guy on the front desk. If he notices the camera phones that are pointed in his direction, he doesn't show it, though he does glance down to me at one point and asks, 'You okay?'

Because of the cameras? I'm used to it whenever I'm around the agency's clients – and my own brothers for that matter. 'I'm good. You?'

In response, he scoffs and gives me that supercilious smirk of his. 'Yeah, Sas. I'm good.'

Inside the gardens, I'm struck by the scent of perfumed flowers, so overpowering, I pause on the boardwalk to breathe them in. Central Park aside, green spaces aren't plentiful in New York City.

'You all right there, city girl?' Colton asks.

I scowl at him playfully. 'I've seen flowers before.'

'Could've fooled me.'

He's annoying, yet my lips betray me as I follow behind him, amused, through the stunning scenery of the gardens. We wind the boardwalk past lush plants and a sixty-foot waterfall.

And I think to myself, *Blake has done this before. She's picked the perfect setting for a new budding romance to be captured by passers-by.*

I catch up to Colton and as we traverse the path, a young couple comes by, the guy unsubtly holding his phone in a way that's obviously filming. He's so busy recording that he squishes Colton and me against a blossom tree. Or he would, if it weren't for Colton slipping his hand onto my lower back and nudging me ahead of him.

When we've settled back to walking alongside each other, I check his hand isn't alight because, damn, he left fire on my skin, even through my linen dress.

Thankfully, my body that still seems to think it's nineteen is interrupted in its latest burst of hormones by the sight of Blake and Megan standing on the bridge, where they said they'd be and...

'Good God, she's stunning,' I tell Colton, who shoots me a look like, *You know she's right there, don't you?*

'A woman who looks that beautiful deserves to be acknowledged,' I tell him in response.

Megan Frost is all immaculate teeth, full lips, perfect honey-blonde hair, petite frame that dazzles in the mini-skirt and strapless top combo she's wearing.

As we get closer, she only appears more flawless. Precisely contoured. Lips painted faultlessly. Not a freckle or fine line in sight.

Damn my thousand-million freckles and inability to perfect the application of make-up to my much-less-plump-than-Megan's cheekbones.

Don't get me wrong, I'm not the kind of girl who thinks she's wholly unattractive, or that I need to look like a supermodel to get a guy, but *dang*, this girl is next level.

Blake leans in for a kiss on my cheek. She looks suave in a shorts and jacket combo.

'Blake, this is Colton.' They shake hands but his eyes are on Megan. Understandably.

'And this is Megan, you guys.' Blake gestures to the sweet-as-candy actress.

'It's so great to meet you both,' Megan says in an Illinois accent as she throws her arms around me in a way that's too overfamiliar even for me. I'm too busy watching the way her pupils dilate over Colton to notice how they greet each other.

Then, we all fall into deathly silence. So quiet, we can hear the waterfall in the distance and a kid calling out for his mama so far away that we can't see either of them.

I do what I tend to do... I cut the tension with words. 'Well, I was worried this was going to be awkward. I'm thrilled it isn't at all.'

It has the effect I hope for, making us all laugh. Even Colton, who watches me as his amusement turns into a smile, and I'm momentarily mesmerized. Again.

He's really kind of beautiful.

Which is great. Because he and Megan are going to look hot together in the media.

This is going to be perfect. I feel it in my bones.

'All right, then. We'll leave you kids to it,' Blake says. 'Don't do anything we wouldn't do.'

She loops her arm in mine to walk us away, and like a mom dropping her kid to a first date, I glance back over my shoulder to see Colton and Megan talking. She smiles. A magazine-cover-worthy smile. And he smiles, showing teeth almost too faultless for his cowboy get-up.

I pretend to myself that I have no idea why there's a part of me wishing Blake had never put this idea to me.

Later, when the first picture of Megan Frost and Colton Quinn miraculously emerges online, I'll stare it for longer than I can explain, and remind myself that he's my client.

This is all a play to get his teammates and club back onside.

To rewrite his disastrous off-season in the media.

All in a bid to land him a decent contract extension and to win me my own client.

9

AUGUST 2026

Colton
She's nice

'She's nice?' Sas asks, repeating my words when we drive away from the Japanese Tea Gardens, two hours after we arrived. 'That's all you've got for me?'

As we pull onto McAllister Freeway, I ask, 'What do you want me to say?'

'Give me some detail. You're like the worst slumber party guest ever.'

I throw a scowl her way. 'I've never been to a slumber party.'

'Yeah, no kidding.'

I'm not the kind of guy who has an easy disposition. I know I can be uptight. I didn't get to where I am without focus and determination. But I can't help laughing at her. Her petulance, I think, which is made worse by my amusement.

She's pretty when she pouts. Maybe because she's *finally* quiet.

Sadly, it doesn't last. She huffs and puffs and tries to blow my house down like a big bad sassy-ass wolf. 'You spent *two hours* with one of the most attractive women on the planet. Give me something.'

'We went for coffee.'

'Whoa, blew me away with that detail.' She swivels in her seat and pulls her knees onto the chair, her short linen dress – sophisticated yet somehow sexy as hell on her – riding higher up toned legs as she does. 'Did you eat?'

'I ate. She didn't.'

'You paid, though, right?'

I feel my eyebrows knit together. 'I might be a cowboy but I know how to treat a woman.'

'Please, you're a jock slut. But paying for her coffee is a good start.'

'Could you put your legs down?'

She looks affronted but does. 'Worried I'll dirty your OCD clean seats?'

Worried I shouldn't be ogling because she's my agent, or acting in his stead. She's my highly strung associate agent, who can't enjoy quiet for longer than one deep breath. And who would probably kick my ass, or try, for making a move on her.

Also, because I'm now apparently not *not* dating Megan Frost.

As if my life wasn't complicated enough.

'That shimmer will be hell to clean off the leather,' I lie, ignoring how enticing the shimmer on her legs looks.

The truth is, it wasn't awful spending time with Megan. She's easy company, if – dare I say it in light of my present company – a little shy. She's twenty but she seems young compared to, well, the city girl sitting next to me. Who, by contrast, seems sure of herself and confident in a way that's as attractive as it is annoying.

Sure, the fact Megan wore skyscraper pin heels to an outdoor walking activity, and that she nursed a hot water with lemon while I ate the restaurant out of food, *could* have been off-putting. But can I be off-put by a fake date?

Honestly, the best part was that, once we'd broken the ice, she talked about herself the whole time – her singing and acting career. It was kind of interesting, hearing about another industry, and yeah, there were some similarities of being something of a teenage star. Mostly, it was nice to not think about football or all the things impacting my game for a couple hours.

Megan has zero clue about any sports and even less insight into who I am, which was ideal.

'When are you seeing her again?'

'Aren't you the one who should be answering that?'

'Oh my God. Are you a complete rookie when it comes to dating?'

'I told you, I don't date.'

'Right. Just a fuck boy. Fine, I'll arrange something. *If* she's even willing to see you again.'

'She needs this as much as I do, Sas.' I glance her way, expecting to see fight or sarcasm in her expression, but what I see is something entirely different.

Compassion, I think.

Unexplainable empathy.

I don't know what she *thinks* she knows about me but everything my family is going through is going to remain just that – family business. Private.

10

AUGUST

Sas
Stay with Me

I'm scrolling my phone intermittently, with eyes on the squad as they continue to battle it out at pre-season camp to be one of Coach Roy's final fifty-three-man active roster. There's one more pre-season game and one week for Glen to announce the final cut.

As camp draws to a close, the biggest remaining battle is for starting left tackle – the guy who'll protect the quarterback's blindside. The Bears' first pick last year retired and there's a choice of a three-year vet or a new first round draft pick, Mat Krasinski. It should be obvious but as I've just told my dad on a call, Mat Krasinski looks fired up and solid. The question will be, as it is for all rookies, can he make the transition to pro a smooth one?

Ultimately, Tommy Thieriot needs to be comfortable with the guys he's got looking out for him when the season gets underway.

Talking ball with Dad is easy; it's what we've always done. Talk football, hockey, baseball, basketball, even golf, but I end the call feeling irked.

In part, because he's refusing to discuss how I might get my first client if I win our wager – will he help me bring in one of his existing interests? Do I have to go scout myself a college player?

But mostly, because Dad hasn't bought into this set-up between Colton and Megan Frost, and I wish he'd just butt out and let me handle it, because every time we discuss it, I start doubting it myself.

The more I get to know Colton, the more I wonder if he can pull off being inauthentic. He's as strait-laced and genuine as a guy comes, so far as I can tell.

I guess I'm relying on his ability to keep schtum in order to navigate this whole thing.

And it is a thing, *already*. Images and footage of Colton and Megan at the Japanese Tea Gardens last week are everywhere. I swear social reels are going to explode.

It's what we wanted, of course. There's no point being in a fake relationship without an audience. But it's been a big hit, fast.

As I'm scrolling the latest, my phone chimes with a message from my oldest brother, Jax. Yup, our parents had sex in Jacksonville, Florida, as well as Kansas City, and it creeps the hell out of us both that we're named after their places of fornication. Though our youngest brother, TJ, drew the shortest stick. Our parents couldn't figure out if TJ had been made in Tennessee or New Jersey, so they covered both bases and named him TJ. He can't even pretend to be the product of immaculate conception.

Jax is two years my junior, yet boundlessly more successful. We're in contact often, despite him spending a lot of time on the road with his hockey team, the New York Dragons. Pre-season for pro-hockey is about to start, which makes picking up the phone to my brother trickier. I take the opportunity now.

When Jax makes the mistake of asking me, 'How goes tricks, sis?' I unleash my rage about Dad.

'He gave me the whole performance and interference chat,' I tell him.

Jax chuckles down the line. A sound I miss. It feels like I've been stuck in a library for the last couple years and since Jax is a starting player for his team, living out on Long Island instead of still at home with our parents, like me, we've not seen each other to goof around as much as we used to.

'Performance is potential minus interference,' Jax confirms.

'Yup. With the underlying meaning being, what I actually need to be doing here in the deep south is working out what's messing with Colton's head, not adding more interference.'

As much as it's cloak and dagger to the rest of the world, my family knows the truth about Colton and Megan. I don't keep things from them. Even if I tried, they know me too well. We're close. Very. Which is part of the reason we're so competitive. The rest is in our DNA.

'Dad's just trying to stop you making a rookie mistake, sis.'

'How so?'

'Isn't it obvious?'

'Clearly not,' I gripe at what feels like another family member not backing me.

I hear air whooshing around my brother's phone and I'd put money on him being at the rink and skating as he's talking to me. 'This goes one of three ways,' he tells me. 'The best result here is for Quinn and Megan to genuinely hit it off and start dating; meanwhile, his game improves. The next best option is that his game improves and even if they don't start boning in real life, everything ends amicably. In either scenario, positive publicity wins Colton favor with Glen and Monte.'

I search the field in front of me now to pick out Colton, working with the position coach. He looks in better shape than he has done in previous practices. He's moving more fluidly. He looks... hot and sweaty and lean and like a man who could have his pick of any girl he wants, even someone as pretty as Megan Frost. And I'm reminded of his own words to me: *I don't date.*

'Go on then, hit me with the worst-case scenario,' I say into the phone.

But I already know what should have been plain as day to me when Blake first mentioned this faux romance.

'They end badly,' Jax says, sounding as casual as ever. 'His reputation is worse than shit. His game isn't making up for it.' He laughs down the line. This time, I *don't* miss the sound. 'Nah, stuff that. If Quinn doesn't play well, there isn't a good option. Either football fans across the globe say he's distracted and not focused on the game, or they hate him for messing around America's darling *and* for playing like shit.'

I tease my brothers all the time about being the dimmest light bulbs in the box. Smart is *my* thing in our family. Though, on this occasion, I've got to concede, Jax has a point.

The point.

Regardless of anything else I'm trying to help here, Colton has got to play well this season, for everyone's benefit. Potentially, all I've done is add an extra variable to the equation.

'Jax?'

'Yeah.'

'I think I'm going to be hanging around in cowboy country for a while.'

Attorney at law, associate agent, turned... babysitter.

* * *

'Are you sure this is okay, Pace?' I ask, dumping my emergency shopping bags in the entrance hall of his *Cribs*-worthy home as he sets down my suitcase. 'I'm a lot,' I tell him, hands on hips as if the stance will somehow drive my point home. 'I can *be* a lot. I'm messy, I'm loud. And having me stay with you while I'm down here, *indefinitely,* is like bringing your work home with you.'

He drops his car fob onto a sideboard – white, to match every other piece of monochrome furniture I can see. I've never been to Pace's home before but it screams bachelor pad, just as I would have expected.

'Sas, your family's always been there for me, since I was a college kid with a whole load of attitude. Do you know how many times your dad has waded in to save my ass?'

'A few?'

'Something like that,' he says with a smirk. 'Plus, if you're staying here to somehow get Quinn back on track, that's music to my ears, firecracker.'

I haven't told anyone except Blake and my family about Colton's fake viral romance, but I have told Pace that I'm sticking around to track Pace's start to the season, *and* to scout some potential clients of my own while I'm here. Someone has to have faith that I'll be winning my own client by the end of the Colton Quinn Project.

'Come on, I'll show you to the choice of bedrooms,' Pace tells me, leading the way through his palatial space, up a wide staircase lined with signed black and white sports prints, to a long hallway of doors.

This is how I come to be staying at Pace's six-million-dollar suburban home, on the outskirts of San Antonio city, with a personal chef and a pool I fully intend to utilize.

11

AUGUST

Colton
The Active Roster

I wouldn't have said my being named on the active roster was in question, but it's a relief to be there. I don't know, I've never doubted my ability to play ball. *Ever*. It's as natural as breathing to me.

But all this crap around the contract extension brings my loyalty into question and I hate that. I don't want to be playing anywhere else. I'm a Bear, through and through.

I just want to ball. Well. I want to put right the shit that went down in off-season, get the guys back onside.

I'm resting back against the corral fence, watching my sister as she gently plods on her horse at the ranch.

'I'm not going to fall off, Colton; you don't have to stalk me like I'm prey to your hawk eyes,' she says, hat dipped low enough that I don't see her do it but I know she'll be rolling her eyes.

'You're six and a half months pregnant, Annie. You shouldn't even be up there.'

'You're over-protective.'

'If I'd been keeping a better eye on you, you wouldn't be in the situation you're in now.'

I know before she brings her mare to a halt in front of me that my words haven't been well received.

She glares at me, bringing a hand to her bump. 'Ya'll need to stop referring to my baby as a situation.'

'I hate to be the one to break it to you, Annie, but being a single mama when your own mama is...'

She sighs when I don't finish my sentence. Long seconds seem to tick in the otherwise still countryside. 'Saying it out loud won't make it any worse or any more real, Colton.'

I stare back at her. Mama's days are numbered and she's still refusing to try a pioneering treatment. My best friend got my sister pregnant then fucked off out of our lives. Daddy's a train wreck. Every foster kid my parents had a hand in raising is long gone or out of state, and I'm— Lord, I don't know if I'm succeeding at anything right now, which is so far outside my comfort zone, I can't even see the goalpost.

'Have you heard from college about your deferral?'

Annie shakes her head – in exasperation, as opposed to an answer to my question. 'I still don't know about going back.'

'Annie,' I warn.

'Colton,' she responds, mimicking my tone. 'I have no idea what next year will even look like. How am I going to look after the baby and study?'

'I've told you not to worry about that. I'll get you help.' I hate that the implication is, Mama won't be here to support Annie. And when she's gone, Daddy's going to be useless to everyone.

'Would it be so bad if I stayed here? Took care of my baby and carried on Sunshine Ranch?'

She reaches out a hand to me and I lift her down from the horse. She comes to stand next to me, all two and a bit of us looking across the plateau at the falling sun.

'The baby's kicking. Feel.'

She places my hand on her bump and I feel my niece or nephew raising hell inside her. For a moment, everything else fades into nothingness. There's a real human in there.

'Your mama's gonna look after you so good, little one,' I whisper to the baby. Then I look up to Annie, her gentle, caring eyes, and I tell her, 'While she's finishing college.'

'You drive me crazy, d'you know that?'

I'm about to tell her, *Yeah, I do*, when my phone rings.

'Sas.'

'Colton.'

It's become our standard greeting. A stern call and response, of sorts. I don't know why but it makes me grin. Maybe it's the thought of how much I know I'm winding her up as she waits for me to speak, knowing I won't break. Getting a rise out of Sas has become a habit of mine recently.

If she will take it upon herself to babysit me and, worse, move in with my teammate so that he can keep up with my progress, one dropped catch and unsigned contract at a time, then I'll see that as a green light to ruffle her pretty little feathers.

It delights me to hear frustration in her voice. 'I've got you a date,' she grinds.

'With the Devil?'

'You'd deserve that. No, with an angel in the form of a beautiful actress.'

'What are my orders, Coach?'

Now I hear amusement in her voice and, I confess, I sort of enjoy causing that, too. She's got a killer smile. Kind of like if the Grim Reaper was offered up my soul on a silver platter.

'Megan is officially moving down here to get settled in before filming starts on the new series and Blake and I thought it would be cute socials fodder if you collect her from the airport.'

As if I don't have enough on my plate. But I've got to admit, there is a lot of attention coming my way from the two times I've been seen in public with Megan so far – first the Japanese Tea Gardens, then a private breakfast feeding at the zoo – and if I get positive attention, the team gets positive attention, and maybe the ears and check books of sponsors prick up for us all. It's also cool that Megan got the gig on the new show, and I'd like to support her.

'Austin?' I ask. And Sas gives me the details of Megan's flight and arrival time.

When I hang up the phone, Annie has that teasing look I've seen too many times in my life. 'So, you and Megan Frost, huh?'

'Mind your own, Annie.'

'Would this be like your first ever *real* girlfriend?'

I start walking back to the house but Annie is hot on my heels.

'I've told you it's just a publicity stunt.'

'Right, because the football star is highly unlikely to fall for the smokin' hot singer-actress.'

Annie pushes me through the skeeter door and into the kitchen, knowing I can't push back, but we both still when we see Mama, standing in front of the stove.

'I'm making jam for the end-of-summer fair,' she explains.

She's lost so much weight in recent months that her blouse and pants engulf her, but the buzz I get from seeing her up and active, doing something she enjoys, is like a jolt of electricity straight to my heart.

I roll back my shirt sleeves and set my cowboy hat down on the table. 'Give me an instruction.'

Two hours later, Mama is so exhausted that she falls asleep on the sofa, with Annie, my old man and me sitting around her watching TV. I carry her up to bed and when she's settled under the sheets, I hold my lips to her forehead. As I do, I realize that no matter how much time I spend with her in the months to come, it will never be enough to make up for the time I've missed because I've been playing football.

It will never be long enough, period.

12

AUGUST

Sas

Laying Hard Boiled Eggs

Pace's Chevrolet Corvette is unreal. Terrifying and unreal.

He let me choose one of his cars to drive today and once I'd pointed to this one – mostly because it's shiny red – he made me do a test run with him.

Now, I'm on my way to Colton's apartment. Despite leaving thirty minutes sooner than my map app told me I needed to, my extra loop around the freeway has meant I'm late.

Of course, the primary reason I'm here at all is to make sure Colton doesn't forget – accidentally or intentionally – to collect Megan from the airport. Therefore, if he isn't here because he's already set off, great. If he is here, I'm still on time to complete my mission.

I get my answer as soon as I arrive outside his apartment building because he's on the ramp exiting the basement parking lot and *damn,* he suits driving a sports car. Top down, shades in place, dark hair styled like it's been done for the front cover of *GQ*.

We both stop, sweet rides facing each other, until Colton holds out his arms as if to say, *Explain yourself.* I kill the engine of the Chevrolet and walk to him. I'm suited today, in a cream two piece I bought as part of my emergency shopping spree when I decided I'd be staying in Texas for a while. I've spent the morning on video calls with my dad, in commercial sponsor negotiations for other clients.

I only remember that now, as Colton gives me a silent once-over, probably wondering both why I'm here and why I look so formal.

'I've come to make sure you don't forget today's arrangement.'

He slips off his shades, holding them by the gold arm, elbow resting on the window frame of his driver's door. It's suddenly extremely warm out here at midday in a suit.

I'm sure that's the reason for the flush of heat I feel rising up my neck.

'As you can see, I'm fixin' to go to the airport. If you'll move your— Is that Pace's Chevy?'

I glance back at the dazzlingly polished car. 'Yup. It's an absolute demon to drive. In fact, I'm pleased you're driving a two-seater. Now I can follow behind and have some fun in this thing.'

'First off, why are you coming to the airport?'

'To take pictures.'

He shakes his head and fires his crazily loud engine.

'What's second?' I ask.

Ignoring me, he flicks his gears into reverse and starts rolling back down the ramp into the garage.

'Where're you going?' I call after him, knowing he can't hear me over the roar of that car.

I follow in Pace's Chevy and park up in a spot next to Colton's Range Rover as he gets out of his sports car and opens the driver's door of the SUV.

'Come on,' he tells me as I get out of my ride.

'What? Why?'

He pauses on the threshold of his car. 'Because there's no way I'm letting you drive that thing to the airport. You'll kill us both.'

'Hey! I can drive.'

'You might be licensed but you live in NYC. You have no need to drive cars like these, city girl. So quit arguing with me and get in here before you make us late.'

City girl? I guess I do think of him as a cowboy. *Touché.*

'I drive wild and fast, baby. You don't know what you're missing.' I finish that statement with a pout, hand on my waist, both recognizing the error of my ways in flirting just now, and hating how much I'm enjoying Colton's hungry eyes assessing me.

We both seem to snap out of the blip at the same time and he gestures to his more sensible, while still being flashy, ride. 'In there, wild thing.'

Huffily, I do as I'm told. Something I don't take kindly to from anyone, let alone the guy who has me stuck down here in this heat because *he* can't behave himself. The guy who is irritatingly difficult to *not* ogle. 'I'll get in your car but only because it's so hot in this garage, I'd be laying hard boiled eggs if I were a hen.'

I climb into the car as he does the same, and when both our doors are shut, he tells me, 'That's disgusting.'

His words sink in and I realize it was a gross reference. Sort of unexpected from a suited attorney who drove here in an extremely swanky car. The ridiculousness of the situation, together with Colton's reaction, makes me snort with laughter.

And that, in turn, makes the most unlikely thing happen.

Colton Quinn *laughs*.

He actually laughs.

It's hearty and deep. The kind of sound that draws you in and forces you to grin.

Even when he stops and he's driving us out of the garage, there's an element of good humor left in the fine crinkles at the corners of his eyes, the deep half-moons drawn on the sides of his mouth, and a lightness so rarely in the air around him.

He suits it.

'So,' I begin, abruptly changing tack to rapidly drag me out of the Colton-sized fantasy bubble I just found myself lost in. 'How're you going to play this?'

'This?' Those tantalizing displays of character disappear from his face.

'Your next date with Megan. You know, the woman we're driving to collect?'

He shrugs. 'I'm picking her up. Isn't that what you asked me to do? I'll drive her to her rental. You can get a picture somewhere along the line, which I'm sure will miraculously appear on social media in the next twenty-four hours.'

'Colton, would you stop sucking on proverbial lemons for like a nanosecond?'

I watch that sickeningly defined jaw of his stiffen.

This man may hold his cards close to his chest but he's not the emotion-less guy I first thought. He feels it, he just doesn't show it. Unless you watch him closely enough.

'It's not a real date, Sas. It doesn't need a playbook.'

'Granted. But it has to *appear* as if it's a real date.'

'Yeah, well, I've told you. I don't date. A woman is another distraction that I don't need in my life right now.'

A nugget. He has distractions. Step one is to acknowledge the problem. Step two is to work the problem, and that's where I come in. 'So, you're a monk now?'

He glances my way, shaking his head, but those half-moons are back. I shouldn't get as big of a kick from that as I do.

But I'm doing my job, right? Making connections. Getting beneath the skin of a man who doesn't want to open up. That's why Dad sent me here after all.

'Do you ever just *stop* making noise?' he asks, but his tone is light.

'Rarely. You know why? Because the more I talk, the more you talk, and I'd like to know more about these distractions you're keeping to yourself.'

Well, that zaps his cheer.

He fiddles with the buttons on his dash and an Andy Grammer song I recognize plays into the car.

'You need a game plan, Colton.' He cranks up the music, making me shout my next words. 'Would it be so bad if you actually enjoyed hanging out with Megan and got to know her a little? It would make time pass much quicker. And who knows, getting some action might loosen you up.'

I know he hears me by the way his chest rises and falls deeply with his next breath. Then he says something I can't make out but I'm pretty sure he's talking about me, not to me.

Most likely, chanting death threats.

* * *

Perforated ear drums would have been less painful than listening to country music at that volume for the remainder of the drive to the airport.

Things I've had reinforced about Colton on the drive here: he's stubborn as a mule, he will *not* be giving me any insight to his *distractions* any time soon, he's still disastrously hot when he's driving, even when that jaw is twitching with irritation, and one curve of his lips makes me immediately forget how annoying I find my client.

We're standing in the Arrivals Hall now, waiting for Megan, me with my phone in hand, braced to collect some footage. Colton's head dipped and his cowboy hat slung low, trying to hide from preying eyes, as he watches the double doors where passengers are making their way to friends, loved ones and cab drivers. I guess his discretion is habit because preying eyes is exactly what we *want*.

Turns out, there's no need for me to point out that little fact, nor to take a video myself. People around us have spotted Colton and are already unsur-reptitiously taking his photograph. If he notices, he doesn't let it show.

It occurs to me that, unlike the people around us, Colton and I are neither friends nor lovers of Megan, which prompts me to tell him, 'Just try to be less... *undatable*, okay? She's traveling solo and putting her faith in you.'

He looks at me like I'm a child who just sat on his pet hamster, licking his lips in a way that simultaneously demonstrates his annoyance and is irrationally sexy. He has full lips. Pink lips. Kis—

Ahem. Channeling Harris. Channeling Harris.

It's the whispers and raised phones of onlookers that alert me to Megan's presence before I see her come through the doorway with her lilac carry-on, looking a gazillion dollars.

She's wearing a white dress: floaty, summery, with ruffled short sleeves and a Bardot neckline. As she spots us, she full-on beams at Colton and he raises the brim of his hat, no doubt to get a better look at the screen star.

Onlookers capture the moment Megan switches her walk to a run and comes at Colton full throttle.

I'm not sure what I'm expecting but it definitely isn't what I witness. In a move that I would think entirely unlike him, Colton opens his arms and lets Megan run into him, picking her up into a hug when they connect.

With the flair of someone who knows how to grab attention, Megan kicks up one leg – cowboy boots, nice touch! – and the fake couple look undeniably perfect for each other.

Which is great.

Super.

Social media will lap it up.

This is exactly the thing both stars need.

Precisely as Blake and I planned.

Exemplary performance all round.

So *why*, as I trail behind the couple like a spare wheel, do I feel surprisingly downcast?

* * *

They barely acknowledge that I exist in the back of Colton's car as we head to Megan's rental. Which is a good thing, really, because I'm gobsmacked. Utterly speechless, for one of few times in my life, because whatever version of Colton I'm seeing and hearing in this car can only be the result of a personality transplant.

He asks Megan about her work, and she relays stories of her days on the set of *To Be Seventeen*. And Colton is having socially appropriate responses. *Weird*.

He's laughing and smiling and asking her more questions about herself. It's not a version of him I've seen at all.

It's one I can imagine bagged him any girl he wanted in college – captain of the football team and *sweet*? Doesn't everyone love sweet and sour? Aren't our brains preprogrammed to devour that combination?

Admittedly, there are moments I'm questioning, like the way his laugh is more of a titter than the full-blown belly laugh I heard earlier, and the teeth flashing smiles that seem unnaturally wide for his cheeks. But, look, there aren't eyes on the couple right now. They don't have to fake it, and yet...

'Bexar County,' Megan says, attempting a Texan accent, as we pass the sign on the roadside.

'Bear,' Colton says in his southern drawl.

'Bear?' she asks sweetly.

And Colton breaks it down for her. 'Down here, we pronounce Bexar, Bear.'

Megan repeats it, not doing a bad job at all.

Colton checks his blind spot as he moves across lanes and though he's wearing shades, I'm sure he casts a look my way through his rearview mirror. I should probably give him a thumbs up or something – *good job, buddy, keep it going* – but I don't. I'll put it down to being flabbergasted.

'See, it came from the Spanish, *Béjar*. Pronounced Bay-har. Over time, there was a phonetic drift to just straight Bear.'

'San Antonio Bears,' I say, for my own ears, I think, until I see Colton focusing on me in the mirror, again.

He gives me a nod. No smile. No words. Nothing like what's happening in the front between this new ideal match.

'Oh my gosh, *totally*. Your football team. That's such a coincidence.'

I refrain from asking, *Is it?*

Instead, I get back to looking out the window and thinking I probably don't need to play the role of Mom supervising these dates going forward.

At Megan's rental – a cute apartment on the outskirts of the city, easy to get to her primary filming location – Colton carries her luggage inside. After she's briefly waved goodbye to me, they go in. And close the door behind them.

I stare at the door. Not entirely sure where to go next on this gooseberry trail. Then I decide to switch into the front passenger seat.

I'm mid-climb across the seats when Colton opens the driver's side door.

'Wouldn't it have been easier to walk around the vehicle?'

Probably. 'I wanted to test the durability of these new pants,' I tell him, legs akimbo.

When we're settled in our seats and pulling away from Megan's new pad, Colton looks my way.

'How was that for undatable, huh?'

I scowl in response.

Is he playing games? Was it all a show for me? For the cameras in the airport?

Surely not.

The chemistry I just witnessed felt... real.

13

SEPTEMBER

Colton
The Season Opener

I'm warming up on the field – warm enough without the exercise, since the roof is open and I'm in full kit. It's our season opener against the Titans this afternoon, at home in the Bears' Alamo Stadium.

Both teams are out on the gridiron with all their support staff. The pre-game entertainment is ramping up between music and I'm quietly singing along to 'Sweet Caroline' as the stands steadily grow fuller. The buzz of a new season is real and it feels good to be back on the turf.

This place is as home to me as Sunshine Ranch. A thought I immediately dismiss because I'm compartmentalizing. Ignoring the stuff I can't control and focusing on the game.

I'm side-lunging, stretching out my groin, when Omar Kubiak, another wide receiver – our starting flanker – sidles up to me.

'Is that you singin', brother?' He rocks his shoulder into mine, cheese-eating grin on his face. 'Hell freezin' over?'

'It's good to be back at it,' I tell him, realizing that I do feel lighter today than I have in months.

I've got some focus and like Sas told me in a voice note this morning, I need to enjoy it. Remember that it's a game I love.

The part I've added myself is that I need to block out the thing I hate about it – the guilt of not being around for my family. If I can do that, I can be the best split end in the league.

Bold? Sure. Arrogant? Absolutely. But true? Hell, yeah.

'I'll bet it is, brother. Playing ball and wearing Megan Frost on your arm. Life ain't too shabby.'

Megan. Right. She's coming to the game today, sitting with Sas, Harris, Daddy and Annie.

'Gotta tell you, though, I thought you and your agent girl were going there.'

'Sas?' I ask, switching to lunge on the other leg.

'Hell, brother, she sees your miserable face and she still shows up to practice every day? That's L.O.V.E. love right there.'

For some reason, I look to the stands, where I know she'll be sitting for the game. But either I don't see her or she isn't in the crowd yet.

'It's not like that,' I tell him. 'She's just...'

What *is* Sas doing in Texas? Babysitting me to stop me screwing up any more? Keeping my fake relationship with Megan under close watch?

'A skeeter,' I say. 'Constantly buzzing around and making noise, ready to bite.' *Always in my head*, I choose to leave out.

'Sounds like she's under your skin.'

I scoff. 'Not in a good way.' Nosy. Reactive. Unpredictable.

'Whatever you say, brother.'

I don't notice that Trent Daniels has come up behind me until he speaks to me for what might be the first time since our run-in during training camp. 'I heard you and Megan are getting traction on the club's socials. Apparently, you've brought a load of chick fans to the club. If you're goin' to get sponsors on our side, keep doin' your thing, dawg.'

My hackles rise as I watch him walk away, but I should be pleased, shouldn't I? Isn't getting my teammates and sponsors onside the reason my fake girlfriend is going to take a seat with my family any minute now?

Another photo opportunity.

Another lie.

I don't like lying. I especially don't feel good about lying to the guys. As sour as some of them are with me, we're on the same side.

Less than an hour later, after one of Coach's shout-talked inspirational speeches, my name is announced into the stadium. Helmet in hand, I run out of the tunnel to ZZ Top's 'La Grange', the club's anthem. I high-five the lines of players flanking me on the field, creating the typical guard of honor, and at the end of the pack, waiting for the rest of the guys to be announced, I secure my helmet and pull on my gloves.

Then, I look to the stands. It's not easy – in fact, it's highly unlikely – to be able to pick faces out of the seventy-thousand strong crowd. But since I arranged the tickets, I know exactly where to find my family, Sas, Harris and Megan.

Immediately, my attention is grabbed by the loudest, most brash of the group. Sas is wearing a football jersey and hollering into the stadium, leaning back, hands to her mouth as she cheers – or wolf cries, or makes whatever loud noise she's making up there. And I can't help but shake my head because she's nuts. The opposite of Harris, who's standing quietly next to her in his smart collared shirt.

'Eyes off your girl, Quinn, it's game time.' A heavy hand lands on my shoulder pad. Pace.

For obvious reasons, while I'm staring at my agent – or agent's daughter – everyone else thinks I'm making eyes at Megan, who I'm only just now noticing is standing on the other side of Sas and waving at me. I wave back, then do a sharp warm-up sprint toward the ten-yard line.

Then I do my best to tune everything else out and get into position, split off from the line of scrimmage, ready for the first play. But when I go deep and catch the first down at the twenty-yard line, my first thought is, *I hope Sas was watching.*

14

SEPTEMBER

Sas
He Really is a Cowboy

Colton makes first down on the twenty-yard line with an outstanding catch. The kind of catch that got him Rookie of the Year three years ago and got him more than a fourteen hundred yards in the season two years ago. The kind of catch that made him a first-round draft pick.

I'm up on my feet cheering – alongside his dad and heavily pregnant sister, Annie – when he looks up to the stand where we're sitting. I've no way of knowing who he's actually looking at but there's a strike of something in my abdomen that feels like adrenaline.

Having grown up around sports and over-achievers, there's nothing I find more attractive in a man than being great at something. Also helpful when said man is six foot four and looks absolutely smoking in his uniform.

Totally unhelpful is when said man is your client and you're here in your professional capacity, with your boss sitting on your blindside and your client's girlfriend – for all intents and purposes – flanking your right.

When your mind is screaming, *Oops, I put my foot in it*, because Blake was right: I haven't grown out of it... I'm totally hot for the brooding sports guy, *again*.

Hands over my open mouth, I slump down to my seat.

Dad leans into my ear and says, 'I know, great, right? This is exactly the kind of play we were hoping for.'

'Oh yeah. Great.' *Fuck.*

At the end of the second quarter, I grab Dad, Colton's dad Sonny, and myself a much-needed beer. Hoping it will put out the flames that seem to be igniting between my thighs every time Colton makes a run, or receives a ball, or glances up to the stands.

Once I've handed out the beers (and soft drinks for the underaged and pregnant among us), I decide to reshuffle the seating, too, and opt to get to know Annie and Sonny better. Or avoid Dad and Megan. Same difference.

'When are you due, Annie?' I ask.

She touches her bump with the kind of glint in her eye that moms have when they talk about their children. The kind of unconditional love that warms me from my toes.

'Middle of November, if I'm on time. You know how these things go.'

Actually, I don't. None of my friends have had babies yet and I don't foresee that kind of settling for myself for a long time. I've spent too much time with my head in academic texts. If anything, I'm ready to step into my smut era.

'I'll still be wobbling around the ranch come Thanksgiving,' she says, finishing with a giggle full of happiness.

'It would be the most precious thing to be thankful for, though.'

'Growing our family is precious every day,' Sonny says, loud enough to be heard, yet distant, as if he's speaking his thoughts aloud.

In the background, the cheer squad finish their routine, and the players come back onto the field. The Bears have made a substitution but, irritatingly, my eyes find Colton with treasonous ease.

'With all the kids out now, and everything else that's going on, things can be quiet some days,' Sonny adds, as if he's talking to no one in particular.

Annie rests a hand on top of her dad's and gives him a gentle nudge.

There's a shared story between them, I can tell. Something that would affect Colton?

'So, you live on a ranch?' I ask, hoping to keep them talking.

'Born and raised,' Annie says. 'I've never left and Colton is back like a bad smell at the moment. Always around. Always hammering or sawing at something.'

I scoff. 'He says *I'm* relentlessly noisy.'

'That's rich coming from my brother.'

'He likes to keep himself busy,' Sonny says in his son's defense, not taking his eyes off where the center for the Titans snaps the ball to their quarterback. 'Make himself useful. That's how us Quinn men deal best.'

There are so many things I'd like to unpick here. 'Is the ranch near the city?'

'No, we're very rural,' Annie tells me. 'Middle of nowhere.'

'I'm confused; isn't Colton living in the city?'

She nods. 'He has his place here but for the last few months, he's been staying at the ranch most nights. Waking at five in the morning and riding his stallion every day before he comes into the city for practice. Driving me crazy.'

'He rides?' My head snaps faster than the football and I locate the cowboy on the sidelines straight away.

'Course, darlin', he's a rancher!' Annie's words are said with such a strong Texan accent, it makes me chuckle.

And everything else that might be useful information from that conversation seems to slip right out of my brain as I realize, this city girl might actually be turned on by a real-life cowboy.

Those washed-out jeans and Lone Star belts he wears. Those checked shirts and that crooked smile. Under a cowboy hat dipped low? Riding a stallion against the backdrop of the rising sun?

Man alive, I'd like him to lasso me right now, then tell me how noisy he'd like to make me in that strong southern drawl.

What the actual...?! I shock myself so much, I drop my beer, making everyone stand around us.

Holy shit, this is a figurative and proverbial mess.

And it's only the first game of the season.

Hoping I don't look as guilty as I feel, I glance to Dad, then Megan, and tell the family of one of the other players how profusely sorry I am to have splashed them.

Sorry, my mind was so far in the gutter, I spilled a near-full beer.

* * *

By the end of the game, I'm wound tighter than a coiled spring.

Honestly, I just need to go back to Pace's pad and cool off in the sanctity of my own bedroom. But Dad wants to see his guys, and Megan is as giddy as I've seen her to go find Colton – the kind of giddy I imagine you'd get if you crossed a unicorn and a glitter fairy. It's sweet, really, just not very *me*.

So, we say our goodbyes to Annie and Sonny, who are awkward with Megan and keen to get back to the ranch – I guess they have a long drive and Annie's probably tired.

I traipse behind Dad and Megan in the direction of the home dressing room. We pass Coach Roy in the cold corridor, leaving with a few of the position coaches, and we wind up speaking to him for a few minutes, until I sense how tetchy Megan is.

'I'll take Megan to see Colton. You can catch up,' I tell Dad, though he follows before we even reach the door.

I knock and cover my eyes when it's opened. 'If there are any small penises on show, please put them away. Ladies entering,' I call.

'Can the big ones stay out?' I hear Max call, making me chortle, finally releasing some of the tension I've been carrying through the entire second half of the game.

'I thought you said ladies, plural,' Pace adds once we've been let inside by security and I've uncovered my eyes to find, happily, all men at least semi-dressed. 'I can only see one.'

Referring to Megan, obviously, because Pace sees me as one of the guys. At least, he likes to pretend to in order to get a rise out of me. Since I am here wearing my jersey with Pace's number on it – he gifts me one every year, always has done – ripped jeans and sneakers, next to Megan's six-inch sandals and mini-skirt, I do look significantly less feminine.

I fist pump Max and Pace, congratulating them on the win. 'Though, you did give up sixteen points.'

'A win's a win, baby!' Max says.

'Ain't that right,' Pace replies, thumping his teammate in the arm. If Pace punched me that hard, I'd fall on my ass, but Max doesn't budge an inch.

'Is Colton around?' I ask.

Pace inclines his head in the direction of the shower room. 'He's always last out of the shower. Does his post-game analysis in there,' he tells me, hopefully not realizing how the thought of Colton naked and under the blazing jets of the shower makes me clench my legs shut.

God, I *thought* the tension was subsiding. It's back full throttle.

'I hope that's the only thing he does in there, man,' Max adds, and my groin tells me before my head registers that he's insinuating a *happy* shower.

'If a brother's gonna play like that, he can jack off in the showers every game,' Omar Kubiak says, walking past me half-dressed in slacks and no shirt, winking as he speaks.

I've seen enough athletes post-game, including my brothers, to know the pump when I see it. Testosterone flies after a win.

Though I think Megan may need therapy after this. The poor girl's jaw is on the floor as she turns her head around the space, the faces, the semi-nude muscle.

Surely an actress has seen men in good shape, but I do have empathy because a football bod can be—

I'm stopped in that thought, *all* sensible thoughts, by Colton 'cowboy' Quinn stepping out of the shower room. White towel around his waist. Water droplets running down his pin-up torso. Towel-drying hair that I suddenly want to drag my fingers through.

'Harris, how you doing?' Pace asks my dad, who's now behind me.

I swallow to wet my dry mouth and focus on my dad – my boss – the agency and our clients.

Except as I hear a wolf whistle, my attention is pulled back to the shower door and the glittery unicorn who's standing on tiptoes to wrap her arms around Colton's neck, lips pressed to his.

For no good reason, the sight steals my breath.

That's what I've wanted to do for the last hour and a half and now Megan Frost – gorgeous, feminine Megan Frost, who I set up with Colton – is kissing him in this locker room full of people.

His eyes are open. He's surprised. And for a brief moment, his gaze connects with mine. Then he closes his eyes and brings his hands onto Megan's petite waist.

It stings somewhere in my abdomen that has no business feeling stung.

I'm saved by Dad, again. Saved from myself. Dad makes strides for Colton and for some unfathomable reason, I follow.

'Don't mean to interrupt,' Dad says. 'I just want to say good game, son. That's the kind of performance we're after.'

They shake hands and Colton's attention flicks to me briefly again. I can barely look at him and suddenly feel like I'm under a spotlight, being ridiculed by my own fantasies.

Awkward. As. Hell. I hold out a hand for Colton to shake. Then think better of it. Colton holds out a fist for me to pump at the same time as I hold up my hand for a high-five.

A high-five? Are we in kindergarten?

He bumps his fist against my hand and it's all cringeworthy. Even *Dad* is looking at me like I'm totally uncool.

This stops tonight. No more cowboy fantasies. Back to grown-up Sas, who has moved on from the days of falling for the brooding baller.

'Are you heading straight back to the hotel, Dad?' I ask, turning my back on Colton.

'Yes, I will be.'

'Cool. Great.' I give him a sort of father-daughter hug meets business-woman hug and tell him, 'I'll see you for breakfast in the morning. I'll ask Pace to give me a ride tonight.'

'Makes sense.'

'Pace,' I call across the dressing room. 'Am I okay to catch a ride with you?'

'Sure thing. You ready?'

One hundred percent. *Get me out of here double time so I can reset.*

I don't look back as Pace drapes a lazy arm around my shoulders and we head out of the dressing room together.

'Do you know how heavy you are?' I ask in the corridor.

He leans onto me even more. 'Firecracker, I'm in pieces. First game back. If I thought you could carry me, I'd let you piggyback me to the car.'

Laughing, I take hold of his hand. 'Come on, old man, let's get you home to your pipe and slippers.'

15

SEPTEMBER

Colton

Kansas City Arrows

It's the second game of the season today and I'm on a coach with the team from Kansas City Airport to the Arrows' stadium.

I've barely seen Sas this week. Hardly heard from her. Despite her and Blake setting up a photo opportunity for Megan and me on the set of Megan's new TV series. Blake chaperoned this one but Sas didn't come.

Maybe she trusts that I'm not going to out the truth or mess this up. I won't, since it seems to be working. Press attention has shifted from ruining my reputation to building it up. Megan has received a flurry of requests for interviews about the series she's filming from an older target market, so she tells me. My teammates are happy to be coming along for the ride as the Bears get more airtime on socials and in the news.

Beyond that, if the truth comes out now, I have to admit to lying to the guys. I didn't want to lie, I wanted to be passive about this whole fake-relationship thing, but every time I allow Megan to hug me or kiss me or I so much as smile at her while knowing there are eyes on us, I'm an active participant in this charade.

It's not sitting well with me. Worse, much worse, than my unease over the whole farce is what's happening at home. Mama's latest scan results have showed her cancer continuing to grow and spread. She's been given a last chance offer to trial a new treatment but if her prognosis worsens, she won't be eligible. It's now or never.

Annie is begging Mama to at least try. Daddy is staying quiet, as usual, but I can see it every time I look at him, how much he hopes Mama will change her mind and give it one last fight.

Me? I wish with every single part of me that Mama hadn't got cancer in the first place. That the ordinary treatments would have worked. That I could get more time with her to rewrite history and actually be around for her, helping on Sunshine Ranch, playing Scrabble over pink lemonade and helping her make jam.

Having Annie on my back for not trying to force Mama into a decision she clearly doesn't want to make has been playing on my mind all week. Should I be doing more? Am I supposed to pick a side?

As my teammates banter around me, in good spirits ahead of the game and on the back of a solid performance last weekend, I listen to music because I can't be bothered to discuss Max's love life, or rather, his latest fallout and make-up with his on-off girlfriend. Avoiding a discussion about who we're sleeping with – or pretending to be sleeping with – is probably for the best.

But as we pass a sign for Kansas City on the roadside, my mind wanders to Sas, for the millionth time this week.

Her incessant ramblings – telling me what to do or not to do, calling me out for eating meat off the bone like a pig, hating on my country music – have actually been a useful diversion of my thoughts. For some absurd reason, I'm getting used to the noise of her, even liking how it seems to take my mind off everything else.

Knowing she was up in the stands watching me play last weekend, some-how, for some reason, kept my head *in* the game. Or, rather, on impressing her.

There. I admit it. I'm totally hot for Sas, like a horned-up teenager out to steal her attention.

There's nothing more to it than that. She's funny, though annoying. She's smart, though a smart-ass with it. She loves sport and *knows* sport. I don't have to explain the minutiae to her the way I do when Megan asks. And she's solid.

She knows herself. Knows what she wants. She's driven. And her body could drive me crazy. Scratch that, it *does*. Whether she's looking *fine* and womanly in her tailoring, or, even more so, when she's in her sports gear and jeans.

The problem today, and I think the reason I don't want to joke around with the guys, is that Sas isn't here to distract me with all that stuff. To pull me out of the devastation of what's happening elsewhere in my life.

Honestly, I'm not sure why she hasn't been around so much this week.

I guess she's working. My schedule is prescribed and restrictive now that season has started. Between that and being at Sunshine Ranch, it's not as if I've been around either.

But... I don't know... I thought she might have messaged. Harassed and hounded me the way she does. I think I expected her to come to the game today and it threw me when Pace told me she hasn't.

Not as much as it threw me watching her walk out of the dressing room with Pace last weekend, though. His arm around her as she wore his number on her jersey. That felt like someone punched me in the gut and I'll be damned if I know why.

She's my business adviser, my agent's daughter. Plus, she's annoying as hell.

But I'd be lying if I said I haven't thought about having just one night with her multiple times this week.

To add insult to the injury of knowing I can't go there, I have to consider the feelings of my fake girlfriend, too. At least, what the world will perceive her feelings to be.

The woman who actually has decided to travel to the game today.

* * *

For the first quarter of the game, whenever I do anything noteworthy, I look in the general vicinity of where Megan is sitting with a co-actress.

In the second quarter, I give up because my frustration over trying to put on a show off the field, while I'm on the field, is adding to the diabolical performance I'm putting in today.

I just can't seem to get my head out of my ass, as Sas would say. And believe it or not, I wish she were here. Because looking into the stands for

Megan only serves as a reminder that I'm having to endure this sham to put things right that I made wrong in the first place.

To put things right because I've been distracted about Mama. Irate about Annie's situation.

And when Sas is around, somehow, she drowns it all out. Knowing she was in the stands first game did that. Today, I'm struggling to stay focused and the team is suffering the consequences.

16

SEPTEMBER

Sas
Tanking the Second Game of the Season

I'm watching the Bears game from the comfort of Pace's made-for-tall-people sofa. So deep, in fact, my feet don't touch the floor when I sit correctly. Instead, they're tucked beneath me as I sit cross-legged in my lounge pants and Bears hoodie, prescription glasses on instead of my usual contact lenses, hair whipped into a messy knot. My laptop has been discarded on the sofa next to me – marking up contracts for the agency is on hold until full time. I've got a bowl brimming with loaded tortilla chips on my lap.

I've put some distance between Colton and me this week. Natural distance, mostly. Season proper has begun now and his training schedule is grueling. Dad's riding me hard with work, too.

But if I'm completely honest with myself, last weekend was not one to be repeated. There were some kind of brain synapses firing and sending confused messages. Emotionally charged messages. Hormonal messages. *Unprofessional.*

I need to focus on the reason I'm down here in Texas – to make sure this press stunt between Colton and Megan goes to plan. To land my own client and Dad's respect, even if he's riding my ass so hard I haven't been able to get to a college game to scope the talent yet.

More pertinently, to get Colton the best deal on his contract extension that we can.

For sure, that means getting inside his head.

It absolutely does not mean letting him get into mine.

Not my head.

Definitely not my panties.

And sitting in the stand watching him play last week, I can't deny that crossed my mind.

But what really shook me was how much I hated seeing Megan's arms around his naked torso, their lips connected.

The green-eyed monster is *not* someone I need or want to hang out with.

So here I am, alone, having given my ticket to the game to Megan and arranged a second for one of her friends.

Perfect. Loaded chips for one, thank you *very* much.

Except I'm onto my second helping of nervous snack shoveling because Colton is playing one of the worst games of his career. That's not on me but you better believe that if I were there, I'd have headed down to the tunnel to ask him where on earth his head is at.

My phone pings with a message as the teams run back onto the field for the beginning of the third quarter.

It's my brother, Jax:

> Not even Megan Frost can paper over the cracks in your man's game, sis.

'Fuck,' I say into the vast living space.

Tossing my phone aside, I wonder for the hundredth time, *What is it that Colton is holding on to?*

As the Bears' defense gets into position on the line of scrimmage, I whisper, 'Come on, Bears.'

But no amount of chanting helps the guys and they absolutely tank the second game of the season, losing 27–9.

To add insult to injury, the cameras pan to Megan in the stands, watching her beau crash out, and she's wearing the kind of smile I'd only be wearing if the Bears had just won the championship.

I hate that it makes me wonder if she's genuinely pleased to be there for Colton.

What will happen between them after the game?
Will he fly straight home with the team?
Will he and Megan stay over in Kansas?
God knows babies are made in Kansas City. I'm living proof.

* * *

It's a little after nine when I hear Pace typing the code in his front door. I'm back on the sofa with my laptop. After a brief interlude for a stress-busting run, I showered, got back into my loungewear and started working again.

'Hey,' I say when he comes inside and dumps his bag by the door. 'How you doing?'

He slumps down on the sofa next to me in his game day two piece, eyes to the ceiling. 'Can't make any better of it now.'

'Onwards and upwards,' I tell him. 'It's early days.'

He nods. 'We never got into the game. Any of us. We can't have Tommy getting sacked as many times as he did today. Mat has some learning to do. And if your tight end and flanker are being man-marked, your split end's gotta go deep and make some plays. Quinn had nothing today.'

'I saw.' I set my laptop aside. 'I've got about twenty minutes' work left to do, then we could carb load and play *Grand Theft Auto*, if you like?'

He looks at me now, tired. 'Would you be offended if I said what I really want to do is light some candles, put some trash on the bathroom TV and soak in the tub for a while?'

'People would never suspect you, would they?'

'Of being in touch with my feminine side?' He pushes up to stand, groaning as he moves. 'It's one of the perks of living alone, firecracker. And if my post-game routine ever gets out, I'll know where it came from.'

I draw an imaginary zipper across my lips.

'Catch you in the mornin'.'

'Sweet dreams, Pace. Message if you want me to bring you up a snack.'

He limp-walks up the staircase, making the kind of noises a man forty years older might make as his joints bend and flex.

It can only have been five minutes before my phone pings with a message. Expecting to have a request for a carb-heavy snack from Pace, I pick it up.

> **COWBOY**
> Are you home?

Frowning at the screen, I reply:

> Yes?

> **COWBOY**
> Let me in the front gate?

My torso literally flips so hard I have to press my hands against it to stop my internal organs diving right out of there. On unsteady legs, I go to the intercom box and buzz the front gate, opening the door, too.

A minute later, Colton steps out of his Maserati and comes to stand on the porch, running his eyes over me. For sure, I don't look like his agent right now.

Meanwhile, my cardiovascular system has started stuttering over Colton in a perfectly tailored gray suit, pale-blue shirt unbuttoned by two, his tousled hair styled.

'What are you doing here?' I ask, feeling the burn of his intense focus.

He doesn't speak until he's so close, he's towering over me. 'Where's Pace?'

Oh. *Duh*. He's here to see his captain. 'In the tub, upstairs. Want me to get him?'

He shakes his head and swallows so deeply, I watch his Adam's apple rise and fall against lightly stubbled skin. *God,* that's sexy. Should that simple move *be* sexy?

Now. Right now. In this moment. I feel justified for having stayed away from him this past week. I can feel my self-control hovering above me, out of my body, watching me to see if I'll act on the sudden ache between my legs and the pounding under my ribcage.

'I need you to clarify a few things for me,' he says, still staring at me.

'*You* want to encourage conversation?' I lean out the doorway, looking left and right, as if I'm searching the area. 'Okay, who are you and what have you done with Colton Quinn?'

I've become accustomed to seeing a reluctant twist of Colton's lips when I tease him but tonight, I get zilch. Not so much as a twitch. There's nothing light about the charged air between us.

'Is there anything going on between you and Pace? Are you two a thing?' he blurts.

I physically recoil. 'Pace? Not at all. He's a friend.' I'm tempted to stop there but as tends to happen, the pause button in my mind is a step behind my voice box that's steaming ahead. 'I'd never date a client. Dad already thinks I need to work on being more professional and less emotionally reactive. Can you imagine how much he'd flip if I—'

Colton's tongue wets his lips in a move that's so disarming, my brain finally hits the emergency stop on my treadmill of verbal diarrhea.

'What are you doing here?' I ask, my eyes reluctantly moving north to the intensity of his focus.

'I needed to see you.'

'Why?' I croak.

'Because for some reason, the noise you make is louder to me than everything else I can hear.'

'Huh, right, so you needed to insult me?' I feel my eyebrows draw closer together. 'Where's, ah, Megan? Forget her in Kansas?'

'I don't want to talk about Megan.'

'Oh really? Then what do you want to talk about?'

He inches closer to me, firing up more of my senses as his mix of cologne and something that's distinctly him envelops me. Taste, touch... They're waking up in anticipation of I don't know what.

'Why haven't you been around this week? Why weren't you at the game today?'

'I've been busy with work.'

'I thought I was work?'

My own tongue now wets my suddenly dry lips. 'You are work. *Hard* work. I'm so busy babysitting you that I get nothing else done. So, I've been playing catch-up all week.'

I walk away from the door, stepping inside the house, and glance up the staircase to make sure Pace isn't around. As I head into the kitchen, I hear the door close and for a second, I wonder whether Colton left.

I start taking things from the units to make myself a hot drink that I don't want, then Colton is in here, leaning against the archway between the living area and kitchen.

'You're avoiding me,' he says.

'Avoiding you? Why would I avoid you?' I focus intently on my mug of steaming coffee that would keep me up all night if I drank it. 'You're my client. I can hardly—'

He's crossed the room and he's standing right behind me. I feel rather than see his presence, the air that moves with his words kissing my neck and bringing bumps to my skin. 'I can't get you out of my head, Sas. I'll be damned if I know why but having you around seems to keep everything else in my head at bay and at the game today, you weren't there...'

I turn to face him. His proximity, his masculine scent, his towering frame, all of it, overwhelming. 'I thought you said I'm so noisy I'm like a breakdown on the highway when you have places to be?'

'You are. One that I can't stop rubbernecking at.' He inhales and exhales so fully, his chest expands against mine. 'I'm starting to think that might be a good thing. Except today, every time I looked up to the stand, every time I saw a Kansas sign with your name on it—'

'That must have been a lot.' I chuckle nervously and watch his eyes narrow.

'It was. You've been on my mind all fucking day and not in a good way. You weren't even there and you *still* drove me batshit crazy.'

'Oh. Well, that's nice to—'

'I'm wondering if the problem is that I can't have you.'

I swallow so loudly Pace can probably hear from the tub. 'Do you want me?'

He leans his head to one side, a lopsided grin twisting on his lips. 'Fuck, yeah, Sas. I want you.'

Huh.

'Well, we both know that can't happen,' I tell him, pinning myself back against the counter, failing miserably at putting distance between us. Much-needed distance because my core body temperature just skyrocketed. The ache between my legs is beginning to throb.

'I know that. It's all I've been thinking about in Kansas. All I fucking thought about through that game.'

'You were unfocused.'

'I know.' His words resonate in one place of my anatomy, and it isn't my head or ears. 'Because I was too busy realizing that what I need and what I want is one night. Get whatever this pull is between us out of our systems and go back to you driving me insane because you never stop hounding me. Rather than because I want to fuck you so badly that I can't think about anything else.'

He steps closer to me and my body betrays me, chin rising, tilting my face up to his. Because I know I can't do this but damn it, I want to.

I really want to. And hearing the same salacious thoughts from his lips is worse than the temptation of caffeine first thing in the morning, the smell of waffles from a food truck, water in a drought.

'You need to fix that because I'm not falling for a player. I'm absolutely not having sex with a client. And I won't ruin what you've got going on with Megan.'

Though my voice is strained, I'm giving myself a proverbial high-five for this fine display of willpower. I've got this.

'There's nothing going on with Megan. You know that, and I've made that perfectly clear to her every time we've seen each other. It's just an act.'

I feel my breaths coming thick and fast, my chest rising, climbing toward his. Who am I kidding? I haven't got this at all.

'I didn't know you wore glasses,' he says, his hand reaching out to my neck, thumb trailing my jawline.

Warm. Strong. Big.

I close my eyes and as I do, I remind myself, I'm wearing glasses because I'm working.

'Colton, don't. You're reeling from a loss. This isn't going to make anything better.'

Yet, I don't make a move away from him.

Because I want this too.

One night.

No strings.

When my eyes open, his are like fire on mine. Fire I feel all over my body. I bite down on my lip as I squeeze my thighs together.

In the distance, I hear music turn on. A reminder that Pace is upstairs. That I'm living with another of the agency's clients.

And I'm staying here to help the one whose brown eyes are piercing mine.

I'm not reeling from a loss, therefore *I* need to be the one to say, 'This would be a bad idea, Colton. Terrible. Awful.'

'Why have you really stayed away from me this week?'

He knows.

The fact he does makes me mad. At myself, not him. But that flash of temper makes me take hold of his hand and remove it from my neck.

'Go home, Colton. I'll see you in a couple days. Right now, you need to cool off.'

We both do.

17

SEPTEMBER

Colton
Post-Game Review

It's Monday morning after our disaster against Kansas City and I'm in the training facility, lifting light weights and focusing on recovery with the rest of the squad.

Some of us move on quicker than others, and while a bunch of the team are goofing around, I'm running over what went wrong on Sunday in my own game.

I'm a good player. One of the best in the league. My goal is to be a GOAT. I'm capable of it.

But I can't get my game straight and I know it's mental. This has been the longest stretch of time in my life where there's something in need of my attention more than football.

I'm disappointed in myself for not being as mentally tough as I need to be. As I thought I was.

I just keep doing the wrong thing and messing up.

'Wassup, Quinn?' Pace comes to sit on a machine opposite me, where I'm resting between reps on the chest press. He grunts as he takes a seat – and that's after seeing the physio.

'Hey. You good?' I watch him as I speak, wondering whether he knows I was at his place last night, calling it about as wrong as I could have with Sas.

'Nothing an anti-inflammatory won't fix.'

I smirk. We all take anti-inflammatories before a game but some of the longer servers, like Pace, pop them like candy.

Speaking of mental resilience, the man in front of me has stacks of it. He's a joker and a jackass at times but I've got bags of respect for Pace. Not least because he's my captain.

'A few of us are playing golf tomorrow. You up for it?' he asks.

'Ah, I can't. I've got family stuff to do.' Like any one of two dozen jobs around the ranch.

'Look, I'm not really a feelings kind of guy but I think living with Sas might be making me wet. So, here goes... You've always played your cards close to your chest and that's cool, man, whatever works for you. As long as you're playing well. But yesterday, your game was off. Way off.'

I inhale, coming to rest my forearms on my thighs. 'Me and about twenty other guys.'

Pace nods, then sniffs as he swipes a knuckle under his nose, as if I dealt him a personal blow. 'Yeah. But these other guys aren't Colton Quinn. Expectations are high, Quinn, and I'm saying, if there's anything you want to get off your chest, I'm here for it.'

There's a lot I could unload. Mama. Annie. Auston. The ranch. My fake girlfriend. But it's all private or secret. The one person who at least knows the full truth about the make-believe relationship, I came onto last night. *Fuck,* I messed up.

Rising from the machine, I pat him on the shoulder and say, 'Good session. Thanks, man. I'm cured. See you in the post-game review.'

'Yeah, any time, Quinn.'

I head to the locker room and find my phone. There's one thing I can attempt to fix.

> I'm sorry about last night. I wasn't thinking straight. I promise it won't happen again.

It's a lie. I was thinking straight, I was just thinking with my dick and the fact it screams to be allowed to play every time Sas comes into my mind, which is a lot.

Even in her loungewear and glasses, with her hair knotted on top of her head, she was a massive turn-on last night. She was rocking the sexy attorney look in those specs.

But no matter what her eyes were telling me, her mouth told me no, so that's the end of it.

My phone buzzes as I'm putting it back in my kit bag.

> CITY GIRL
>
> Already forgotten. Enjoy the tape!

I grin at her message.

> ME
>
> I'm in for a roasting.

> CITY GIRL
>
> See, you will get some action after all.

Is she flirting with me?

> ME
>
> Thought you said it was already forgotten?

> CITY GIRL
>
> ...typing...

Her lack of response speaks volumes. She might not be willing to go there, and I understand all the sound reasons why. But I don't think the pull is one-sided.

And I wish that thought wouldn't make my dick hope.

No good can come of it.

My phone finally vibrates, and I check for Sas's reply.

Only, the message isn't from Sas.

> MEGAN FROST
>
> Hi you. I have my new script and wonder if you might walk through it with me? Mx

Suddenly, that game of golf sounds like an easy get out of jail.

* * *

I've always thought golf was a way to socialize and compete on a lesser scale than playing ball.

Turns out, golf is also pretty damn sexy, when your agent is unexpectedly part of your group.

Sas is teeing off from a forward tee box. There're some low handicaps among Pace, Max, Trent, Omar, Tommy and me. Yet Sas is holding her own with ease.

It's *golf*. Golf isn't sexy. It's an old man's sport. A cooldown and recover sport. But I'm having to avert my focus every time Sas bends over her ball. I'm having to ignore the way she handles that long driver like a pro.

So, she's good at something. Fine.

So, her checked pants fit her hips and ass perfectly and let me see exactly how her body moves through her swing. Cool.

So, that tight-fitting polo shirt hugs perky, rounded breasts. Doesn't bother me at all.

I lean my head from side to side, creaking my vertebrae as I do. Just tension from Sunday's game. Nothing more to it.

I'm supposed to have a girlfriend, anyway.

'How come you're staying out in the sticks, brother?' Omar asks, mirroring my stance as we both lean on the heads of our clubs, waiting for Sas to take her shot.

I let slip that I wasn't staying in town at the moment when Tommy offered me a lift. News travels fast. Though I'm not the only guy not living nearby, I am the only one with an apartment going to waste.

'My folks have a ranch and I'm helping them out.'

'Can't you pay someone to do that for you? That's a long commute every day.'

'Long story,' I say, leaving it there, instead of telling him that it's high time *I* put the time in for my family. That I could hire additional ranch hands but I want to do it, even if it is killing me alongside training.

We hop on the buggies, Sas sitting up front with me as I drive us to our next shots.

'He's right, you know,' she says. 'Omar, I mean. It can't be helping your game doing manual labor in your downtime.'

I watch her in my peripheral vision, feeling her focus on me. Unexpectedly, I want to tell her the truth. I want to explain that my mama is dying and this is the least I can do.

When we park, Tommy and Omar hop down off the back of the buggy and I'm left staring at Sas.

'I've got all the time in the world for a long story, Colton,' she tells me softly. In a way that makes my heart beat faster, because I think I might say the words. I might say aloud what's haunting me.

'Quinn, it's your shot,' Pace calls.

With my next blink, the idea of opening up disappears.

Mama wants her prognosis to stay private. The last thing Annie needs is to be exposed to the world for getting knocked up to a pro-baller she isn't even dating.

18

SEPTEMBER

Sas
Dinner With Coach Roy

I'm sitting on Glen and Millie's sofa, stuffed to the brim of Millie's famous – to my family – seafood risotto and homemade garlic bread. I'm staying over at their palatial suburban home, in order that I can partake in the wine and not need a cab back to Pace's pad.

It's a bit of a chicken and egg story as to who got together first – Mom and Dad, or Glen and Millie. Dad and Glen played for their college football team. Mom and Millie met in their junior year and became best friends. I'm not sure I've ever had the *full* story in all its eighteen plus detail, but it goes something like, Dad propositioned Mom and Millie made eyes at Glen at the same end-of-season house party.

Fast forward a decade and Coach Roy and Millie became my godparents – Roy never played pro-ball like Dad did; he went directly into coaching.

One of the benefits of staying over tonight is that I'm already wearing elasticated loungewear, which I need after Millie serves me a dish of tiramisu. She titters as she takes a seat with her own bowl, in the opposite corner of the sofa to mine.

I know better than to waste one of Millie's signature puddings, so I dive in.

Glen sets down an Irish coffee on the table next to his chair and digs into his portion, too.

He looks the way he does during season – tired eyes, a little too red in the cheeks. He'll have spent the day reviewing tape for the coming weekend's game and honing the book of plays for it with his position coaches.

'So, young lady, are you going to tell your godmomma what you're really doing down here in Texas? I know you must be missin' the City,' Millie says.

She catches me off guard – although I should have anticipated the question – and I use the obscene mouthful of coffee liqueur-soaked dessert as a delay tactic. All the while, I'm mindful of Glen's eyes on me – more a sense than literally seeing his intrigue.

'A couple of things.' I shrug, feigning nonchalance. 'First, I'm keeping an eye on Colton Quinn, though it's nice to spend time with Pace and Max, too. Secondly, I'm keen to get to some college games and peruse the talent for potential representation by the agency, and me specifically.'

'Don't you need to be in New York to work?' Millie probes. There's something in her slightly narrowed eyes – an expression only someone who knows her well enough would recognize – that tells me she's not wholly believing of my tale.

I shake my head, swallowing another mouthful of delectable hip-widener. Is she onto the fictitious Colton and Megan narrative?

'Does anyone need to be rooted anywhere these days?' I chuckle. 'Unless you're the head coach of a football franchise,' I add, daring to look Glen's way. 'I can work from anywhere and since I'm back living with Mom and Dad in suburbia post-college, and until I can afford something in the city, it's nice to have the luxury of Pace's empty house most of the time.'

I try not to dwell on that asshat Patrick who is probably reveling in me being out of sight down here and going along to a ton of career-building meetings with senior agents.

'There's nothing going on between you and Pace, is there?' Glen asks, dragging my attention from my work nemesis and making me almost choke on my food. He sounds more like my father than godfather.

'No. He's more like a best friend or big brother.'

Glen sips his coffee. 'Good, because he's one hell of a tight end and he's a strong leader, but his reputation with the ladies is—'

Pace is a hook-up only kind of guy.

'Glen, you absolutely do not need to give me the birds and the bees talk.'

Millie and I laugh as he stammers an incomprehensible response, cheeks aflame, more than if he was hollering instructions from the sidelines of the championship final.

'I could have told you that, Glen,' Millie says. 'Because try as this young lady may to deflect, I know Colton Quinn doesn't need round-the-clock babysitting, and I am *not* blind. That boy is sweet on the eye.'

Now my skin flushes to mirror my godfather's. As I refute that there's anything romantic happening between me and my client, I remember his proposition at Pace's door on Sunday night. The way it tormented everything south of my ribcage. I remember today on the golf course, watching the muscles of his arms bend and flex. The way his butt clenched with every swing of his club.

'Whether he is or isn't, he's dating Megan Frost,' I say, in a bid to move the conversation along.

'Oh, you know, now that you mention it, I think I did see something about that online.'

'Well, all I know,' Glen says, 'is that he had one hell of an opener against Pittsburgh and he had one of the worst games he's played against Kansas City. Can all your babysitting shed any light on that?'

'How do you mean?'

'I mean, do you know what got into the kid in the off-season and am I at risk of having that version of him on my roster for another sixteen games?'

'I'm working on it, I promise.'

He sets down his bowl, pats the arms of his chair and rises to his feet. 'Good. Because Lord knows the kid can play. And I'm telling you like I told Harris, I *want* to keep him and give him the money he deserves, but if Quinn can't give me consistently high performances, I don't have a leg to stand on with Monte. If he plays like he did against Kansas, he'll be moving on by the end of the season.'

'That's the last thing he wants,' I say, looking up to Glen. 'If you cut him in half, he'd bleed San Antonio Bears.'

Glen nods somberly. 'I know that. But my hands are tied unless he comes up with the goods. He caused himself a lot of damage with Monte and his teammates in the break.'

'I really think there's more to it,' I say.

'I agree. So, find out what it is. Make him talk. It's not his physical ability that's the problem. It's that his head isn't in the game. Whatever worked for him against Pittsburgh, I need that guy on my offense.'

Millie rolls her eyes. 'Oh all right now, Glen. Head on up to bed and let me gossip with my goddaughter.'

Glen ruffles my hair as if I were still ten years old, then makes his way to bed.

'Now tell me,' Millie says, twisting on the sofa to face me and pulling her legs up beneath her. 'If you aren't down here for Pace and you aren't interested in Colton, who are you *really* into, girlie? Because you are *not* living in the deep south just to get more space, and you could fly down here for work as often as you need.'

This makes me ask the same thing of myself... *Why am I here?* Colton and Megan seem to understand what they need to do. Colton's so busy doing whatever it is he does at home on the ranch and training that he doesn't have time to get himself into trouble. And Millie's right, I could catch a college game anywhere in the country.

I refuse to believe I'm here because Colton twists my stomach into the kind of knots it's impossible to ignore. I know better.

Ergo, I *have* to believe I'm here to get him talking. To understand him better and help his game emotionally.

An hour later, lying on Glen and Millie's spare bed, I send Colton a message I don't expect a reply to until morning.

> I meant what I said earlier. I'm all ears for a long story, if you're willing to tell it.

Despite the late hour, I get a response a few minutes later.

COWBOY

> Don't worry about it. Not much to tell. I'm with Meg right now. Speak soon.

19

SEPTEMBER

Colton
She Kissed Me

Megan comes back from the toilet in the steakhouse where we've had a late dinner by the river. I relax when she's back with me. We might not be a real couple but I'd protect any woman, any person in trouble, and she's getting a lot of extra attention recently. I'm a big guy but more than that, at home in San Antonio, I have something of a protected status. A town treasure. Weird but true.

My phone pings and I quickly glance at it before pocketing the device.

> CITY GIRL
>
> That's great. Hope you're both having a good time.
> Don't do anything I wouldn't do.

She signs off the message with a winking emoji.

I don't know what Sas would or wouldn't do – except that I know she won't let me enjoy one night with her – but my own message landed with her.

It was childish to let her know I'm with Megan at this time of night and give her no insight. To not tell her that Megan and I came out late to avoid any crowds (my decision). That I reluctantly changed my mind because I felt guilty about playing golf today when I should have been helping on the ranch or supporting Megan with her Texan accent and dialect because that's part of our deal.

I've let people down today, so I suppose staying in town tonight and helping Megan is sort of penance.

Actually, though, it's been surprisingly fun. Megan's a nice girl. We have no chemistry. No fire. No electricity. Or whatever it is that makes you want to take someone to bed. But spending time with her is okay. We've shared a few laughs. I've been entertained by her stories.

As we request the check in the restaurant, I can admit that today has been something of a relief. Hanging out with the guys and Sas was fun. Not least because Sas kicked everyone's ass, including Trent's. I happily lost my early lead to her, or rather, I stopped thinking about my lead, because I was too engrossed by my agent.

I was halfway to Sunshine Ranch when Annie called and told me that Mama was already in bed and the horses had been mucked out, so there was nothing pressing for me to do. Simultaneously, Megan messaged begging for help running her lines because there were parts of it she just wasn't getting. So, I made the decision to bring her out for dinner.

Once I've settled the check, I help Megan into her light jacket. As we're leaving the restaurant, she slips her hand into mine.

I'm not a hand-holding sort of guy, especially with people I don't know all that well, so it feels off, but she glances up to me through her long lashes and asks, 'Is this okay?'

It'd be hard for anyone to refuse her charm. 'Sure.' But I don't want there to be any blurring of lines, so I add, 'This is why we're meeting in public, right? To keep up the pretense.'

'Right.' She beams at me and I think another guy would be lucky to be holding her hand. Just not this one.

We walk by the river for a short while, running through her lines. I think she's genuinely nervous about her new job. It's her first major adult role since the high-school drama.

'One last time,' she says, after what feels like the millionth time that we've crawled through the scene, me correcting her pronunciation and her pleading with me to breathe some life into the characters I read out.

As I've maintained, playing a role doesn't come naturally to me, but it doesn't help that the whole time, I have half a mind on *why* when I sent that message to Sas did I want her to believe that I'm *with* Megan right now?

Am I bitter that she knocked me back? Honestly, she's right. It would be messy.

Or do I want to make her jealous? Because I've spent the entire day wondering if she's into any of my teammates. Thinking of the havoc I would like to wreak on her body. Believing that getting lost in her might be the thing to get me through this season.

My mind being on Sas is what kept my head off other things through the opening game and when she wasn't around in Kansas, I didn't like it.

None of this makes any sense to me.

She's loud. She's incessant. She's *city*.

My polar opposite.

Megan and I have looped back to my car. 'Well, I don't think you're going to be the next big thing in Hollywood, Mr. Quinn, but I do feel better about filming tomorrow.'

'My stage is a gridiron, Meg.' I reach for the passenger door to help her inside and she flashes those immaculate pearly whites.

'You're good people, Colton.'

Just as I'm thinking my job is almost done, she reaches up to grab my neck and her lips press against mine.

She catches me so unawares, it knocks me off balance, and my big old frame bumps into hers. I drop my hands to her waist to steady her, *us*.

When she pulls back from me, she's smiling mischievously. 'There's someone over there with a phone camera trained on us,' she tells me.

Ah. I side-eye the passerby.

'Plus,' she adds, climbing into the car, 'I wondered what it would feel like to kiss you properly, without a dressing room of silverbacks around us.'

She buckles up as I ask her, 'And?'

She shakes her head. 'You are without question deeply in the friend zone.'

Laughter so deep bellows out from my stomach. When I sit into the driver's seat, I tell her, 'I think you're great, Meg. Any other guy—'

She presses a hand to my chest. 'It's fine, Colton. I think the same. Hand-holding only from now on.'

I walk her to the door of her apartment and in a move I've never done myself and only ever seen in movies, I take hold of the hand she offers me and bring it to my lips. 'Good luck tomorrow.'

'Thanks. I'll be seeing you, then?'

'You know where to find me.'

'On the line of scrimmage?' she asks, gentle eyes gleaming.

I chuckle. 'You're learning.'

The friend zone works nicely for me.

* * *

It's three days before I next see Sas. I've been training and working on the ranch, and she's been working – she works damn hard as far as I can tell – so it's unsurprising that we've barely communicated. But I've checked my phone more than usual, waiting for something from her. A sign of life. A sign of jealousy. A relent on her turning down my idea of us having one wild night together.

I was pathetically happy this morning when she said she wanted to speak to me about a TV commercial Megan and I have been offered. Since she's been in meetings all day, she offered to call me tonight and I suggested she come over here instead.

I wanted to see her because even if she hasn't changed her mind about crossing the line with me, I'd like to know we're cool. That I haven't completely ruined our working relationship, too. I want to see the whites of her eyes. And that deep blue of her irises.

Though when I open my apartment door to her, her eyes aren't the first thing drawing my attention. She's standing in front of me wearing a short black dress with a silk tuxedo neckline that dips teasingly low, though not low enough to be unprofessional, only knock-out businesswoman.

'Hey, come in,' I say, as if I'm not thinking I ought to call 911 because this woman is fire. As she steps by me, all I can do is watch her feet clad in red-soled pumps that I swear to all things mighty I am trying not to visualize digging into the small of my back as we—

I bite down on my knuckle, maybe trying to remind myself what's real. Possibly to give my mind something to eat that's not her because hot-damn, she's enticing.

'This is Jason,' I tell her, closing the door and gesturing to the kitchen area, where my personal chef – who's being patient as hell with me recently as I call on him hit and miss – is preparing three portions of seafood fettucine. It's Friday, a carb-loading day, and I wasn't sure if Sas would stay for dinner, so I asked Jason to cover all bases.

'Jason, this is Sas. You'll know her life story by the time you leave tonight because she never stops talking.' I pretend to ignore her slack jaw, smirking as I pass by her and make for the refrigerator.

'Drink, Sas?' I ask once she and Jason have exchanged introductions. 'Club soda, Jason can make up some kind of infused water, beer, wine, tea, coff—'

'Look at you, playing the extrovert.' She slips a large burgundy purse from her forearm and sets it down on one of the stools at my kitchen island. 'Club soda is great, thanks. I'm driving.'

I pause, glaring at her around the open door of the refrigerator.

'Relax, I've borrowed Pace's SUV,' she tells me. 'Though I'm perfectly safe in a sports car.'

I set her drink in front of her, trying not to gawp down the front of her dress, or at the smooth skin of her crossed legs, or the way her calves are shaped in those heels.

'Don't give me anything else to worry about,' I say before my brain has engaged. I consider backtracking, playing it down, but fuck it, the horse has bolted.

'I'm surprised you keep a stocked refrigerator here, since Annie tells me you're nearly always at the ranch when you're not playing or training these days,' Sas says. She sips her drink then wags a finger between Jason – who is now plating up the pasta – and me. 'How does this work? Do you go out to the ranch, Jason?'

Jason glances up from his task in hand and I shrug – go ahead. 'We work it out,' he tells Sas. 'He's catered at training and in the hotel the night before and morning of game day. The meals around that, sometimes I batch cook or give him a recipe for.'

'You cook?' she asks me. But before I can respond, she adds, 'I know how much you star players are shielded from the mundanities of real life.'

She doesn't mean anything by it, but she's hit a nerve. I feel my muscles tensing in response. Everyone thinks I don't feel and don't react – at least they did before I caused Auston a trip to the ER a few months back – but I do. I hear, see, feel everything and react like a human being. I've been called a robot before but that's not true. Cut me and I bleed.

The difference between me and other people is that I've learned to contain my emotions and control them. That's what being brought up around a house full of foster kids will do for you. You learn that they need attention more than you do. That their emotions are heightened. That their voices need to be heard more than yours in that moment, and so, you internalize, you learn to keep things to yourself. To spare your family more trauma. To protect yourself from the abuse that might get hurled your way out of, often understandably, uncontrollable feelings.

I do it now. I pretend like Sas's words didn't mentally send me home to the ranch and what's going on there.

'I make a mean spinach and mushroom omelet,' I tell her, though focusing on Jason's three dishes of food, which he's topping with cracked black pepper. 'I didn't know if you'd want to eat with us, so Jason made you a plate.'

She looks from the plate of steaming food to me, to Jason, back to the food, to me again. 'That's scarily thoughtful of you, thank you.' To Jason she says, 'Not you, Jason. It's super kind of you to go to the additional effort, but Colton here probably can't imagine anything worse than listening to my unrelenting racket over dinner.'

I turn away because I don't want to show her the smirk that plays on my lips. The woman can drive me from hurtin' to smirkin' in the time a Mustang goes from zero to sixty.

Carrying my plate and my own club soda to the dining table, I mutter, though loud enough for Sas to hear, 'Talking your enemies to death is your superpower.'

'See,' she says, coming to sit opposite me on one of the two long wooden bench seats either side of the table.

In my living-dining area, we have a panoramic view of San Antonio at dusk as the lights of the city come to life. It's the primary reason I bought this place. The main reason I love it. But it doesn't beat the sound of crickets, cicadas and the vast open plains of rural Texas.

Jason serves up three plates of pasta and when Sas hums around her first forkful, I swear every part of my body that's below the tabletop is pleading to get closer to this woman. My chef catches me ogling and humor creases the corners of his eyes.

'Oh my gosh, Jason, this might be the best fettucine I have *ever* tasted,' she says, twirling a second helping of ribbons around her fork. I ought to jam my hands over my ears if I'm going to keep it together. 'You have to give me the recipe.'

This leads Sas and Jason into conversation about everything from nutrition to college, from Jason's upbringing to his romantic life. Sas really could talk the hind legs off a donkey, but as I watch her and listen to her, I'm also in awe of how comfortable she is in her own skin. How easily she can draw anyone into conversation with her. A level of confidence I've only ever found on a football field.

Forty-five minutes later, after I've loaded the dishwasher to allow Jason and Sas to continue chatting, Jason heads out, waved off by his new BFF.

'I was wrong,' I tell her from where I'm resting back against the kitchen counter. 'Your superpower might be making other people talk themselves to death.'

The short, snorted laugh I receive in response brings a lightness to me that I'm not able to hide from her this time.

She locates her purse on the stool and takes out her laptop. 'Shall we chat about the commercial?'

'Sure. Sofa?'

'That works,' she says, suddenly reaching absurd decibels.

As we come to sit on the curved sofa, angled toward the view, Sas positions herself as far away from me as possible, which I'm delighted about.

I showered and sprayed not long before dinner, so I *know* I don't smell bad.

Instead, I'd guess she's keeping her distance because she's unnerved.

She's affected by me, *us*.

She is absolutely not over my proposition last week and, though I won't renew it, the fact she might be feeling *something* between us is a massive turn-on.

One that I set aside as I ask, 'What's the deal?'

Sas walks me through the details of an offer for Megan and me to pose as a couple doing laundry to get my kit clean from dirt stains – which I point out aren't so much of a thing when we primarily play on fake grass –

in a prime-time commercial for America's number one liquid laundry detergent.

'What do you think?' Sas asks, almost forcing me to admit that I haven't been listening, because I've been mentally taking her out of that tailored dress for the whole time she was speaking. 'The money on the table is good. And it's great that these deals are still on offer, what with...' She twists her hand through the air in a way that irks me.

If she's going to bad-mouth me... to my face... own it. Don't hide behind a gesture.

Pushing up to stand, I move to the window. The view is spoilt by this conversation. 'I don't think it's for me.'

'Give me strength,' she mutters. 'Why not?'

Folding my arms across my chest, I turn to face her. 'Because Meg and I would look too much like a couple.'

Sas rises to stand and mirrors my pose. 'More than holding hands and kissing along the river walk for the entire world to see on social media?'

Two things occur to me simultaneously. One, social media makes fast work of spreading news about my personal life. Two, Sas is bitter. Maybe even... jealous?

'As it happens, I think you should turn it down,' she says.

'Then why are you here?'

'Because my da— Harris thinks you should do it. He thinks detergent is a softer image than the one you've displayed in recent months and it could be good for you.'

'He's on board with the fake relationship now?'

'Not exactly but since you *are* having a relationship with Megan—'

'I'm no—'

'You might as well capitalize on it. *I*, on the other hand, think that your relationship with Megan is too big a deal for detergent. You want big money commercials. Luxury brands. You cheapen your worth by contracting with Waves.'

God, this woman is infuriating. She never lets me *speak*. It's like being a kid in a crowded house. My temper causes me to tell her, rightly or wrongly, 'I'm getting used to you turning down a sure thing for me.'

She dumps her hands on her perfectly curved hips. 'What's *that* supposed to mean?'

'That this whole contract-extension bluff isn't working.' Though even as I say it, I'm cognizant of the other sure thing she turned down. *Me.*

'The team are coming around, the sales of merchandise with your name and number on it are great, and, in case it didn't hit you over the head like a mallet, you actually took a day off on Tuesday and socialized with your team-mates, like an actual functioning, feeling human being.'

There it is again: the assumption that I don't feel. I wish I didn't but it isn't true.

'I went to golf so I didn't have to spend the day running lines with my fake girlfriend.'

'Pfft. Really? Because you two looked pretty cozy to me.'

Too right she's a green-eyed monster.

And damn straight I'm hot for it.

'*She* kissed *me*,' I say, closing the space between us, until I can hear her stubborn exhale.

'What are you, thirteen? If she did kiss you, it's because you gave her a signal. And who could blame you? She's gorgeous.'

I'm not even listening to her words, only the lack of conviction they carry. Sas is into me, and the odds on this one night that I'd like with her are looking up. At least my increasing pulse rate and core body temperature think so.

'She is attractive,' I say much more calmly than I feel. 'But there's nothing going on. I don't want her.'

Sas looks up to me, draws her pink tongue along her lips and swallows. *Say yes.*

'Colton...' She presses her fingertips to my chest, searing my skin through my shirt as she applies the kind of pressure that tells me she's fighting the fission between us.

'I won't ask again, Sas, because you told me no. In my book, when a woman tells a man no, it means no. But dammit, I want you to change your mind...'

She fixes her electric eyes on me, straightens her shoulders and inhales so hard her breasts rise toward me. 'My dad already thinks I'm too emotional and unprofessional, Colton. A one-night stand with his client isn't worth undermining everything I'm working for.'

She turns away, closes the lid on her laptop, stows it and, in those devastating heels, strides toward my door.

'One night is all I can offer,' I tell her.

'I'm not asking for more, Quinn. I'm saying no to anything.'

Now I'm *Quinn?*

On the threshold of the exit, she about-turns, the expression that gives Pace reason to call her a firecracker drawn on her face. 'Do you want the detergent gig or not?'

For two reasons, I tell her, 'Yes. I'll do it.'

The first is to piss her off.

'Fine, I'll set it up.'

The second is because there's a chance she'll run, that I've come on too hard, scared her with her own desires – because her words might tell me she doesn't want to go to bed but everything else about her tells me otherwise.

A commercial deal gives her a reason to stick around. It gives me a chance to change her mind.

Regardless, after the game in Kansas, I think I need her buzzing around my head just to make me play.

'Great,' she tells me.

She lets the heavy door crash closed behind her, and for reasons I'm not sure I comprehend, I'm left grinning after the feistiest woman I've known.

20

SEPTEMBER

Sas
My Tummy Flips

I take my seat at the Bears game in Alamo Stadium, which is lit by floodlights as the sky is already turning midnight blue. To clarify, I'm not here because Colton said he wants me at his games, but to watch *all* the agency's clients.

Plus, I should see the opposition teams. I'm here to watch the Denver players, too, even if I do have a soft spot for the Bears (and maybe want them to win the championship).

No, I'm not here for Colton specifically. In fact, I'm still pissed at Colton. For multiple reasons. The first, he's doing that stupid laundry detergent commercial that I advised him not to take. Second, he showed up at Pace's door and propositioned me. Not just propositioned but told me he wants to make me his one-night stand.

It's not that I wasn't flattered. Honestly, there was a beat where I thought I'd dive on him and rip off his clothes. My irritation comes from him dismissing my role as his agent, or associate agent, at least. He's my *client*. And to proposition me, no matter that I might have had inappropriate thoughts about him too, makes him just another man in this field who doesn't respect what I'm doing. Adding himself to a long list of men, which often includes my own father, who make me question whether this job is really for women.

'Sas!' Annie waves, her other hand resting on her baby mountain, as she approaches our seats from the steps.

I help her get settled, noting that she's out of breath. It must be like carrying a weight belt around twenty-four seven being as pregnant as she is. Colton's dad, Sonny, is close behind her and shakes my hand, a little formally, before he takes his seat. At least one man still sees me as a career woman.

Annie's wearing a cute summer dress with an elasticated belt and ruffled sleeves. I tell her she looks pretty. She really does, despite her blushes. I leave out that she has the same shade of eyes as Colton.

They both have striking brown eyes with flecks of gold that remind me of galaxies in the universe, though there's a thicker black ring around Colton's that somehow makes him seem more intense. They share the same wide smile and straight teeth, though Colton's lips are a little plumper. Kissable, some women might think. And Annie has the same thick cocoa-brown hair as her brother, though she has highlights to brighten hers. Neither of them looks much like their dad, so I can only guess they take after their mom.

I like Annie a lot. She's a straight talker, like Colton, but she smiles more, the air about her is lighter, and unlike her brother, who prefers not to speak, Annie is chatty. It's easy making conversation with her. When we pause after our initial greetings, I offer to get her and her dad a drink, though they both tell me to relax.

I think Sonny is keen for the walk to the family area and free bar.

'Who're we waiting for today?' Annie asks, glancing to the two spare seats next to me.

'Harris is coming and I guess the other seat is for Megan?'

We both roll our eyes. Me at the fact that my dad doesn't come to this many Bears games in a row any season – he has other clients and other teams to watch, though he's always on the road for football. Clearly, he's checking in on me.

Annie, I think, is rolling her eyes at her brother's pretend girlfriend. Although even I'm starting to believe the increased media attention around the couple that's making their relationship look like more than Colton is letting on to me.

Another reason why I absolutely cannot cross the line with him. There's another person involved and the last thing I want in my life is a messy love triangle.

Colton's dad comes back with drinks and hands me a beer in a plastic cup as the team's anthem starts bellowing into the arena for the players' entrance.

As I thank Sonny, I see my own dad making his way into the stand. Behind him, someone I've seen before, a PR executive the agency hired for Pace once, when his off-field reputation was... questionable. But I know that Pace has been on the straight and narrow for the last few years, since he made Captain. And I know that Max tows the line often, but he rarely crosses it.

So, by process of elimination, my guess is that Sean Boyle is here with regard to Colton. Something my dad has chosen not to let me in on, which augments my already prickly mood tonight.

Dad doesn't trust me.

Yet he kisses me on the cheek and has the kind of musk he gets from traveling most of the day. But less the long-day smell, and more the way he greets me like I'm his daughter in front of Sean, has me quickly bypassing pleasantries. I'd rather he shook my hand. Also, I'm too angry to want his PDA right now.

'You remember Sean, don't you, Kansas?' Dad asks as Sean extends a hand to me.

'Nice to see you, Sean.' I say the words with a forced smile, all the while glaring at my dad. Asking him why in hell he didn't give me a heads up. *Why blindside me? Why am I even down here babysitting Colton if my dad is making plays behind my back?*

I'm wearing ripped jeans and a Bears jersey, for God's sake. If I'm meeting with a PR executive, I want to be in my office wear.

Dad takes the spare seat immediately next to me, either intentionally distancing Sean from my ill-temper, or because he wants to excuse his actions quietly for my ears only.

He confirms it's the latter when he leans into me and says, 'If Colton's doing commercials with Megan now, he's upped the ante. We need to engage Sean. If the shit hits the fan on this whole media relationship—'

'It won't,' I snap.

Though in all honesty, it might. And now Colton's immature point-scoring with me means he has Sean Boyle working for him.

I don't know everything about Colton – I'm not convinced many people do – but I think I know him well enough now to guess he's not going to be happy about engaging a PR firm.

'Way to be on the same page as me, Dad.'

There's bite to my words, though my eyes are on the field as the best players are announced ahead of the game. A surge of something makes my tummy flip as I anticipate Colton running onto the gridiron.

Dad speaks close to my ear as we stand to applaud the team. 'You've got a lot to learn, Kansas.'

Annie cheers as her brother is announced and he sprints out of the tunnel, through the guard of his teammates. My insides betray me, doing some kind of dance for him. He glances up to our seats, kissing his fist and holding it up. It's the same move he did when Megan was at the last home game, and he must know she isn't here tonight.

Which means he must be sending the kiss in the direction of his sister and dad. But I can't tear my eyes away from him. And for a second, I completely forget myself. I wonder what it would feel like if he was sending his affection my way.

As soon as my senses come back to me, I realize I need to leave Texas.

I'm catching some kind of desire that I can't and shouldn't have for the testing split end. And I no longer need to babysit his behavior because Sean Boyle is about to be all over it. No good can come of me staying in San Antonio.

All our guys play out of their skin in the first quarter. The Bears are 10–3 up, Colton having scored a touchdown with an overhead catch very few players could take. He looks like the player I know he can be. The player he was earlier last season.

'Looks like he's got his head straight tonight,' Annie says to me in the break before the second quarter.

I glance her way as her dad slips out either for a drink or the bathroom, or both.

'He's got a lot going on. And I know I'm not helping matters.' She plants both hands on her unborn baby.

'He's worried about you?' I ask, genuinely curious. 'Is everything going okay? You don't have to answer that.'

'That's all right. Baby is fine. Growing like a small elephant. He's clearly going to take after his daddy. But Colton's sour with me. About multiple things but mostly, I think, about college. I want to drop out. I just don't see how I can look after this little one solo and finish my senior year.'

'Do you have any support? The dad?'

As she inhales and exhales a fast, shallow breath, her nostrils flare and her eyes seem to glaze over. 'Colton hasn't clued you in on that?' I raise an eyebrow and she shakes her head in response. 'I assumed he'd have at least let you in on my dirty secret. My brother should have been a left tackle the way he protects everyone else's blindside and forgets himself.'

She sighs, giving me the kind of sad half-smile I've seen on Colton.

'No, it'll just be me.' She shrugs. 'That's what you get for having faith in the wrong guy, despite all the warning signs.'

I should heed a few of those myself. 'What about your family? Your mom, dad? Colton is here.'

I wonder as I say the words if this is why Colton is so desperate to stay in Texas next season. I've seen how much he loves Annie.

'It's not that straightforward, though, is it? I mean, people won't always be around.' Her eyes suddenly dart to me with something else in them – fear? 'People have their own obligations.'

'So, you and Colton are fighting?'

'He says he'll pay for help so I can finish my final year.'

'But you don't want it?'

She strokes her tummy. 'Family means more to me than anything. I want to be the one who's there for my baby before anyone else.'

'You could defer? Even if you've no intention of finishing, it gives you an option, right?'

'You sound like my brother.'

I give her a soft smile. 'Well, he's a smart guy and he loves you. A college education isn't the be all and end all, but deferring leaves the door open for you to make a decision further down the line. You might want to have a career with your degree one day. For your sake and your little one. I could do something else but I couldn't be an attorney if I hadn't been to college. It gives me a choice, that's all. Women have a tough enough ride as it is. Maybe you open doors for yourself and Baby, too, one day.'

The game restarts and my eyes immediately find Colton standing off from the offense on the line of scrimmage – my stomach leaps.

'But hey, it's your decision. Not Colton's. Not anyone else's. And regardless of what you decide, you're going to crush mom life. Look how much you love the baby already.'

As I watch her brother break free and take a catch for first down, I think maybe I should have listened to him more, too. He didn't want this whole charade with Megan; he just wants to renew his contract and stay in Texas to help his sister. Now, Sean Boyle is going to ramp up this fake romance like nobody's business.

So, I spend the remainder of the game pretending that I'm not totally into my client, that I don't melt into my seat every time he looks into the stands, and that I'm not wedged between my dad and Colton's sister as I reluctantly lust after him.

What I need and what I want is one night.

Oh boy. I need to be the stronger person here.

* * *

I wish I could leave with Annie and Sonny after the game. It's late, Annie's tired, and they'll see Colton tomorrow, when he stays at the ranch. Tonight, he'll stay at his apartment. Really close by me, at Pace's house.

It would be so easy to give in to—

'Sean, I'll take you to meet Colton in person,' Dad says, not at all inviting me, or even acknowledging me.

So, to spite him, I put on my best toothy smile and say, 'Great idea!' I cock my head at Dad as I lead Sean into the stadium's passageways.

Except as we approach the dressing room, my hands are clammy with nerves. Primarily because I think Colton is going to hate having a PR consultant onboard. Secondarily, a very close second, I can feel my hormones firing at the thought that Colton, who always showers last, might still be sitting in just a towel behind this heavy blue door.

The security team check in with him, then let us into the dressing room on Colton's say so.

I instantly regret not wearing some kind of eye cover because this man gets more buff every time I see him. And he's wearing nothing but a Bears-branded towel around his extremely hench waist.

I need to get on a dating app.

I need to have this conversation with my eyes closed.

Then I need to go home and sort myself out.

After that, I need to date and find another outlet for this increasingly pent-up frustration.

Dad reaches him first and introduces Sean, which gives me a chance to compose myself. *This is ridiculous.* I. Do. Not. Want. A. Thing. With. Colton. Quinn.

Not even one night.

'Sean, hey, thanks for coming out,' Colton says, and *this* is what finally pulls me from my stupor.

'You knew Sean was coming?' I ask, knowing my frown lines have put in an appearance.

'Yeah, Harris arranged it. I approved the game tickets.' He says this nonchalantly, and I realize he thinks I knew, too.

They cut me out entirely.

Even if I tried, I wouldn't be able to take the thunder out of my expression.

Glaring at Dad, then at Colton, I tell them, 'Looks like you don't need me. I'm going to take off.'

'Sas?' Colton asks, stepping toward me as I move away. He's questioning. Wondering what? Why I'm pissed?

As if it's not easy to see that I'm down here working my ass off and being cut out professionally by him and my dad. Should I be happy that I'm seen as pointless?

Why am I even wasting my time in Texas? Catching stupid, hormone-fueled feelings that don't need to be caught.

Sports guys are the pits.

'Colton?' I reply, boring holes in him.

We're facing each other, neither one of us moving. There's a charge in the air that shouldn't be there between an agent's assistant and a client.

I realize this must appear odd, as I clock the eyes of the few remaining players in the dressing room looking our way.

But my dad and Sean are standing right behind Colton. Other guys are in the dressing room. This isn't allowed to be anything other than a professional stand-off.

I see the moment Colton concedes, his shoulders sinking. 'Goodnight, Sas.'

'Sleep well, Colton. Great game.'

21

OCTOBER

Colton
Show Me the Love, Guys

I'm playing house with Megan, acting out a scene of us bickering over my dirty shorts in a staged kitchen, a lime-green screen behind us.

'Show me the love, guys,' the director says. 'Ramp up the touchy feely.'

Megan is a natural at this, smiling, happy, getting into the role of my domesticated significant other. While I couldn't act my way out of a paper bag. I feel stiff, wooden, and not in a good way.

It's awkward touching her, hugging her, kissing her cheek as if we're a real couple. I'm trying not to think about how many people are going to see this commercial when our performance in front of the twenty or so people in this studio is embarrassing enough.

I'm standing behind Megan, her back to my chest, and playfully speaking into her ear, though for the benefit of the cameras.

She raises her hand to my cheek and looks at me with pretty eyes, as the real her tells the real me, 'Just relax, babe; you're doing great.'

'I don't want you to feel uncomfortable,' I whisper.

She turns to face me and smiles sweetly. 'I don't. This is my bread and butter. It's what I do. You've got this.'

She kisses my cheek, and I nod, grateful for the pep talk, though something about the move makes me cast my eyes to the back of the room, behind the cameras and crew, to where Sas is standing by Sean Boyle, both of them drinking complimentary coffee.

Sas is still pissed at me. She's been grunt-talking to me ever since she found out I knew about Sean's representation. Less at Sean being onboard, more, I think, at the fact she wasn't in the loop. Which, I have to say, isn't entirely my fault. Maybe I should have spoken to her, but I think that's more on a friendship level than a professional one.

Harris is my agent. He's my number-one contact at the agency.

But Sas, I'm realizing, has become someone whose company I enjoy. And there aren't too many people in that bracket.

So, aside from the fact I'm increasingly hot for the woman I can't have, I wish she wasn't fuming at me.

I wish I'd listened to her and turned down this whole stupid gig. More than that, I'm hoping she knows that all this fussing between Megan and me is for show. We're role-playing, even if the girl really can act. She almost had me believing we're a couple at some points in this painstaking hour.

When I look her way, Sas is watching me. So is everyone else in the room really, but she darts her focus away from me as if she's been caught in the act of something taboo. It gives me hope that she might one day cave and let me get this unrelenting need to take her to bed out of my system.

'More eye contact with Megan, Colton,' the director calls. I do as I'm instructed, but not without one more glance at the most attractive woman in the room.

My reasons for taking this commercial are still valid. This is what we're all working toward, isn't it? A new version of me? A new image? One that's the opposite of the guy I was made out to be in the off-season? One that improves the image of the Bears, gets my teammates back onside, makes the club want to improve their offer and extend my contract come March?

The way Sas is clearly griping at Sean quietly at the back of the room, though, makes me think I'll leave my side of the argument in my head.

No good will come of airing my truth.

Story of my life.

'Touch up for Megan's make-up?' someone in the production team calls. 'You're doing great, hunny. The camera loves you. I want to see a little more of you guys behind closed doors, Colton. Free and easy. As if it's just the two of you at home, okay?'

Fuck my life.

Everyone has something to say. Everyone wants to be the loudest.

And I don't want any of it.

22

OCTOBER

Sas

The Guy's a Sleaze

I would rather chew on maggot-infested pickles than be within even viewing distance of Sean Boyle. The guy's a sleaze. Worse than that. He's *fleas* on sleaze.

'It was a good idea to play the old fake-relationship card, Kansas. It was an even better idea to bring me onboard. This is my field of expertise. Soon, the whole world will not only believe that Colton and Megan are dating, they'll wish they were them,' Sean tells me, between smacking on a croissant like a salivating dog with no teeth.

We're standing by the refreshments table in the back of the studio where Colton and Megan are filming their new happy-couple-themed laundry detergent commercial. I've managed to stand myself in the only cool-ish spot, next to an industrial-size fan. While there are no windows in the studio, the artificial lighting, the number of bodies in the space and the boundless amount of recording equipment are adding to the hot temperature outside. I feel as if I've been dropped in a donut fryer.

Maybe it's something to do with the three chocolate iced donuts I've consumed while watching the sickeningly lovey-dovey performances of Colton and Megan.

Colton, *who,* I remind myself, told me he *can't* act. That he *won't* act. That he's authentic.

He even had me fooled, until he went behind my back in hiring Sean.

Reluctantly, I turn to watch the PR exec wiping pastry flakes from the corner of his mouth and brushing down his expensive suit.

'You know, Colton doesn't want to outright lie. I had to convince him this whole thing was a good idea at all.' I'm pleased I matched Sean in tailoring today. My silk blouse and high-waisted pants aren't helping my core body temperature, but they are making me stand taller next to my new nemesis. 'He's comfortable going along with it but—'

Sean sneers in that way city slickers do and inclines his head toward the sexy couple, who have their hands all over each other, their faces barely an inch apart.

'He doesn't look uncomfortable to me. In fact, I'd say those two are well on their way to making my job a whole lot easier.'

I drag a breath through my nose as the muscles in my jaw tighten. Because I don't like Sean and the way he cut me off.

But I look back at Colton and I have to admit, his smile seems genuine. He's awkward in front of the cameras but he doesn't look *un*happy with Megan.

Sean sucks his thumb, making a popping sound as he extracts it from his mouth. 'I can read people, Kansas, and I'm understanding exactly why your dad thought you needed me to wade in here.'

'Oh yeah? Are you about to tell me I'm a rookie, Sean?'

One side of his mouth curls up. 'No. I'm about to tell you that you're on the verge of making a rookie mistake.'

He has my attention now, and my fiercest frown.

'I've seen the way you've been watching Colton all afternoon. I saw the way you looked at him half-naked in the changing rooms at Alamo Stadium. And I see the way he watches you right back.'

I didn't know my temperature could rise any higher, but it does, and I'm sweating, my heart thumping against my ribcage.

'I think Colton and Megan can absolutely help each other out in the reputation stakes. She makes him look sweeter. He makes her look more interesting, sexier and more mature. But guess what would make this whole thing blow up in everyone's face?'

My eyes must look like slits to him because my view has become dark, ominous. 'I'm sure you're going to tell me.'

He nods. 'If it comes out that Colton Quinn has been screwing the pretty new girl at her daddy's agency while he was dating one of America's sweethearts.'

My palm twitches, keen to pick up a pastry and stick a few more flakes to his face. The rest of me is stilled by his words. In part, because he's a dick. Mostly, because I thought I was hiding the fact that, since Colton told me he wants me, I've thought about little else.

Even so, I won't go there because...

'How dare you question my ethics?'

He laughs in a way that's both sinister and aggressive.

'Kansas, if I'm running the show down here now, why are you still in Texas making eyes at my guy?'

I plant my hands on my hips, instantly wishing I hadn't but not able to move them or I risk looking uneasy. 'I'm in Texas to scout new clients.' Even though I've not yet had a chance to do anything about that. 'And I am *not* making eyes at anyone. I would never *screw* one of my clients.' Doubting my own resolve, I swallow. 'I'm also here for other reasons you don't need to understand.'

'Sure. To make him talk, right? To get some kind of explanation for him being caught out in the off-season? Newsflash, sweetheart: he's just being a pro-baller. There's nothing more to tell.'

I glance back at Colton now as he laughs with Megan and some of the crew.

What the hell am I doing risking my reputation over this guy, who is clearly happy to play another game?

'You want to run the show, Sean? Be my guest.'

'I don't need the blessing of a junior associate, sweetheart.'

'You're a jackass, Sean. Anyone ever tell you that?'

He chuckles darkly. 'All the time, kid. All the time.'

With a growl of frustration, I turn on my heel to storm out of the studio. Only, when I reach the exit, I turn back to the buffet table and stuff a napkin with two more donuts for my ride home.

Fuck Sean Boyle. Screw this whole damn male-dominated industry.

* * *

'Jackass doesn't even cover it! I should have given him both barrels.' I'm in Pace's kitchen, striding up and down, stopping only to take a cold can of club soda from the refrigerator, then continuing my rant and supporting strut.

Meanwhile, Pace is reclined on his sofa, *Grand Theft Auto* paused on his large TV screen, watching and listening to me relay my run-in with Sean at the studio.

'Sounds like you did give him one,' Pace tells me, a smirk playing on his lips as he takes his hands behind his head.

'I left feeling like he had the upper hand.' I pause my heel-clicking to pull the ring on my can, then resume the march.

'The man's a jerk but he's good at his job,' Pace says.

'Is that enough, Pace?' I gripe before guzzling down club soda too quickly and forcing myself to gasp my next breath. 'Is it okay to be good at your job but be an awful human?'

He sits up and pats the sofa next to him. Though I feel like I have too much kinetic energy to sit, I do slump down on his deep, comfy furniture with a sigh.

'I'm sick of having my professionalism questioned.' I side-eye him. 'God, I shouldn't even be ranting like this to a client, should I? Maybe Dad has a point.'

'You're venting to a friend, Sas. Friends first, work second. You know that.'

I sip my drink this time, then fiddle with the ring until it snaps off and I push it into the can. 'Maybe that's the problem. I've tried to be friends with Colton and perhaps that's not what I'm supposed to be doing down here. I thought I could get to know him better and understand what's happened in his life to upset his game.'

Pace takes the can from between my hands and plants it down on the coffee table between us and the TV, where his game controller and a dish of chips rest.

'You're going to cut yourself with that thing.' He twists back to recline and flops his legs over mine.

'You're heavy,' I complain weakly.

'I know. Heavy enough to stop your fidgeting.' We both chuckle. 'Look,

Colton isn't a talker. You've been sent on an impossible mission to get him to open up. I'll admit, I liked him when he first came into the squad. He could come out with a smart-ass one-liner sometimes and have me doubled over. But that's not who he's been for a while now. He doesn't hang out with the guys anymore, so he can't win favor. If he can't open up to his teammates, you've got no chance.'

'You choose to tell me this now?'

He shrugs. 'I like having you around. Besides a chef and a cleaner, I don't often have company in this big old place for one.'

'You need a dog.'

'Or a someone.'

I raise one eyebrow at him. *You? A someone?*

He gives a short laugh. We both know he won't give up the dating game any time soon. He's always said women are too much of a diversion of time and energy during playing season.

'Listen, being objective, you can't ask people to change their opinion of you and expect that they'll do it. You've got to earn it in the way you act. If you want Harris and jerks like Sean to see you as the undying professional, make them.' He holds up two palms. 'I happen to love who you are, but... and I mean this from a good place... I can see that sometimes, *maaaayyyyyybe*, you're reactive to situations. Attorneys, agents, they're supposed to be the ones who keep their cool, when the prima donnas like me lose ours.'

I give him a gentle smile, not in the least offended but actually thinking he might have a point. Sean is taking care of Colton's reputation now and if I can't make him talk, why am I here? Because I can't give up a lost cause, or because I've caught feelings for a man I shouldn't want?

Loath as I am to admit it, Sean's right that if Colton and Megan did form a real connection, it would make this whole thing perfect.

'I think I'm going to go back to New York.' I look at Pace, who makes a sad puppy-dog face but doesn't object, which I take as affirmation that it's the right thing to do. 'Dad has to see how hard I'm working and he can't see it from here. Until he does, nothing will change. He won't take me seriously.'

I leave out that I ought to get away from Colton because seeing him with Megan today was... not fun. I wasn't jealous but I was... *Fuck,* I *was* jealous.

Which means even more than proving myself to my dad, I need to make sure I don't do anything stupid until these lusty-lou feelings have disappeared.

'Why can't you coach Colton like this, huh? *You* could be the person to get through to him.'

'Because Colton doesn't want to hear it. He is the way he is.'

'Maybe he's shy? Thought of that?'

'Ball players aren't shy, Sas.'

'I agree, he has an arrogant streak. In fact, I'd like him to ramp it back up consistently on the field. But something's thrown him off, I'm sure of it, and I think he could use an arm around his shoulder.'

'I'm not it. I'm here for a good time, not a long time.'

'You're his captain.' I drop a hand to his foot and flinch. 'Yuck. You need to talc those toes. It's a fungal farm up in there.'

Pace chortles, wiggling his toes under my nose until I push his legs to the floor.

'Give him a chance, Pace. I honestly think there's more to him than just an angry, brooding man-whore.'

With that mic-drop, I go in search of my laptop to book flights home.

* * *

I know I'll be back in San Antonio to watch the guys, but I don't know when and I'm unlikely to be back for a lengthy swathe of time. I'll scout players from New York, once I've convinced Dad to let me have my own client, whether or not Colton gets a better offer from the Bears, because it's out of my hands now.

I've packed up everything, despite Pace saying I could leave some stuff in his guest bedroom. Lying face down on top of my luggage to pull the zipper shut, I realize I've bought a few more outfits down here than I should have. That, and I've acquired a lot of Bears merch through Pace.

Eventually, I complete the deed and start wheeling my case along Pace's hallway toward the stairs. Over the sound of my wheels on his wood floor, I hear two male voices. One Pace. The other—

I still at the top of the stairs, looking down to where Colton's standing with Pace, carrying a colorful box of twelve donuts. I recognize the get-up of the store, which is miraculous because I am 100 percent distracted by the man wearing washed-out jeans, a buckled belt and a tightly fitted white shirt that displays every. Delectable. Inch of him.

'I'll get your luggage,' Pace tells me, bounding up the stairs three at a time. At the top, he pats my shoulder and tells me, 'I'll give you a minute. Shout me when you're ready to leave for the airport.'

'Are you looking for me?' I ask Colton, wishing I could tear my attention from him and his just-showered-looking mussed-up hair as I make my way into the lounge.

'Are you going somewhere?' he asks in response.

'Home. To New York.'

He frowns. 'Why?'

I act more nonchalant than I feel, pretending my throat hasn't dried at just the sight of him, as if my body hasn't decided I'm leaving, I'm safe, so it can just go whole hog and admit to wanting the very bones of this man.

I shrug, my casual tee pulling out of my ripped jean shorts as I do, and I try to ignore Colton's gaze wandering to my midriff. 'Because I don't need to be here anymore.'

'Is it because of the commercial yesterday?' he asks. 'Because I'm not entirely sure what I've done wrong or Sean's done wrong but I think I have an idea and these...' He holds out the box of brightly iced donuts. 'Are a peace offering.'

I don't mean to but my hands seem to plant on my hips of their own volition. 'What makes you think I'm pissed?'

'Because I've made a career out of reading the game, and you're the kind of person who wears her plays on her face. I can guess everything you're thinking just by watching the change in your eyes. Their color, their severity, the creases that form when you're angry.'

His words make me look away from him. I really *hope* he can't read everything I think and feel when I'm around him.

I stare at the box, then finally up to him, and watch a lopsided grin – an annoyingly sexy, lopsided grin – tease his lips. God, this version of him is the one that makes me forget my rationale for anything.

'I saw how much you liked donuts at the studio yesterday.'

I feel a pout draw on my lips. 'I'm going to take your donuts, not because I'm a donut lover, but because I do feel like you should extend a peace offering.'

He nods, handing them over, and I try not to gobble-up one of these delectable-smelling sweet treats right away. This is my new professional era, after all.

'I'm not good with the female psyche, so I'm going to guess you're either pissed because I came onto you, but why now? Or because I agreed to hire Sean and you didn't even know it was a possibility? Both options are confusing to me.'

'Confusing? How can either— You know what, it doesn't matter. I'm really leaving because Sean has taken over the PR stuff now, so you don't need me for that. Honestly, the main reason I was down here was to try to get to know you and understand what's got your game off and, I don't know, see if I could help somehow. But—'

'You do help, Sas.' He takes one of his giant strides toward me, making me grateful for the large box of carbs between us. 'You, and your incessant talking, your attitude, and the fact that I can't stop thinking about getting you—'

We glance to the ceiling as Pace makes noises moving around above us.

Good. Let's not finish that sentence.

Except, Colton raises a hand toward my face and I think I'm going to let him touch me, until he pulls his hand away.

Close shave.

But he's staring at my lips and I know because I'm watching him in a similar way.

'You're a distraction, Sas. A huge one. So loud that you drown everything else out.'

'Oh, so now I'm loud again—'

'Let me finish.'

I nod, trying to stay focused on his eyes, though they're just as alluring as his lips.

'I need you to stay because when you're not around, the volume seems to crank up on everything else and it affects my game.'

'What, so I'm like your muse now?' I snort, nervously and wholly unattractively. Not that I'm trying to *be* attractive to Colton. The exact opposite, in fact. Which reminds me... 'The agency has other clients who need me, Colton. I'm a professional adviser. And I'm sorry if I've given you any reason to think it's okay to proposition me, but this...' I motion between us, one hand gripping the box between us needlessly tightly, my thighs pinched together. 'It's not an option. It's never going to be an option.'

God, Dad's right; I have a few things to work on. Not falling for clients being *numero uno*.

Colton leans his head to one side, an arrogance I've seen on the field that I hate to admit, I find strikingly hot. 'It's not an option?'

I feel heat in parts of my body that I really shouldn't. That forces me to tell him, 'No. So, thanks for the donuts. I was annoyed that you and Harris cut me out of hiring Sean. I felt like you went behind my back, professionally.'

He sobers now. 'Harris is my agent, Sas. And I'm grateful for everything you do but ultimately, he's the guy who's represented me for the last three years.' He holds out his hands. 'Isn't this a good thing? Isn't it what you asked of me – to date Megan, let the media think it's real? Wasn't it me who didn't want this in the first place?'

'It's working, isn't it? The noise about you in the media is positive. You've got new endorsement opportunities. Sales of the Bears' merch with your number on it are up, and all this reflects well on the club for your teammates.'

'Exactly. That's what I'm saying. So, I'm leaning into it. Like you wanted.'

'Like *I* wanted? Ultimately, this is all to benefit you, Colton.'

He shakes his head. 'Right, and there's no upside for you if this goes to plan?'

'I'm not in this just for the money.'

He stares at me. 'That makes two of us. I'm in this to stay with the Bears.' He holds his next blink, in frustration, I think. 'I should have just accepted their first offer.'

As he drags a hand back through the hair I'd really like to pull, I remember Annie. He wants to stay in Texas to support her. Suddenly, the twinging in my stomach is less lust and more... caring.

'I wish you would have just opened up to me, Colton.'

Our eyes connect and that feeling in my torso gets heavier, deeper somehow.

'Maybe you just have to take my word for some things, Sas.'

He doesn't want to expose Annie. He wants to protect her story. I feel for him, but... 'Whatever you say to me can stay between us.'

We're locked in some kind of moment and I think, as his lips slowly part, that maybe he will talk.

'So, will you stay?'

'No. If you're not going to let me help you, there's nothing more for me to do here.'

'You're happy here. And I thought you wanted to catch some college games to check out the new talent. If I re-sign with the Bears, you get a client, right?'

Oh, he's good. He knows how to get into another player's head.

'I can go to college games in New York. While dazzling the agency with my hard work.'

He watches me for too long, until we hear Pace coming down from the mezzanine and say, 'Sas, we should probably head to the airport.'

'Great, yup, I'm ready. Thanks, Pace.'

'I can take you,' Colton says, quieter now that Pace is bringing my luggage down the stairs in the background.

'There's no need. I have a ride. And twelve donuts I don't want to share.'

He smiles gently. Panty-meltingly. 'All right. But promise me you're not leaving because of what I said after the Kansas game? I said it. I meant it. I want it. But I'm also not trying to get in your head and fuck with you. You said no and I heard you.'

He's leaning closer to me to speak quietly, and I inhale the scent of outdoors on him, mixed with something darker, smoother, manly.

'That's not why I'm leaving. It's already forgotten.'

'So, you're not worried about what you'd do if you stayed?'

I swallow so hard I'd be amazed if he didn't hear it. 'Not at all.'

But the longer those chocolate-brown eyes gaze into mine and his scent feels like it's all around me, the more my resolve wanes.

I'm immensely grateful for Pace appearing at my side and saving me from myself. 'All set?' my roomie asks.

'Mmhmm, sure.'

When I shift my focus from Pace back to Colton, Colton is holding out his hand. 'Thanks for everything, Sas. I guess I'll see you around.'

I take his hand and feel it like an inferno against my palm. The way he applies gentle pressure to my hold mirrors the squeeze I feel between my legs.

Get me out of Texas before I destroy my fledgling career.

23

OCTOBER

Colton
It's Y'all

'Have a great night, you all,' Megan tells fans, waving them away from our table in a sushi restaurant in the city.

She explained to them that she's practicing her Texan accent, so as to not sound strange when they approached our table to ask for her autograph, presumably.

'It's y'all,' I tell her once it's just the two of us, again, sitting in the window table, where passersby can snap us in a happy-couple moment.

She flicks her ringlets. 'Right. I need to remember that one. So obvious.' She flashes me a mischievous grin. 'Or maybe I was just checking you're actually listening to me tonight?'

I wince. 'Sorry, I've not been the best company, have I?'

'Even for you,' she teases. 'What's up? A problem shared and all that...'

'Nothing.' I try to end the conversation by putting another forkful of seaweed salad in my mouth. 'Why does anyone eat this stuff?'

'Well, it's tasty, and it's packed full of vitamins, minerals and antioxidants.'

I stare at her and think, I'd rather be eating trash takeout with Sas. Even better, watching her freak out across the table from me as I suck meat from a bone.

'He smiles!' Meg says, not realizing that it's remembering Sas's looks of disgust that's entertaining me. 'I know you'd rather ask me questions all night than have me ask you something, but I'd like to think we're friends now.'

I rub my chin, the days-old gruff scratchy. 'I guess last weekend's game is playing on my mind.'

'Given I have zero clue about football, you'll have to interpret that for me. I mean, I know the Bears lost and all, but the rest...'

'I played awful. Worst game of the season.'

'Everyone has a bad game, though, right? I mean, some days on set, I can get a scene right in three or four takes. Others, it's like twenty and it's already getting dark out by the time I've got it right.'

'Yeah, something equivalent.' And I think, if Sas were still in Texas, she'd be beating me up for that performance, telling me what I did wrong, how to improve, how I'm putting my contract extension in jeopardy.

Oddly, her pressure is good; it works to drown out the other stuff and make me focus. *She* makes me focus.

But now she's gone and there's still all the other stuff. Like worrying about Annie's future, and Mama's bloods getting worse, and the fact I might need to concede that I can't keep working as hard as I am at the ranch. That I might need to hire more help but that help would find out Mama is sick, which is the exact opposite of what she wants. It's all so deafening without Sas.

'You like her, don't you?' Megan asks, pulling me from my own head.

'Who?'

She leans her head to one side while flicking her eyes to the roof. 'Who? Sas. You like her. You miss her.'

I puff out my next breath and bury my gaze in this godawful antioxidant dish of food.

'I don't blame you. She's great. Clever. Hilarious. No holds barred.'

I fork my food like a petulant child. 'We work together. That's all.'

'Then why are you being so defensive? And so absent?'

'I don't mean to be.' I rub that gruff again – I really ought to shave. 'I'm frustrated that I'm not compartmentalizing well and it showed in my game this weekend.'

'That's such a fallacy, don't you think?' she asks. Then answers her own question, as she often does. 'I mean, people say compartmentalize but it's hard to focus when things aren't straight at home. So maybe if you sort out whatever's going on with you and Sas—'

'There's nothing going on.'

'All right. Sure. But say, *hypothetically*, if there *was* something going on and you got that sorted, maybe your game would reap the benefits, too.'

'God, you're starting to sound like her.'

She scrunches her nose in amusement like a cute bunny. 'All that time sitting in the stands with her must be rubbing off on me.'

I sigh. 'Look, there's nothing going on with Sas and me. She's made clear she wouldn't cross that line. I also don't do girlfriends. It's messy and disruptive. I'll have all the time in the world for a relationship once my career is done. And, in case you haven't noticed...' I gesture between us. 'I'm sort of seeing this actress with a questionable southern accent.'

Megan laughs and the sound is so light, I feel my cheeks rise reflexively.

'If it were me, I'd talk to her.' She pauses to swig some gut-churning-looking green juice. 'If you don't, she's not going to come back to Texas, and you're going to play bad for the whole of eternity.'

I shake my head at her as she fights to pick up rice with her chopsticks but really, she's got a point. If Sas left because I won't talk, maybe I need to give her something.

* * *

ME

Hey

Yup, this is what I message to Sas after not speaking to her for a week and a half, since she went home to New York.

I'm sitting in a rocking chair on the front porch at the ranch, Bear snoring by my feet, stars decorating the night sky, the moon so bright it's silhouetting the horses and barn. The homey sound of crickets chirping to attract females is ever-present yet never seen. The air smells of Mama's citronella candles.

I set my phone aside on a table my daddy made from spare wood with one of our fosters years ago. Mama has always been the voice, the love, and my old man not much of a talker. But he'd use his skills with his hands to give the foster kids projects to focus on. He was great at that stuff.

For some reason, it's only just occurring to me now that maybe that's what he's been doing for me over the last six months – finding me jobs on the ranch.

Mama's been well enough to come outside and lightly putter around today. We're reopening the ranch for respite from Monday and the place is in pretty good shape, at last.

There's been a temporary hiatus and we've all been trying to convince Mama not to reopen, but she's determined. So determined that I know I'll make sure the Sunshine Ranch charity continues after...

It's been good to have her alongside us today. So good, I hate to even acknowledge that maybe she's doing the right thing in not trying new treatments. She might get a few more months of being well enough to enjoy life.

I rest back in the chair, steadying the movement by putting my feet up on the fence, and take a swig of beer from my bottle – I allow myself one or two here and there during season.

CITY GIRL

Hey, back!

I'm obviously not expecting a reply because I near jump out my skin when my phone vibrates, the sound resonating against the table and deafening in the darkness.

When I see her name on my screen, I doubt myself. What if Megan and Annie were wrong and Sas doesn't really care whether I give her any kind of insight now? What am I trying to achieve anyway?

I stare at her name, scratching my head, as if that will make me come up with some sound reasoning. And I suppose it works because I remember what I'm going to tell her...

ME

The cheerleader that got kicked off the squad, Molly. She wasn't just a random hook-up. We've known each other since kindergarten. We both had some stuff going on and agreed to a one-time thing.

She made a mistake telling another girl on the squad who she thought was a friend. I asked Harris to try to fix it when it leaked but it was everywhere, too quick to stop it.

> When she was kicked off the squad, I took the blame, but it didn't make a difference. I offered to pay her salary for as long as it took for her to find another job and I put in a word to get her on another squad. I messed up but it wasn't the way the press made it look.

I haven't told anyone that, because I intended to take the fall. I still do. People expect this kind of thing from footballers but it's career-damaging for Molly. Granted, in the round with the other things I got slaughtered for by the media closed season, it's also not helping my career and it's resulted in this PR farce I'm stuck in right now, but it would have been worse for her.

I wait for a response, not really sure what I'm expecting as I watch those *typing dot dot dots* appear, disappear, then reappear.

CITY GIRL

Why tell me now?

ME

> It's a lame sort of thank you, for whatever you said to Annie. She told me tonight that she's going to defer college, and she told me it's because of something you said.

In fact, Annie told me she wants to have the option of a professional career and lead by example for her baby. Words I can imagine coming from Sas. She'd be a great mama. Take no shit but give a massive one. A lot like my mama, I think as I find the Big Dipper and Little Dipper in the sky.

CITY GIRL

I'm sure she would have found her own way to the same conclusion eventually. I'm working on this idea myself. Taking a horse to water but letting it drink.

She's talking about me, I think. Or if she isn't, she could be. She wants me to talk, open up. As much as I don't want to, I want her to know that if I was going to be open with someone, I think it could be her.

CITY GIRL

Thank you for telling me about Molly.

Those dots appear again. While I'm waiting for her next message, I can admit to myself that it feels... I don't know... *nice* to have shared that with Sas.

This time, her reply takes longer and I'm wondering what *she's* thinking. Does she believe me? Does she believe I'm not just a fuck 'em and don't care about 'em kind of guy?

Does she think that if *we* had a night, if she *wanted* to go there, it would be more than just me getting my kicks and that's it?

I actually care about her. I like her a lot. And I *really* want to go there with her.

I just don't have anything more than one night to offer. For a thousand reasons. Her career and the fact I know how much it means to her being high on the list.

Perhaps telling her about Molly will show her that I am concerned, I *do* take an interest in what matters to her?

> **CITY GIRL**
>
> I assume I'm not allowed to share this with Sean and have him rewrite the media's narrative?

Shaking my head at the screen, I answer my own question – maybe not.

> **ME**
>
> I told you as a friend. Sweet dreams, Sas x

I stare at that kiss for longer than any sensible man should. Are we friends? Are we adviser and athlete?

Did I also give her some insight because what I really want is for her to come back to Texas? Because I play better when she's here. Because I— Because I was starting to like her buzzing around. *Her.*

I'm so fucked.

24

OCTOBER

Sas
New York Dragons

The Dragons won their first hockey game of the season and my brother, Jax, got a goal and an assist, so he's as high on life as he usually is when his team is playing well. In fact, Jax is always high on life. Like one of those perpetually hyperactive, good-mood kind of guys. I love him for it. But he can be a lot, too.

We're in a VIP section of a bar on Long Island, not far from the Dragons' stadium, well-enough hidden to protect the players from any unwanted attention.

The guys are having a couple drinks to unwind, nothing crazy. It's actually worked out well that I'm home. I've never missed Jax's first game of the season as long as he's been pro. Before then, too.

But he's rightly teasing me now because I've been staring at messages from Colton for too long, indecisive about what they mean and what I should reply.

Colton's told me what happened with the Bears cheerleader, Molly, in the off-season. He cared about her. Arguably, they made a mistake hooking up. But the bigger mistake was that she told anyone about it.

The thing is, it plays into the kind of guy I think Colton is. Which makes me wonder whether the other stories from his off-season are true. Why did he get fined for non-conforming uniform? Why did he sock Auston Rogers in the face?

If there are other interpretations of those stories, is the truth behind them also why he isn't playing well?

And he isn't playing well. He's playing terribly. He was substituted at half-time last game.

Why did I have to mention Sean in my reply to him? All I'll have done is encourage him to rebuild that tiny fraction of wall he just let down.

'Sas will have one!' I hear Jax shout across the space – over a dance version of 'Tiny Dancer' being played by the DJ – then a shot glass full of clear liquid is being held out in front of me on a tray by a waiter. Something tells me it isn't H$_2$O.

'Not for me, thanks.'

'It's punishment for you being unsociable,' Jax calls, closing in on me.

'Fine.' I snatch the glass and knock back the shot of tequila. 'Happy?'

My brother's hovering over me now and though I pull my phone from his view, he must glimpse enough because he asks, 'Who's Cowboy and why's he wishing you sweet dreams with a kiss?'

'He's Cowboy Get-Lassoed from Never You Mind Ranch.'

Jax chortles. 'Ah, I've missed my most irritating sibling.' He drapes a heavy arm around my bare shoulders, exposed in my strapless LBD – my go-to outfit in the city when I can't decide what to wear.

'Please. *I'm* the least irritating of the three of us,' I retort.

'If you do say so yourself. So, who is he? An app hook-up? Or Colton Quinn?'

My eyes dart to my brother's. Not that I've done anything wrong. But it sure feels like I'm being caught red-handed.

'I knew it. There had to be more to you staying in Texas than babysitting him and Megan Frost.'

'What are you talking about? That wasn't even what I was doing. Not exclusively.' I turn away from him under the guise of locating my cocktail from a nearby table. I should have been on the lookout for new talent, because there's no way Dad's going to just gift me one of his clients even if Colton gets a better contract offer, which looks in serious jeopardy recently. I made zero tracks with that because... my attention was elsewhere.

'You know Dad will flip, right?'

I drain my cosmopolitan. 'Fine, it's Colton.' My empty glass meets the tabletop harder than intended. 'But there's nothing happening between us.'

'Even though he's saved as Cowboy in your phone.'

'It's just a name. He *is* a— We're not having this conversation. This is no different to me messaging Pace. I've been living with him for weeks and you aren't tormenting me about him.'

He drops his arm from my shoulders and points at me, his fingertip meeting my nose. I slap his pokey little digit away, rattled. 'That's because Pace is like the sibling we never asked for but got anyway. He's safe as houses. He wouldn't dare mess with my sister. But Quinn... Not a good idea, Sas.'

'You don't know him.' I realize coming to his defense doesn't exactly support my argument.

Jax cocks his head to one side, as if to say, *Case in point.* 'I do know that to the rest of the world, he's dating Megan Frost. I know he's Dad's client. Just don't say I didn't warn you.'

I scowl as he walks away, backwards, slipping into the fold of his team-mates, again with a victorious grin on his smug face.

> ME
>
> I don't think I'll be getting to bed any time soon. I'm at a club celebrating my brother's first win of the season.

I take a selfie, holding up my empty glass, and send it with the message.

> COWBOY
>
> Such a city girl cliché! X

Another kiss, which I'm still analyzing when his next message pings through.

> COWBOY
>
> By contrast, I'm sitting in a rocking chair, nursing a bottle of beer, listening to crickets surrounding the ranch and staring at the big dipper x

> ME
>
> The big dipper? Is that a euphemism? X

Dang. I didn't mean to add the kiss. *And am I brazenly flirting?* I stare at my glass as if it's the cocktail's fault. Then decide, *fuck it*, and hold up the empty to the barman, who nods in acknowledgment. There are some perks to hanging out with my brother and his team.

COWBOY

I'm sitting on my parents' porch, Sas. What's wrong with you? Take your mind from the gutter x

Tickled, I fire back:

ME

Such a cowboy cliché

I imagine the sides of his mouth turning up. Lips that I've decided I really want to kiss.

COWBOY

You look insanely hot btw x

I know I'm smiling like a lovesick teen, which my brother confirms when I glance in his direction and he shakes his head at me, all lip-pouty and supercilious. I don't know how he *dares* have an opinion on anyone else's love life.

Love life? Slow down, Sas.

All right, I concede, this is a bad idea. A rabbit hole I don't want to fall down. A warren I can't afford to be trapped in.

ME

Now whose mind is in the gutter? X

COWBOY

I've not tried to hide it x

His words throw me back to the image of him standing in Pace's doorway, asking for one night. I cross my legs tightly, but the move doesn't alleviate all my symptoms – the pang between my thighs, the way my breasts feel as if they're swelling, my nipples hardening, the skin of my neck suddenly waking up, and a sensation like something is alive and wriggling through my tummy.

Maybe if we just had one night. Got it out of our systems. I don't tell anyone, nor does he. Then it can't go wrong.

This wouldn't be like Colton and Molly. It would just be two consenting

adults, having one wild night, in secret. It doesn't need to ruin his public relationship with Megan. My dad never needs to find out.

Just the thought of it has my panties wetter than the drink that's just been
placed in front of me. Even if I tried to stop this from happening, my body has
already gone there.

Good thing then I had the sense to get out of Texas. Here, there's only me
and my vibrator. Mind sex doesn't count, right?

* * *

I wake up in the guest bedroom of my brother's apartment on Long Island.
Through one eye, I glance around at the scene that looks as if I had a really
good night with a hot man between my thighs – shoes kicked off in different
directions, expensive dress cast across the drawers, panties hanging over a
chair. Sadly, I didn't. But I can say definitively that my right hand and my
brain's conjured images of a certain split end had a relatively good time all the
same.

But here it comes... the inevitable... something akin to one-night stand
guilt.

Honestly, it's necessary. A reminder that Colton and I banging it out of our
systems would be a shockingly, disastrously, terrible idea.

Sitting up, I rub my eyes – realizing I didn't bother to take off my make-up
last night – and press the base of my palms to my temples, hoping to stem
some of the cosmopolitan explosion happening in my brain. I knew I
shouldn't have had that last one.

This is good. I feel awful and guilty, both things that serve as a staunch
aide-memoire that I absolutely cannot and will not go there with Colton.

There's too much at stake – both our careers, his very public career and
love life, my respect (self and professional) – to throw caution to the wind for
one night of...

Oh, I bet it would be so good.

Passion.

Madness.

Wild limbs sweaty and tangled up.

Fingers pulling, tugging, scratching.

Mouths biting, nipping, sucking.

Dropping my hands over my face, I fall back against my pillows. This has to stop. My brain has got to get back in the game. The game of me being an attorney and superstar sports agent in the making. *Not* the Colton Quinn fantastic sex game.

Reaching for my phone, I see it's nearly ten in the morning and I thank God it's Sunday.

Coffee. Coffee and the fresh pressed orange juice that my brother's house lady buys from the local bakery and stocks in his refrigerator.

I pull on a pair of shorts and a Dragons' hoodie and drearily pad to the kitchen, where I thank the heavens for the small mercy of the orange juice.

I set the filter machine off percolating. Then, turning into the wide-open living space, I hear murmured voices, followed by a sheepish-looking blonde, who appears from the hallway to the bedrooms. She's wearing a Dragons' jersey over what looks like a very short dress or skirt and she's carrying a pair of strappy sandals and a clutch.

'Oh, hi!' she says. 'I'm just—' She points to the front door.

I hold up a hand, not taking my mouth from my glass of juice until she's closed the door behind her and Jax appears, hair mussed and yawning, as he pulls on a t-shirt with his boxer briefs.

'Really, Jax? When you knew I was staying over?'

Now I am grateful for my cosmo-coma.

'It wasn't my fault. She came on to me. And I tried to keep the noise down. I even put my hand over her mouth when she started screaming my name.'

I pick up the nearest thing within reach, which happens to be a banana, and throw it at my brother.

He catches it, laughing. 'Don't be sour just because you're getting boned by Dad's client.'

'I'm not getting anything by or from anyone.'

'Actually, that does make more sense. No one who's getting enough sex is this crabby.'

Rolling my eyes, I do a one-eighty to the coffee machine. If the choice is between being accused of having taboo sex or being called crabby because I'm not, I suppose I have to take crabby.

'Let's go get breakfast; I don't have anything in. Or maybe I do, I'm not sure. But I don't want to make anything.'

I pour us both coffee and slide a mug along the countertop. 'I want to be back for the Bears game, though. They've got the early kick off.'

'Oh yeah, don't want to miss your boyfriend in action.'

'Fuck off, Jax.'

* * *

A few hours and a significant pancake stack later, I'm confident it's no longer my hangover making me feel queasy but watching the Bears get tanked in Miami.

The entire team is having an off day, but Colton is a stand-out stink fest all on his own. Mistimed runs, dropped catches, negative yardage.

'Get your head in the game!' I yell at my brother's vast wall-mounted TV.

He leans across me to steal chips and dip from the bowl in my lap during the final quarter, before shuffling back to his corner of the sofa. 'You sure you want to get boned by this guy?'

'For the last time, Jax, there's nothing going on between Colton and me. I work for him. That's it.'

He crunches on a chip, chortling because he knows he's getting under my skin. 'Good thing too, because I've seen Megan Frost on screen as many times as I've seen Tommy Thieriot get intercepted this game.'

Huffily, I ram another snack in my mouth. But he's right; the cameras are eating up the Quinn-Frost romance.

As we intended.

But within the relative safe space of my own mind, I confess, the thought of them in Florida together, under the sun, at the beach, maybe sipping a virgin pina colada on account of Megan being underage, it... is doing something to me. Making me feel off. Making me feel something I don't want to feel because it's not who I am or what I'm about.

That unwell feeling is confirmed once the game's over and images of Colton and Megan start to surface on social media, hand-in-hand in the Sunshine State.

Dear Doctor, what's wrong with me?

Well, Kansas dear, you have a severe case of... the green-eyed monster.

I am without doubt jealous of Colton and Megan. Real or pretend. The sparks sure look authentic, and I don't like it.

Which is why, when Colton messages me in the evening when I'm back home at Mom and Dad's place, my stomach leaps.

Why, when I read his words, my heart tries to hammer its way out of my chest.

He might be the only medication to treat my condition.

> **COWBOY**
>
> Please come back for the St Louis game. I can't play without your noise, city girl x

Or at least a fix.

I don't reply right away. I don't because I'm trying to stop myself from agreeing to something stupid. But even while I'm not typing it, I know I'll say yes.

Luckily for me, two days later, stars align to give me the perfect business excuse to head back to Texas.

25

OCTOBER

Colton
To Be Clear...

I'm standing in Arrivals at the airport in Austin, having paid the driver who was waiting for Sas and told him that she has another ride. Win-win for him. And for me, it's the least I can do. She's flown down here because I asked her to come back, because I need her around if I want to play well. Especially this weekend when the Bears take on the St Louis Archers.

What I didn't anticipate was that I'd feel like a kid at Disneyland for the entire drive out here. That the sensation would only ramp up. And that standing here in the airport, my internal organs would be having some kind of wrestle to be let out of my torso at the thought of seeing her.

It's the surprise element. Everyone loves giving surprise gifts. It's the antic- ipation of seeing a person's reaction to the gesture. That's all this is. Sas isn't expecting me to be here and that knowledge has got me... excited, I guess.

I'm leaning back against the store front of a coffee chain, cowboy hat dipped low, trying to remain as surreptitious as a guy my size can be. But I'm so wired, my fingers of one hand are tapping my belt buckle, toes of one foot bouncing my boot up and down off the ground.

The sound of my phone ringing startles me. Tugging it from my butt pocket, I smile and swipe the screen.

'Hey, what's up?' I say, way more casual than I feel, I hope.

'When do you ever answer the phone like that?' Sas asks, calling my bluff. *Damn it.* 'Anyway, I've just landed in Texas, and I was thinking on the flight that maybe we could catch that college game I've been meaning to get to. You know, since I'm down here for business, I should make the most of the time.'

I'm staring at the double doors of the Arrivals exit, waiting for her to appear. If the club doc took my blood pressure right now, he'd have me sitting on the sidelines for reasons other than my diabolical performance the last two games.

'Sure, makes sense. They're playing out of state this weekend though and I can't travel far before the game on Sunday.'

'Oh.'

Now I'm grinning again. 'You could stay down for the week and we could catch the mid-week game or their home game next Saturday? Plus, I have a bye next week.'

Silence.

'Sas, you there?'

'I'm thinking.'

She's wearing heels. Despite the buzz and hum of the airport, the sound of her shoes clicking against the ground meets my ears. The woman knows how to strut. And now I'm wondering what she's wearing. One of those tailored dresses that hugs every perfect curve of her body?

'I thought the line must have gone dead,' I tell her. 'I've never known you to go a second without talking.'

'Oh ha *ha*,' she's saying into the phone when she finally pushes through the doors, wheeling her luggage behind her.

As she pans the row of cab drivers looking for her pre-booked ride, I stand up straight and try to take a deep, steadying breath. She's wearing a red dress. *Red.* Sleeveless, with a zipper down the neckline. Down to her cleavage and those perfectly round—

Lord, I need to rein this shit in.

I need her here so that I can play. The last thing I want to do is overthink flirtatious messages, kisses on the end of each one, and scare her away again.

The fact remains, even *if* we went *there* – and fuck do I want to go there – it would be one night. No one needs to catch anything more than a good time.

I wait and I watch, enjoying the view, calming my surge of testosterone, chuckling as I see her temper rise when she gets to the end of the line and hasn't located her driver.

'Urgh, why are drivers always late?' she gripes into the phone.

'Did you look everywhere?' My cheeks are aching. 'Try by the coffee stand.'

'By the coffee stand? If he's grabbing coffee while I'm wai—'

Finally, she sees me and stills. Then a smile like fire draws on her painted red lips and she slowly makes her way toward me, phone still to her ear.

'Someone must be trying to give me the full Texas experience because they've sent me a cowboy.'

I'm still chuckling when she finally reaches me and says into her phone, 'I've got to go; I've found my ride.'

I slip my own device into the back pocket of my jeans. 'It'll be the ride of your life, city girl.'

Her eyes narrow but the smirk around her highly fucking kissable mouth betrays her as she points at me. 'To be clear, I'm here on business. We have a meeting with a potential new sponsor on Monday.'

I'd love to bite that finger. Instead, I bite my tongue. 'Strictly business.' Then I reach around her and grab her luggage. As we make our way to the exit, I see her watching me in my peripheral vision. I know she feels this pull, too. Watching her fight it is hilarious.

Eventually, I cave and glance her way. 'Hi.'

I'm rewarded with a beaming smile. 'Hi.'

It's crazy that I could have missed someone who drives me up the wall as badly as I've missed Sas these past couple weeks. I need to play this cool. As cool as my big fat cat grin will allow.

'Thanks for coming to get me. It's a nice surprise.'

'Don't get used to it; spontaneity isn't my thing.'

'That's how I know this is going to be a long old drive listening to your country tunes.'

We reach my Range Rover and I pop the trunk, swinging Sas's luggage inside as I tell her, 'You bet your ass it is.'

Coming to stand boot to toe with me, she takes the hat from my head and plants it on her own.

I watch as the sexiest damn cowgirl I've ever seen moves around to the passenger side door, listening to her laugher. That sound beats the hell out of crickets at dusk on the open plains. And *that* takes some beating.

It is a long old drive to Pace's place, not because of my country tunes, and not because Sas is filling me in with extreme granular detail on her time back in New York. Because the whole time, my eyes wish they could watch her instead of the road. My fingers feel purposeless where my arm rests on the center console, aching to touch her in that dress.

As painful as the journey is, there's a lightness about her, us, *me* that I like and I'm gutted when we arrive at our destination. I want whatever this feeling is to stay. Since I pulled up at Austin airport, I haven't thought about the game tomorrow or, specifically, that I'll be coming face to face with Auston Rogers for the first time since our off-season bust up.

This is what she does. She distracts me in the best way. A way only she can.

So, when we're standing at the trunk of the car on Pace's driveway, Sas's luggage on the street between us, I ask her, 'Stay with me?'

She physically rears. 'What?'

'Come stay at my place. I won't be there the whole time anyway, with the game, training and being out at the ranch. You'll mostly have the place to yourself to work.'

She's staring at me in a way that makes me think she's either going to give me attitude, or she's contemplating the idea. I can't tell.

'Stay with me, please.'

Suddenly, her chest is rising and falling so hard it's pushing against the zipper in that red dress. And that simple change of breath has me worked up, again.

'That wouldn't be a good idea,' she eventually says and, honestly, I get it. If really nothing can happen between us, it would be a terrible idea.

And if something did, it would be a disaster. One night is one night. It's not supposed to be one night, then you wake up the next day and you're living together.

So, I nod – *okay.*

But I'm not ready to be done here; I only just got her back. So, as she wheels her suitcase toward the porch, I call after her, 'Donuts!'

'Huh?'

'Let's go get donuts. And a milkshake. I've got a game tomorrow; it's basically prescription.'

She shakes her head, brow scrunched, and continues to walk away from me. But at the entrance, she turns back. 'Give me a few minutes to say hello and grab a quick change.'

My mind starts doing high-fives up there. Mentally, I'm twirling on the spot and swinging my ass like a rock 'n' roll touchdown celebration.

But to Sas, I check the chunky watch on my wrist and ask, 'Is that twenty minutes in girl speak?'

She flips me the bird, right as the door to Pace's house opens.

26

OCTOBER

Sas

San Antonio Bears vs St Louis Archers

I take my seat in the stands early enough to watch both the Bears and St Louis warming up. This is the reason I'm here. Colton asked me to fly back for this game.

Yesterday was... unexpected. From Colton surprising me at the airport to us sharing donuts sitting beneath a tree and him telling me stories about growing up on the ranch. I tease him about being a cowboy, but the ranch sounds idyllic.

Though I can't deny that when he was instructing me how to lasso, all I could think was, *I'd like you to lasso me.*

It feels like there's been a shift between us. Things are less antagonistic. They're less strained. Part of me thinks it's because every conversation, every double entendre and every intentional or accidental touch holds less reluctance and more promise.

Colton and I are going to have sex.

I know because there's no way we can't. No way I can keep my sanity and continue to walk around with this heavy load of need in my core. There's only so many times I can avert my gaze and think of the most mundane documentaries when he's close to me. There's a limit to how many times I can squeeze my legs shut before they weld into a chastity belt.

The feeling is mutual. He told me as much weeks ago.

And knowing that as soon as I relent this agonizing wait for the inevitable will stop makes it a harder torture to suffer.

Even now, from my position in the stands, watching him stretch and warm up down there on the Alamo turf, I can't think of a better way to risk messing up my career and my self-respect in public.

Plus, if we agree it's just one night – one night of mind-blowing tumbling in the sheets, his strong body hovering over mine, the smell of sex in the humid air, frantic, wild – then no one needs to know. Only us.

'Oh boy, this gets harder every game.' Annie's panted words come to me from the end of our row and I go to her immediately, offering a hand to help. 'How is it possible that I still have a month to go?'

'Are you sure there aren't twins in there?' I ask as she lowers herself into her seat, one hand holding on to me, the other on her lower back.

It's just the three of us today – Annie, Colton's dad and me. Megan is in LA and *my* dad is watching a game in San Francisco.

Once Annie's settled, Sonny appears and hands me a beer. Colton's family are such easy company. By contrast, my family is highly strung. I should channel the Quinns more.

It was weird how New York seemed to have a less invigorating buzz about it and more head-battering noise when I was back these past two weeks. Maybe it was the pressure of having Dad watch my every move in the office, or my brothers constantly trying to get me fired up, or my mom asking me questions about *everything*.

Though I would have balked at the suggestion in summer, Texas is really growing on me now. It's a different pace, a slower pace, and I like it. *Weird.*

'How are you guys?' I ask.

To which Sonny puffs out a breath. 'Tired, Sas. Very tired.'

I expected to get a reply from Annie, not Sonny of even fewer words than Colton. That's more than he usually says in four quarters.

'I'm sure Colton told you we've opened the ranch for respite season. It's always tiring the first week or two back at it.' He looks away from me, staring out at the field. 'But especially this year.'

I wait for more, but it never comes, though I do notice a few extra creases around Sonny's eyes. A slightly grayer pallor than usual.

Annie gives me a barely-there smile that seems to hold something in it besides happiness. A story, which she starts to share...

'At Sunshine Ranch, we offer respite for families caring for sick loved ones. Sometimes, whole families come stay and we distract the kids with activities if they're able, to give the parents and the kids a break. Older kids often come alone, either to have a break from being primary carers to their parents, or sometimes, where their siblings are sick. Sometimes, kids who are sick themselves come along for a change of scene.' She really does smile now. 'They all love the horses. And they love making jam and pecan pies with Mama.'

Her smile fades and she reaches out to squeeze Sonny's leg through his stonewash jeans. He doesn't look her way but places his own hand on top of hers.

What am I missing?

'Is that why your mom doesn't come to the games? Do families stay over at the weekends?' I ask.

Before Annie can respond, Sonny and I stand abruptly from our seats as on the field, Colton, normally cool, calm and collected, is squaring up to none other than Auston Rogers.

We're too far away to hear what's being said but they're shouting and now their teammates are getting between them and pulling them apart.

And this, I think, is why Colton wanted me down here. Through all my mind being in the gutter and enjoying being back around him, I forgot to ask how he was going to find coming face to face with Auston Rogers today, after giving him a right hook in the off-season.

'Oh boy, I was afraid of this,' Annie says, finally standing between her dad and me. 'Daddy, can you get down there and talk to him?'

'How do you propose I do that, Annie? Your brother needs to mind his own business and keep his powder dry, otherwise you'll both end up stuck on that ranch with me.'

Annie gasps. 'Daddy!'

'It's true, Annie. Auston has already done enough without bringing Colton down with him.'

On the field, Colton is being dragged away by his position coach, Tommy and Pace. It's taking all three of them to put a wall between Colton and Auston.

'What the actual *fuck,* Colton?' I mutter into the air, my words drowned by the het-up home crowd, siding with him.

We have a meeting with a sponsor on Monday. A *big* meeting that Dad has, remarkably, let me handle alone. Even though it's just an initial meet, it's a big deal for me, for Colton, for us all.

And he's currently on the field *fighting?*

His coach thrusts a drinks bottle at him – supposedly a literal and prover-bial request for him to cool the hell off.

Should I have anticipated this and tried to talk to him about it? Was my head so full of raging hormones that I missed this completely?

I'm mad at myself but I'm irate with Colton.

He has eyes on him from every angle and there's no mistaking that he was the one to approach Rogers.

What on earth went down between them? And what's *Sonny's* beef with Auston?

And *why* in the name of God Almighty is Colton *still* seeking out Auston and trying to stare him down on the field?

At best, he'll end up fined. At worst, he'll wind up suspended.

I can sense Annie's tension as she worries her lip, hands on her bump.

'Annie, what happened between those two?'

There's a moment of indecision, I see it, until eventually, she sighs. 'Well, if he won't tell you.' She holds her hands out from her tummy. 'My baby? It's Auston's baby, too.'

Come again. I'm blinking as fast as my brain is trying to process. *How have I not heard about this? How has the press not heard about this?*

'You're with Auston?'

Annie scoffs. '*Ohhhhh* no. That's the problem.'

'She's good enough to knock up but not good enough to marry,' Sonny says, his accent thicker than ever.

'Daddy! Do you have to? Don't you think it's embarrassing enough without your own father thinking—'

'Now, hey, I didn't say anything about what I was or wasn't thinking.'

'You literally just said—'

'Annie? Annie.' I take her hand and with it, her attention. 'What happened?'

She lowers into her seat and I do the same as Sonny heads off for a closer view of the field where the teams have settled back into their warm-ups. Or cool off, in Colton's case.

'Colton and Auston were best friends right through college. Roomed together, played together, did everything together. Auston would come stay at the ranch in college breaks and I... stupidly thought that he was in love with me.

'We kept things secret for a while because we didn't think Colton would like it. Then they both got drafted to pro teams and Auston moved to St Louis.'

She looks up to me and I see in her eyes now how hurt she still is. 'I was devastated. He came to visit sometimes, and we'd... you know. I was so smitten with him that I took whatever he'd offer. Then in spring, I found out I was pregnant and Lord knows it can't be anybody else's child.'

'So, Colton was mad enough when he found out you guys were together that he punched him? That just doesn't seem—'

'That's not how the story ends. See, I thought that when I told Auston about the baby—'

Her eyes gloss over. I take a small packet of tissues from my bag, offering one to her while glancing out to the field to make sure Colton hasn't gone in for a repeat with Auston.

'He doesn't want anything to do with the baby or me, Sas. Colton thinks it's all his fault that I ever met Auston in the first place. He's angry that his best friend could just walk away. Gone without a trace. I don't hear from him at all. I'm going to have his baby and he's ghosted me.'

'Annie I— I don't know what to say. That's—'

Rage feels like it boils every part of my insides. How could *any* man do that to a woman carrying his child? But a man who was a family *friend*? A man Annie was actually *with*?

I stand, eyes on Colton, and all I can think is, *Damn right*. He was looking out for his sister. He must have felt a thousand times the anger I feel now because I barely know Annie by comparison and I don't know Auston Rogers at all.

I know he can't feel my eyes on him. He might not even be able to see me.

But Colton turns to look my way and there's a twinge of something new in my chest when I feel like our eyes connect. Something raw and real and an urge to be with him. Not to sleep with him, but just to tell him *I know*. I know and I get it and I wish you weren't still being forced to do things you don't want to do to put right something that was never your fault in the first place.

But I can't go to him. I can't get any closer to him than Sonny can. All I can do is hope that the Bears absolutely trash Auston Rogers and the Archers.

When the players head into the dressing room, there's another moment between Colton and Auston. They're shoulder to shoulder and being encouraged apart by their respective teams.

I'm worried about Colton. I'm even more worried about the impact this is going to have on his game.

'For a long time, I tried to convince myself he just needed to come round,' Annie says. To me, I think, though she's focused on the field in front of us as the stands continue to fill for kick off. 'I thought, surely it's just shock, right? We'd been seeing each other on and off for years and I don't believe he didn't feel anything for me. Even if he didn't love me, I thought he cared.'

I bring a hand to rest on her knee. I've been so concerned with Colton that I've skimmed over Annie's broken heart.

'Urgh, pregnancy hormones,' she says, taking my tissue out of the pocket of her dress and giving her nose a hearty blow. 'I promised myself I wasn't going to do this today.'

'Annie, you have every right to feel however you feel, pregnant or not. He broke your heart and the way he continues to behave is frankly—'

'Abhorrent? I know. I concede now. I've made excuses for him. I've hoped and waited. But he knows my due date. He knows his baby will be born soon and he hasn't even asked how things are going.'

I shift on my seat to face her. 'You, Annie Quinn, may be the strongest and loveliest woman I know.'

She gives a short laugh. A sad laugh. 'You think so?'

'I do. I think you're smart and funny. Sassy and interesting.' I turn the end of her curled hair in my fingers. 'You're beautiful and kind. And you have an incredible family, too. You're going to be a fabulous momma bear to that baby. There's no room for a dick like Rogers anyway.'

Her pretty lips turn up a little more but there's no sparkle in her eyes like there is when she's happy, and I hate Rogers for it. I don't even know him and

I hate him, so I can't imagine how his ex-best friend is feeling right now as he runs onto the gridiron to 'La Grange'.

Come on, Bears. Do it for the Quinns.

But they don't. Colton is having a disaster. Omar isn't playing well. Pace looks slow and leggy. Our running back wouldn't make it to a coach stuck at a red light. Tommy Thieriot must be infuriated down there because he has no good options.

By half-time, the Bears are lucky not to be down at least 0–20. The defense is working hard and that's the only reason the score is at 0–14.

I'm mad. Cross with the Bears. Irate at Rogers. Frustrated with Colton for letting this whole thing bring down his game instead of firing him up to beat that jackass. And annoyed because he's already blowing that meeting on Monday before we even turn up.

I'm so wound up that I storm from my seat and into the tunnels, using my lanyard badge to get me as close as I can to the dressing room. Close enough that I can hear banging inside and Coach Roy shouting with all the strength of his lungs.

'Get your shit together and get back out on that field!' he yells, slamming the dressing-room door as he steps into the corridor, his face a worrying shade of purple.

'Glen!' I call past Security and the film crews that have been sent out of the dressing room, presumably before he unleashed on the players.

He double-takes. 'What are you doing here, Sas?' he snaps, which I let slide, in the circumstances.

'Let me speak to Colton.'

'It's half-time in a game. You can't speak to Quinn now.'

I nudge the security guy out of the way and move closer to my godfather, hands on hips in my Bears jersey – technically, Pace's Bears jersey. 'Do you want to win this game or not, Glen? Because I want those guys to slay. So, I'm about to march into that dressing room and tell Colton to pull his head out of his ass for long enough to make some yards and stick it to Auston Rogers.'

He points at me. 'Now you listen, Kansas, that boy is lucky to be on the field at all after the stunt he pulled before the game.'

Rearing as if he poked me in the face, I slap his digit down and point my own right back at him. 'You may be my god-daddy, Glen, but don't you get all pointy-pointersome with me.'

He grabs my finger. 'And you may be my god-baby, but if that finger gets in my face one more time, girlie.'

I snatch my hand back. 'Then what? You'll ground me? Not let me play out with my friends?' When his nostrils flare with his next breath, I soften my tone. 'Look, I know what went down between Colton and Auston. That's why I want to speak to him. This isn't his fault. Please. Let me have thirty seconds with him before he goes back out there.'

He sighs but I know he's relenting. 'Thirty seconds.'

Pushing onto the toes of my sneakers, I kiss his cheek. 'Thank you. Love you.'

Through grinding teeth, he mutters, 'Love you.' Then he heads back to the dressing room and opens the door for me.

A heap of startled and confused eyes turn on me from both players and coaching staff but Glen says, 'Ya'll need to get your asses out there. Not you, Quinn. Sit *your* ass back down.'

Colton doesn't sit. He stands. Eyes fixed on me as everyone else gears up for the second half. For a fleeting moment, I think, *Damn you look seductive in that uniform*, but I push it aside. Because *I* am a professional. And that is precisely what Colton needs to be in the third and fourth quarters.

I move to him until we're standing face to face, waiting for the space to empty.

'What are you doing in here?' he asks.

'I've got thirty seconds to tell you to pull your head out of your rear.'

'Sas, I don't need to hear it, all right. I just got a leathering from Coach.'

'Yeah, well, he didn't say this... I'm pissed at you.'

'Oh believe me, he did say that, and not as politely as you.' He turns to collect his helmet.

'Annie told me, Colton. She told me about her and Auston and how you guys were best friends.'

'She told you?'

'Yes, and I want to rip his fucking balls off for both your sakes.'

His arm that was holding his helmet drops to his side, as if with physical relief. I want to hold him so badly. An urge I hadn't expected, but it's here.

Just seeing how tightly he's been clinging on to that to protect Annie makes me want to... jump his bones, honestly.

I try my best not to because it's half-time in a football game, anyone could walk in at any time, and even the fastest man alive couldn't orgasm in what's left of my allowance from Glen.

'I'm annoyed at you for not telling me,' I say. He goes to speak but I hold up a hand. 'A-bah. I understand why you didn't but I wish you had. I would never have forced Meg— Urgh, that's not a conversation for right now. I'm mostly pissed that you're not out there absolutely annihilating Auston Rogers's team right now. You've let him get in your head and what you should be doing is shoving that football so deep where the sun doesn't shine on him that—'

'I get it. And I wish I was doing that but, yeah, he's screwed with my head and I'm...' He holds out his arms. 'I'm human, Sas. For a long time, I thought I could compartmentalize in some kind of superhuman way, but I can't.'

I step closer to him and take hold of his face, feeling my own heart race as much as I see his doing at the touch. I've never wanted to kiss anyone as badly as I want to kiss Colton right now.

'Then let's change your focus.' My breathing is coming thick and fast as my brain processes the words I'm about to say. 'You go out there and stick it to Rogers the way only Colton Quinn can.'

'Sas—'

'You finish this game with at least seventy-five yards and two touchdowns... and I'll give you your one night.'

He blinks twice in quick succession. It registered. Instantly, he's breathing like he just sprinted the full length of a field. His free hand comes up to my hip and grips, tugging my body to his, so close I have to look up to his lightly stubbled jaw.

'Seventy-five yards,' he croaks.

'Two touchdowns,' I say, just as hoarsely.

'Then I get this after the game?'

I nod. Barely able to form a rational thought, let alone a word.

'Where will I find you?'

'If you get seventy-five yards and two touchdowns, I'll find you, cowboy.'

There's a loud thump on the dressing-room door. 'Quinn. Get out here.'

He lets go of my body and makes to leave, but not before looking over his shoulder and giving me that dazzling lopsided grin.

And I'm left thinking, *I am going to hell because all I can think about is sinning.*

* * *

'Did they let you see him?' Annie asks once I've shimmied past her and back into my seat.

I feel every blood cell in my body make a beeline for my cheeks. 'Briefly.'

'What did you say to him?'

'Well...' I stay standing, shoving my hands in the back pockets of my jeans because I suddenly really need to fidget.

Did I say what I think I said? Did the words really leave my mouth?

If Colton pulls this game out of the bag, are we going to... fuck?

My heart is racing faster than if I'd drank ten energy drinks.

'Hopefully, what he needed to hear,' I say as the third quarter gets underway.

The Bears won the toss and deferred, so they have possession. Tommy has the ball and he's looking for the pass, but my eyes are watching Colton make the kind of run few men are capable of.

My body is tense, knees locked, as I watch the football glide through the air toward him.

Fists clenched, I watch him catch and tuck, then he's rushing for the end zone, avoiding a tackle from the defense and—

'Yeeeeeeessssssssss!' Annie is screaming, jumping much more vigorously than she ought to be in her condition, and near choking me with her hold on my neck.

But I don't care because Colton's first touch of the second half is pure magic.

Sonny high-fives me as we watch a replay of Colton winding his ass in the end zone to celebrate his touchdown.

I don't know for sure but something about that dance feels like a personal message.

I'm still watching him give attitude to the St Louis sideline as the Special team round off the play with a successful kick.

When the teams settle back into the game, Annie rocks her shoulder into mine. 'Whatever you said, it sure worked.'

I smile at her in a way that I hope masks how every part of me was set alight by that touchdown. How every cell in my being is glued to this game and wondering if Colton has got what it takes.

Whether I have what it takes to follow through on a promise. Knowing that there isn't a moral compass strong enough to point in the opposite direction of the things I'm imagining letting Colton do to me. Things I've imagined multiple times in my own bed at night.

As the quarter goes on, I'm up and down in my seat like a frickin' yo-yo on speed, mentally clocking Colton's yards.

It was a huge ask for him to finish this game with at least seventy-five yards and two touchdowns. That would have been a good game for him with*out* having had a shocking first half.

So maybe I was trying to push him but knowing he'd fail. Maybe I was only *pretending* to be ethically gray.

Yet, everything south of my brain is currently wound tighter than my Rolex spring.

By the end of the third quarter, the Bears are up 20–17. Annie and I are both *literally* on the edge of our seats going into the final quarter and I can't help noticing the irony that *she's* on edge because she's slept with a guy out there and *I'm* on edge because I really, desperately want to.

But this is the only way I can concede, right? I have to make him believe I lost a bet. That I've not been sitting watching him for the last two hours thinking, even if he doesn't score another touchdown and make seventy-five yards, I want to jump his bones anyway. Not because of the player he isn't but because of the man he is.

Jesus. I'm utterly lost to hormones.

The Bears lose momentum eight minutes into the final quarter when they give over possession to the Archers and now, I'm fixated on a different player and for an entirely different reason. Every time Auston Rogers completes a pass, I want to take that ball and wind it so far up his—

Annie places a hand on the fists I didn't realize I've clenched on top of my thighs. 'You okay there, hun? You kinda look like you're gonna run down there and give my ex what-for.'

I unclench and take hold of Annie's hand. 'I'd like to. He's a piece of—'

'Let it go, Sas. When you sit with it for a while, you know, it makes more sense. My brother's the exception to the rule. Fool on me for thinking I could change a baller.'

'Annie Quinn, *no*. Sports guys just happen to be publicly really good at their passion. You know as well as I do that they're human beings first. All of this' – I gesture around the stadium – 'could be gone with one bad injury, one awful season. And it's a short-lived career. You and your little one mean more than throwing a ball around a turf field. This is on Auston.'

Sure, I've been burned by sports guys doing their thing in college, but they were all meaningless relationships. Mini-heartbreaks as a rite of passage. This is adulting. It's real life outside the bubble of school. Annie is bringing a child into the world.

She nods, hands on her bump, but I still don't believe she thinks she's good enough for Auston, and I hate that. She's not only good enough for him, she's better. Significantly so.

'And d'you know what? Your brother is going to give it to him so bad.'

She laughs heartily – a relief, I think.

Then I'm back on my feet watching the clock count down the final two minutes as the Bears get a second down on the twenty-yard line.

They've won. At least, it's highly likely they'll win from here. But for a multitude of reasons, I want Colton to score another touchdown.

I want to feel his hands on me. I want him to handle me the way he expertly handles that football. I want him to take me to my end zone and hammer the—

Sheesh, enough football euphemisms, Sas.

Tommy calls the play behind the line of scrimmage and there's movement. I'm watching Colton twist and turn away from the defense – two guys marking him on account of him playing out of his skin this second half.

The ball is snapped and in Tommy's hands.

Tommy makes strides, then sets himself up. Colton breaks free.

And the ball coasts into his waiting hands like there's no one but Colton and Tommy on the field, as if they're in practice. Smooth. Flawless. Controlled.

Smooth.

Flawless.

Controlled.

I feel every microsecond of the play beneath my panties, where I'm going to have a very skilled man, hopefully not long from now.

As Annie and Sonny jump around alongside everyone else in the family area, I stare at the field, at Colton.

He holds the ball to his chest and falls backward onto the turf, into the end zone, before he's piled on by his teammates, who know there's not enough time on the clock for even Tom Brady or Patrick Mahomes to reverse the scoreline on this game.

He did it.

Seventy-five yards – by my best calculations.

Two touchdowns – by the assessment of seventy thousand fans currently screaming his name.

27

OCTOBER

Colton
We Made a Deal...

I'm so wired, wired wouldn't even recognize me.

I just played one of the best halves of football I've played in a Bears jersey. Auston got what he deserved. For Annie.

All thanks to Sas.

I'm applauding the home fans who've stayed back after the game to chant my name around Alamo Stadium. It's a fickle game sometimes. But it feels good to hear their songs again. It's the stuff a boy's dreams are made of.

But as soon as I head down the tunnel, even as Max hangs an arm around my neck and gushes in my ear, all I can think about is Sas.

We made a deal. A deal I want to cash in on. I want it so bad that Sas managed to drag me from a dark place at half-time.

What she put on offer, *her*, was like hot-wiring my ride. I don't know how I didn't get hard for the entire crowd to see after that first touchdown, because all I was thinking was how I'd moved one step closer to getting Sas naked, sweaty, legs wrapped around me, fingers in my hair.

Shit. I turn to face my cube because football shorts don't help a horny guy out in a packed locker room.

I chat with the guys; we're all joking around. And it feels *nice*. Maybe

I've reached a point in my career where I feel comfortable among fellow vets. Or I'm just extra buzzed tonight. Whatever, I try to just enjoy joining in.

I shower and dress into my jeans and shirt. But every time the dressing-room door opens, my entire focus shifts to it. Where is Sas? She usually comes to say hi to the guys after the game.

Has she changed her mind? Was the whole deal just to get me to play?

The thing is, I realize as I fasten my thick watch around my wrist and spray myself with aftershave, I'm gutted if she's changed her mind.

But I'll be more devastated if she stays away from me because of it.

We don't have to spend the night together. I wouldn't have done it before making absolutely sure that she was into it anyway. She's turned me down once before.

But she came all the way down to Texas because I asked her to. She did something for me at half-time tonight that no one else could have managed. And we won the game.

If nothing else, I'd just like to hang out with her and get an opportunity to share the win with her. To say thanks.

I hang back in the dressing room until there's no one but cleaning staff around. Sas hasn't come. She hasn't messaged.

ME

Everything okay? X

I hesitate before hitting send. I don't want her to take it as an insinuation. I genuinely want to know she's cool. That *we're* cool.

Nothing. Not even typing dots. So, I head out to the underground parking lot to find my Range Rover.

It's near empty down here now. I hop inside my car and toss my man-bag on the passenger seat. As the engine starts, I sigh, both hands on the wheel. *Did I blow this?*

I click the car into gear and reverse out of my space.

'It's a good thing you live in the country, cowboy. Your car wouldn't last five minutes if you left it unlocked in New York City.'

I slam the brakes on, eyes darting up to my rearview mirror. To the woman sitting in my backseat, looking prettier, hotter, damn fucking sexier, than ever before.

'It's a good thing we're in the south then, city girl.' How I remain cool as I say that is nothing short of a miracle.

I watch as one side of her mouth tilts up. 'Good game.'

My lopsided grin is a match for hers. 'I had some incentive.'

Her eyes darken right before the interior lights wind down. But I can still see her in the mirror; I know she isn't reneging.

'Are you going to drive us to your place, or is this going down in the middle of the parking lot?'

'Don't tempt me,' I all but growl, before pulling out of the building and away from Alamo Stadium.

Controlling a car while completely hard and trying to avert my gaze from the woman I am insanely hot for in my rearview is a serious test of will. Getting through this is equivalent to winning the championship with my own one-man team.

'Are you blushing, Colton Quinn?'

I frown in response, because, yes, I *am* blushing. It's an alien feeling to me but my cheeks feel like I've been horseback riding under the August sun all day long.

'There was no sign of this nervous guy after the Kansas game. Or were you all bravado then?'

I suck in my gums. She's teasing me the way she can, but I'm too strung out to play along.

'Are you going to show me the amazing one night you promised?'

Right there in her words, there's something that makes me pull over to the side of the road, midway between the stadium and my place.

'What are you doing?' she asks as we watch each other's reflection.

I get out of the car and move to open her door, offering her a hand. She hesitates, confused, but steps out of the car, into me. I shut her door and walk her back against the gleaming metal.

Damn, she smells good. Like her, whatever her expensive perfume is. I could get drunk on it. Her hair cascades down her shoulders and I can't stop myself from trailing my fingers through it. When I look back to her, she tilts her chin up, lips parted slightly.

I could kiss her like this, right now. It's dark out; no one can see us.

I *want* to kiss her more than anything else in this moment.

But... 'After the Kansas game, you said no, and I told you I wouldn't ask you to spend a night with me again.'

Her tongue slips out of her mouth, along the line of her pink lips, and I watch her swallow deeply. Her eyes fix on mine as my fingertips trace the line of her jaw and down her slender neck, coming to rest in the crevasse between her collarbones, exactly where I want to taste.

'We don't have to do this, Sas. Screw the deal. You got my head back in the game. The Bears won. That's enough for me. You did your job.'

Her next breath is so deep, her chest rises against my torso, those fine breasts pressing into me. But I don't let the feel of her cloud my judgment.

'I want to take you home, I really do, but I'm not going to touch you unless you tell me you really want it. That this isn't just a bet you lost.'

Watching me, she must be able to see how serious I am. There's no gray area for me when it comes to sleeping with a woman. She's in or she's out and there's nothing in between. Especially Sas. Especially when there are so many reasons this is a bad idea and we both know it.

She holds her hand over mine on her breastbone and hooks a finger behind my belt buckle, encouraging me closer to her.

'Are you sure there's nothing real between you and Megan?'

'Nothing. I promise.'

'She knows that, too?'

'She told me kissing me is like kissing a brother.'

I half expect her to laugh but she doesn't; she only nods, uncommonly quiet. 'One night?'

'One night.'

'No one needs to find out?'

'They won't from me.'

She rises to her tiptoes and nudges her nose against mine, then gently nips my chin between her teeth, driving me fucking wild with that tiny move.

But I need to hear the words.

Leaning her head to one side, she presses her lips to my neck and I think my knees might buckle under the sensation.

'Colton. Take me to bed. For no other reason than I really want you to.'

With her words, I'm completely undone. All resolve lost.

As some kind of animalistic sound leaves my chest, I nudge my body into hers, pressing her back against my car, and *finally*, my mouth meets hers.

She groans and takes hold of my shirt in her fists, yanking me closer. A sweetness that tastes like it's distinctly hers and the gentle bitterness of beer are insanely moreish. My hand slips into her hair and tugs her mouth more firmly against mine. Our tongues meet with the kind of slickness that's tormenting. Teasing me with thoughts of where else I'd like to taste her.

I'm hard as nails as my crotch meets her stomach, and when she pushes up, encouraging me to take her legs around my waist, I doubt even denim can contain me for long.

'This is what you've been holding back?' I ask, my words deep and guttural, right before my mouth finds her neck.

The way she moans makes me lose myself, pressing her into the car to stop my arms from letting her go. She makes me want to liquify, to melt into her, desperate to be in-fucking-side her.

'Now you find your voice?' she asks, making me smirk. Even when we're dry humping against my car on the side of the road, she's got attitude.

'I always have a voice. Unlike you, I don't verbalize my thoughts before I think them through.'

'Oh really? And what are you thinking right now?'

I show her with my mouth, kissing her in a way that's as close to fucking as a man and woman can come with their clothes on.

Hell, if this keeps on, I think I could finish the job.

Dragging her lip between my teeth, I lower her to the ground, both of us breathing heavily, foreheads pressed together. 'I'm thinking there are other places I want to kiss you. So, I'd like to take you to my place, where I can go down on you until you're begging me to be inside you.'

She presses her teeth into her own lip, eyes hooded, then tells me, 'Once you go down on me, I want to repay. I've had to look at this body in nothing but a towel too many times. I want to get acquainted with what's just beneath here.' She runs her fingers inside my jeans, from my hipbones to the front of my pelvis, and I'm unravelling under her touch.

Then it's gone.

'Oh God, unless... is now the point where you tell me your dick doesn't match the rest of you? Like, it has some kind of weird kink in it. Or it's all balls and a matchstick down there.'

I rear, brows furrowed. 'I don't have a weird dick.'

'Are you sure? Because if you only have your own equipment as a reference point then—'

'I've grown up in football locker rooms, Sas. You think I don't know what a good dick looks like?'

Her silly grin fills her pink cheeks and dances in her eyes. 'So *that's* why you're always last out of the showers.'

'Lord, you really have no filter, do you?'

She tugs me toward her by my belt again and taunts me with her open mouth barely touching mine, her tongue flicking against my lip, driving me wild.

'Get in the car, Sas.'

She gives a short, naughty giggle and turns to open the door she's leaning against.

I hold it shut. 'There's no way you're riding in the back. Come up front with me.'

'Can I drive?' She wiggles her eyebrows.

'Absolutely not. But I want to be able to feel you up on the way home.'

With a hearty laugh, she walks around the car and climbs in next to me, her body twisted, knees bent up to the seat as she talks to me.

I can't wait to get her home. Kissing her hasn't sated anything. Knowing how much she wants this – feeling how much we want to be with each other – has made it worse.

28

OCTOBER

Sas
One Night...

The air is so hot in this car I feel like a fajita sizzling on a grill pan. He said he wanted to feel me up – well, he is, but barely. As he drives us home, his fingers trace lines across my knee and up my thighs, but over my jeans. It's not often enough, or high enough; it's not *enough* to tame the wild he's brought out in me.

If he'd have wanted to go up against the car at the side of the highway, hell, I'd have taken the risk of being picked up by a state trooper.

I'm charged like I've been plugged into the national power grid.

Pace calls me a firecracker, but I feel like a firework, waiting to be set alight by Colton. Waiting for the ultimate climax.

He signals to maneuver off the highway, then that teasing trail of his fingers is back on my legs, making the ache between them worse. I grab his hand and gently bite his knuckle, turning my tongue around the end, relishing the way his eyes narrow and he shifts in his seat.

Now you know how I feel.

'Sas, you'd better make quick time out of this car because I'm about to burst out of these jeans.'

His expression is so serious – as if needing a seamstress would be the worst plight known to man. It makes me chuckle and my heart beat faster all at once.

Colton pulls us into the underground garage and kills the engine, then leaning his head back on the seat, he turns darkened eyes on me.

He slides the chair backward and tells me, 'Get over here.'

What do you know, very occasionally, maybe just this one time and circumstance, I'm okay with being told what to do.

Eyes locked on his, I shimmy over the center console as gracefully as I can manage and place my knees either side of him on the chair.

His lips curve up in that delectable half-smile and he nudges my hips closer to him. Then his hand is back on my face, cupping my jaw, like he was by the roadside.

I'm not sure who makes the first move but our mouths crash together. Hot, messy, teeth-clashingly frenzied. Fumbles and groans and the kind of sounds from us both that make my hips thrust deeper against him without my brain's active messaging.

It's impulsive and feels so good that I don't think we'll make it out of this garage.

'God, Sas, I've waited weeks for this.'

His hands slide up my hoodie, over my ribs that are expanding and retracting at a rate of knots.

'Is it worth it?' I pant.

He looks up to me, eyes as dark as I've seen them, the lights from the garage forcing the car to cast a shadow across his face, making his already chiseled features more distinct. Admittedly, I'm lust-drunk, but he might be the most attractive man I've ever been with.

His response is to un-cup my breast from the lace of my bra – thankfully, one of my finest, by chance – and take the tight tip between his teeth. Dragging, licking, sucking my sensitive flesh, he makes me feel like this was worth every second of the chase.

At least, that's how *I* feel – back bowed, neck taut as my head lolls with the feel of the incredibly hot guy between my thighs.

'Let's go upstairs,' Colton eventually says, breaking my moment of sheer unadulterated bliss. 'If I've got you all night, I want to use every minute of it making you go out of your mind.'

I smirk. 'That, and it must be pretty uncomfortable for a man your size to try to contort himself into a sex position in this car.'

He laughs and kisses me roughly one more time, before opening his door and carrying me like a monkey from the driver's side, planting me down on the hood of his car.

I wrap my legs around his waist in a vice grip and make him kiss me again, in a way that only he has kissed me before. If nothing else happened between us tonight, this kiss alone would sate me because it's combustion-level hot.

We ride the elevator to his floor, thankfully uninterrupted, meaning his hand in the ass pocket of my jeans and the way I nibble the lightly stubbled, sweetly spiced skin of his neck go unnoticed by anyone else.

Because as slack as we're being, we have to remember that the world thinks Colton has a girlfriend – who isn't me.

I try to push that thought from my mind, which is easy to do when we step inside his apartment and he's instantly back on me, lifting me onto the sideboard in his hallway, thick crotch pressed hard against me as he fucks me with his mouth. Somehow turning on low lights around us, as music – appropriate mood rather than country bumpkin music – starts to play into the space.

'I can't believe this is what I've been holding out on,' I moan or groan. Heck, I don't even know if my words are comprehensible.

'Did you forget to apply a filter again, or did you mean to confess that you've been dying to fuck me as much as I have you?' Colton whispers into my ear, before nipping my lobe in his teeth.

I don't answer because he picks me up as if I'm weightless, sets me down on his kitchen counter, and starts to unfasten my jeans.

'Shirt for pants,' I tell him, wanting to see that body that's driven me crazy countless times in the changing rooms.

If I get one night of no holds barred, I want to take full advantage.

Colton painstakingly slowly removes my sneakers and peels my jeans down my legs, then unbuttons his shirt by two and holds up his arms to give me what I want, letting me take him out of his top. I run greedy eyes over his firm chest and draw my index finger right down the gap between his pecs and his abdominal muscles that go on for days, until they sketch a V that tucks teasingly into his stonewash denim.

I replay his own moves, nibbling and licking, sucking my way down his torso until I drag a moan from him that touches down right in my end zone.

He takes my Bears hoodie over my head and arms, and this time, when he kisses me, our chests are flush, skin on skin, and *this,* this is where I've wanted to feel his body – on mine. His heat coursing through me more than the San Antonio summer sun.

As his mouth works mine, his taste and the touch of his tongue obliterating my sensory limit, his hands work down my sides, thumbs hooking into my lace thong. He draws the material down my legs, his lips following the same path, until his hand on my stomach is encouraging me to lie back and he brings my heels to the edge of the counter.

'Are you going to tell your chef to give this work surface a thorough wipe down before I have dinner here again?'

He smirks – the last thing I see before he buries his face between my thighs, making me groan, hands in my hair, spine arching, pushing my hips up to meet every stroke, every lick. The ease with which his fingers slip inside me is no surprise; I don't think I've ever been this greedy for anyone.

There isn't a comprehensible thought in my mind, only stars and bright lights, as I clench my fists in his hair and call out his name.

I'm vaguely aware that he scoops me up onto him and carries me through my comedown into his bedroom.

'Didn't have you pegged as a missionary guy,' I taunt when he lies me down on his crisp gray sheets.

I can't help but notice that his room has been interior designed. There's no way Colton managed to make this room look country chic. No footballer could make the longhorns above the bed and the Texas flag cushion on the wingback chair look fancy. This room has had a woman's touch. Since I know he doesn't do girlfriends, my money is on a designer.

Even the feel of his bedding is luxurious and welcomingly cool under my skin. It must feel good if I'm capable of registering the sensation with six foot four of absolute hunk lying on top of me, forearms either side of my face, hair messed from my climax fingers, lips shining under the lamp lights with my taste still on them.

I'm not wowed by athletes, no matter how good they look in or out of their uniform, but I'm wowed by Colton and how he looks like he's just given me one hell of an orgasm.

'I'm not a missionary guy. And in a minute, I'm going to roll you over and fuck you until that headboard is coming through the wall. But first, I just want to be inside you, Sas.'

Just. Like. That. My mouth is too dry to continue toying with him. He rocks himself against me, his hard length sliding across my wet clit, making me squirm again.

'Condom,' I remind him, already feeling bereft from the loss of him.

'That's why we're in here,' he tells me, before planting his lips against mine.

I lock him in with my legs around his waist, holding his heavy body against mine. The weight welcome and heady.

Then I swallow his groan before he unpeels my legs from him and walks backward from the bed until his butt meets a tall chest of drawers and he pulls out what he's looking for. As he sheaths himself, his eyes run hungrily over my body, and I swear I've never felt so desired or desirable. Desperate for him to come back to me.

When he does, he runs kisses north from my ankle, *way* north, until he meets my nipple. When I sigh from the decadence of it, his cock finds my slick lips, my tight bundle of nerves firing on all cylinders.

'Are you sure?' he asks, eyes fixing on mine.

'Fuck, yes, Colton. Let me have you.'

And he does. Torturously slowly, controlled and deep, just like him. He slides into me, groaning as he rolls his hips to take us deeper, his forehead pressed to mine.

He waits, eyes closed, my lip pulled gently between his teeth, until I'm raising my hips for more, squeezing my thighs around him.

'Fuck me, Colton.'

Finally, he moves in and out of me, grinding deep, filling me completely, both of us breathing into each other, mouths parted, lips touching.

I grip his ass, digging my fingers into his cheeks, enjoying the plump flesh as I pull him further into me.

'Jesus, Sas, you feel so fucking good.'

Then he does what he promised: slipping out of me, he turns me to face the back of the bed, where I grip the headboard, my hips pushing back and begging for more. Holding my breasts, he sinks back into me and goes at me harder, faster, until I'm seeing blinding lights again.

There's biting and nipping, panting and begging from us both. Only when my orgasm rips through me does Colton let go and come with me, making a sound that's guttural and untamed.

When we're both sated, he rests on my back, still pulsing as we come down from the kind of high I've never experienced with a man.

It was more than the act. It was... somewhere I'm not willing to overthink.

I wait for sleepiness to settle over me, but it doesn't come. Unusually, I don't want to rest. I want to kiss more and touch more and do all the things until we're ready to go again.

This wasn't one time; it was one night.

I'll be damned if I'm going to miss out on a repeat of *that*.

We shower, washing each other, groping each other through the heat and slickness of soapy water, where I take my turn to repay him going down on me. Then we go again, barely making it out of the bathroom and onto the rug in Colton's bedroom.

We snack and realize the time. So, in the early hours of the morning, we nap, using it as a necessary break to recharge. We both know what daylight brings, so as dawn comes, we make love again. This time in the bed, with Colton wrapped around me like a spoon, whispering into my ear and kissing my neck as we take our time, the frenzy abated.

Until finally, after that third time, he rolls onto his back and I come to rest on his chest, tucked under his big arm. Our legs are entwined under the thin sheet, clothes and bedding discarded clumsily around the room.

As I gently stroke his chest, he lightly draws circles around the back of my hand. There's a smell of sex and nudity around us, mixed with fancy soap and fresh bedding. And with Colton beneath me, it's a pretty nice place to be hanging out.

'Thank you for tonight,' Colton says, breaking the near silence but for our calm breaths.

I know exactly what he means – the game, Auston – but I choose to say, 'You're welcome, cowboy. I'm glad you enjoyed the romp.'

He guffaws so hard, I bob up and down on his pec.

'All right, thanks for that, too. Thanks, three times. But mostly for getting my head straight tonight at the game. You saved me from drowning out there.'

I nod, playing with the thin line of hair down his stomach, going way down under the sheet. 'I wish you'd told me about Auston and Annie. I know you're a private guy. I get it. And I know you were protecting Annie, but I can help. Look how you played tonight once you knew Annie had told me. You played as if a weight had been lifted from you.'

'No, Sas, I played like a man on a promise.'

Now, I laugh hard.

'But you're right. It is nice that you know and that Annie was the one to share her story. I guess...'

'You didn't know if you could trust me?'

'No.' He sighs. 'Yes. I'm not good with speaking up and I find it hard to know who to trust. Especially with this whole thing with Megan.'

'I get that.' I roll over on top of him, chin on my hands. 'Whatever made you feel like you don't have a voice?'

He tucks my hair that's fallen forward behind my ear. 'It's not that I don't feel like I have a voice. I know I have a voice and a platform to use in the right way.'

He stares at me for a while and I think maybe, if I don't do my usual, if I take a leaf out of his book and stay quiet, he might have more to say.

'My parents have always supported me and all their kids as best they could. Annie and me, sure, but also all the foster kids they've given a home over the years.'

'I didn't realize you grew up with fosters.'

He nods. 'Always. Sometimes one or two. More often a couple of longer-term placements and a bunch of respite kids.'

'That must have been chaotic at times,' I say, thinking I'm possibly understanding where this is going.

'It was. It could be great fun, too. And I never wanted for anything. My folks took me to every meet, every practice, every game. I don't know how they managed it around everyone else.' He presses a kiss to the tip of my nose, making my eyes close and a shiver course through me, in the best way. 'But my parents had a lot on, all the time. Cooking, shopping and cleaning for that many kids. Appointments with doctors and counsellors, social workers, new schools. All of it. Often, our fosters had a lot of needs and trauma and I guess I realized how fortunate I was.'

'So, you stayed quiet in the chaos?'

'Something like that. I helped out at home as much as I could and I figured I took up enough energy from my family without being another demand.'

'That was a lot for a kid to understand.'

He shrugs. 'In some ways, it made me grow up quickly. That and football. I had to get savvy. But lately, I've been looking back and wondering if I was too quiet. If I wasn't there often enough. Maybe what I thought was helping my family was actually just me not being there.'

'Old habits die hard, right?'

'Right,' he whispers.

The only response I have is to reach up and kiss him, because I see now that there is no conceited pride about Colton; there's only warmth and thoughtfulness, intelligence. I kiss the little boy who lost his voice and the man he became regardless.

And there's something here, in this kiss, that reaches deep inside me and contorts every piece of me in a way that might not be reparable.

Forever changed.

With the realization of danger, I reluctantly push up from Colton, taking the bedsheet with me and leaving him in all his naked glory.

'Where're you going?'

'To the bathroom,' I tell him. As he brings his hands behind his head, stretching those deliciously taut muscles in his torso, I wonder if I shouldn't hop right back on that bed with him. But it's time to cut my losses before contorted insides become something worse.

Better to take with me only the welcome soreness between my legs than a messed-up bag of emotions I'm not in a position to deal with.

'Then I'm going to head out. I should try to get back before Pace realizes I didn't stay there last night. If he hasn't already.'

Colton inhales, chest rising. 'One night, right?'

He knew it. We both did. He asked for it. That was the basis on which I agreed to have a night of... undeniably unforgettable sex.

I just didn't expect the aftermath of one night to be this devastating. The look on Colton's face, like he doesn't want our one night to be done at all, is killing me.

'Right. One night,' I say, the words breaking as they leave me, before I turn my back on the guy who has utterly rocked my world.

I already know my head and heart have crossed a line I drew. A line that was there for good reasons.

29

OCTOBER

Colton
About Last Night...

We're watching tape from the weekend's game, as we do every Monday morning. I know I had a hell of a game second half but I really stank up the gridiron first half and that's what the coaching staff are focusing on right now, giving me a grilling in front of the guys.

It's cool. I deserve it. The fact is, I redeemed myself second half and helped the team win the game.

Daniels raises his hand when the dressing down is nearly done. 'Coach Roy, can I propose that we send Sas into the dressing room with Quinn every half-time? 'Cause whatever she said or did in there, man...'

Whistles and a barrage of verbal quips ensue – mostly derogatory about what a woman can do to me in thirty seconds. Even the coaches are smirking.

'Come on, y'all, she's a professional. Don't talk about her like that,' I say, hiding the fact my hackles are up because that's exactly what they want.

'Not least 'cause that firecracker will come at y'all if she catches wind of it,' Pace adds.

'You know she will,' I tell him, all the while trying to read his expression.

Is it knowing? Has she said something about last night? Or does he like her?

'Plus, Colton's got a girl. So, no wisecracks outside this circle, all right?' Pace adds.

His eyes are still fixed on mine and I think, *What do you know?* I hate lying and since Sean Boyle has been involved with my PR, what's happening publicly with Megan has become less gray and more flagrant lies. It's not the kind of man I am or want to be. Especially in here, with my teammates.

'Aye, aye, Captain!' Daniels says with a salute.

It sits heavy in my gut, so heavy I look away from Pace and the others, preferring to lie to my own feet.

We're all dismissed from the review room and Pace hangs an arm around my shoulder. 'You look tired today, Quinn.'

'Big game yesterday.'

He nods. 'Sas looks tired today, too.'

I raise one brow. I'm hardly surprised; we got no sleep last night. Tiredness today is a welcome reminder of how fucking incredible last night was. We matched each other with every beat, every stroke and lick, touch and grind. She was all in; we both were. I had no idea quite *how* into it I was going to be.

I'm unsettled by it today. I'm not sure how or why yet but I think seeing her at our meeting with the potential new sponsor this afternoon might be the only thing that can right me. I need to see her.

'Quinn!' Coach Roy snaps me out of my reverie. 'A word in my office.'

Pretty sure I know what this is about.

Two minutes later, sitting on the opposite side to Glen's messy desk – papers everywhere because he's a tech dinosaur, trophies lining his shelves, medals dangling from them, plates of honor nailed to the walls – I'm feeling like the bad kid in class.

He leans back into his seat, hands on his stomach beneath his Bears training suit, then lifts his branded cap and scratches his thinning hair.

'Coach, before you say anything, I want to apologize for what happened before the game yesterday, and for the state of my game in the first two quarters.' I hold up my hands – I surrender. 'I'm sorry, it wasn't good enough. It wasn't like me. And I'm grateful that you stuck with me for the second half, Coach.'

His eyes soften, some of the creases smoothing out with his temper.

Mama has always said, head anger off with an apology. Ice to a fire. She's rarely wrong.

Coach nods. 'I appreciate that but you're lucky you got your game straight, son.'

'I know. And, honestly, I have Sas to thank for that. She's... Ah... She's...'

He puffs out his cheeks on his next breath. 'She's my goddaughter and she's working for you. She's got a lot of eyes looking out for her down here, Quinn. You understand what I'm saying, don't you?'

I clear my throat. 'Yes, sir.'

'I don't read everything that's printed in the papers and online but I do understand you have a girlfriend and the pair of you are making headlines. Don't get my goddaughter messed up in something, all right now?'

'Yes, sir.' I swallow deeply because the enormity of the situation is sinking in.

There is no Sas and me. It *was* one night. That's what we agreed. And this feeling like my insides are a jet plane in free fall every time I think about her needs to stop.

To everyone else's mind, I'm with Megan.

'All I meant, Coach, is that Sas is opening my eyes to a few things. Some stuff with Auston being one of them.'

'Are you going to share?'

Eyes to the ceiling, I exhale slowly. Sas knows and it's for the best – I felt lighter yesterday for sharing. Coach won't spread Annie's story.

So, I tell him. I finally tell someone about my ex-best friend and my sister and my niece or nephew who's on the way.

Coach stares at me and shakes his head. 'That's what happened in the off-season? You found out about all this?'

I nod.

'I can't condone what happened in springtime, or yesterday during warm-up, son. You've got to switch it off on the field and do whatever it takes off the field to make that happen.' He rises from his seat, a towering frame – less muscle but still as big as he was when he played center. 'But as a man, a husband and a father, I'm not sure I would have acted any differently.'

I stand opposite him. 'Thanks, Coach.'

'You can go.' He dismisses me and I head to his door. 'And Quinn?'

'Yes, Coach?'

'There are fifty-two guys who would have your back in a heartbeat if you'd just let them. You tell them to keep schtum, they will. It's been a few years since I played but I do know this... what's said in the dressing room, stays in the dressing room. I know you've taken some heat for things that happened in the break but if you talk to your brothers—'

Something occurs to me in the moment, takes me back to Sas lying on my chest in the early hours of this morning, and I tell him, 'It's not that I don't want to talk, Coach. I just... don't know how to.'

'That's easy, kid. Open your mouth and let the San Antonio breeze move your tongue around.'

I know someone who does that often.

His words and the thought of Sas's unfiltered conversations force my lips up. 'Yes, sir.'

* * *

It's after five when Sas and I are walking out of Alpha Impact, broadly having agreed a lucrative sponsorship deal. Well, Sas has, because, as I tell her when she asks me if I'm happy with the key terms of the deal, 'I legit only listened to the first five minutes of that meeting.'

'Colton!' She snorts, momentarily losing the rhythm of her stride as we make our way to where my Maserati is parked.

'You had it under control. Once I realized that, I did nothing except stare at you in this knock-out dress and think about fucking you in those killer heels.'

We reach the car, and she isn't laughing anymore. Standing on opposite sides of the hood, we silently challenge each other to be the one to fold first. Bluffing that what happened last night, into the early hours of this morning, won't happen again.

'We said one night,' she says, hands locked around her leather laptop case, which is blocking my view of the mind-blowing curves of her hips.

'We did. But technically, it was morning,' I reason.

She pouts and I brace myself for a tongue-lashing. Not at all expecting her to say, '*Technically*, it is still the same day.'

My eyes forget how to blink. My mouth forgets how to close. 'I am so on board with this logic, I can't tell you.'

She chuckles but it's short-lived, before she bites the lip I remember dragging through my teeth. Lips I want to devour right now.

'One last time?' I ask, ready to get down on one knee and beg if I have to.

'One more time.'

30

OCTOBER

Sas
Three's a Crowd

As soon as we're in the elevator of his building, Colton is on me, and I am *not* complaining. I knew the moment I got back to Pace's house this morning that I wouldn't be able to stop thinking about being with Colton until I *was* with Colton. One more time.

That's all I need. One more fix to get him out of my head.

Not a fix, because a fix would imply an addiction, and I am absolutely *not* addicted to the way his lips are teasing the sensitive skin of my neck. I will *never* be so completely obsessed with the way his hands are feeling me up over the skin-tight black dress that I can't stop. I *totally* didn't choose this dress for the meeting today thinking that this very thing might happen.

This is just a... hit. A quick indulgence for good times' sake.

Still, I'm watching us in the surrounding mirrors of the elevator cart, immensely turned on by the sight of him all over me. His shirt taut across his back muscles, my painted nails tugging on his thick hair. His body coating mine.

The ping of arrival is unwelcome, until I realize we'll get to his penthouse quicker if we get out of the elevator.

How I concentrated in that meeting with the directors of Alpha Impact is unfathomable. It was a feat of female design. Multitasking at its absolute best. Because all I've wanted since I walked out of Colton's apartment this morning is to be back in it. With him. In his bed. In his hot, sweaty arms, being taken like I never have before.

He makes quick work of letting us inside. I go to kick off my heels to protect his wood floor but he hooks my leg over his hip.

'Hell no. These are staying on.'

I love how he speaks to me, with the kind of confidence in the moment that I haven't known even with ballers in the past. It's unlike the pre-watershed version of him. More like the kind of man who can play pro-ball with the biggest and fittest in the world.

The guy who won the game yesterday.

I know, I know, I'm not in the market for a sports guy, but what if the problem with the guys I dated in the past was more that they were in college and only looking for a lay than the fact they were on teams?

In the alternative, I'm pathetic, a glutton for punishment, a type-caster and yes, my type is... Colton.

That southern drawl. I don't even like being in the south. I'm a northern girl. A city girl. But dang, this cowboy is making me want to ride.

'Come with me,' he says, taking me by the hand.

I watch my feet move like I'm drunk, concentrating on each step as I follow him through the apartment. I think I might be drunk on *him*.

In his bedroom, he hits a button on a remote control and his blind draws over the window, then he presses another and the soft orange hue of low lighting turns on. With another click, the space fills with the kind of music that somehow turns me on even more.

Colton walks me to a full-length wall mirror and turns me to face it, his chest pressed to my back. He wraps my long hair around his hand and moves it to one side, giving him access to my neck.

'Watch how fucking incredible you look,' he tells me between nips and presses of his lips to my skin. He's hard against my ass, his hands cupping my breasts.

Everything he does builds me closer to a sensory explosion.

As he draws down the zipper at the back of my dress, I brace myself, hands either side of the mirror. I follow our reflection as he takes my dress to the floor and unfastens his pants to push them down his thighs. I feel him spring free against me, my breaths short and ragged as he moves my silk underwear to one side.

I hear the tear of foil and feel his fingers run the slick length of my sex to make sure I'm ready.

'I'm all yours, cowboy,' I tell him, receiving a deep growl in response.

Then he slides into me and I get lost in the sight of him, *us*. His body wrapped around mine, his head hung back with ecstasy, hands clasped around my breasts as he starts to move inside me.

I can do this to him.

Already, I feel myself rising. All reservations forgotten.

And I think, maybe one more time won't be enough.

Maybe there's no number that will ever be enough.

Maybe this *is* an addiction.

Because the way I feel with Colton in me, over me, around me, is not something I can forget or move on from.

We ride each other to our peaks, eyes locked in the mirror. He's right; this does look fucking incredible. Sexy as hell. Outrageously hot. A complete undoing of my sensibility.

I'm still in the wistful fuzz of raging hormones when the apartment intercom buzzes. Head to my back, Colton grumbles at the interruption, but he checks his watch.

'Damn it!'

We separate abruptly.

'What is it?' I ask, grabbing my dress from the floor and holding it over my body as if Colton hasn't seen every naked inch of me.

His expression tells me that he doesn't want to answer. 'Meg. We're supposed to be having dinner. I lost track of time.'

'I— Oh— Right.'

I pull on my dress and struggle with the zipper, until Colton, having pulled up his pants, finishes the fastening for me.

I shouldn't feel like I'm being kicked out of his place, as if I'm some kind of mistress, or worthless second. This is a one-time (ish) thing and Megan is his *media* girlfriend.

But I just had one of the best orgasms of my life and I can't help that it *does* hurt. Ridiculously. Senselessly. But truthfully. It hurts.

'Have I got time to slip out?' I ask, feeling cheap.

He looks at me all doe-eyed and puppy-dog like. 'Sas, I'm sorry. I don't want you to go. You shouldn't rush off anywhere. This is just—'

He scratches his head, looking around the bedroom.

'Exactly what it's supposed to be, Colton. It's fine. We both knew what this was.' I straighten my dress, willing my eyes to stop stinging. 'We've had a legitimate business meeting together. Let Megan in. I'll say hi and be on my way.'

He looks as if he wants to speak, but this is Colton; he only finds his voice in the bedroom. In any event, what more is there to say?

I shrug and he nods. Give him his due, he looks as uncomfortable with this unhappy ending as I am.

By the time Megan makes it up to the penthouse, I've been to the toilet, flattened my just-sexed hair, and fixed my smudged lipstick.

'Megan, hi!' I say, coming out of the bathroom. 'How are you?'

'I'm great,' she says in her newfound Texas accent, which is definitely improving from her time spent with Colton, and on set. 'It's so good to see y'all.'

My smile feels false and I hate feeling like I'm lying to another woman's face. 'You, too. I'm actually about to head out. We've had a meeting and I left my car here.'

Megan looks between us and I'm sure I'm just being overly sensitive, but I think she *knows*.

'Come to dinner with us. We're not doing anything particularly special. Just a photo op and some work on my lines. It'll be fun to catch up. Won't it, Colton?'

'Ah— I—' Mr. Not At All Playing This Cool winds up blowing a raspberry. A *raspberry*. 'Sure.'

'No,' I protest. 'It's your couple time.'

But Megan loops her arm through mine. 'Nonsense, who doesn't love a thruple these days? Let's go.'

Just like that, I'm playing third wheel. The gooseberry. Three's a crowd. To my client, who I'm screwing, and his faux girlfriend.

What could possibly go wrong?

Colton drives us in his Range Rover. Naturally, I sit in the back and let the happy fake couple ride together up front. If there are any cameras, it would look absurd for Megan to be sitting in the back.

I hate that it even bothers me the slightest amount. I guess I have orgasm comedown emotions or something.

Brought on by me.

This whole situation is entirely my doing.

I said one night and should have left it there. Now, I have to look my dad in the eye and act like I haven't had four spine-tinglingly amazing rounds of Colton.

Respect to Megan, though, who spends almost the entire ride out to a swanky vegan place half-twisted on her seat to chat with me. Mostly about herself and her show, but that's fine. Discombobulated spaghetti would have more direction than my brain has right now, so letting Megan talk works for me.

If my vital organs were less spun out, I might recognize that this is what Colton does – he lets other people fill the silence because his mind has been full of a cheerleader, who he cares about, losing her job, and his sister being knocked up to his ex-best friend, who's acting like the absolute pits about it. All while trying to shield everyone from public scrutiny.

In fact, if my mind weren't so drunk on the last twenty-four hours, I think I'd be looking at the man who's staring at me through his rearview mirror with an apologetic expression and thinking, *Colton Quinn, I could fall for you. For real.*

But my mind is... a mess.

Probably a good thing, too.

When we arrive at the restaurant, it's no problem for American football star Colton Quinn and award-winning actress Megan Frost to add a guest to their booking.

The restaurant is chic – not at all Texas vibes but city vibes: white table-tops sit on chrome legs. The tables are relatively close together to fit in more guests. The kitchen is open and the chefs can be seen along nearly the entirety of the back wall. It's a spectacle.

Purposely accidental-looking trees pop up between the dining spaces in large standing pots, decorated in twinkling lights. Chilled vibes music subtly plugs any quiet moments, of which there is one, when other diners spot Megan and Colton... and me. Before hushed words are spoken and surreptitious camera phones placed strategically on tabletops.

This is awful. I should have refused to come.

Especially when Megan takes Colton's hand and the duo follow an overzealous restaurant manager to our seats. It's not the display of affection that bothers me, obviously. It's the fact I'm trailing behind like a child to parents, the black sheep, the ugly duckling.

I'm thrilled when we're settled at one of three tables slightly shielded from other guests by a curtain of fairy lights. I purposely position myself with my back to the other diners and let the media's favorite couple face their fans.

Once a member of the wait staff has passed us each a menu and shared the chef's recommendations, I tell Colton and Megan, 'I don't know how you stand the attention. Every pair of eyes in this place is on you two.'

'It's awful,' Colton says.

As Megan simultaneously says, 'It's all part of the job.'

They share a laugh at their differences, and I think, Colton looks genuinely relaxed around Megan.

And she's truly lovely. She includes me in every conversation, has the kind of easy manner that makes it unsurprising that she's a critics' choice favorite. I find myself listening to what she has to say, not bothered that it's 95 percent about her. She's really quite captivating.

I'm only startled out of my fixation with her when Colton's bellowing laughter, so uncommon, hits my ears like a slap. It steals my attention and I find myself smiling at him. Not at whatever Megan said to draw the laugh, but at the man wearing the cheek-splitting grin. Happy looks good on him. Happy smells good on him. Happy tastes—

His knee suddenly meets mine under the table, our gazes locked, and he reaches up his arms like a teenage boy on his first date about to do the yawn and slide. I watch with anticipation, waiting for his arm to come down around my shoulder, and it will be welcome. As welcome as the warmth of his leg against mine beneath the table.

As he watches me, his arm lowers in the direction of my chair.

But midway, I remember, he *can't*.

And I think the look on my face serves as his reminder that we're in public. *We* aren't the couple. He and Megan are.

Then his other arm comes down toward Megan's chair, and he looks a bit like the statue of Christ the Redeemer, extremities spread wide, as solid as reinforced concrete.

He pulls both limbs back into his body and starts eating the vegan food in front of him, which honestly seems to pain the carnivore with every bite.

'I can't do this,' I tell him. Then to Megan, I say, 'Meg, Colton and I had sex.'

The poor girl nearly chokes on the lychee from her mocktail. 'You did?'

She's looking from me to Colton, who mutters, 'Way to apply that filter, Sas.'

'I'm sorry,' I tell them both. 'No one else can know, for *all* the reasons, and I shouldn't have blurted it out but I don't want to sit here and pretend. I like you, Meg, and I want you to know that I made sure there's nothing going on between you two. If there had been, I swear I wouldn't have crossed the line.'

She plants her hand on my arm. 'Are you kidding me? I'm thrilled about this! Colton and I have absolutely nothing in common. He knows nothing about show business, and I really can't stand sports. Or exercise, for that matter.'

I chuckle, though still feeling uncomfortable and kind of missing Colton's knee pressed to mine. He has physically recoiled at my outburst. I try to ignore the devil on my shoulder asking why.

'Seriously, Sas, Colton and I literally talk about me, or run my lines, or we talk about you.' She shifts her focus to Colton. 'I'm so pleased you finally told her how you feel.'

Colton lets his head fall back. 'Jesus, Meg.'

'Oh. Have you not told her? But you've slept with her. How could you not tell her that you like her?'

I hold up a hand. 'Hi. Still here.' But I can't bring myself to look Colton's way. Does he *like* me? I mean, sure, he likes me. We've had sex. Mind-blowing sex. Multiple times. But does he *like* like me?

He clears his throat. 'It was a one time. Or one night. Or one-day thing.'

I'm not sure what's worse, honestly. That he might like me. Or that he might not.

Flip, my head really is a wreck.

'So…' Megan slurps the rest of her drink through a short straw. 'How was he? When we've kissed it's felt like kissing my brother.'

I stare at her with horror. She stares at me with anticipation. And Colton buries his face in his hands with a groan.

I'm not sure who breaks first but we all end up laughing together.

It's a relief to tell someone, even if that someone is technically Colton's girlfriend.

I don't want to lie to her. Colton's right; withholding the truth from my dad, my friends and family might not be so bad. I mean, our one night (or day) has been and gone. It won't happen again.

But to sit here at dinner with Megan, enjoying every look and under-table graze I receive from Colton, felt like an outright lie.

Through the main course, with the proverbial bomb dropped, Megan shares that she's actually kind of digging one of her co-stars. 'Course, I don't have the benefit of him knowing that I'm not genuinely in a relationship with Colton.'

Through dessert, she starts talking in her nondescript southern accent and I think it's decent, honestly.

By the time we head to the car, it doesn't feel too bad getting into the rear seat this time, and I hang back to make sure I'm not captured in shots by the waiting cameras outside.

'Sean,' Colton mutters under his breath as he turns on the ignition.

'He's doing his job,' I remind him in the rearview mirror.

'You're defending him, now?'

'No, I can't tolerate the man, but he *is* good at his job and his job here is to make the world think you and Megan are a happy power couple.'

'And to make me look cool and edgy,' Megan adds with a beam.

'If only people knew Colton is so far from cool and edgy,' I say, only half in jest.

He shakes his head, though I see humor dancing in those wickedly inviting eyes as he drives us to Megan's rental.

She kisses and hugs us both when she gets out of the car and calls, 'G'night, y'all!'

'She's really sweet,' I tell Colton as I clamber less than gracefully in my movement-inhibiting dress into the front passenger seat.

Colton watches me the whole time, my body immediately responding to his attention. *Traitor.*

I need to put some distance between us. A chance to put the flames out.

So, when we pull into his underground garage, I immediately zap my keys to unlock the sports car I've borrowed from Pace.

Colton leans back against the hood of his car. Calling my bluff, I think. 'You're not coming up?'

I shake my head, backing up to Pace's car, not daring to open my mouth and find out precisely how I'll relent. Knowing there's a significant, reckless part of me that wants to head upstairs.

'Best if you don't?' he asks.

I nod, opening the car door.

'So that's it? That's our one day.'

My chest aches as if all that veg has given me indigestion. 'Like we agreed.'

'Sure.'

He watches me lower myself – again, a bit tricky – into the car, really tumbling the last few inches. And I watch him through my mirror as I drive away, rubbing that strike of indigestion with my fist, truly not knowing how I found the willpower to leave.

It's only when I'm alone, in the dark, the radio playing Sabrina Carpenter's 'Juno' (ironic), that I remember what Megan said.

He likes me.

Which is even more reason to make sure the events of the last twenty-four hours are *not* repeated.

31

NOVEMBER

Colton
Corn Dogs and Nachos

Since I'm driving in from the ranch, I get the rookies, Jad and Terry, to pick up Sas and bring her along to the San Antonio college game.

She wanted to come but said we couldn't be seen alone in public too often – by which I think she meant she's afraid of what'll happen between us if we're alone too often – so I arranged for Jad and Terry to come along, too. They both know some of the guys in their senior years playing for SAU and their Louisiana opponents.

Mama was happy today, getting involved as much as she had the energy to do with the kids at the ranch. Since we've reopened, we've also got more staff helping with chores and admin, which is freeing up some of my time. I'm still around as much as I can be, and I *want* to be there, but I've got to admit, when I'm sore from playing, it's nice to have someone else on hand to do heavy lifting and mucking out animals.

Annie's getting huge, ready to pop, so she spent most of the morning sitting under an umbrella, drinking homemade lemonade and reading stories to the visiting kids.

It felt busy and nice. And, I don't know, I'm feeling kind of lighter this week.

I did what Coach told me, too. On Wednesday, I spoke to the team, apologized for what went down between Auston and me at the weekend, and explained why. It was easier than I thought, even though it was about Annie and *her* story. I'd asked her first and I told the guys it was for their ears only.

I don't know what I expected but the resounding support in the dressing room, as opposed to a bunch of pissed men because I could have lost us the game last Sunday, was... *nice.* They made me feel like they've got my back. I'm not sure what made me think that they wouldn't, but it was still a welcome response – except maybe Trent thumping my back so hard he might have dislocated my shoulder if I hadn't been wearing my pads.

I park in the lot for the sixty-thousand capacity ground. Despite my SAU cap and hoodie, I'm spotted within seconds and spend a while signing autographs and having selfies with people.

Sas was right; if she and I had turned up together and alone, tongues would have been wagging. We'd explain it away as work but I don't want to have to.

Instead, I don't see her, Jad and Terry, until I get to our seats in the stand. She's also wearing SAU stash – cap and hoodie – her long hair falling down across one shoulder as she guffaws with my teammates.

Damn, she's pretty.

As I'm watching, I get noticed again and wind up signing more autographs before I can make my way over to her.

Conscious of the eyes and camera phones trained on us, I fist-pump Jad, then Terry, then the woman I had my hands and lips all over earlier in the week.

'Hi, buddy,' she says, forcing me to narrow my eyes on her, enjoying the way her skin flushes.

'You doin' all right, *dude*?' I ask.

'I'm good. Jad's just telling me about his latest foray with dating apps.'

Between joking around with the guys and Sas, it's surprisingly easy to keep my hands to myself and stop my mind from wandering. The first two quarters fly by as we chat about the game and the players, me telling Sas who I think is someone she should be interested in and Sas having her own well-informed views. It's like hanging out with another one of my friends, a baller. It's totally chilled, even while I think she looks awesome in her get-up, and I can imagine months, years even, of us going to sports games together. As friends, obviously.

At half-time, Sas disappears. In her absence, Terry tells me he thinks she's wicked, and I agree. But I remind him that she's here for work. To which Terry informs me that Sas will be hanging out with all the single guys who are going to Pace's pad for Big Game Sunday tomorrow, since it's a bye week for the Bears. And she won't be *there* in her professional capacity.

Pace invited me to the hang-out. It felt as if he was extending an olive branch after I told everyone at training about Auston and Annie, because, honestly, I've not been a huge fan of Pace before this season and I don't think he's been my biggest advocate either. But Sas gets along so well with him that maybe I should change my opinion.

Still, it's bye weekend, so I'm intending to go out to the ranch and spend time with my family, which was the excuse I gave Pace when I turned down his invitation. I don't know why it's only occurring to me now that Sas will still be around tomorrow, before she goes back to New York on Monday.

Speaking of... she makes her way back toward us and I rush to help her come along the row, taking a tray loaded with food from her, which gives her the opportunity to take the plastic glass of beer she's holding between her teeth into her hand.

'Is that a beer for me?' I ask.

'The beer is for the grown-ups,' she replies. 'All this food is for my growing boys.'

She chuckles and it's the damn sweetest sound I've ever heard.

'You really didn't get us a beer?' Terry asks.

'No.' She takes three bottles of water from the middle pocket of her hoodie and hands them out to the three of us. 'I understand it's bye weekend but do you guys really want to have pictures of you drinking beer during the season going viral on social media?'

We're all doing some form of rolling our eyes, though we accept our bottles of water like chastised boys and sit down in our seats. Sas dishes out corn dogs and chili tortilla chips to each of us.

I remember how good these corn dogs are from college. After a day of studying, I'd often head out of the library and pick up one of these bad boys. The perk of burning through calories on a daily basis has to be corn dogs and chili chips, though I probably won't tell my nutritionist chef about this.

As I audibly appreciate my corn dog, I feel Sas's eyes on me, and I don't know what comes over me but I shoot her a wink, which she accepts with a hearty laugh.

'Nostalgia in a brioche?' she asks.

'Big time,' I tell her through a mouthful of hog.

Jad leans forward, calling from the end of our row, 'Hey Sas, are you single?'

My ears prick up like I live in a Hobbit shire as she empties her mouth before responding.

'Depends, who's asking?' she says.

'What about a pro-baller?'

Straight faced, she replies, 'Not my type.'

And I nearly choke on the last bite of my corn dog.

When she settles back next to me, ready for the third quarter to begin, I lean into her ear and say, 'I consider myself a very lucky exception to the rule.'

She stands to applaud the players running back out to the field, but I see the rise of her cheekbones in her profile.

San Antonio win by a narrow margin. Sas has made plentiful notes on her phone to discuss with her dad. I remember her words back in the parking lot the first time I had lunch with her and Harris. If she improves my game and we get the contract extension we all want, then she gets a client of her own, preferably a Texan, which would also mean she has more reason to spend time down here.

Maybe our goals aren't so out of sync.

At the end of the game, we all leave the stadium together but having been photographed as a group of four all evening, it feels safe enough for me to offer to drive Sas home.

We part ways with Jad and Terry, me grateful for their presence because it meant I got to hang out with Sas, doing something we both enjoy.

Then it's just us, in my car, her giving me grief about Chris Stapleton playing through the speakers, even though she admits that 'Tennessee Whiskey' is an awesome song.

I was planning on driving back out to stay at the ranch to get a head start on work early in the morning, but as we drive away from the crowds dispersing back to college, I have an uncommonly spontaneous idea. One that has my pulse rising.

'Can I take you someplace?' I ask.

When she agrees, I change direction and head out to a spot I used to come when I was in college, and before that, when I first learned to drive. A place where the air is clear, the sky is dark but decorated with a smattering of twinkling diamonds. Where the view below is peace and calm defined. A quiet place, where the noise of any day dissolves into the habitat and is replaced by the chirp of crickets.

We drive to the top of my hill and I kill the engine. I have a spare jacket in the car, which I lay out on the hood. Hopping on up to the space beside it, I recline onto the car, looking up to where constellations are drawn in the sky, increasing clearly, and I pat the jacket. Sas comes to lie next to me and watches the same view of the stars, her arms behind her head, a reflection of mine.

'It's beautiful here,' she says.

I agree. Even more so for being here with her.

'Come on, level with me: how many girls have you brought up here after a college game?'

I shift onto my side and Sas does the same, so we're facing each other in a way that feels relaxed and intimate. She's stunning always but under the light of the moon, here in this place, she's mesmerizing. I have to fight against my fingers wanting to reach out and brush her hair back from her face, because I don't think that level of closeness is where we are.

'You're the first person I've ever brought here. Male or female.'

Unusually, she doesn't say anything. She doesn't even react, just continues to look at me with big eyes I want to get lost in.

'Thank you for letting me into your secret place.'

A short nod is all that I can respond with because, for whatever reason, I'm lost for words.

'You know, I think I could fall in love with Texas just a little bit,' she says.

I feel my lips rise, nowhere nearly as expressive of my happiness as her words just made me feel, and I truly don't know why. It's not as if she's saying she could fall in love with me. Just Texas.

I hold out my index finger and thumb, a tiny gap between them, and ask her, 'Just a tiny bit?'

She holds up her finger and thumb against mine until we form a love heart shape between us. 'A minuscule amount.'

For all the reasons that existed yesterday and still exist today, I know I shouldn't, I know I can't, but I really want to kiss her. I watch her lips, wishing this was less complicated. But if I *was* willing to introduce the distraction of a girlfriend during game season, with everything else that's going on in my life, it would be Sas.

'Try not to overanalyze this, Sas, but I really want to kiss you right now.'

I wait until she makes the move, her fingers coming to trace the line of my lips: soft, slow, welcome. Then she inches forward and that's enough for me. I lean in the whole way and press my mouth to hers, my common sense completely outsmarted by the way I need her whenever she's around. And when she's not.

32

NOVEMBER

Sas
The Best Tex-Mex For Four Counties

'I've got you,' Pace says as I bump open his door with my ass while carrying a box of groceries in my arms.

Pace has arranged for all the single Bears to come round for game day, since it's bye weekend. It's also international game day, with matches being played overseas too. First kick off is at 9 a.m. and they'll go on into the night, virtually back-to-back all day.

I think there are seven or eight of us hanging out for the day and as Pace relieves me of my load, I check my watch. I was hoping to be much quicker picking up the groceries but I wandered around the store in something of a daze, my head still on the hood of Colton's car last night. The stars, his lips, his hands, his body coating mine, shielding me from the chill of the night, hiding me from the realities of why we shouldn't have been kissing. Allowing me to get lost in him completely.

Not that the guys will care, but now I feel a little pressured to get breakfast and coffees on the go before they arrive shortly. For one thing, Pace has been assisted with all this domesticated stuff for a lot of years, so I dread to think what he'd cook up if I left it to him. Also, I want to help him host. It's as much payment as he's willing to accept for all the time I've spent staying with him since pre-season.

I'm heading back to New York tomorrow, at least for a while, so this is my last chance to do something nice for him.

'How was the game yesterday?' he asks as I'm putting away the shopping and setting out eggs, bacon and avocado next to the oven top.

I'm pleased that I have a task to focus on because my cheeks glow like they would if I were talking about boys at a slumber party.

'I enjoyed the game; I watched some decent players, ones the agency should reach out to when we're able.'

As the words are leaving my mouth, I'm thinking about the way I sat in the stands with my legs pressed against Colton's, feeling his heat through both our denim. The way I spent the night after the game kissing him under the stars. How I wanted more than anything to go back to his place when he dropped me back here last night and drove out to the ranch because he'd promised his family he'd have breakfast with them this morning.

Pace and I are making idol chit-chat, the way we do, the way we have for years. Me asking about how his date with a physio from another team went last night, him asking about me and my life outside Texas. Until his phone pings with a message and I watch him view the screen with confusion, then look up to me.

'Quinn's coming today,' he says. 'He must've changed his mind about having something better to do. He never hangs with the guys these days. First golf, now a bye weekend hang-out. I guess he's in the market for some better BFFs than his last one.'

It's as if all the blood in my system has rushed to my stomach, making it hot and busy and sort of hyperactive. Colton's coming over.

'You know, best friends who won't screw your sister and leave her alone and knocked up,' Pace adds.

The meaning of his words finally registers. 'Colton told you about Auston?'

'I assumed you must know. Putting two and two together, I'm guessing that's something to do with the reason you charged Coach Roy and went all alpha firecracker on Quinn at half-time last weekend?'

He's thrown me completely. 'Yeah, I guess I'm just surprised he told you. Colton's closed off, locked with a cast-iron chain.'

'Not just me,' Pace adds. 'He told the whole squad. Asked us to keep it to ourselves, which we'll do; he's a brother. Then he apologized for the way he played the first half on Sunday.'

'What did you say?'

'The same as every other guy in the training room. That if Auston had fucked with one of our siblings like he did Annie, we'd have killed him, and if someone wants to mess with one of our guys and his family, he picks a fight with all of us.'

I rest back against the countertops, arms folded across my chest, not defensively but giving myself a cuddle, because despite the expletives, this feels like a moment, a warm moment.

'I'm glad he told you all. And for what it's worth, I think that's exactly the response he needed to hear. He's a good guy, Pace, and I think he could use a few people having his back.'

Pace slaps his hands down on the countertop and pushes up to stand. 'I'm just pleased he stuck it to Rogers in the end. Gotta tell ya, I wouldn't want to be Rogers next time we play St Louis.'

I'm not an advocate of violence ordinarily, but Auston deserves whatever he gets.

'I'm gonna go shower before the guys arrive,' Pace says, leaving me to fix breakfast.

I watch him go, all the while fighting against the beam that threatens my lips. Colton's coming here for the day. This is just one of the guys, hanging out with the other guys, and I happen to be here, making breakfast for them and chilling with them.

* * *

By the time I've rushed to shower, I can hear voices downstairs already, so I make a snap decision to put on some make-up and leave my hair wet. It'll dry soon enough. It's pathetic how giddy I am that Colton's coming today. I mean, it's just a bunch of guys chilling, right?

I pull on a pair of denim cut-offs and, given it's game day, one of my Bears jerseys. The fact I twist it into a knot at the back to make it fit me better has nothing to do with comfort and everything to do with Colton.

Downstairs, Terry and Max are here and the front door is wide open for the others to let themselves in.

'Are you all in for eggs, bacon and crushed avocado?' I ask.

There are resounding yesses, so I get the breakfast underway, while Pace makes a round of coffees; he's surprisingly particular about how he takes it.

Jad and Omar arrive next. The guys claim their spots on the ginormous U-shaped sofa, with me hovering behind them drinking coffee, one eye on the food. The first overseas game in London is gearing up to kick off on the wall-mounted cinema screen.

'Hey Sas, Terry's got something to ask you,' Jad tells me, chuckling as he slouches on the sofa, massively manspreading.

'Hit me,' I tell Terry.

'Jad, the fuck?' he shouts. 'I don't, Sas.'

'Yeah, he does,' Jad counters. 'He wants you to look at his dating profile and fix it so his ugly face finally gets a swipe.'

As it happens, Terry isn't bad looking. Far from it, in fact, but these guys don't need smoke blowing up their asses, so I tell him, 'I can't work miracles.'

We're all laughing at Terry's expense, raucous enough that we don't hear the arrival of Tommy and— *Damn,* Colton looks *fine.*

Does he get hotter?! Am I a six foot four cowboy girlie now?

I don't even think I'm subtle as my eyes greedily roam from those large boots, up and over long, muscular legs that feel disastrously amazing when they're driving his crotch against me. The crotch I pause on for a moment too long, I think, before dragging my gaze up to his belt buckle, where his shirt is tucked in and covering that perfect V. Those strong forearms I've held on to as he's held my breasts are exposed by his rolled-up sleeves, just the right amount of veins on display. Finally, I ogle right on up to the chiseled face that's fixed on me, a knowing, mocking smirk on his lips.

I'm an opinionated woman, and I have a lot to say, but I always play by the rules. Logical. Pragmatic. Yet with Colton, I'm having to dig deep to even pretend to be professional.

This secret we're hiding, that accidentally grows every time we see each other, feels like crossing all the lines in the best way. It's ragingly hot.

I should be greeting him the same way as I have the rest of the guys instead of gawping at him and thinking, I wish last night had ended with more than incredible kissing and dry humping on the hood of his car.

Knowing that our one day and our accidental date last night won't be the end of it.

Even though I know it should be.

'Aww, Colton brought donuts and pies,' Terry says. 'What a doll. Bake them yourself, did you, hunny?'

I'm pretty sure he'd flash Terry the bird if his hands weren't full of sweet treats.

'My sister's nesting, apparently. It's homemade pecan pie and bought donuts.'

He hands off the pie to Pace, who thumps him on the back in thanks. Then he turns to me and holds out a box of twelve brightly decorated iced donuts. 'These are for Sas because this woman knows how to enjoy a donut or four. You'll have to ask her if she's willing to part with one.'

I grab the box from him with a grin. 'I happened to have been having a bad day that day. But I will take your donuts, Quinn. And your commission,' I tell him with a wink, dragging from him that deep belly guffaw that I love to hear on him.

I make a help-yourself breakfast and spread it on the dining table for the guys to load up their plates in time for the first quarter of the London game. We're all scattered around the sofas, me wedged between Terry and Colton, my laptop on my knees.

I have one eye on the game and with the other, Terry and I are reviewing his dating profile.

'You need to tone down the football,' I tell him.

'Tone it down? That's about the only thing he's got going for him,' Jad torments from his spot on the arm of the sofa – usurped by the vets from his comfier position.

There's an interlude where everyone is shouting at the screen when the official makes a bad call. Then we're back to it and Terry says, 'Chicks love football, Sas. You're here with all the guys, aren't you?'

'I happen to be an exception to the rule. For one thing, it's my job. For another, I've been brought up around sports, between my dad and football and my brothers and hockey. But trust me, if you're looking for more than one night, you need to play down the bad boy football image. Footballers are great for a good time but every girl knows she's going to get burnt eventually.'

As soon as the words have left my mouth, I feel Colton's eyes boring into me. I want to protest, *What?* We said one night and I have many reasons for it, getting burnt being just one of them. Not by anyone who mattered but enough times to know the drill.

He's already told me he's not the kind of guy who does relationships, anyway. But instead, completely unlike me, I decide to hold my tongue and bury my own attention in the laptop, though I don't miss the way Colton's thigh nudges closer to my bare legs, crossed beneath me on the sofa.

What is he trying to tell me? That he can show me a good time? Yeah, I know. In fact, the memory of every time we've had fun does something under my shorts that I really don't want to let on to in present company.

By full time, Terry's new look dating profile is complete. By the end of the second game of the day, he's already had many new swipes.

'I don't want to say I told you so but the evidence speaks for itself,' I tell him.

I'm having a really good time, goofing around with the guys, griefing the players and the officials on the screen, and generally hanging out with Colton. He's lighter than I've known him in the company of the guys and I wonder how much of that is down to him sharing Annie's story with them. It's good for him. Not for any reason other than his friendships. But if the knock-on consequence is that he gels better with the team on the field too, then yes, I've hopefully helped him move a step closer to the contract extension we all want for him.

Toward the end of the third game, I declare that I'm going to start making my chili in the kitchen, intentionally letting my leg slide against Colton's when I rise from the sofa. Blatantly sticking out my ass a little as I go.

He's been tormenting me for hours by nudging into my side, thigh to thigh, his arm casually draped around the back of the sofa, dangerously close to my shoulders. So yeah, I engage in a little butt flirt, and I know the message has been received when I glance back across my shoulder, smirking, and find his eyes firmly on the globes of my ass.

I feel sexier with his eyes on me in denim shorts and a football jersey than if I was all dolled up in a VIP club in New York. Crazy.

'D'you need help?' Pace asks.

I shake my head. 'My treat.' Then, for some reason, in my best southern twang, I put my hands on my hips and say, 'I make the best Tex-Mex for four counties, y'all.'

'You know which state you're in and how many guys are from the south here, don't you, city girl?' Colton asks.

I turn to face him, hands still on my hips. 'Oh, I'm fully aware, cowboy.'

I watch his lips rise. 'Way to read the room there, Sas.'

Chuckling all the way into the kitchen, I think to myself how flirting with Colton is as much fun as I've had with my clothes on.

I should also keep a lid on it in company, but a little flirting never hurt anyone, right?

My music is playing just loud enough for me and I'm wiggling my hips as I move around the kitchen, preparing a chili to slow cook for dinner.

'You know, my mama genuinely makes the best jam for four counties.'

I don't know how long Colton's been standing here, watching me go about my business as he leans back against the kitchen units, but I don't mind it at all. In fact, I'd say my body's response is 100 percent glad of his being here.

'Want some help? I really am good at cooking Tex-Mex,' he says.

Are you kidding me? Why is the universe trying to shatter my resolve?

He takes those large strides of his in my direction, slowly, purposefully. When we're only inches apart, him looking down on me, me trying my hardest not to stare at those lips that kiss me so good, he says, 'I do a few things well.'

Don't. I. Know. It.

I'm sure there must be some kind of sassy retort to this but right now, my lips have parted, breathing shallowed. He runs a hand across my hip, low enough to be hidden by the counter, not at all missed by me. His voice is low, quiet, deeply and irrationally erotic, as he tells me, 'You look smokin' in a Bears jersey but you'd look even hotter wearing number eighty-two.'

I feel like our connection is melting me and I'm suddenly very aware of all the sensitive spots on my body.

Then someone clearing their throat snaps me out of it. Colton and I both startle, jumping apart when we notice Pace, standing with his arms folded across his chest and scrutinizing the scene.

'Is there something happening here that I should know about?'

'No,' I say reflexively, as Colton says, 'Nothing that's your business.'

Jesus. Now, of all times, he decides to find a voice. *Now*, he chooses to antagonize Pace.

Pace glares at his teammate. 'I'm your captain.' Then he shifts his admonishment to me. 'I told Harris I'd look out for you down here. And in case you haven't noticed, you're under my roof.'

'We're just making chili, man,' Colton says.

'Yeah, looked like that's all that was going down.'

Max suddenly appears in the space, taking in the showdown. 'Whoa, what did I walk into?'

'I'll ask you again,' Pace says, face like thunder. 'Are you two getting into something that's a fucking awful idea?'

'Hold up!' Max says, while literally holding up his hands. 'You two?' He motions between Colton and me.

'No,' I tell them all. 'There is genuinely nothing going on between Colton and me, okay?'

Would I like there to be? That's an entirely different question. *Is there?* Really. Truly. No. We said one night, and it's done, whether he'd like me to wear his number or not.

'Now would you all get out of the kitchen so that I can prepare food. Otherwise, pick up a knife and start chopping.'

When none of the guys move, I clap my hands. 'Let's go. Make a choice.'

Max decides to help but Colton and Pace leave us to it. When Colton looks back across his shoulder, I glance away. We're done. We never really started. This can't happen. Even if he does buy me donuts and cook, and dress like a hot cowboy, and touch me and kiss me in ways no one ever has before. Even so... because of Megan, and my career, and the fact he doesn't want a relationship.

For all these reasons, we're just client and associate, friends who had a very short-lived flurry of fire.

Yet, despite knowing better, regardless of my resolve to drop this, I'm buzzed when Colton makes a fuss of my food, and I spend more of the day laughing and joking with him than I do anyone else. Even when we're not trying, there's an energy between us.

So much so that after the fourth and final game of the day, when the guys are leaving, I wish I could go with Colton. And the way he looks at me at the door when Pace and I are saying goodbye to everyone makes me think that he wishes I could go with him, too.

When the door is closed and it's just me and Pace, I know it's for the best. This thing, whatever it is going on between Colton and me, can't continue.

So why am I super giddy when I think up a plan to squeeze out a few more seconds in his company?

'I'll take out the trash,' I tell Pace, already wrestling the garbage sack from the under-sink trashcan.

'I can take it,' he tells me.

I hold on to the trash bag more possessively than I used to hold on to my texts in law school. 'I've already got it.'

Then I'm rushing outside, hoping to catch another glimpse of Colton. It's ridiculous when I've spent the entire day with him.

A smile threatens to tear apart my lips when Colton, Jad and Terry are still saying goodbye on the driveway, Colton's Maserati the last car in the sequence they need to leave.

I hold up a hand, call out, 'Bye guys,' and my breath catches with the way Colton's focus lands on me, the hunger I see, and with it the disappearance of my willpower.

I hear Jad and Terry pull away from the house from where I'm tucked round the side, dumping the trash into the outdoor facility.

I sense the heat of Colton behind me before I feel the whisper of his breath on my neck. 'Is this for my benefit?' he asks knowingly.

When I turn, his shoulders are arched over me, his face so close to mine that all the air in my lungs is expunged.

I'm not sure who makes the first move but we're pressed together, my back against the wall, Colton's entire body touching mine. I thrust my hands into his hair, pulling on the thick ends, and tug his mouth to mine, my entire body melting into his as his tongue wraps around mine, warm, wet, a reminder of the heat we've shared in his bed.

There's nothing else in my mind, only him. Only us. His touch, his taste, the way he completely consumes me.

He breaks our contact, his voice low and gravelly, 'Come back to my place.'

I want to. Desperately. But... 'I can't, Colton.'

'Why?' he asks, forehead resting on mine, his breathing as ragged as if he's just caught a Hail Mary.

I sigh. 'Do you know how much pressure I've felt growing up with two hockey All-Stars in the making, a dad who was a pro-baller and now has one of the best reps in sports agency in the country?'

'Funny enough, I do know pressure, Sas. Mine wasn't family rivalry, granted. But the pressure to succeed when my parents gave me so much, *that* I know well.'

I nod, teeth digging into my lip, conflicted. 'I just want to be great at something, you know? Like they all are.' I nudge him away. 'I need to get back inside.'

But he grabs my hand and tugs me back to him, so close, my chest rises and falls against his and I drown in the eyes I've fallen deep into.

'For what it's worth, you're fucking dynamite in bed.'

My laughter strips away all the conflict I feel and the beam I receive in return makes me feel like I *am* great at something.

I'm starting to think I want to be great at something more than just my job. I want to be great at making Colton happy, which is truly terrifying.

I watch him leave, feeling discombobulated – lost and relieved, bereft yet lighter.

Inside, I close the door behind me and lean against it, eyes closed, hands touching the skin of my neck, my collarbone, my jawline where he's just explored with his mouth, trying to calm the tightness I feel in my chest.

'You know there're security cameras all around this house, don't you?'

I yelp, startled when I open my eyes to see Pace leaning against the wall and watching me. He's holding up his phone.

'Don't worry, I stopped watching as soon as I realized what the notification was. But you can't tell me there's nothing going on between you and Colton.'

My mouth is suddenly drier than Death Valley.

'What are you thinking, Sas? He has a girlfriend.'

Oh boy.

'Why don't I make us both a hot drink?'

* * *

An hour later, lying in my bed, I nervously fire a message to Colton.

> Pace knows everything. He saw us on his security camera.

In a way, I suppose I'm pleased that Pace knows something's happened between Colton and me because now I don't have to lie about that or Megan. But saying it out loud to someone else makes this thing real, whatever this thing is. No matter what this thing shouldn't be.

So, I'm chewing my lip, bouncing my phone off the comforter as I wait for Colton's response. He's a private guy and he, like me, knows that we're not looking for a relationship here, just one night (and a bit).

That's why, when my phone vibrates and I read his response, it makes something inside me knit.

One simple word. That's all he replies.

COWBOY

Good x

33

NOVEMBER

Colton
I've Fallen

I feel drunk. I've felt intoxicated for two weeks, since that kiss with Sas outside Pace's place on bye weekend. It's the kind of buzz that makes me train harder, that made me run faster in our away game in Tampa Bay, but it's one that I can never burn off.

It's here all the time, boundless kinetic energy. When I'm working on the ranch. When I'm doing something as simple as eating dinner with my folks and Annie or watching trash TV that I can't focus on. When I'm out to dinner with Megan and going over her lines, listening to her tell me about her crush on her co-star but I'm only half-present.

My mind is in New York with Sas, and I know she's thinking about me because we speak every night on the phone. Me sitting out on the porch while she's getting ready to go out to dinner and cocktails with friends.

Her life in New York is the exact opposite of mine down here in the south and I have no idea whether we're compatible. I know that my head is in a different place to hers. I'm ready to break all my rules, to mess up whatever Sean's plans are for Megan and me and our whole PR farce. Sas isn't ready, that much I know, but I'm not sure if she's even close or if she ever will be.

I know she likes me. I know there's a pull on both sides. We don't sit on the phone every night discussing legal contracts and endorsement deals; we're learning about each other in a way I've never done before. I've never wanted to explore a girl's life this deeply. In a way I don't think anyone's tried to get to know me, either. The smallest of details, the biggest feelings.

Pace has given me the almost older brother chat. I get it, this thing between Sas and me is messy but regardless, I won't hurt her. If he could get inside my head for just a minute, he'd know that's the last thing I want to do.

I'm pleased he knows. There's no label on what's happening with Sas and me, I can't put one on it, but I also can't ignore the way I feel about her.

I'm falling. I've fallen.

It's new and unexpected. I wasn't looking for it. But it's real and I like it.

And if she's told Pace the truth about us, this is more than nothing to her.

I've been worried about girls being a distraction to my game. Or, more accurately, about feelings being a distraction to my game, and as far as my life at the ranch goes, that's exactly what's happened. But when it comes to my game, Sas seems to negate all the other hurt I'm holding on to, so long as I stay in the moment with her.

That's why I played out of my skin in Florida and the Bears took home a thirty-point win.

It's the Sunday morning of our next home game and I'm buzzed for it, completely fired up. Things are okay at home. Annie seems heavy but happy. Mama has increasingly more vitality since moving on from her last round of treatment. She's still weaker and slimmer than she was, and her hair has a fun fuzzy texture that we joke about as it starts to grow back, but she feels closer to her normal self than she has since the day she told me about her diagnosis.

There are more helping hands on the ranch to lessen the load on my old man and me, so I'm still spending as much time there but I get to spend it with my family, something I haven't done enough for as long as I can remember.

But over and above everything, I think I'm mostly fired up because Harris and Sas will be at the game today.

I'm going to see her. Even if all I get to do is see her and speak to her face to face with her dad hot on her heels and Pace scrutinizing my every move like a grizzly bear in need of salmon.

I just want to see her.

I don't know who this version of me is or where he came from, but I don't dislike it. In fact, I like it. I like it a lot.

'La Grange' plays as I run out of the tunnel to the cheers of the home crowd. A supportive crowd has always been a by-product of me wanting to make my family proud and do myself justice on the gridiron. Today, none of that seems to matter as much as me peacocking Sas, where I know she's sitting in the stands with Annie and my daddy, Megan and Harris.

At the start of the season, I felt the enormity of the void where my mama should be – up there with the rest of my family. Sas can't fill that place, I'll always want Mama to be healthy and at my games, but Sas is plugging a hole I never knew existed. One I don't even think *did* exist before her.

The Indianapolis Oilers win the coin toss and start the game with possession, which they don't have for long before our defense intercepts a pass. We're less than three minutes into the game when Tommy calls a shallow cross play for our second down and finds me in open space. I receive the pass, tuck the ball and put my head down, outgunning the Oilers' defense to the edge of their ten-yard line.

I want the ball, I'm hungry for it, and I know it's coming my way as Tommy calls, 'Hut one, hut two.'

The ball's snapped and with some quick feet, Tommy finds me in a spot where I can fall into the end zone.

My teammates are on me instantly, celebrating, but all I care about is searching the stands for Sas. I can't see her in the sea of jumping bodies, but even knowing she's among them, cheering me on, makes me feel invincible.

The Bears have all the momentum in the game. Indianapolis might as well have stayed home. Toward the end of the fourth quarter, the Bears are scoring points for fun. Our defense is having a hard-earned rest after the rough start we had to the season.

We're not being intentionally unsportsmanlike, but we are having a good time on the field, all of us bantering, laughing and joking, even while we play hard. By contrast, frustration drips off the Oilers' defense. They're tired and miserable. We've all been there. On days like today, you count your blessings when you're on the right side of the scoreboard.

It's our first down with just over two minutes left on the clock and Tommy calls a play that has me running deep. Adrenaline seems to be boosting my speed because the Oilers' safety can't keep pace with me today.

I receive the ball on their thirty-yard line and there's only one zone in my sights. I've got my blinkers on, driving forward, and don't see the cornerback coming at me. Not until I'm smashed sideways, head clattering off the ground and the cornerback's helmet. In what order, I've no idea. It all happens quickly, including the darkness that filters from the sides of my vision.

Until everything goes silent. Black.

34

NOVEMBER

Sas

He's Proud of Me

Dad hugs me when the Bears get another first and ten. The whole offense is playing off the charts but Colton is next level.

'This is what we've needed,' Dad shouts above the animated family and friends of the players around us. He points to me. 'If you've helped get him here, kiddo, I'm proud of you.'

I accept another hug but I'm wondering how much I have helped, if at all. I've encouraged him to talk, the Megan thing is working out for sponsorship and hopefully, a combination of those things is getting his teammates on side. Whether anything else going on between me and Colton is helping his game, I don't know for sure, but I'm certain I gave him an incentive against St Louis.

On the one hand, I'd like to think so. On the other, when this thing ends, does any positive impact die with it?

But above all that, my dad just said he's proud of me. *Me.* Not my brothers. Not his clients that he worships. Me. He's proud of *me.*

I smile as he holds my face in his hands and shakes it, fueled by endorphins.

'Even I know he's having a good game,' Megan says, leaning into my ear when we resume our seated positions. 'And I don't have a clue about football.'

Annie and I both laugh. It's so true. Megan asks a thousand questions, on average, every game. But I also like her spilling the tea about her onset crush, and that she wants to torment me about Colton and me. Nothing's happening, I repeatedly tell her, having to make it clear to Annie too, because Megan isn't hiding the secret from Colton's sister. But their hushed whispers add even more excitement to the whole thing.

At least, that's what I'm putting my churning insides down to. Honestly, it might be solely that I'm going to see Colton in less than an hour, once the game is done. Even though my dad is here and I'll have to let Colton and Megan do their couple's show, I'd just like to be in the same room as him. To see in real life the smile I've been watching on video calls from New York. To smell his scent, feel his warmth and see his towering frame (preferably only half-covered by a towel).

The ball is snapped and passed to Colton, who blazes toward the Oilers' end zone. But I'm on my feet as I anticipate what's coming, the contact from the Oiler's cornerback imminent.

He smacks into Colton, who goes down hard, both players crashing heads before Colton impacts the ground.

He doesn't get up.

Megan and Annie gasp. My dad and Sonny are on their feet. And I push through the row of people, making my way down the steps, as close as I can possibly get to the sidelines and the Bears squad.

Pace and Terry get to Colton first and they're frantically waving the medics. I hold my breath as I watch the replay of the tackle. High and late. A blatant attempt to get the player, not the ball. And I watch Colton's head get hit once, twice, three times in the collision.

I don't blink. I don't move. The stadium is as quiet as the Alamo ever gets.

It takes an eternity before Colton's limbs move. The medics sit him up but have to catch him when he falls back. My hand feels as if it's holding my chest together as I wait, with seventy thousand people, to see that my – client? Friend? – is okay.

Pace jogs over to the sidelines and he clocks me in the stands. He points to his head and I'm sure he calls, 'Concussion.' Then he gestures to the tunnel and I have no idea if he's telling me Colton will be taken off the field, or if he's telling me to go down there, but it doesn't matter because I'm already making my way in the direction of the Bears' medical room.

By the time I've navigated the corridors and security – who are familiar with my face by now – Colton has already been assessed by the concussion experts.

He's sitting up on one of four beds in the room. Relief floods me, dropping my shoulders from my ears on my next exhalation.

'Hey, cowboy,' I say gently, not knowing how he's feeling but able to tell from his pallor that the answer is probably not great. Still, the curve of his lips when he sees me – gray as he looks – is liquifying.

One of the team of docs in the room comes toward me, 'You can't be in—'

'She's good,' Colton says. 'She's my... ah... she's... ah... my...'

The same doctor trying to get rid of me strides to Colton's bedside and whips out a small torch. 'Are you confused?' he asks, shining the light in Colton's eyes.

Despite the severity of the situation, I have to cover my mouth to stop a chuckle escaping.

'He's my friend,' I tell the doc. Thinking as I do that, I probably should have said client.

The doc looks between Colton and me, then shakes his head. 'Good. He's got a concussion. He's going to need to be kept under a watchful eye for the next twenty-four hours. Will you be his *friend* for the next twenty-four hours?'

'To be continued,' I tell him, then make my way to Colton's bedside. 'Look at you. Not happy being the star of the show for your performance, you've got to go and get a concussion, too? You're *such* an attention seeker.'

'Hey, Clint, is she allowed to talk to me like this when I'm a patient?' Colton asks the doc.

Clint smiles as he takes off his gloves and trashes them. He and the others leave the room, leaving only Colton and me.

'There's nothing wrong with you,' I tell him, taking out my phone and calling Annie. 'Let me update your family.'

He nods, then rests his head back on the bed as I make the call. Despite the smiles, he's clearly uncomfortable. Reflexively, I reach out and gently stroke his temple as I tell Annie, 'He's got a nasty concussion but he's okay.'

Colton leans into my palm, eyes closed. It's the simplest of moves but it contorts something in my chest. I'm glad I'm here for him. Pleased he wants me here.

'He needs to have someone stay with him for the next twenty-four hours,

Annie, but he can't drive. Could you and Sonny maybe wait for him and drive him out to—'

'No,' Colton says. 'Annie needs to go home and rest. I'll be fine at my place. I feel okay. It's not the first time I've taken a knock to the head.'

Always looking out for everyone else. I run my hand from his temple to his jaw and watch his eyes close like a satisfied puppy being stroked.

'Don't worry, Annie. I'll stay with him tonight and give you a call in the morning to let you know he's okay.'

I wish her sweet dreams, then narrow my eyes on Colton. 'You had better be a good patient, cowboy. No funny business.'

Even slightly distant in his gaze, the way he looks at me makes me want to break my own rules right here and now.

He runs a hand up the back of my thigh, encouraging me closer to the bed. 'Don't tell the others, but you're the hottest medic.'

Though I'm fighting against my amusement, I tell him, 'No strenuous exercise. The first rule of concussion.'

'I guess that means you're on top.'

Now I do laugh. 'You are going to be a terrible patient, aren't you?'

'As soon as this headache lifts.'

With my typical act-now-and-think-later approach to life, I bend over him and press a magic healing kiss to his forehead. As I do, he raises his chin, catching my lips with his. I should pull back, check that no one's looking, but my body betrays me, moaning into his mouth, eyes closing rather than observing our surroundings.

God, I've missed him. It's not even been two weeks.

A throat is cleared loudly, then I hear Pace's voice at the door. 'Actually, Harris, before we check on Quinn, I've got a question... about... err... *me?*'

I jump back from Colton, rubbing my lips as if hiding evidence of our faux pas.

Colton looks completely nonplussed.

Pace opens the door again and this time shoots me an expression that says, *Are you kidding me?*

Yup, that was slack, and stupid. Dad could have seen if Pace hadn't acted quickly. Anyone of the Bears' staff could have seen.

But no takie backies, because even as I hear Dad ask, 'How're you feeling, champ?' I'm wishing the room would empty and I could fall back into that kiss.

I'm so screwed, I think, as I mouth *Thank you* to Pace.

* * *

I drive Megan home, standing back for cameras to catch her and Colton leaving the stadium together, then take Colton and me to his place.

By the time we settle onto the sofa, he looks exhausted – probably from a combination of exertion and the triple head blow. I like that I can be here for him. I adore how cute Colton looks with mussed-up hair and sleepy eyes. And I love that I have the flexibility with work to stay south for a few extra days – helped by Dad thinking I'm partly involved in this shift in Colton's game.

'So, how can I persuade you to stay awake for a little while longer, on the doctor's orders?' I ask Colton, who has slumped down on his sofa but now turns his head where it rests on the cushions to look at me.

We both know he's in no fit state for fondling but still he wiggles his eyebrows at me.

'You promised to be a good patient.'

'I'd be the best patient you've ever had.'

'All right, stud. I was thinking more like a club soda or herbal tea and a movie?'

'A dirty movie?'

'Colton Quinn!'

He chuckles, the cutest sound. 'Club soda and a non-dirty movie sounds good.'

I set us up with snacks and drinks in the lounge and borrow a t-shirt of Colton's that fits like a dress on me.

Less than five minutes into the film, Colton shifts to lie across my lap, all dopey and doe-eyed. 'I could get used to you looking after me,' he says.

I kind of like it, too, but I tell him, 'I wouldn't. It's temporary.'

'Really? 'Cause from my perspective, you deal with my business, you make me the best Tex-Mex for four counties, you nurse me better, and you service me in the bedroom. You're the complete article, city girl.'

With his body tucked against me and his lips in striking distance, he's making it extremely difficult for me not to lean down and kiss him. 'You're really testing my resolve, aren't you?'

'I hope so.'

I can feel my body shifting toward his, but I stop myself for so many reasons. 'I think you're clear to go to bed now. Let's get you up.'

He squeezes his eyes shut and I reach out to steady him when he stands, but he recovers, and while I follow him to his bedroom, and we clean our teeth in his en suite together – me using an airline freebie he has in his toiletries stash – he seems okay.

Once he's in bed, I make to leave. 'Shout if you need me or if you feel funny in the night, promise? I'll just be next door.'

'Do nurse duties extend to spooning? Just cuddles, no funny business.'

I bite my lip, wanting to say yes. 'No, I don't think they do.'

Then I leave before he can protest. We said one night. My dad almost caught us earlier. To all but a few people sworn to secrecy, Colton is dating Megan.

Yet I stare at the ceiling in his guest bedroom, turning my one platinum ring around my finger, wondering why I'm here if I know all these reasons we can't be together. Why have I been speaking to him on the phone every day from New York? Why was I nearly sick with the anticipation of seeing him today and why, when he got injured, was I terrified until I saw him sitting on that bed and smiling at me?

As I'm lying here, I hear Colton moving around. I cast the bedding aside and pad out to the hallway.

'Are you okay?' I say on seeing him, wearing just his boxer briefs, the floor lighting casting decadent shadows across his defined muscles.

'No. I can't sleep and I don't like lying in bed alone when you're right here.'

I sigh. 'Colton—'

'Just cuddles.'

'You're so needy,' I say, trying not to grin as I stride past him and to his bedroom.

I've been in here before. In his bed. But when I lie on my side and Colton wraps his big body around me, it feels... different. Dangerous. Yet not at all unwelcome.

'Sas, are you still awake?' he asks after some time of me basking in the comfort of his arms.

'Hmm.'

He falls silent for so long I wonder if *he* has fallen asleep, until he says, 'My mama doesn't come to my games anymore because she's sick.'

I feel his face turn into my neck, his breath warm where I swallow, not sure what to make of his words.

'She has cancer and she's stopped her treatment.'

I don't know what to say, for once. Instead, I find his hand on my stomach and interlace my fingers with his – *I'm here.*

'I found out toward the end of last season. When I was fined for wearing a band on my uniform. That's why I was wearing it – in her honor.'

When his game fell apart. Before the headlines suddenly changed from being about the exceptional player he is to negativity.

'It messed with my head for months. It's still messing with my head and it's why I spend as much time as I have been at the ranch.'

I shuffle in his arms to face him, an inch between us.

'But somehow, you make everything else bearable.'

He's concussed, I know. I've seen how unusually emotional sports guys can get when they're concussed. But this feels bigger than medicine. It feels like something he's needed to get off his chest, something he's needed to tell someone.

And I'm so pleased it's me.

I reach out to cup his jaw. 'Thank you for telling me. I'm sorry, Colton.' I think of Annie and her baby on its way. Of Sonny and how stoic he is – like father, like son. And of Colton, going through all this in his own head.

My heart breaks for them all.

When I press my lips to his, it isn't sexual, it isn't a precursor to something else; it's just a kiss, full of emotion and support and admiration. And when I feel wetness between our cheeks, I don't know who the tear belongs to, me or him.

35

NOVEMBER

Colton
Concussion Never Felt So Good

Harris dropped by on Monday morning before heading to the airport bound for California to see another client. He told Sas to stay and work from Texas for a few days, offering her as a nurse and cab service to get me to and from my appointments with the Team medics each day until I'm signed off as fit to play.

I don't want her to run around after me, she's already gone way beyond, but I won't pretend I'm unhappy about getting to keep her here a while longer.

It's small things, like the way my place smells of her perfume after Harris dropped her things from their hotel. The way she moves around the apartment making coffee, which she holds between her palms as she reviews legal contracts on her laptop. That she chooses to wear my jerseys and sit cross-legged on the sofa to watch movies in the evenings, always with a bowl of something sweet for us to snack on.

I kind of like her toothbrush sitting by the sink in my en suite, even though she could use the main bathroom. And I love that she's sharing my bed at night, despite our agreement to no funny business.

I know it's a short-lived bubble. I can't train, there's no Megan, I can't work on the ranch and though I cherish my family, it does feel like a brief respite. There are no questions about what Sas and I are or aren't; we're just being in each other's company, no one to hide from, no one to interrogate or opine on us.

Truly, concussion never felt so good.

It's Wednesday morning, the day before Thanksgiving. Sas is working in the dining room at the training facility, while I'm being assessed by the concussion specialists, but I already know I'm out for tomorrow's game in Tennessee. I know from the near constant dull ache, the tenderness when I touch between the base of my head and my neck, and the way I feel dizzy when I stand too quickly or for too long.

But it wasn't until Sas telling me on the drive here that I started seeing this as an opportunity, rather than a pain in the ass.

'When did you last get to spend Thanksgiving with your family?' she'd asked.

And she's right; I've played through Thanksgiving for the last few years.

Though she didn't say it in words, since we've talked about my mama's prognosis over the last couple days, I knew from the suddenly heavy air in the car that we were both thinking the same thing. This will likely be Mama's last Thanksgiving.

So, as I answer the clinical questions I'm asked from my position on the treatment bed, muddling some basic memory recall exercises, I decide to see the silver lining in all this.

Once I'm officially declared out of tomorrow's game, I take Sas's advice and go to see Coach Roy.

'He's human,' she'd said. 'He cares more about his family than anything else in the world, trust me. If you open up to him, he'll let you sit out the game at the ranch with your family. Annie and your mom will be fine without you, Colton. They're tough as old boots. But talk to Glen and make the request for your own benefit.'

She's right, of course. She knows her godfather well.

Coach welcomes me into his room with proverbial open arms and though I trip over my own words and cough my way through moments in which my voice breaks, I tell him about my mama.

'I only wish you'd told me sooner, son,' he tells me, and I can imagine he *is* a good family man. A good father to his kids. A decent godfather to Sas. 'You spend tomorrow with the people who matter most. Be thankful for them. The team and your position on it will be waiting for you as soon as you're fit to play.'

That's how I come to be packing an overnight bag, my old man on his way to pick me up, while Sas, in my lounge, sounds increasingly animated talking on her phone, rather than calmly waiting for her ride to the airport.

When I head out there, she's pacing the floor, phone to her ear. I drop my bag on the sofa.

'There's nothing at all flying? What about Newark? Nothing? But it's Thanksgiving tomorrow. Yes, I appreciate there's a storm and I do know that's not your fault, I'm just— Are there any other options, no matter how convoluted they might be?'

She spots me and holds out her free arm, her eyes more upset than angry, a mismatch for her voice on the call.

'Okay. I understand. Thank you. No, don't rebook me for Friday. I still want to try to figure this out.'

'What's going on?' I ask when she hangs up, though I think I caught the gist.

'The storm is so bad the airports in New York and the surrounding area are grounding all planes or diverting to different airports. But if I take a diversion, I risk getting stuck somewhere alone on Thanksgiving.' She drops down to sit on the sofa. 'It's okay. I'll call Millie to ask if she's going to the game or staying home. I can tag along with her and see Glen after the game. At least I'll get to see someone for Thanksgiving, even if it's not my family.'

'I'm sorry, Sas, this is all my fault. What can I do?' I come to stand behind her, my hands on her shoulders, rolling my thumbs over her tense muscles.

'It's not your fault. I wanted to be here for you.' She leans her head against my forearm – another of those little moments I'm getting too used to. 'I don't know that I have any other options. I'll just fly home when I can and have a belated Thanksgiving.' She sighs. 'I'll call Millie.'

'Sas...' I pause, wondering if what I'm about to say is too much too soon, for her. But when she leans her head back to glance up to me through her long lashes, I think, *Fuck it*. 'Come to the ranch with me. My family would love to have you. Your city vibes will make things interesting.'

She turns, kneeling up and facing me. 'Are you sure? I don't want to intrude. I know you guys are private. Honestly, I'd be fine at—'

I press my finger to her lips, silencing her. '*I'd* like to spend Thanksgiving with you.' Beneath my touch, her lips gently curve up, even if I can see her nervousness, too. 'Go pack your bag, otherwise you'll be stuck wearing my jerseys or Annie's maternity dresses for the next couple days.'

When I call ahead and tell Annie and Mama that Sas is coming with me, Annie squeals so loudly I have to hold the phone a full arm's length from my ear.

I guess I've never taken a girl to the ranch before.

Label or no label, I can see why Annie might be spirited about it.

Still, I ask her to keep a lid on it when we arrive. Even though this feels like a pretty big deal to me, I remind her that Sas and I are just friends.

'Oh right, y'all are just friends who can't keep your eyes and hands off each other,' she says, and I hear the beautiful sound of Mama laughing with my sister, albeit at my expense, right before they hang up.

36

NOVEMBER

Sas

This Might Be the Most Serene Place I've Ever Been

Colton wasn't kidding when he said his country-music fetish was mild by comparison to the rest of his family. I've spent the entire drive out to Sunshine Ranch with two of the least talkative humans on the planet – even worse when they're together, seemingly – listening to uninterrupted Kenny Rogers, Willie Nelson, Waylon Jennings and ZZ Top. I know because the only words Colton and Sonny have spoken on this journey have been to educate me on Texas-born musicians.

But when we turn off the road and onto a dirt track, the sound fades into the background of the magnificent setting. We're more than a million miles away from New York City. As if we've been transported into another world entirely.

Undulating hills are punctuated with occasional trees and grazing animals as the sun starts to lower in the sky above, casting shadows that produce a sweeping color palette of greens and browns. The Quinns' house is like something out of a cowboy romance – a significant yet humble white country home, with the kind of porch Noah Calhoun might sit on in *The Notebook*, and a white picket fence that those southern-born singers love to get vocal about. Well, when they aren't singing about neon signs and whiskey.

We pull to a stop out back of the house, by a large corral, inside of which huge glossy-coat horses graze on grass. Beyond them is a significant barn, doors open so I can see right through from one side to the other, the hollow framing the lush landscape beyond.

I step out of Sonny's truck and fill my lungs with air that feels clean, fresh. And I close my eyes as I absorb a silence that would never exist at home.

This might be the most serene place I've ever been.

It's easy to see how Sunshine Ranch would be an idyllic place to come for respite. It's home and escape all at the same time.

Being here for just the beat of a heart, Colton already makes more sense to me. His calmness, his honesty. The way he can just *be* in quiet.

Not for the first time this week, I think I fall a little closer to disaster.

'Like it?' Colton asks, coming to stand next to me, where I'm holding on to the corral fence, I think partly to steady myself.

I bend to ruffle the ears of a collie whose tail is wagging as he sniffs around me. 'Far too quiet for me,' I tease.

I know he doesn't believe me because I'm becoming quite accustomed to Colton's expressions, the quirks of his personality reflected in the most subtle of twists and turns of his features.

'Girls, we're home,' I hear Sonny call out inside the house.

'You've met Bear now. Are you ready to come meet my mama?' Colton asks.

I'm nodding but inhaling with intent. I'm not sure what I'm expecting. I've been actively trying not to come into this with a preconceived idea of Colton's mom. She's sick and I know she's had treatment that caused her to lose her hair. That it's growing back now but she's frail and different levels of weak from one day to the next. But I've never met anyone who's dying.

In addition to all that, moms are a big deal, right? When I think of the guys I've dated who've met my mom, it's been largely because she's met them by accident or incidental to something else, like she's been visiting me on university campus or we've all been at one of Jax's games.

Technically, meeting Mrs. Quinn is an accident brought on by a storm, so I shouldn't overthink it. Colton said he wanted to spend Thanksgiving with me, but he wouldn't have asked if I hadn't been stuck in Texas.

It's safe to say, I'm nervous. I meet people from all walks of life, every day. I network with people for a living. Yet somehow, the idea of meeting the woman who brought Colton into the world seems... I exhale hard. 'Yup. Ready.'

Colton chuckles, hanging an arm around my shoulders. 'She doesn't bite, Sas.'

He heads through the fly screen first and I think he's surprised to see his mom in the kitchen with Annie, each of them wearing aprons and doing food prep. I am, too, based on what he's shared with me this week.

Sure, his mom looks pale next to the rest of her family, and I can tell her hair is new growth, but her eyes seem bright, her smile for her son huge.

He bends to hug her and kisses her cheek. It's the kind of hug that lasts longer than an ordinary greeting of family who see each other most days.

'How are you feeling?' she asks him, her hand reaching up to his forehead.

'I'm seeing ten of you,' he torments her.

She pats him playful. 'The more the better.'

Could this guy and his family mess with my emotions any more?

'This gorgeous lady must be Kansas,' she says, turning to me, arms outstretched.

Without thought, I step into her hold. 'It's just Sas, please. I don't need to think about what my parents did in their hotel room in Kansas City that night.'

His mom laughs, heartily, bringing her hands to the sides of my face. Across her shoulder, Colton is stealing food from the counter and shaking his head.

'Like I said, no filter. She's very *city*.'

I scowl at him while feeling the fuzziest buzz inside – he talks about me. Even if it is derogatory.

'Sorry, I'm not always PC,' I confess.

'A bit of spirit is exactly what this home has been missing of late. I'll call you Sas. And you can call me Mama.'

Both Colton and I cock our heads to one side, as if in mechanical sync.

His mom wafts a hand. 'Too soon?' She chuckles. 'All right, then, Caroline for now.' She twists the ends of my long hair through her fingers. 'Would you look at your pretty hair,' Caroline says. 'I used to have long hair like this.'

'Well, I have a bunch of girlfriends in New York who only wish they could pull off the short look like you can.' I point to her gray hair. 'Not many people have the bone structure for it.'

She titters again and I wonder if I was just wildly inappropriate, until she tells me, 'I'll be sure to give them the name of my stylist, hunny. His name's Chemo.'

As if we're the only people catching the dark humor in the kitchen, Caroline and I laugh.

'Thank you for having me for Thanksgiving, Caroline, especially at such short notice.'

'Nonsense. The door of this ranch is always open, hunny. Especially to a *friend* of my son. Ain't that right, Sonny?'

'I already said that,' he calls from somewhere in the house.

She leans into my ear as if to share a secret, though doesn't speak quietly. 'I can tell I'm going to be able to get out all my suppressed cancer jokes for a couple days. My family are a tough crowd.'

'I have two brothers who are more brawn than brains,' I tell her. 'I'm all about the inappropriate humor.'

'My kind of woman,' she says, heading out of the room, looking a little fragile as she moves. Fragile but full of spirit.

'Hey, Sas,' Annie says softly, taking a pan off the heat before giving me a hug. 'It's good to see you.'

We're both stretching over her full-term bump as she says, 'Ouch! He kicked. Did you feel that?'

'Actually, I did.'

She takes my hands and places them on her round tummy, where my palms are whacked by some part of her baby's anatomy.

'Have you felt this?' I ask, turning across my shoulder to Colton, finding him smiling after us.

'Once or twice,' he says. Happy. Relaxed.

It's amazing how he just fits here. The way those stonewash jeans and that big old belt buckle look just right. He belongs to all this warmth and beauty.

Before I fall down a well of screaming ovaries, I look back to Annie. 'All right, Annie.' I roll up the sleeves of my ribbed top. 'Put me to work.'

'No! You're a guest; go sit down. I'm doing pasta for dinner. Real easy. The rest is prep for tomorrow.'

Glancing to the farmhouse-style countertop, I spot a hefty pot of pecans and gasp. 'Are you making pecan pie?'

'Sure am.' She rubs her hands down her apron.

'This is *the* pecan pie? You've got to show me how to make it. You could have your pick of baby daddies from all the single Bears. They fell for you big style when you sent over pie for bye weekend.'

'She absolutely cannot,' Colton says, pushing off the counter, suddenly less relaxed as he brushes between us both and steals a handful of pecans. 'No more sports guys. Especially not a Bear. Or anyone I know. Or— Nope. Just no sports guys. *Ever.*'

Annie and I look at each other and snigger.

'And you...' He leans into my ear. 'If you want the recipe so that you can start cozying up to another Bear, think again.'

Sometimes, he surprises me, catches me completely off guard with how brazen he is. How he just doesn't care about hiding that he likes me. And while I make an exaggerated eye roll, inside, I'm delighted. Even as I know I've got no business lusting after him.

Still, I can't resist as he heads through to his mom and dad in the lounge... I speak loud enough for him to catch it. 'You know, Annie, Terry is on the lookout for a girl right now. He's nice. I think he'd make a good baby daddy.'

Annie and I lean together, falling apart as we hear Colton muttering away behind the wall.

'Now, this pie. Put me to work,' I say when we're composed.

Annie brushes her arm against mine. 'Why, so you can burrow yourself even deeper in my brother's heart?'

'Just his stomach,' I tell her.

'You know that's the way to make a man fall in love, darlin'.' Caroline comes behind us. 'If we're making pie, I need to help.'

I shake my head. 'I really learn best by doing. So why don't you two ladies grab yourselves a drink and take a seat at the table where you can call out my instructions.' When they glance between each other, unmoving, I tell them, 'Please? It's the least I can do. You've let me come here last minute and I would have never turned up to your home empty-handed if I'd had notice.'

For the next hour or so, I get to know Annie even better, and I learn where she gets her chatty-cat personality from. Where Colton takes after Sonny –

quiet and stoic – Annie is a reflection of Caroline's welcoming and talkative personality.

Colton intermittently putters around the kitchen, stealing food and, I think, mostly checking on me. Honestly, I'm fine. I love it here. I adore his family. His mom is hilarious. And the subtle hip grazes and lower-back touches when he's leaning over me under the guise of thieving more pecans are more welcome than they should be.

We eat pasta at a big oak dining table. Caroline tells Sonny he isn't allowed to eat from a tray when they have guests. So, I soften the blow by joining him in having a beer – everyone else out on account of pregnancy, illness and injury.

After dinner, Caroline's energy seems to wane. Her conversation tapers off and her eyes look heavy. Then I hear her subtly tell Sonny she's ready for bed as Colton and I tidy the kitchen.

'I'll take you up,' Colton says. Caroline winces as she pushes up from the table and shuffles to say goodnight to Annie, Sonny and me.

I watch as Colton walks behind his mom to the staircase. Then at the bottom, he leans down and she wraps her arms around his neck, before he scoops her into his arms and carries her upstairs.

I'm left biting down on my gums to fend off tears as the stark reality suddenly hits me – this gorgeous family will look very different by next Thanksgiving. Annie won't have her mom around to support her with her first child. Sonny won't have a wife to share his home with.

I finish cleaning with a lump in my throat that won't subside, thinking about these guys, thinking about my own family and how much I love and miss them. More than anything, admiring Colton, Sonny and Annie for getting on with life when I think I'd want to curl into a ball and bury myself under a comforter, pretending all the bad stuff wasn't happening.

'I'm going to switch to the sofa,' Annie says, holding her back as she stands from the table. 'Stop cleaning now, Sas. You've more than earned your dinner.'

'Which you didn't need to do in any case,' Sonny adds, also standing.

I give them the most genuine smile I can muster. 'I'm going to admire the starry sky for a few minutes. It's a novelty to have no light pollution.'

37

NOVEMBER

Colton

It's the Most Like Home This Place Has Felt in a Long Time

When I come downstairs after helping Mama to bed, Annie points me in the direction of outside to find Sas.

She's standing by the corral, hands resting on the fence, chin tilted up to the dark night, smattered with precious gems in millennia-old patterns.

I'm torn between going to her to make sure she's okay and just watching her be. But I know tonight has probably been a lot for her. I only dropped on her two days ago that Mama's sick, and while my family and I are used to the idea now, it might have been a shock to Sas.

She's been incredible since she arrived, slotting in as if this is *her* home and *her* family. Never giving the impression or making us feel like there's anything other than normal happening here at Sunshine Ranch.

It's the most like home this place has felt in a long time. The warmth, the sounds of happiness, the sight of uninhibited love and affection. I feel full and hopelessly hopeful.

Eventually, I come to stand next to her at the fence. My hands come down to rest close to hers, just shy of our fingers pressing together, because as much as I want to be able to touch her freely, as much as I've realized I want everything Sas is willing to offer, I don't think she's here with me. I know she isn't. And I've got to keep the depth of what I'm feeling quiet.

Don't make a sound that might scare her away.

'Are you okay out here on your lonesome, city girl?'

She gives a short breath out, shaking her head, then shuffles her hand so our pinkie fingers are crossed over.

She does feel more than a one-night stand. I just don't know how much she feels.

Her gaze falls from the sky to the horses nearby. 'Jesus, Colton. Am *I* okay?'

She sniffs and only now do I realize there's a glistening tear silently rolling down her cheek.

'Hey,' I whisper, turning her to face me, running the pad of my thumb over her soft, wet cheek. 'What's this?'

Those deep blue pools are even darker in the night but every bit as mesmerizing.

'I'm sorry that you've all been going through this. I wish there was some way I could help.'

'Sas, the very last thing I ever want to see on you is tears, especially if I'm the cause.'

I press my lips to her brow, knowing it might be too intimate but doing it anyway because I can't not. I tug her into my chest and wrap my arms around her, feeling her warmth through my shirt and her short, ragged inhale. Until she physically sinks into me. She fits so perfectly into my hold, as if she was made to be here.

'You being here is helping, Sas. That's the most animated I've seen my mama and Annie for months. Annie hasn't griped at me once.'

She leans her head back to look at me. 'Why would she?'

It's me who fully breaks our hold. My next words seem too heavy with Sas in my arms. Leaning my forearms back on the fence, I tell the night, 'She thinks I should be trying to convince Mama to continue treatment.'

'Is it still an option?'

I swallow deeply. 'I don't think so. It's time to accept it. And Mama's brighter now that she's getting the right end-of-life care than when they were trying to treat the cancer.'

Sas mirrors my position, her hip grazing mine. Enough contact to remind me she's here. But not too much. This talking thing is new to me, and I think she gets it. She sees me for the boy I've always been, I think, not the pro-baller who's supposed to be bold, confident and unbreakable.

I *am* fallible. I'm beginning to realize that, thanks to Sas.

'It's hard for you all but it must be really hard for Annie right now, Colton.'

Her words are gentle, even though I recognize that she's rationalizing with me. Oddly, it doesn't make me want to shut down, close my ears. I'm listening. I'm here for her sense and reason.

'I doubt she's mad at you. She's hurting. Auston has really done the worst imaginable – which is *not* your fault, and she knows it. But she's staring down the barrel of being a single mom and while I know you and your dad are going to be a huge part of the baby's life, Annie probably can't imagine not having her mom around. I know I'd be on the phone to my mine for advice all the time if it were me becoming a parent for the first time.'

God, she'd make an amazing mama. I glance her way but a feeling so intense comes over me, forcing me to turn back to the horses.

'I need to go easier on her,' I manage eventually.

'No, Colton. You all need to go easier on yourselves. You have a beautiful family. Your mom would be devastated if she thought that this would break you apart.'

Something like fire burns my eyes. I stare deep into the night until it rescinds. She's right. Mama needs to know we'll be okay when she's gone. Not that we'll spend our lives bickering and not speaking to one another.

With an inhale, I push back off the fence. 'I'm going to put the horses in for the night. Want to help?'

She smiles at me. The sweetest, gentlest smile. 'I do.'

I pause at those words, realizing for the first time that I want to hear them again one day. In a grander moment. In front of our friends and family.

I'm in love with her.

With my vital organs palpitating, I decide on the spot that I'm in this for the long game. However long it takes me to win her over.

I'm all in.

One by one, we walk the horses inside, me telling Sas their names and how we came to have them. By the time I lock the stall door on the last mare, the mood has lightened between us.

Sas can do that. She can shift my emotions, the whole feel of a room, by her presence alone. I've never met anyone who can do that. She isn't all sweetness and glitter, yet I feel light as air around her.

That's what I'm pondering as I'm making my way to the archway out of the barn, when I feel Sas's hand take hold of mine from behind. She encourages me back to her.

'Kiss me,' she whispers.

We're less than a foot apart, my heart thumping so hard it could knock her over. Because I think this kiss might be different. It might be the one I've been waiting for.

I want to take my time, enjoy it, because I don't know if it's a first or a last kiss of its kind.

My fingertips find her temple, my eyes find her expectant ones, and when she raises her chin, nose nudging against mine, I finally give her what she's asked.

I lower my mouth to hers, slowly, gently, my eyes falling closed with the soft contact. It's one press of our lips. One moment in time. But to me, it feels like time stands still entirely.

Our mouths move together, tongues tentative against each other. I know there's more on her side than there has been before. I don't know how much more but I feel it.

I encourage her back against a joist, her stumbling slightly as she goes, her laughter short, a brief interlude from the intensity of what I'm feeling.

Then her humor is gone as her body meets the wood and her palm comes up to cup my jaw. I take her other hand over her head and shift my body to where I want it, touching hers in every place possible.

I get lost in her touch, in her kiss, in her breathlessness when my lips meet the sensitive skin of her collarbone. I get lost in *her*, moaning when her hands slip under my shirt. I know where this is going, and I want to take my time, even as my body screams at me with urgency.

I lower her hand, leading her to the steps, up to the mezzanine over the stalls, where I'd hide out as a kid when the chaos of the place became too much.

A place I've always found peace, with a person who brings me more peace than I've ever known.

On bales of hay, I lay down one of the blankets we keep up here, and Sas sets herself down, us both knowing how this ends.

She takes off my shirt and I lift her top over her arms, then I crawl over her, drowning in the sensation of her naked skin against mine, taking my time to feel her, kiss her, explore every inch of her torso, before I undo the fastening of her jeans and her mine.

Here in the barn, in my place of quiet, with the stars decorating the sky above us, we move together in a way I never have. Bare. Raw. All-consuming.

If this thing between us isn't going to last, it will have to be her who ends it.

I hope she never does.

38

NOVEMBER

Colton

I'm Thankful For Today, No Matter What Tomorrow Brings

I watch Sas from the doorway of the kitchen, her back to me as she stands before the cooker. I'm thinking simultaneously, *damn,* she's beautiful, and that I can't let on how I really feel about her. How she's the last person I ever want to go to bed with and see first thing in the morning.

That would terrify this city girl with her thousands of reservations. A few months ago, I'd have been afraid, too. I still am. But mostly, I'm afraid of going in too heavy and scaring her away.

'Where is everyone?' I ask eventually.

She gives me the kind of beam that makes me feel wider than an offensive lineman, faster than a running back, taller than I already am.

'Your mom and Annie are outside drinking hot water and lemon with their feet up – on my absolute insistence. Sonny's collecting eggs from the hens to replace the ones I'm about to poach, now that you've got your lazy ass out of bed.'

Chuckling, I push off the door frame and go to her, wrapping my arms around her from behind, where she's stirring the water in her poaching pan. I drop my lips to her hair that smells of her shampoo – coconuts and vanilla.

'I can't remember the last time I had a lie-in. I also can't remember the last time I slept so well.' I feel her cheeks rise against mine, even if I can't see that dazzling smile, and I think, *Yeah, I'm sure I'm smiling big because of you, too.* 'Can I help?'

'No, I want all the glory. I'm an impeccable poacher. Go spend some time with your mom and Annie. Or calmly fondle a hen's ass. Things will get crazy around here as soon as that little pair of lungs arrive.'

I plant another kiss on her temple. 'Happy Thanksgiving, city girl.'

She rotates in my arms now and lights me up with the tenderness of her kiss on the tip of my nose. 'Happy Thanksgiving, cowboy.'

Acting like she doesn't steal my every breath, I reach around her to thieve a muffin from one of the plates she's already set up, feeling, for the first time in months, like some of the pressure is off. She's got this. Even if all she was doing was being here, her vivaciousness and the voraciousness that I recognize from the only other lady who gives me orders, sick or not, would lighten any room.

'You don't really think hens lay eggs out of their ass, do you?'

She whacks me with the towel on my way out. 'Stop stealing food! One day, you'll retire and I'll laugh when your food theft means you put on two hundred pounds overnight.'

'There'd be more of me for you to love,' I say through my mouthful of food.

Then I hear Mama's voice from the porch. 'I've been telling him this for a quarter century, darlin'. He gets worse.'

As Sas laughs, I tell her seriously, 'Thank you. I appreciate you.'

That stops her amusement, as if no one ever thanked her in her life. She waves a hand, turning her back on me and confirming my assumption that people don't often support Miss Independent.

'Now my own mama is giving me grief, huh?' Outside, I kiss Mama on the cheek, then do the same to Annie, and drop a hand to my nephew. 'Happy Thanksgiving, y'all.'

Dad comes back with a bucket of white eggs and after we've eaten Sas's flawlessly poached eggs, Annie preps the turkey to be put in the oven for dinner. That'll be after we watch the Bears' first game of the season without me.

I know I can't play, the choice has been taken away from me by doctors, so I can enjoy being with my family and Sas without guilt or resentment.

On this day, this year, I'm right where I'm supposed to be. I'm thankful for today, no matter what tomorrow brings.

After the game and dinner, before the final light of the day has disappeared but my parents and sister are snoring to various decibels on the sofa, I take Sas to the corral. Before we settle the horses inside for the night, she lets me take her for a trot around the land, her sitting snugly between my thighs, my hands covering hers on the reins.

It's a new kind of bliss, even if I do get a lot of cowboy jokes thrown my way.

'You're the one wearing my hat,' I tell her as I lift her down from Luke's saddle.

'Don't be such a big baby. Just 'cause I called you out, country boy,' she tells me.

'You talk too much,' I fire back, looking down over her, tugging her into me.

'*You* don't talk enough.' She raises her chin.

'You're an attention-seeker.'

She pouts. 'You're a brooder.'

'You're fucking beautiful,' I almost exhale.

And I must win because she lifts my hat from her head and kisses me in a way that makes me want to take her right upstairs to my bed.

* * *

I don't know what time it is but it feels like the middle of the night when there's a knock on my bedroom door. Then I hear Annie's voice. 'Colton?'

She sounds stressed, worried. Something in her tone makes me sit bolt upright, tipping Sas off my chest in the process, until she and I are both sitting straight-backed, staring at the silhouette of my sister in the doorway.

'So much for sleeping in the guest room,' Annie teases, relaxing me one notch down from fever pitch.

'What's wrong, Annie?' I ask. 'Are you okay? Is Mama okay?'

'Actually, I think I might be— Ooh, ouch, bleeping balls.' She pants through what I assume is a contraction.

While I freeze with the reality that my sister is in labor, Sas leaps out of bed, turning on the light, seemingly oblivious to the fact she's wearing only lace underwear.

I toss her my shirt from yesterday and pull on my jeans. Meanwhile, Annie's contraction subsides. 'There are some things in life I do not need to see,' she chastises us.

'Annie, you are about to bare all to anyone willing to put their head between your legs,' Sas says in true uncouth fashion.

Annie giggles. It might have been funny to me any other day but right now, I'm internally freaking out as I ask my sister as calmly as I can, 'What can I do? Should I get Mama?'

Annie shakes her head. 'Let her sleep. It's a first baby. This could take a while. I just don't want to be—'

'We're here,' Sas says, stroking my sister's arm, now dressed slightly more PG. I think her softness could win anyone over and it seems to stop my sister's spiral before it begins. 'Now, I have two man-whore brothers, no sisters, so you're going to have to give me some directions. Should we take you to the hospital?'

'She's having a home birth,' I say as Annie has another contraction and practically mauls Sas, who amazes me by not buckling under the strength of Annie leaning on her, panting and grunting her way through the pain.

When it wanes, she tells us, 'We need to call the midwives and set up the birthing pool.'

'The birthing pool sounds like a man job,' I tell them, relieved to have an excuse to get away from seeing my sister in pain. I know I'm leaving her in safe hands with Sas. This woman has got her shit together, always. She's a fucking marvel.

39

NOVEMBER

Sas
Every. Single. Emotion.

'I've been crotch groped on a subway, followed around college campus in the dark, and I've skydived over Lake Taupo, but watching a woman give birth may be the most terrifying experience of my life,' I say out aloud, knowing before Colton calls me out that I'm oversharing to him and his dad.

The three of us are standing around in the kitchen. Honestly, shell-shocked.

The midwives are tidying away the birthing pool in the lounge while Annie and her brand-new baby boy, as yet nameless, lie on the sofa having skin time and feeds.

Caroline doesn't seem perturbed in the slightest as she sits on the end of the sofa rubbing Annie's ankles that are across her lap. In fact, she looks every bit the doting grandmother. Clearly, she remembers her own experience better than Sonny, who seems as stunned by the events of this morning as Colton and me.

He's poured himself a whiskey on the rocks and I'm pretty sure, if it hadn't been for his concussion, Colton would be drinking one too.

They're both frighteningly pale. Casper the friendly ghost has more color.

It's a couple hours later, once the baby has roused Annie from her much-deserved recovery nap, that we're all sitting in the lounge, which now looks ordinary, rather than like a scene from *American Psycho*.

'Do you want to take him?' Annie asks Colton.

Though I see his trepidation, even as his big sturdy frame rises from a lounge chair, I also know that this man will be a very hands-on uncle. I've no doubt this little boy has zero option but to become one of the best footballers of all time, under his uncle's supervision.

When Colton nervously reaches out for the baby, I expect that he'll tuck it to him like he just received a game-winning catch. This big man in control of a tiny little person. But what I don't expect is that, watching him rock the baby in his arms, every single part of my anatomy that defined my biological gender explodes like a firework on the fourth of July.

The footballer I can't resist. The cowboy who surprised me. The quiet man who's started to talk. The only man who's ever shown me the kind of highs in the bedroom that he has. The compassionate, empathetic, wildly handsome man holding a newborn baby.

Dear ovaries,

Rest in peace. You had no chance.

Yours sincerely,

The woman who has caught more feelings than she ever would have predicted.

* * *

Days after Annie gives birth, Colton is cleared to play in the Bears' next game, which I watch from home in New York.

I try to go back to my life as it was – working hard in the office, making sure my dad can see how serious I am about becoming a fully-fledged agent, getting in at first light and leaving after dark. But I notice that the sky isn't clear. There are no stars over Manhattan like there are over Sunshine Ranch.

For a couple weeks, I go back to what I used to do, grabbing a cocktail or dinner with my girls after work. I go to Jax's game and head out with the team to celebrate their win, staying over on Long Island. Mom, Dad and I catch TJ's college game. It's his senior year and he's a captain, also the leading D1 scorer so far this season. I enjoy it all, or at least I try, but it feels like something shifted in Texas. As if I left a part of me there with Colton and his family.

No matter where I am or what I'm doing in New York, the smallest thing, like the sight of pecan pie in a bakery, or even a pecan in my oatmeal toppings in the morning, seeing a horse on Ralph Lauren's store front, or one of my girls ordering chili when we go out for Tex-Mex, makes me think of the Quinns.

Colton messages me first thing every morning and I message him last thing at night, even if we've spent an hour on the phone already.

His last two games have been some of his finest displays of athleticism since being drafted. Though I know the truth behind the pictures of him and Megan that go viral from the Alamo Stadium, they also strike a chord with me deeper than they ought to. Jealousy. Hurt. Longing.

I think I might be homesick for Texas. Or worse, lovesick for Colton.

Either way, it doesn't matter because I'm in New York, where I live and work. Where I'm trying to prove my worth to my dad and the agency.

Colton is in a contract-extension year, working his ass off playing in Texas, helping Annie through the night with his nephew, and his dad and the other non-profit workers on the ranch to keep the place running just how Caroline likes it.

We have different lives and unless or until I have a legitimate excuse to fly south, we're long-distance... People who work together, friends who've shared benefits.

Which is exactly how it's supposed to be.

But when Colton messaged me a week after the baby was born, holding him in the smallest Bears kit I've ever seen, with an even tinier number eighty-two on the front, and told me he's called Nelson Quinn, I'd never been happier to receive a message.

ME

He has a name!

P. S. Please don't tell me he's named after Willie Nelson x

COWBOY

Ha. I wish I had.

Nelson is my mama's maiden name.

X

I'd swallowed a big, fat wedge in my throat, pleased that we weren't on a video call.

In part to cheer myself up but mostly to make sure Colton couldn't dwell on the reason his nephew had been named after his mom, I replied:

> Your mom is related to Willie Nelson?!?!

Even though he didn't immediately reply, I knew he was laughing in his rocking chair on the ranch porch, shaking his head at my lack of etiquette.

I've thought about those messages a lot over the weeks that have followed – and about Colton's warm, welcoming family that is full of goodness and love. Every time I've turned down an invitation to go out with the girls and listen to stories of their dates gone wrong, I think of them. Whenever I've come home to an empty house because Dad has been travelling for work and Mom has been out socializing.

Nothing has seemed as important as it had before Thanksgiving. My daily life has felt trivial next to what I experienced at the ranch, with Colton, with Annie, and what they're going through as a family.

When my dad told me in the office one night that he was proud of my work ethic. When he took me to a meeting instead of that bonehead, Patrick. When he said I was going the right way about being trusted to have more autonomy with clients and he agreed that Richie Davenport of SAU is someone we should contact as soon as we're able, I should have been thrilled. It was what I wanted. What I'd been working toward. The reason I'd been in Texas all summer.

Yet, my smile and gratitude felt... if not false, then overplayed.

I wanted to be in Texas. In a home that wasn't mine, with a family that didn't belong to me. It was an unfamiliar feeling and one I didn't know that I liked.

I'm a city girl but I'm pining after the country.

* * *

When Christmas comes, it's a welcome break from the hours I've been burying myself in the office and the same old routine of the last four weeks.

My brothers are home: TJ for a week and Jax for the day. Both sets of grandparents come over and Dad actually sets his phone aside for short periods of time.

As is our family tradition, the first champagne cork is popped late morning, when we're all dressed smartly in uncomfortable clothes that Mom likes us to wear for Christmas Day. I'd rather be wearing a hoodie and lounge pants, but Christmas Day is Mom's day. For all of the things she does for us, wearing uncomfortable clothes today is a small price to pay.

By noon, our chef, Gio, and Marta, our all-round house lady, serve a tray of delectable canapés, which we eat as we open our first gifts of the day. Our tree is as tall as our high suburban ceiling. Decorated with designer baubles, it carries the distinct smell of Christmas pine that overshadows even Mom's plentiful reed diffusers.

'This one's for you, sweetpea,' Mom says, nudging a large wrapped gift box along the wood floor to where I'm sitting on a highbacked chair.

'For me?' I set down my flute on the marble coffee table. 'From who?'

My gran – Dad's side – leans forward and turns over the gift card attached to the box. 'It just says Sas.'

As I question the other eyes in the room, no one seems to be owning up. But there's no need, because when I unwrap a stack of LPs – Willie Nelson, ZZ Top, Meat Loaf and more – sitting on top of a brand-new LP player, I know exactly which country boy sent this gift.

'When did this arrive?' I ask.

In my head, I imagine Colton hiding behind a wall, ready to pop out, kiss me on the lips and tell me, *Merry Christmas, city girl.* But I know that the next time I see him will be on our television screen in a few hours' time. Still, there's a sensation in my stomach that I haven't felt since I was in Texas. A connection to him.

I miss him.

I can pretend all I want but I've never missed Pace or Max like this. I've never missed my brothers or even my parents like this.

It's a new and heady kind of longing to be somewhere else, with Colton.

'Marta, do you know when this gift arrived?' Mom asks as Marta reappears to top off our glasses of fizz, her own eyes looking a little glossy from the fizz Mom told her and Gio to help themselves to while they're cooking. They'll go home to their own families shortly.

'A few days ago,' she says. 'I put it right under the tree as instructed by the note that came with it.'

I don't realize I'm biting my lip to quell my smile as I stare at the face of Willie Nelson wearing a cowboy hat until Mom tells me to stop. It's one of her pet hates.

But when I glance up to her, she winks and shrugs her shoulders. She's been trying to get out of me who I'm speaking to each night on the phone.

Little does she know, I absolutely cannot tell her.

I do take my phone out now, though, and message Colton. He's already wished me merry Christmas this morning, but he never mentioned a gift.

> Willie Nelson? X

I feel a buzz as soon as I see those typing dots. It must be early enough before his game that he still has his phone on him.

COWBOY
> Only the best for you, city girl xx

ME
> I didn't get you anything… x

COWBOY
> Sas, the only gift I want is you xx

My next breath is short and shallow, barely there. I want that, too. Regardless, I reply…

ME
> You know that isn't an option x

COWBOY
> I've forgotten every reason why. Or maybe I just don't care anymore xx

ME
> Megan x

COWBOY
> So we publicly break it off x

> My job. My dad. The fact that sports guys don't do relationships x

COWBOY

> The last one is a non-point x

I sigh. I agree. I'm not actually afraid Colton wouldn't make a good boyfriend. Not anymore. I've seen him with the people closest to him. I *know* him.

But my job and my dad remain the biggest hurdle.

COWBOY

> I'm ready to run through defenses for you, Sas.

> Let me x

I stare at the screen, trying to ignore my dad's blazing glare.

Colton stood in the doorway of Pace's home once and told me he wants me, but this, I know, is different.

COWBOY

> Are you there? Don't go quiet on me.

> I want this. All of it.

> Every thanksgiving.

> Kissing you in the barn whenever I want.

> Coming home to you working on our sofa in those tiny little shorts and one of my jerseys, wearing those sexy lawyer glasses.

> Helping Annie with Nelson.

> I want all of you.

> Xx

I could ask, why now? After months of quiet. After weeks of flirting like we're friends with benefits. But I know why. He's just said what I've thought a million times in the last month.

Because everything changed at the ranch on Thanksgiving.

I felt it – and now I know he did, too.

I can't reply. I don't dare. Because as my thumb hovers the keys on my phone, all I can think is, *Me too.*

And the primary reason I can't say I'm all in too is staring at me across the room right now.

'Who's the gift from?' Dad asks, stone-faced.

I swallow deeply, meeting his stare. Not afraid of him. He's a marshmallow. But afraid of the corner I've boxed myself into.

I'm at a crossroads. Do I lie and keep my job, keep making my dad proud in a way he's never told me I have before? Keep everything level for Colton's contract extension year, even if he has decided to be reckless?

My phone rings in my lap, vibrating without a tone, and I stare at Colton's name moving across the screen – *Cowboy.*

Jax, who's refilling his glass with bubbles, not offering a top off to anyone else, starts laughing as he reads my screen across my shoulder.

I think I'd like to pull all the wheels off his favorite toy trucks, like I did when I was eight years old. Because I know what's coming...

'It's from her cowboy boyfriend,' he teases. 'Our little Kansas has grown up and gone and got herself a man.' He laughs harder the sterner my scowl grows.

Scratch that, I want to go and stick a pin in every single one of his footballs and spray paint all his favorite hockey sticks with expletives.

'Are we finally going to find out who this man is that you've been spending so much time on your phone with?' Mom asks, playfully side-eyeing my grans, as if we're at one of her ladies who lunch dates and Colton is the current subject of gossip.

She adds to the torment as I venture a glance to Dad, who's now boring holes in me.

And I make my final decision. Whatever's going on with Colton and me might not work anyway, even if I put everything on the line and risk my job, my relationship with my dad; even then, this might not work.

'It's from Pace,' I lie as my phone finally stops vibrating.

Then I immediately pack the gift away, stick my phone in the pocket of my short skirt and make to leave the room, because I don't want to sit in front of my family while I'm blatantly lying to their faces. We aren't perfect but we don't lie to each other.

I head through to the dining room, where the ten-seat table is set fancy for our turkey feast. Holding on to the back of a chair, I close my eyes and breathe through pain in my chest, my fist drawing circles against my breastbone. Hurting Colton is agony.

If I don't want him, *us*, then why does every part of me ache so bad at the thought of letting him go?

'Is there something going on between you and Pace?'

I yelp at Dad's voice in the archway to the room.

'What? No! We're friends. I've been staying with him. The gift is just… it's an inside joke thing, that's all.'

Now Jax appears behind Dad. 'Sure it is.'

'Sas, if I find out there's something going on with you and one of my guys—'

'Oh my God, Dad. How long have I known Pace? How long have *you* known Pace? He's like a brother.' I narrow my eyes on my biological siblings as TJ joins Jax. 'Like one I wish I'd had.'

Jax chortles. 'Yeah, yeah. Don't get your panties in a twist just because I know about you and—'

Dad's phone ringing into the room cuts off Jax in the nick of time. 'I need to take this.'

'On Christmas Day?' TJ asks.

The response is evident when Dad puts his phone to his ear.

'Do you have to be such a jackass?' I gripe at Jax. 'And stop laughing like that. You're a condescending five-year-old.'

'Ah, come on, Sas. If I can't poke fun at my sister, what can I do?'

'I don't know, maybe not drop me in it.'

'Ha! I knew it was from Quinn.'

'Shut up!' I whisper-shout.

'Hold up. What have I missed?' TJ asks.

'Urgh.' I look to the ceiling.

'Sas is about to get in deep shit with Dad for boning one of his clients.'

'Wait. What? Which one?'

'Stop! Both of you. I think you need a lesson in how the body works if you think I'm capable of *boning* anyone.'

'You know,' TJ says, 'I don't think I want to imagine you boning someone.'

I move back to the lounge, where my mom and my grandmothers have their proverbial ears pricked up.

'Are you going to spill the tea?' Mom asks.

Jesus.

Ironically, I'm saved by Dad's return to the lounge. He pockets his phone and drops into another highbacked chair, one leg crossed over the other.

'That was Colton Quinn,' he tells me, with an expression I can't read. 'He's told me to explore the possibility of a contract in New York.'

'What?' I think I should sit because I suddenly can't feel my legs, but I'm all at once frozen like Olaf in the middle of the room. 'But he— Colton doesn't want to leave Texas.'

Dad raises his shoulders. 'Well, I had a charity golf event a couple weeks ago and the GM from New York was there. We got chatting and the possibility of discussions about Colton when the negotiation window opens was thrown into conversation. I mentioned it to Colton and he said he'd think about it. Today, it seems he's open to the idea.'

'But his sister has just had a baby. Auston Rogers's baby. And he wants nothing to do with them. And Caroline, their mom, is *dying*. What is he thinking?'

Now Dad's expression is recognizable. It's something like anger and frustration. 'Didn't you think to tell me any of this about one of my clients?'

'I— Ah— *No*. Because it's not my story to tell, in either case. And I shouldn't have told you just now, except to stop you from having those conversations with New York.'

And now I need to tell Colton that my big fat mouth has run away with itself again. I need to forewarn him.

I need to stop him from making a bullshit move to prove to me that he wants *us*.

But I ring and ring and ring... It's his turn to ignore me.

The next time I see him is when he's on the television screen warming up on the turf in Louisiana. My tummy would ordinarily be stuffed more than the turkey Marta presented to the middle of the dining table. Instead, it's near empty because my biggest indulgence of the day will be watching the man who has me so strung out that I can't eat.

Jax, on the other hand, has switched his denim for a stretchy waistband

and drops down to the middle seat of the sofa, manspreading across the two spaces either side of him.

'Come on, everyone,' he calls, loud enough that my parents and grandparents making their way through from the dining room can hear. 'Let's watch Sas's boyfriend play some football.'

I pick up a sofa pillow and whack him with it. 'Could you not? He's *not* my boyfriend.'

'Oh we know he isn't, sweetpea,' Mom says, increasingly tipsy, though likely to slow down her top offs of wine, since the staff have gone home for their own Christmases now. 'We've known Pace a long time. Don't let your brother get to you.'

Except he *does* get to me, and he knows it. That's why he waits until Dad is sitting in an armchair facing the large flat screen on the wall to say, 'I'm not talking about Pace. I'm talking about Quinn.'

I make sure I strike him as hard as I can with the pillow, again, before turning to see Dad's stone face.

'Quinn? Colton?' he asks.

'Dad, don't listen to Jax. He's full of sh—'

Jax is laughing so hard his head might fall from its stupid-person stanchion.

'Kansas,' Dad begins, in that way only dads can. 'Are you having a relationship with Colton?'

I shake my head. 'No.' Really true. Do I want to be? That would be a trickier question to answer.

'So, him suddenly showing an interest in New York—'

'Absolutely nothing to do with me. I don't understand it at all. Maybe he's in for the business tactic, you know? Play the teams off against each other. Or maybe he's worried the Bears won't make a better offer.'

'Quinn's playing the best football he's ever played. As if the Bears don't want him,' TJ adds, clearly incapable of reading the room.

My brothers really are dumbass jock-whores.

But I'm not looking at them because I'm watching Dad, who has always called me a terrible liar, and I see in his face now that he doesn't believe me.

'What about all the PR work we've been doing with him and Megan, on *your* suggestion? What happens when your fling blows up and I've got to choose between a client and my daughter? Have you thought about any of this, Kansas?'

Every. Single. Day. Since I met him.

Dad pushes up from his chair. 'I've been so proud of your professionalism recently. The way you've grown and learned. I saw real potential in you.'

'I have grown and learned, Dad,' I protest as our audience chooses now to be silent.

'I don't think I've ever been more disappointed in you. Act first and think second. It was a mistake bringing you into the agency.'

Through blurred vision and stinging eye sockets, I watch my dad stalk out of the room.

'I don't see what the big deal is,' Jax says. 'You're both adults. And it's clearly working for the big man.' He points to the screen where Colton just received the ball from the first snap of the game and got a new set of downs.

I want to watch the game with the others but my dad's disappointment is bigger than what's happening on the screen.

I've fucked up.

Maybe that's the reason tears silently roll down my cheeks. I've let myself down.

I watch the game from my bedroom, knowing that I've got to choose between my family and Colton. Dad has left me no choice.

Even when I overhear Mom and Dad in the kitchen later, and she asks him, 'Don't you remember when you fell for someone you shouldn't have?'

She means her. Mom. A cheerleader for his football team.

'That's different,' Dad tells her. 'We're married. We have three kids.'

I decide not to get a glass of water and instead, lean my head back against the wall and try not to imagine being married with kids, Colton and me. Because I remember the way he held Nelson as a newborn baby, the way he was at ease in his Texas ranch, riding horses, tending hens. I want it. All of it.

'You think she likes him that much?' Dad asks.

'I think she's sought your approval her entire life. She's wanted to show you that she can be great at something. I don't think for one second that my kind, smart daughter would risk that if she hadn't really fallen for Colton.'

I have fallen for Colton. But wanting him for a few months is nothing by comparison to a lifetime of trying to prove myself to my dad. Mom's right; I wanted to show Dad that I can be great at something. And I will.

40

JANUARY

Colton
Men Can Be So Stupid

'I blew it,' I tell my mama and Annie. I'm standing on the porch with Nelson curled like a crescent moon on my chest, sleeping. My sister and mama are rocking gently back and forth in their chairs. 'I knew the New York thing would scare her. I pushed her too hard, too soon.'

'For what it's worth,' Annie says, 'I'm proud of you.'

Mama smiles. 'You did exactly what I told you to do, son. You put yourself out there.'

I run my calloused thumb along the fine black hair at the bottom of Nelson's head. Soft like silk. He's going to be a heartbreaker one day, I know it already.

Better to be a heartbreaker than heartbroken, kid.

'Any bright ideas as to what I do next?' I ask.

'You wait,' Mama says. 'You've planted the seed and now it's up to Sas to let it grow.'

'Inspirational, Mama. Thanks.'

She and Annie chuckle, and despite the fact Sas hasn't spoken to me since Christmas night when she told me again that nothing more could happen between us, I smile at the other women in my life.

'She'll come round,' Annie says. 'I see the way she looks at you.'

Mama reaches out and takes hold of Annie's hand just as Dad comes from inside with two bottles of beer. He hands one to me. It's a Monday, day off tomorrow, so I take it in my free hand.

'Do you know how happy y'all make me?' Mama asks.

I swig my beer, knowing I'm emotionally, unexpectedly, fragile enough right now without hearing one of her speeches.

'I sat in this house the day after Thanksgiving, thinking I'm more thankful than ever before, because that day, I knew... y'all will be just fine when I'm gone. I watched y'all pull together and show more strength than I've ever seen in you, to bring my gorgeous grandson into this world.'

Annie starts to cry and Dad hands her a tissue. 'Come on, Mama, my hormones are still all over the place.'

Mama rubs Annie's chin, gently turning her lips up. 'I'm so thankful to have seen you become a woman, Annie. Grateful to have met Nelson. Joyous at seeing your daddy have a grandson to dote on. And you...' She looks to me with an expression I know is truly unconditional love. I know because I feel it for her. 'You, my son, are a wonder. Your grit and determination have always been an inspiration to me. But I'm at peace now, having met the woman who has turned your frown upside down. That's how I know that you haven't blown it, as you put it. You just need to give her time to see how much she loves you back.'

That's a lot to take in. A lot to process. A lot of tears and words in my head to suppress. But one thought says to me loudly, *She's right*. I do love Sas. I'm in love with her. Unconditionally. In New York. In Texas. Whether she's an agent, my agent, or whoever she wants to be. Even if she decides that's not with me.

I love her in this moment, and I think I always will.

* * *

'Do you really think this will work?' I ask Megan.

She's hatched a plan to get Sas in Texas and talking to me. The two of us are sitting at my kitchen counter, figuring this out. Meanwhile, Pace, Max and Terry are grunt-gobbling Annie's pecan pie like pigs eating from a trough.

It's the first Tuesday of January and the guys and I have been out for a round of golf. I think Annie and Mama were so keen to get my grumpy ass (Mama's words) off the ranch that Annie took a mini break from her new role as round-the-clock baby feeder to make two pecan pies for my teammates. Then I had to say yes to golf, if only to deliver the pies.

Actually, the fresh air and coming clean with the guys about Sas and Megan has been good. It was their suggestion that I call in Megan to help. They said chicks need to give advice on dealing with chicks. But I'm pretty sure they just want to get to know Megan, now that she's *available,* even if the rest of the world still thinks that she and I are dating.

Messy.

Very messy.

Not that the guys seem to care.

'I absolutely do,' Megan says, hitting send on her message to Sas with the level of dramatic flair I've come to expect from my friend. It's much less jarring and more a Megan-ism these days.

She takes a fork to my slice of pecan pie for about the gazillionth time, shaving the smallest slither of dessert – it doesn't count if it's not a full bite, she tells me. She moans around the taste of food, which is fucking hilarious to watch because she knows that she's got three large men lapping it up all around us.

I shake my head. She pout-winks in response.

'Walk me through this plan again,' I say.

'God, Colton, could you *listen*? So, I've invited Sas to the wrap-up party for the show next Sunday. It's going to be, like, all red carpet and fancy and star-studded, so, naturally, it's the perfect opportunity for Blake and Sean to set us up for PR.'

'You and I?' I clarify.

'Yes.'

'But I thought Colton wasn't going?' Terry interrupts, spraying crumbs from his mouth in a way I'd say just ruined his chances with Megan, if he had any.

'Are all footballers this dumb?' Megan asks.

'Just the rookies,' Pace tells her, he, Max and I enjoying the joke at Terry's expense.

'Good to know I'm in the market for a vet,' she teases. 'Now, you're right,

Rookie, Colton *won't* show. And why won't Colton show? Anybody? First correct answer gets another slice of pie.'

'Because he's making a point to Sas that he's done with fake-dating you. He wants out of you and into Sas,' Max says.

I level him with narrow eyes for the crassness of that statement.

Megan holds up a finger. 'To be clear, Colton has never been *in* me.'

'I know the next part of the plan,' Pace says. 'And since this whole thing is about Colton getting into the equivalent of my sister's pants, can I get extra pie regardless?'

Megan nudges the plate his way. 'That probably does justify pie. Go on then, enlighten those of us who can't seem to get the detail here.'

Forking the remainder of the pie rather than cutting another slice, Pace tells us all, 'Sas gets pissed that Colton doesn't show because, you know, that's what Sas does. Then at some point, she hunts him down like an elk to give it to him, and Colton tells her, to her face, that it's her he wants. Some kind of romantic-comedy music plays from somewhere in the distance, they kiss and run off into the sunset. Or, in this case, Colton runs off to play for New York like a di—'

'Okay, okay, we've got it,' Megan interjects.

'Man, you know I don't want to leave the Bears. No matter where I am, I'll always be a Bear. But Sas needs to know that I'm in this. If she'll put her career on the line, I'll do the same. Like I told you, all I've done is said Harris can plant a seed in New York.'

Pace shakes his head. 'See, *this* is exactly why I don't do relationships. Not until I retire.'

'Can I ask a question?' Terry says, holding up his hand as if he's in a math class.

Megan nods.

'What if Sas is like genuinely just out? What if she was just screwing Quinn and she's not into him like that? What if she turns down your invitation?'

His words make me instantly nauseous, until Megan sighs and says, 'Men can be so stupid. Sas found every excuse she could to stay in Texas for weeks at a time. She loves him, you hippo. And she *won't* turn down the invitation because if I'm right – and I'm more often right than not when it comes to girl stuff, trust me – Sas has been sitting in New York waiting for an excuse to come down here and end things with Colton properly, face to face. She's cooler than a text-message ending.'

'You think she's coming to end it?' I ask, spine straightening as I push back from the countertop.

'Well, duh, of course she is.'

'Lord, now I'm confused again,' I say, dropping my head to my arms on the counter.

'She's coming to end it because she's been forced to choose between her dad and you. His fault, not yours. But when she sees you...' She claps her hands three times, and I think I'll take that as a positive message, choosing to not delve any further into the many ways this plan could go disastrously wrong for me.

41

JANUARY 2027

Sas
He's an Idiot

Megan's wrap-up party, as it happens, coincides with some of Max's sponsors flying into Texas from LA to renegotiate their deal – a Sunday meeting to fit around his schedule, because the Bears played yesterday. Even though I'm still not Dad's favorite person since Jax's unhelpful outbursts at Christmas, he's travelling elsewhere, and since I wanted to come to Texas to support Megan – and her PR relationship with Colton – Dad suggested I take Max's meeting, too.

I'd take it as a win, as if Dad's extending an olive branch, but when he asked me to take the meeting, he said, 'It's a given anyway. The Bears are killing it. No one expected them to be placed fourth going into Wild Card weekend. If they win this coming week, they'll make it to the divisional play-offs, again. Max will be made a good offer off the bat. There won't be much for you to do.'

It made me feel all warm and fuzzy inside.

Still, as Jax continues to erroneously state, I did bone his client.

Megan told me to dress fancy tonight, so I'm wearing a black strapless plunge dress, thigh high, that I picked up in the Bergdorf Christmas sale. I absolutely chose it because I thought it was chic yet made me feel sexy. But

I'd be lying if I said I hadn't stood in the fitting rooms on Fifth Avenue wondering what Colton would think of me in this dress.

I guess we'll find out soon because I'm making my way into the five-star hotel in San Antonio chosen for tonight's wrap-up party due to the opulence and superb rooftop views. The same reasons I chose it as the venue for that first and fatal lunch meeting with Colton.

I'm nervous to see him. So much so, I'm on the verge of chickening out, even as I smile at the concierge, my legs moving me forward into the venue. I hold my shoulders back, knowing there are cameras everywhere, waiting to catch a glimpse of the cast and crew. Also remembering that with my hair pinned up, an arched spine would be a bad look – it's the kind of thing my mom has drilled into me since school.

If it hadn't been for Max waiting for me to get changed at Pace's house after our meeting ran over, and driving me to the party, I probably wouldn't have had the balls to come.

'It's just a party, Sas. It's supposed to be fun,' he told me from the driver's seat of his sports car.

Fun is the last thing this party is going to be because I know what I need to say to Colton when I see him. Exactly the same thing I've messaged him since Christmas. There can't be anything more between us than client and associate.

But I also know that when I see him, my body will default to the one setting it knows around him – I want him, in every way imaginable.

'Sas, over here!'

I swivel on my thin heels to see Megan holding up a hand, then picking up the chiffon overlay of her floor-trailing dress to high-heel jog toward me.

'Wow, you look fantastic!' I tell her.

She really does. Her outfit accentuates her figure and height, whilst shimmering contouring highlights her symmetrical features and Hollywood smile.

We hug and cameras flash somewhere around us. 'Thanks for coming,' she says.

'Free champagne and fancy food? How could I resist?'

She slips her hand into mine. 'Great company too, right?' She speaks in her learned Texas twang.

I laugh. Megan's me me syndrome is genuinely endearing. 'Where are we going?' I ask, reaching out to accept a glass of fizz from a waiter.

'To the rooftop. The view is great.'

I remember. I also remember that the man I was sitting opposite the one other time I've been here was even more attractive.

'Where's— Ah, should we wait for—'

'Colton?' Her smile widens, though I can't reciprocate it. I feel nauseous. I've walked away from guys before. Why is this time making me feel ill? 'He isn't coming.'

I tug her hand right before we get to the elevators. 'What do you mean, he isn't coming?'

'He changed his mind.' She shrugs and steps into the cart, where hotel staff hold open the doors.

'But Blake and Sean think he's coming. They've told the press to expect pictures of you two in your finery.' I follow her into the cart and the doors close on just the two of us. 'Megan, it will look really bad if he doesn't show. The media will report it as a relationship breakdown.'

She stares at me, and I think understanding is dawning on her, until she tells me, 'Sas, we know that. It's kind of the point.'

'Kind of the point, how?'

She places her hands on my cheeks and encourages me into the elevator. 'Colton Quinn is mad for you. He doesn't want a fake relationship anymore. He wants a real one. With *you*. He's done pretending.'

He's an idiot.

* * *

I know that stomping across the training field in my work heels is not a good look, especially when they keep slipping into the fake turf and making my legs shaky. Though they could be shaking because I'm marching toward a squad of fifty-three players and all the coaching and medical staff that come along with them, hell-bent on tearing Colton a new one.

I hear someone saying, 'Oh boy.'

And someone else say, 'Get down, boys, this is about to get ugly.'

There's some mention of firecracker and I hear a long, drawn-out whistle from another direction.

Yeah, well, I *am* that angry. The fact that Colton wouldn't answer his phone to me last night and all this morning, while my own phone has been blowing up with Sean Boyle's number, has made me even more pissed.

Colton is bent over as if he's about to start a sprint exercise with the other receivers, but he glances my way. He *sees* me. But he ignores me and prepares to run again.

Oh no he didn't!

'Kansas, what are you doing here?' Coach Roy asks.

'I won't be long, Glen. I just need a minute with that dumbass over there.'

I continue past my godfather, my heels giving me hell, but Colton starts his drill, paying no credence to the fire I feel inside.

I know why I'm so angry. It isn't just because he didn't show last night and I've had Sean breathing down my neck about it. It's more than that. The fact he didn't, *won't* listen to me. He and I can't happen and knowing that he wants us to is only making it harder for me to take.

So, in my temper, I pick up the nearest thing to me, which happens to be a football. I even surprise myself when I launch the ball at Colton. I'm more stunned when it smacks him flush on the side of his helmet.

He stops in his tracks and finally faces me. There are murmurings and gripes all around me, but I have my blinkers on.

'What are you doing?' he asks.

'*Me*? What am *I* doing?' I pick up another ball and throw it at him, hitting his shoulder.

'Nice arm,' he tells me.

'Thanks, I played for the women's team in college.'

'Course you did.'

He takes off his helmet as I pick up another and launch it in his direction. He catches this one. 'Stop throwing balls at me!'

'First New York and now *this*? I've spent the morning on the phone to Sean, getting it in the ear about you doing a no-show last night.'

I drop my hands to my waist as he comes my way. He takes my elbow to lead me away from the squad and though I snatch it out of his hold, I do follow him to a quieter spot on the training field.

It's an outdoor field and it's the part of training where media are allowed to watch, so I know the timing of this spectacle isn't the best, but neither is the crap he pulled last night.

'I'm sorry you've had to deal with Sean. I'll speak to him and tell him the whole thing with Megan is done.'

'You...' I'm so furious I can barely think straight; I'm just watching beads of sweat roll down his beautiful face. He's wearing his pads under his jersey and I'm dying inside because if I have a type, it's this. My type is Colton Quinn. 'You and Megan lured me down here. You never had any intention of going last night, did you?'

'No.'

He's as honest as ever and as calm as ever. A fucking pacifist while I'm irate.

'I'm done with it. The only woman I want to be photographed with is you. The only woman I want to have on my arm is you. The only person I want to kiss is you.'

God, he's making this hard. Making my eyes sting like I'm some kind of crazy person who can't control her emotions. Biting down on my gums, I shake my head, willing myself to be objective. Rational.

'Colton, I've told you, even if there was no fake relationship, you and I can't be together. My dad can barely look at me because he knows something's happened between us. He told me he made a mistake hiring me.'

Colton takes a step closer and reaches out for my face. I push his hand away.

'Do you know how that felt? When all I've done is try to make him see that he can trust me, that I'm a professional, now because of us, all my hard work has been undone.'

'I'm sorry he said that, Sas. I am. Everyone can see how hard you work and if he can't, then he's a fool.'

'He's my dad.'

'Fair. I shouldn't say that but it's true. And if he makes you suffer at work because of me, if this between us can't happen because he's my agent, then I choose you, Sas.'

'What are you saying?'

He moves so close now his heat is radiating off him, into my skin. Even in my heels, I'm looking up into deep brown eyes that are so genuine, I could fall for him all over again.

'I'll get a new agent if that's what I have to do.'

I close my eyes to help me think straight, blocking out the image of him.

'Colton, my dad is one of the best agents around and this is a contract-extension year for you.'

I feel his hand on my cheek and reluctantly open my eyes to the sincerity of his. I wish it were this easy. That he could just fix this for us.

'You said it yourself, if I play well, the rest falls into place. Why do you think I'm incentivized to play the best football of my life right now?'

'I won't let you mess this up over me.' I free myself from his touch and start walking backward away from him. 'This is your career, Colton. It's your life. We were just—'

He reaches out for my wrist and before I know what's happening, I'm flush against his chest, his hand in my hair, his mouth on mine, and there are gasps and cheers and wolf whistles all around us.

But I know that among them are camera clicks and the promise of stories of Colton cheating on Megan. Stories of Colton and me that will now make news headlines and reels.

I push back from him. 'Colton! For God's sake!'

'I don't care anymore, Sas. There's not a guy on this squad thinks that you and I don't fit.'

'They know?!'

'Everyone who knows me can see that I'm head over boots for you.'

The ache in my chest at his words is almost unbearable. 'But the world thinks you're head over boots for Megan Frost.'

Hand over my lips where his have just been, I turn to walk away. Only now, of all times, my fecking heel sticks in the turf and my shoe is pulled from my foot.

'For fuck's sake,' I gripe, bending to pick up the shoe, and limp-walk off the training ground, not daring to look back or pick my head up.

42

JANUARY

'Hey!' I say from my position on the sofa, computer on my lap, when Pace walks through his front door. 'You're usually home right after training. You're not staying away from your own place because of me, are you? Because I know what happened today was a shit show and I can go to a hotel.'

'Relax.' He drops his training bag on the floor next to the sofa and comes to sit. 'I want you here. Max and I took Quinn for nine holes after training, that's all. He needed it.'

'Oh. Is he...?'

'Okay? He's somewhere on the intersection of scratching his head and gutted.' He swivels to fully face me, pulling a knee onto the furniture and casually draping his arm over it. 'He's ready to upend his life for you, Sas. You and I both know he doesn't want to be in New York, but he'll go if that's what it takes to win you. Or keep you.'

'I'm not a prize he can pick up for winning a rodeo, Pace.' I sigh. Colton has never made me feel like that. Not even close. 'I don't want him to move to New York. I adore who he is here. At the Bears. At home on the ranch.'

'I don't know if it's my place to tell you this, but Quinn called Sean right after you left training and told him to fix it so that him kissing you isn't the next viral reel.'

I nod. I've turned my phone off. It's a matter of time before Sean and Dad start calling to berate me – if they haven't tried already. And I can't be bothered with messages from Mom and the girls at home when they get wind of that kiss. But I have been stupid enough to check online from my laptop and what I've found already is *not* good.

'There was media at training, Pace. Not even Sean can fix this one.' I look to the ceiling, resting my head against the back of the sofa. 'To everyone who doesn't know the truth, Colton just cheated on America's sweetheart.'

'I agree; if Sean can't make it disappear, that kiss is pretty good fodder for trolls.'

'It's already out there.' I huff my next breath. 'You should read the comments. People wanting to know who I am. Some people connecting dots and deciding Colton and I have been going behind Megan's back for months. One comment called me a home-wrecking whore.' My eyes well with tears.

'Hey, hey. Where's my firecracker, huh?' Pace asks, tugging me against his shoulder. 'They're keyboard warriors with nothing better to do with their time than drag other people down, Sas. They aren't worth shit. Trust me, I've had my share of social batterings and they always fade away with the next thing. And Megan's cool. She was in on this whole plan to get you back down to Texas. I'm sure she'll come up with something.'

I swipe the back of my hand across my wet cheek. 'Meg's amazing, but it's not just that, is it? Imagine how my dad is feeling right now. He'll be furious. And my career... I'm going to get a name for sleeping my way through clients before I've even had a chance to contract my own.'

Pace nods thoughtfully. 'But we can't help who we fall for and when. And it's like you say to us guys, if we play well, the rest is just noise. Same for you, right? If you're good at your job, who gives a fuck who you date?'

I scoff. 'I know one man who will.'

'Harris will get over it when he realizes how serious you and Quinn are about each other. And so will the rest of the world.'

I look at him now. Is he right? Will this blow over? Can Dad and Sean fix this?

More importantly, how serious are Colton and I about each other? He's set his stall out. But where am I at?

'Exactly how many people were in on this plot to sabotage my career?' I ask Pace, more playful than the words would look on paper, which surprises even me.

He shrugs, coming to stand. 'All of us. We've got our boy's back.'

Despite my awful mood, my lips turn up. 'If something good has come of this season, I'm pleased you're all there for him and he's letting you in.'

Pace nods. 'Me, too. He's good people.' Then he moves toward the kitchen. 'Club soda?'

When I say yes, he pops the ring on both cans and hands one to me.

'You know, if Quinn messed up, we all did. I understand that Harris has your balls in a vice, and I see both sides of that coin, but sometimes, I think it would be nice to have someone to come home to.' He slurps his drink. 'I don't think it's to be sniffed at.'

I set my laptop down and kneel up to face him across the back of the sofa. 'Pace, I love you.'

'Love you too, firecracker.' He winks. 'If my opinion means anything, I think you and Quinn could make a real go of things.'

'I came down here to tell him it's not going to happen.'

'Do you love him?'

I blow out my next breath through my lips. 'I know I was crushed when he didn't show to Megan's wrap-up party. When I'm not with him, I want to be, and when I am with him, it feels like we'll never be close enough.'

He nods. 'I'm a perpetual bachelor, so my advice probably means jack, but I'd say when everything else is done – his career, yours – isn't that the feeling you want on your death bed?'

I think of Caroline and Sonny and I imagine there's nothing they'd want more in the world than more time together.

'I'm thirty-three, Sas, and I've finally started to wonder what comes after football. But with everything Quinn has going on in his life right now, maybe he's seen the light sooner than I have. He already knows what really matters.'

That's what I think about for the rest of the evening, while Pace's chef makes us dinner, while we eat, while I'm lying in his guest room staring at the ceiling, willing sleep to come, trying not to look at my phone and see just how big of a disaster today has become.

* * *

I guess, at some point, sleep did find me, because I wake with a start from a dream that I forget the second I open my eyes.

I'm in such a daze that I don't remember not to look at my phone, until it's too late.

The screen has blown up with messages and call notifications from my girlfriends back home, my brothers, my mom and, obviously, my dad.

Wincing, I open my social media apps one by one, and what I find is even worse than I could have imagined.

I already know the kiss is out there. Accusations of cheating, hating on Colton, standing with Megan, it's all there and plentiful. But worse than any of that is the stories Sean has used to divert attention.

The moment I see them, I feel sick.

He's exposed Annie and Auston.

He's told the world that Caroline is ill.

And the only way Sean knows any of that is because I told Harris at Christmas.

My *dad* has told Sean.

Everything Colton was trying to protect is public because of me.

Suddenly, nothing else matters except making sure he and his family are okay.

Of course they aren't okay.

But I need to be with them. I need to apologize and somehow, someway, make this better.

I tug on a hoodie and a pair of yoga pants and hot foot it to Pace's bedroom.

Knocking on the door as I let myself if, I ask his face-down form, buried in his pillows, 'Pace, can I borrow a car?'

'Always.' He groans. 'What time is it?'

'Just after seven.'

'Jesus, Sas. It's my one day off. I need my beauty sleep over here.'

I ruffle his hair. 'You're gorgeous, Princess. And I'm sorry but the proverbial shit just hit the fan.'

He shifts to look at me and I hold up my phone. 'Ah, fuck. Take a fast one. The keys are in the usual place.'

43

JANUARY

Colton
She Doesn't Know How to Take Her Time Doing Anything

I'm out riding, cowboy hat lower than my eyes to shield from the early-morning sun. Luke trots lazily as I spend the time thinking and processing everything that's happened in the last twenty-four hours. I'm a good way from the house when I hear the unmistakable roar of a luxury sports car coming up the dusty driveway of the ranch.

From my vantage point, I recognize it as Pace's, but the speed it's travelling at tells me who's driving – that woman doesn't know how to take her time doing anything.

'What do you say, boy? Should we go back? Or don't we want to know what she has to say today?' I pat the horse on his neck and I'm not sure if his happy nasal exhale is confirmation that we should turn back, but I choose to take it as such.

I jump down from the stallion's back and unsaddle him, all the while trying to stay unruffled. I just need to get out the words that I want to say to Sas.

She's sitting on the porch with my mama and Annie. I know how they'll have reacted to her being here after my conversation with them before my ride this morning, but I hope I'm right.

Rubbing my hands on a rag as I make my way from the barn to the porch, I try to control the slight tremor in my extremities.

Is it normal to be this nervous around a girl? Probably, when we've both screwed up so badly.

Sas's hair is pulled into a ponytail. She's make-up free, wearing Bears merch and yoga pants. She's as stunning now as she looked in the pictures from Megan's wrap-up party when she was in that black dress.

She rises from her seat, where Bear has been sitting next to her, and makes her way toward me, as slow as I've ever seen her move, hands in the front pouch of her hoodie. It's a version of her I'm not used to seeing. She's nervous, too.

Leaning back against one of the corral posts, I wait for her to reach me, one booted foot crossed over the other, watching her and wondering if today is the beginning of the rest of our days, or the beginning of the end.

Before she even reaches me, her scent catches on the breeze – not perfume, not shampoo, yet something that's distinctly her. Something I want to hold in my arms every night and wake up to every morning.

She's biting down on her own gums, cheeks sucked in as she shakes her head.

'I'm so sorry,' she says.

Immediately, all the tension I was holding leaves me.

'Colton, I had no idea Sean was going to do this. If I had, I would've done everything in my power to stop him.' She slips her hands free and holds them to her chest. 'Please know that the very last thing I would ever want to do is hurt you or Annie, or your mom, your dad or baby Nelson. Any of you.'

I nod. My throat is suddenly dry. 'I know. It's okay.'

She moves closer to me, until she's standing right in front of me, her eyes full of a sadness I never want to see on her.

'No, Colton, it's not okay. This is my fault. At Christmas, I told my dad about Annie and Auston, and about your mom and her prognosis. I had no idea he'd told Sean but I should've guessed as much, and I should've seen that Sean could do something like this.'

'Sas, it's okay.'

'Colton, stop. Just stop being so calm and so nice and so goddamn perfect. I talked you into the whole PR stunt with Megan. I crossed the line when I fell for you, and as soon as I realized how hard I've fallen, I should've left.'

She takes another step toward me, which is a complete contradiction to the words leaving her mouth.

'I was supposed to get under your skin and find out what went wrong in the off-season, why you started out playing this season so badly, and I did that. But in the end, it wasn't because of a job or because Harris asked me to. It was because I wanted to know everything there is to know about you. But I shouldn't have taken what you shared with me in confidence and given it to my dad.'

'I appreciate your honesty, but I said yes to the arrangement with Megan, and I said yes because I was too shy or proud or too something to be open with my teammates and my coaches about what was going on in my life. I expected people to be honest with me when I wasn't being honest with them. That mistake's on me. Yesterday, you didn't want me to kiss you, especially not in front of the media. You knew what would happen. You were right and I ignored it. I was headstrong when I should've listened to you.'

'But Sean wouldn't have been able to—'

'I called Sean after you left the training ground yesterday and I told him to fix it and do whatever he had to do to protect you. The shit people were saying about you online was—'

'I don't care about that. I mean, I did yesterday, but Pace reminded me of what's important. *You* and your family are important, Colton, not a bunch of idiots I don't know and I'll never meet. The people here, at this ranch, matter to me.'

'It matters to me that you don't suffer the consequences of my actions.'

She leans her head to one side. 'Like you have mine?'

'I stand by my decision to tell Sean to sort this. And no, I didn't expect that he would take something so personal about me and my family and use that as click bait, but he was acting on my instructions to fix things.'

'You've done nothing to deserve this, Colton. Nor has Annie or your mom.'

I reach out for her arm and encourage her to move closer, parting my legs until she walks between them.

'And all you did was give my agent information I should've told him myself. I should've kept him in the loop and relayed to him whatever he was entitled to do with that knowledge. As of first thing this morning, Harris and I have fired Sean. Neither of us will be working with him again.'

'You've already spoken to my dad?'

I can't resist reaching up to move a rogue strand of hair from her temple and brushing it back from her face, feeling more confident when she closes her eyes and leans into my touch. The sun casts a golden glow across her soft, freckled skin.

'Yes. I also told him that you're great at your job, and maybe we've both got some things to learn but that none of this mess is on you.'

'You didn't have to do that. I don't deserve it.'

'Yes, you do. My life is better since you convinced me to start opening up to people, Sas. My relationships with my family, my teammates.' I take a deep breath and look into her eyes when she reopens them. Pools of midnight blue I've gotten lost in more times than I can count. Not nearly as many as I'd like. 'I also told your dad that if he ever makes you choose between the agency and us, or makes me choose between you and the agency, I choose you. I'll choose you and stand by you every time.'

She drops her forehead to mine and I smell the sweetness of Annie's mint water on her next breath.

'If we've got stuff to figure out, I want to figure it out together. I want to be with you, Sas.'

She raises her chin until her nose is touching mine. Reflexively, I slide my hand up her neck, to the base of her head.

'I won't spend my final days wishing I'd invested more time appeasing a public I don't know. Or squeezing an extra six figures out of a contract when I already earn enough money to make us a damn good life. I'll only wish that I never wasted a moment of time that I could have spent with you.'

She closes her eyes, her words against my lips, her mouth grazing mine, as she says, 'I choose you, too.'

With her confirmation, I wrap my other arm around her back and bring her flush against me, because I need all of her. Her lips meet mine and I deepen the kiss as she moans, or I do, and we're holding on to each other as if we can't get close enough.

She presses her lips to my neck as I hold us together and tell her, 'I missed you so much.'

'I missed you, too,' she whispers. Though I knew it, hearing her say it makes me feel as if I'm levitating.

Until she pats me on the back like one of the guys might do in a manly post-touchdown hug. 'Now, we've got work to do.'

She pulls back from me as I ask, 'What work?'

'The very last thing I would have ever wanted is to hurt you and your family. I'm here to support you, all of you. I want to fix this as best we can. So, what do you want, Colton? You're in control. Tell me how you want to play this and I'll put everything I have into making it happen.'

I rub a hand along my day-old gruff, then glance to the porch, where Mama and Annie are, unashamedly, trying to eavesdrop, even if they do have the decency to dart their focus away when I clock them.

'I think it's up to them,' I say.

She nods. 'I agree. And just so you know, I have apologized to them both for what's gone down.'

'Thank you,' I tell her, reaching down to take her hand and kissing her hair before we make a move for the porch.

'Don't you want to know how they reacted?'

'I already know.'

'Well, your mom was great.'

'I know.'

'She said it's about time it came out. You've protected them for long enough and now it's their turn to look out for you and me.'

I nod. 'I know.'

'Annie, I might still need to work on, but she doesn't seem to hate me.'

'Like I said, I know. I talk to my family these days, especially about you.'

'Huh. Well, I did have to bribe them both. I told Annie I'd never refuse a request for babysitting services whenever she wants them, including night feeds.'

I chuckle. 'She would have settled for a lot less than that. I think in some ways, she's pleased she doesn't have to hide it anymore.'

'She did say the town might stop looking at her like she's a hussy.'

Now my chuckle turns into a bellowing laugh.

44

JANUARY

Sas
Wild Card Weekend

We spend the rest of Tuesday morning in a bubble, not looking at phones or laptops, just playing with Nelson and hanging out with Colton's family. But everything has changed. Every look holds only promise. Every touch is full of hope that hasn't been there between us before.

It's impossible not to be happy at Sunshine Ranch, among the warmth of the home, where despite everything, I only ever feel included, welcome and secure.

I know I've made the right decision.

Colton is all in, and so am I.

The rest we'll figure out.

And that's what we spend Tuesday afternoon trying to do.

* * *

'Would you look at you two?' Megan coos when Colton kisses my temple in his apartment, where we're making drinks and snacks, expecting this whole game plan to take some time. 'I did so well, didn't I?'

Colton and I turn to her, where she's sitting with a shimmering pink laptop on Colton's dining table with a cheese-eating grin.

'At what?' Colton and I ask in sync.

Megan wafts a hand and makes clear her exasperation, as taught in theatrical school. 'Sorcery. Match-making.'

I laugh, conceding that she was the catalyst of everything that has followed between Colton and me. I set down a lemonade in front of her and tell her, 'A token of my appreciation.'

'Like lemonade is going to cut it.' She takes a sip. 'You can repay me by making me your maid of honor whenever you two get married.'

I cough my next sip of drink, coming to sit opposite her. It's far too early to have those conversations, but I do know that those precursory three words are on the tip of my tongue. They've been there for weeks.

When the timing is right, I'll tell him. But right now, 'Let's focus on hatching a plan for Colton's first intentional statement on social media *ever*.'

Megan interlaces her fingers, pushes her arms away from her and clicks her neck. 'Don't worry, I'm a pro when it comes to wooing the public.'

With input from Colton and me, she comes up with a plan to go live on her socials with Colton. I can tell he isn't wholly comfortable but we're all in agreement that this is the best foot we can put forward.

'Go over it one last time so I don't come across like a total dick,' Colton says, more nervous than I've seen him before any game of football.

'We'll explain to our fans that we're great friends, that you've helped me with my accent and showed me around while I've been in the south. But ultimately, we're no more than friends and haven't been for some time.'

He nods, over and over, as if he's letting it sink in. 'Are you sure we can't go for a written statement on your account?'

'Urgh.' She rolls her eyes. 'It won't be enough. Keyboard warriors would only ever say that I'm saving face or covering for your cheating. It has to be live to prove that we're on good terms.'

He's nodding again, his silence speaking volumes about his reluctance.

So no one is more surprised than me when evening comes and they go live from Colton's lounge. He looks surprisingly at ease, genuinely laughing and joking with Megan in a way that only hardened trolls could pass negative comment on.

It's clear, because they aren't acting, that Colton and Megan have a genuine connection. No lying, no cover stories, just two buddies – who happen to be famous – giving a casual update to the world.

Even during their live, I watch on my phone as well-wishers are out in force in the comments. So much so, it makes me wonder whether they'd ever needed Blake, or me, and definitely not Sean.

Everything is going swimmingly, until Megan says, 'I couldn't be happier that he's fallen for my good friend, Sas. They are the cutest, you guys.'

Colton snaps his head to me and I bury my face in my hands as he laughs – it happened on IG, so I guess it's official. Colton Quinn has fallen for little old me. And *that* is enough to drown out all my reservations.

* * *

Today feels like even more of a test than Megan and Colton's statement, because I'm in Las Vegas for the Bears' wild card game. And my dad will be here any minute.

I'm already in my seat for the game. Sonny has the spot next to me but he's currently standing as close as he can get to the gridiron, watching the teams warm up.

The Bears have done so well to have fourth seed after their start to the season, but that also means they have the closest matched game of the weekend. I'm as proud as I am nervous for them. Colton, Pace, Max, all the guys I've gotten to know much better over this season.

But that's not why I have a chill, despite the mild climate. It's not the reason my legs are bouncing against my seat. *Those things* are my body's reaction to knowing I'm going to stand up to my dad in a way I never have. Not simply giving him my opinion on how to achieve an end result we both agree on. Today will be the first time I've seen him since making the decision that I'm standing behind Colton and me. I want us.

Maybe for the first time ever, Dad and I aren't aligned on something that really matters.

Intermittently, Colton glances up to where I'm easy to spot in the family and friends' area because I'm a relatively lone wolf. Megan is coming but hasn't arrived yet. She's convinced me to head out after the game to either dance away our sorrows or dance in celebration and, honestly, I'm not sure if she means in respect of the game result, or my inevitable conversation with my dad.

On account of the game being away and Nelson still being so young, Annie hasn't travelled.

I notice Sonny glance up to our seats, as if he's ready to come back to sit, then his focus shifts elsewhere and he thinks better of it. Which tells me who he saw.

Sure enough, within seconds, my dad is making his way along the row to me, almost twinning my outfit in dark jeans and a Bears zip-up. If our guys are still playing at this stage of the season, it calls for merch over work attire.

'Hey,' I say when he nears me. We don't hug or even touch like we usually would if it were just the two of us at a game together.

It's already fractious and I haven't even begun to state my case.

'Hi,' he says.

Stubborn meets stubborn. *Like father, like daughter*, Mom would say.

Maybe that's why he's visibly taken aback when I blurt, 'I'm sorry.'

In fact, he looks as dumfounded as he's ever looked, still as a statue if it weren't for his rapidly blinking eyes.

'I should have told you the truth about Colton and me as soon as there was anything to tell.'

His shoulders seem to drop as his chest deflates. 'You should have. More to the point, you never should have—'

'I tried, Dad. Believe me. I tried to not feel anything for him. I tried to walk away. But I couldn't.'

'At Christmas—'

'At Christmas, when you asked me, I should have been honest. I was in denial, to some extent. I thought that I could leave it, walk away. Get out of Texas and get Colton out of my head, but the thing is, Dad, I haven't felt the way I do for Colton about anyone, ever.'

He clears his throat. This clearly isn't what he was expecting or the kind of conversation he wants to be having with his daughter, but here we are.

He brings a hand to his jaw and rubs it, the way he does when he's thinking through a legal or business conundrum. I haven't forced him to consider personal drama conundrums with me, but I guess this one is a hybrid of the two. I'd bet he's thinking being Patrick's boss is a lot easier than being mine right now.

'You've put me in a spot here, Kansas.'

I nod. 'I know, and for that, I apologize, but I can't and won't apologize for wanting to be with Colton. I won't call us a mistake.' I hold out my arms. 'I've made my decision, and I hope that doesn't mean I can't work for you at the agency anymore. That's what I've wanted for a long time, you and I working together, you showing me the ropes.'

He finally meets my focus, his eyes narrowed on me. 'If this thing between you and Quinn ends badly—'

'Dad, you've met him, right? You know what it takes to get to his position. He's one of the most determined men I've ever met. And you've told me enough times how annoyingly headstrong I am—'

'You take after your mother.'

I give a short laugh and he very nearly breaks a smile, easing the tension between us.

'We both want this and if we can't make it work, it won't be because we didn't give it our all. I honestly can't imagine a life without Colton in it in some way.'

He turns to the field and we both see Colton glance up before catching a ball that's tossed to him.

'Your mom keeps reminding me that sometimes, people who aren't meant to be together fall in love.'

'Like you and she did?'

Even on his profile, I see his lips fight a smirk.

'I was excited to have you come to work at the agency, Kansas. Maybe I didn't show it but I was hoping you'd come to the agency over all those offers you got from law firms.'

'You were? I felt like I forced you into employing me.'

'Well, I didn't want to put pressure on you. I wanted you to have choices and explore your options, but I've always known you were the smart one of your siblings.'

I scoff. 'Come on, Dad, that's not exactly a mark of achievement.'

We chuckle. Actually, my brothers are smart. They're just idiots, too.

'I want you to stay on at the agency,' he says, glancing my way. 'Working for Colton, too, if that's what you two decide is right.'

I can't hide my smile.

'But promise me one thing, kiddo. If things don't work out for you two, you'll stay professional. Don't put me in a conflict situation, because Colton says he'll choose you over the agency, but I'll always choose you, Kansas. You'll always be my number one. You have been since the moment you were born.'

Now it's my turn to be surprised, as I fight against a big-ass lump in my throat and the sensation of needles pricking the backs of my eyes.

Professional or not, I step into his chest and delight in the feel of his arms around me.

'I love you, Dad.'

'I love you, too, kiddo. And I hope things do work out between you and Quinn. Anyone who's willing to stand behind my girl like that is all right in my book.'

I stand back from his hold and plant a kiss on his cheek, then rub my lip color from his face with the cuff of my top.

'I'm also sorry about the way Sean attempted to fix things. He was more focused on keeping the lucrative thread of Megan and Colton alive than looking out for his client. He shouldn't have used information I shared with him in confidence and I shouldn't have trusted him with those details in the first place.'

'Thank you for saying that. I appreciate it and I know Colton does, too. He's also sorry about the way he and I came out.'

He nods. 'And I suppose you still want to talk about signing Richie Davenport as your client when Colton inevitably gets his extension deal?'

'Naturally.'

He shakes his head. 'You did good work down here.' He gestures with his head to the field. 'Go Bears.'

Smiling, I copy him. 'Go Bears. Oh, and Dad? I made a promise to Colton's mom, by way of apology. So, if the Bears win today, I could use your help next game.'

Brow furrowed, he nods. Then we proceed to do what we're good at – watching our guys win as if it's the last game of their lives. We spend the next few hours jumping up and down, cheering and hugging, sharing a drink or two with Sonny, as the Bears put on one of their best performances of the season.

They crush the opposition 10–34 and I'm still dancing to the full-time music when Dad leans into my ear and shouts over the raucous crowd, 'Let's hope the Ravens beat the Archers later, otherwise Colton will be facing Auston Rogers in the divisional finals.'

* * *

Naturally, the post-game conference puts Colton in the hot seat, lights and cameras all trained on him, as questions come thick and fast. Not entirely unexpectedly, the press doesn't want to discuss the two incredible touch-downs he scored, the plays he nailed, or the yards he gained to help win the game. They all want to talk about Caroline, Megan, and mostly, Annie and Auston and how Colton will feel now it's been confirmed that he'll be facing his old friend in the divisional play-offs next week.

Dad and I are dressed in our workwear today, me tucked away as best I can be because whispers in the room have already confirmed that the press in attendance know who I am – the girl from the training ground video. The woman Colton kissed. The woman who everyone thought – before Megan's cunning Live – had been a co-conspirator in Colton cheating on Megan. Now, the person he's dating.

I want to tell them all to stop hounding him. I want to wade in and protect him. At one point, I must make a move for the table where Colton is standing, alone, in front of a microphone, because Dad places a hand on my arm to stop me.

'He'll be hating this,' I whisper.

'He's a pro. He'll handle it.'

So, when Colton looks around the space and finds me, I mouth to him, *You've got this.*

He takes his Bears cap from his head and runs his fingers back through his hair – sexy as hell, even if he is uncomfortable.

'Look, I get that you guys want to know about my personal life and I'm coming to understand that's part of the game.' I exhale as he speaks with confidence. He *does* have this. 'Maybe if I'd been open, the news would be more accurate. I appreciate your well wishes for my family and so far as next week goes, it's another game the Bears want to win. My focus is on that. And my preference is still to talk about the game we all love.'

The next question comes. 'Colton, great game today. Possibly your best in a Bears jersey. Can you talk us through that back pass from Tommy? Was that something you've worked out on the training field?'

Colton smirks. 'Now that's how to get a man onside. Open your questions by blowing smoke up his ass.'

The room laughs, lapping up this open, confident, self-assured man that I am unequivocally smitten with.

45

JANUARY

Colton
The Best Game of My Life

It's a week that feels overshadowed by media speculation about Auston and me coming face to face again. Now they know the reason why I can't stand to be on the same planet as the guy, let alone the same field, it's as if the fact the Bears and the Archers are facing off in the divisional play-offs doesn't even matter.

The coaches check in with me daily. My teammates are surprisingly empathetic, in their own grunting, chest-beating, back-thumping sort of way. Sas does exactly what I asked her to do the second I knew we'd be playing St Louis this weekend – she distracts me like only she can. I get lost in her, in us, whether we're talking over dinner, watching Archers plays on repeat on the sofa – I love how much she gets the game – or whether she's taking me to places I didn't know it was possible to go when night falls.

'I'm good,' I tell Pace on Friday, our last full day of training before the game. 'Annie and Nelson are great. That's what matters. Auston's a fucking idiot and I'm glad he's not in their lives. They're better off.'

We fall into walking lunges as we stretch with the rest of the squad.

'Does Annie think so?' he asks me.

'Depends if you're asking about her life or Nelson's.' We switch legs. 'Honestly, I think it depends what time of day you ask her and whether she managed to get any sleep that night.'

'Man, her hormones must feel like a spin cycle right now,' he tells me, which is surprisingly perceptive. So unexpected, it makes me raise one eyebrow at him.

'What? You don't think I have any semblance of emotional intelligence? I've been on this planet more than thirty years. More to the point, I've lived with Sas for most of this season and that girl is a woman's woman.'

That makes me smile. I love how supportive Sas is of other women, especially my mama and sister, even Megan. Who am I kidding? If Sas likes someone, she'll move heaven and earth for them regardless of their gender. I adore that about her.

* * *

When game day comes, I'm zoned in. The way I've prepared, the way the team has prepared, and our blinkered focus on getting the job done today is the same as always.

I'm sitting in the changing room in my own locker stall, music sounding into my ears as I visualize the plays we've been running in practice all week, anticipating where the Archers' defense will be in relation to me each time.

I've blocked out the stuff with Auston, almost to non-existence. He's not worth it. I know that now. No self-respecting man is doing what he has done and continues to do to Annie. But Annie's good, Nelson's incredible, so screw Auston.

There is one thing about this game that keeps creeping into my thoughts, though, no matter how hard I'm trying to compartmentalize, and that's the people who won't be here today.

Annie will be home with Nelson. My mama hasn't made it to a game all season. She probably never will again. I've accepted it and I have to push it aside for now. She'll watch the game from home, this time.

I'm kitted up and ready to get out there. Coach Roy will give us his final rallying speech soon, not that any of us need it; we're all pumped. My head is rocking to the tunes in my ears as I wring my hands together, warming them up for the show.

Coach walks up to me, stealing my attention from my hands.

'Quinn.' I see his mouth move, so I take out my earbuds. 'I'm breaking with protocol today. You've got a visitor.'

I know my expression shows my confusion. *Sas?* Has she pulled her goddaughter rank on him again and somehow talked him into seeing me? If so, I hope she's going to give me one of her *talks*. Because, hell, if she wants to offer me sex in return for bringing my A game today, I'm here for it.

I follow Coach's focus to the dressing room door and sure enough, Sas steps inside, making my lips curve up. She wraps everyone around her little fing—

But when she opens the door wider and moves aside, the next person I see takes the air right out of my lungs.

I'm incapable of even forming the word... *Mama? She brought my mama?*

Sas clears the way and my dad steps into the room, with Mama's arm wrapped across his.

I'm off my ass and in front of her so fast it's as if I slid through the air.

'I couldn't miss your big game,' Mama tells me, letting go of Dad to reach her arms around my neck.

I bend into her hold and it takes everything I've got not to cry in front of my entire team and coaching staff, because I never thought she would see me play again, ever.

I hold her probably too tightly, unable to tell her how much this moment means to me, trying to tell Sas and my dad in a look that I will be eternally grateful to them both for making this happen.

Not until right now have I realized that I've felt as if my mama was snatched away from me by illness. We never got to *choose* to stop doing things, on our terms. She disappeared from my games overnight, and this... might go some way toward making that right for us both.

When Sas's eyes fill with unshed tears, I look away from her, thinking I'll find the stoicism I need in my dad, but he rubs the pad of his thumb across his wet cheek and all I can do is hold my mama tighter still. As if I'm a boy who needs the safety blanket of the woman who raised him.

'I love you,' I manage to whisper in her ear.

'I love you too, son.' She leans back and holds my cheek in her palms. 'Now go stick it to those Archers.' She looks beyond me and into the dressing room. 'That goes for all y'all. Give 'em hell.'

A chorus of, 'Yes, ma'am's and, 'Sure thing, Mrs. Quinn's and, 'You got it, Mama' sounds around us, lightening the moment.

* * *

Knowing my mama and Sas are sitting in the stands puts extra fire in my belly. The Bears get an early interception and a pick six that immediately throws the trajectory of the game in our favor.

As the defense leave the field, Trent Daniels, of all people, who started the season hard on my case, thumps me on the back and tells me, 'That one's for your sister, man.'

He leaves me grinning as I strap on my gloves and run onto the field with the offensive line. Daniels just made Auston Rogers look like a rookie and whether he did it in my sister's honor or he's just pleased he happened to stick up the proverbial bird to Rogers on her behalf, I'm grateful.

By the end of the first quarter, once Rogers has been sacked twice, brutally, I know for fact that my guys on defense have got my back. Not just the Bears but *my* back. That's something I wouldn't have bet a dollar on at the start of the season and even as I focus on the second quarter, I'm also able to comprehend that Sas is the reason the guys are on my side.

I was right to an extent; if I play well, I earn respect, but she's the one who taught me that I have to be open with the guys if I want to have a solid bond on and off the field.

Sas is the reason Auston's getting what he deserves today.

By the time we head in for half-time, we're up by ten. The Archers are giving us a tough match, but the momentum is with the Bears. I'm having the game of my life and while I'm trying to stay focused, I'm also fucking delighted that my mama is seeing this version of me. I am what I am because she made me.

Coach still gives us a hard time in the dressing room but ends his rant with his version of asking for more of the same.

And that's what we give him. We start the half with possession and fly through our first two downs.

Until Tommy calls our next play, but the Archers' defense has the read on him. They close him down, forcing him to move with the ball, and he's walloped from his blindside. It's a hard hit and I know it's bad before Tommy even hits the deck.

Our running back is first to him and immediately signals to the medical team. By the time I get there, Tommy is still face down on the ground, limbs unmoving.

He's talking, which is something, but he's in pain, and the medics are speaking in hushed tones about stretchers, Tommy's back and his neck.

All we can hope at this stage is that it's precautionary, but when he's stretchered off the field, I know Tommy will be out for some time.

His injury immediately changes the course of the game. Our rookie quarterback replaces Tommy and though the ball has been sticking to me and the other guys on offense like we're Spidey, now our game is falling apart.

We give up possession and at the end of the third quarter, the Archers are back in the game. We ask about Tommy over drinks but there's no word yet – or we're deliberately being kept in the dark.

So, while we never give up the fight, the fourth quarter is dominated by the Archers.

It's how the game goes sometimes.

We give it everything but when the final second counts down on the game clock, the Archers are up by one point. The win is theirs. It's their family and friends who rush the field.

I console our guys, as they do me, but once I've spoken to my teammates, I locate my family and my girlfriend in the stands.

Helmet tucked under my arm, I run the width of the gridiron and jump the sideboards, climbing the stands as fast as my lagging legs allow.

Today didn't end with the result we were hoping for, but it's been the best game of my life.

I find my mama and wrap my big sweaty body around her. This time, surrounded by people I love, I let my tears fall. I cry into her shoulder because she's here, and because at some point, she won't be. There'll never be enough time, but I have this time with her, right now.

I don't know how long I stand in my mama's arms but when we eventually let go, I find the other woman in my life that I am fiercely in love with.

Reaching out to her face, I immediately pull her to me and press my mouth to hers, kissing her as if no one else can see us, trying to convey how grateful I am for what she's done for me. Today. All of it.

And when I'm finally ready to peel our lips apart, I drop my forehead to hers and tell her what I've known for a long time. 'No matter what that score-board says, I won tonight, Sas. I love you, city girl. I love you so fucking much.'

She doesn't need to say it back, it won't change how I feel, but when she closes her eyes, she shakes her head and tells me, 'I love you too, Colton, and I'm so proud of you.' She takes hold of my shoulder pads and rocks me gently. 'For tonight, and how you've handled yourself all week, and for the way you've bounced back from everything all season. You're a cut above average, cowboy.'

I feel like one heart isn't enough. I need a back-up and a spare to cope with how much I feel for her.

This season started out with us aiming for a more lucrative extension on my contract. Now, all I want is to play ball with great teammates and all my favorite people around me. Hell, I'll play for free if I have to.

46

APRIL

Sas

Spring Dance at Sunshine Ranch

Waking up to Colton almost every day when we've been together such a short amount of time should feel like a lot, right? But stirring in his arms, whether we're in his apartment or here at the ranch, is the most natural thing in the world to me. It's the days I wake in New York that seem out of kilter now.

Humming with contentment, I curl tighter against him and kiss his chest. We still have logistics to work through, but I love it here, with him, with Annie and Nelson, Caroline and Sonny. I'm even starting to be less fearful around those unfathomably large horses.

His arm tightens around me and his lips press to my hair, his eyes still closed. He's the most beautiful man I've ever met, inside and out.

Naturally, he got his contract extension, with an extra 15 percent on his first offer – helped in part by him being offered big from New York. I would never have let him go but I appreciated his show of commitment. I didn't and don't have to change my life for him; he's made that clear. The fact is, I want to.

Honestly, Colton was happy about the new deal and we celebrated it hard with Dad and Sonny in tow, but all he wanted was to sign for the Bears. He genuinely doesn't care about the extra money, except that he'll give even more to the ranch and other charities. The money was never the driver for him. I understand that now, and if Dad and I had listened to him a year ago, maybe we wouldn't have had so much strife to contend with.

But as Colton likes to remind me, 'Everything happens for a reason.'

And now that I have the day-to-day conduct of our agency's brand-new client – tenth overall draft pick for Louisiana, Richie Davenport from San Antonio college – I have even more reason to spend time in the south with my boyfriend.

I've completely forgiven myself for falling for him these days. When the universe created this man, I'd already lost the battle of ethics.

'Morning,' he mumbles. That southern twang warms me more than the sun beaming through the bedroom windows.

'Big day today,' I tell him. 'Are you ready?'

He takes his arms behind his head, finally opening his eyes to mine as I prop myself up on his chest.

'It's going to be the biggest and best spring dance at Sunshine Ranch yet. That's a lot down to you helping to organize everything and getting the guys to help out. It's your big day too, reluctant cowgirl.'

I chuckle every time he calls me that. I'm not sure I am reluctant anymore. And I still like when we dress up and head into the city for dinner and drinks. But being out in the country with the endless views, the tranquility of it, the smell of grape soda in the air, even the relentless sound of those freakin' crickets, it's become my favorite place to be.

I run a lazy finger across his chest, tracing the arc of his pec. 'You know, we still have some time before we need to—'

He flips me like I'm a featherweight, my back to the mattress as he comes to hover above me. 'You don't have to ask me twice.'

He captures my laughter with a kiss. Close will never be close enough to this cowboy.

* * *

Colton has Nelson strapped to him in a carrier, the not so little baby napping against his uncle while Annie and I were getting ready and helping Caroline into a dress for the occasion.

Some of the Bears are already here and sipping on homemade lemonade under one of the gazebos tents they helped erect yesterday. They make a fuss of us girls when we come outside and I love the glow that spreads across Annie's cheeks under the attention. She deserves the confidence boost.

Colton is the first to tell Caroline how pretty she looks but Pace and Max, even Daniels, are next in line to fuss Mama Quinn.

I slip under Colton's arm and look around the ranch, decorated with bright colors and flowers. Inflatables and fairground games punctuate the animals and areas for food and drink. There are fire pits to be lit in the evening and haybale seating around them.

He could have spent money on having a team of professionals come in and take over the party planning, but he wanted to do this for his mom. Earlier in the week, I wasn't sure we'd ever get to this point but with the help of his teammates, Colton pulled it off. The beam that's been fixed to Caroline's face all week has made every minute of effort worthwhile.

The families who are regulars to Sunshine Ranch begin to arrive around midday. The grills start smoking. My own family arrive among the bedlam – Mom, Dad, Jax and even TJ. They've come to show their support for a great cause and, I think, Colton.

It doesn't take a genius to work out that I intend for Colton to be in their lives for a long time, long after his days of playing have been and gone.

More Bears turn up, plus the coaching staff and Megan, which delights the kids and their families, who relish the picture opportunities with the stars and their heroes.

The whole day is filled with warmth and happiness, great food and later, some of Sonny's awful home-brew beer.

More than once, I step back to take it all in. All these people coming together to give Caroline the final spring dance she wanted.

In the early evening, fairy lights around the trees, the fence posts, the porch and the barn are turned on. The fires are lit, despite the warm spring air. Annie puts Nelson down for the night inside and the younger kids leave.

A band plays – country tunes, obviously – on a stage set up in the field, and Colton and Annie teach my mom, Jax and me how to line dance.

When the tempo drops, Sonny breaks that stoic guard he always has up and asks Caroline to dance. For a moment, I don't think there's a person on the ranch who doesn't have a lump in their throat watching the couple in love after all their years together move to the slow rhythm of the music.

My dad leads my mom onto the makeshift dance floor and Pace asks Annie if he can take her for a twirl – not without a word of caution in his ear from her big brother first.

Then that very same big brother finds me sitting on a haybale with TJ near the band. That half-smile that blows my mind is teasing his lips when he reaches out his hand for me to take. I come to stand in front of him and he pulls his other arm from behind his back.

I take from him the new season Bears jersey and unfold it, grinning when I see his number – eighty-two.

'You're giving me my first number eighty-two jersey to wear?'

His smile disappears. 'No, Sas. I'm asking you to make mine the last number you ever wear.'

Heart pounding in my chest, I pull on his jersey.

This is it. This is what it feels like.

Eyes fixed on his, I tell him, 'Forever.'

Then he seals our eternity with a kiss.

* * *

MORE FROM LAURA CARTER

The story continues... Will Annie get her happy ever after? You can order the next book in this series now here:

https://mybook.to/LauraCarterNewBackAd

ACKNOWLEDGMENTS

Wow, I can't believe I'm writing the acknowledgments to what will be my fourteenth published novel. How did this happen? I'll tell you... with an army of incredible people.

First, to my parents – as Colton says, I am who I am because you made me.

To my gorgeous babies – it's been a busy old year but you are a constant reminder of what's important. Thank you for making me laugh every day. I love you unconditionally.

To Sam – there's no one else I'd rather drink beer with at sports games, or watch sports documentaries with on the sofa, whilst arguing over who gets the last square of dark chocolate (me, always me). You're my favourite team player. Love you, babe.

Alan and Diane – thank you for being the cavalry and changing plans at the drop of a hat to help us out. I'd never be able to run two jobs and a household without calling on you for help when the wicket gets sticky. I'm extremely grateful for you both.

Monte, John and your Jags-loving families – there would be no San Antonio Bears or St Louis Archers if you hadn't helped me out with the American football geography! Until the next Jags game!

Louise – where would I be without your football for dummies support?! I hope I haven't let you down.

Authors who don't know me but whose sports romances I love – thank you for writing books full of romance and adrenalin that I can get completely immersed in.

To the authors who do know me and support me. You know who you are and without your ears for venting, your jokes for laughing through the slogging days, and the arms you wrap around me when I need them, I'd never finish a book. I'm always here when you need me in return.

Emily, my incredible editor at Boldwood Books, I am so lucky to work with you. Thank you for loving Colton and Sas (and the world I decided I couldn't leave alone) as much as I do. And to Niamh, marketeer with a vision, the entire editorial, sales and production teams at Boldwood, thank you for making this sports romance pivot a reality.

Rachel Lawston – what can I say? I am in love with your illustrations and this one is no exception. Your talent knows no bounds. Thank you!

Tanera and Laura. I feel like a broken record but I'm going to write it again: you truly are the dream team and there's not a day I don't feel safe in your capable hands. That extends to the Darby crew, too! You're all amazing.

Friends and family who cheer me on from the sidelines, I'm super grateful for you. An extra special mention to Little Jen, who has all her own stuff going on and *still* comes to every book signing with me, *buys* every one of my books, and gives me a safe place for venting voice notes whenever I need it. You know I will *always* have your back, too.

Readers – you thought I'd forgotten you, didn't you? NEVER. I have ideas but I also have real life to contend with and sometimes I have to ask myself if I am strong enough to keep up the juggle. Then one of you will send me the exact message I need at the exact right time. You keep me going. I would write all the words regardless, but it is such a wonderful feeling to know that you will read and fall in love with them. Thank you for your time, your money and your support.

Until the next one... Pace and Annie's story... Love, Laura x

ABOUT THE AUTHOR

Laura Carter is a top 10 Amazon and internationally bestselling author of romance and romantic women's fiction. She lives with her family in Jersey, Channel Islands.

Sign up to Laura Carter's mailing list for news, competitions and updates on future books.

Visit Laura's website: www.lauracarterauthor.com

Follow Laura on social media:

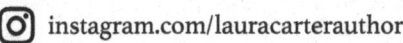 instagram.com/lauracarterauthor
 tiktok.com/@laura.carter.author
facebook.com/lauracarterauthor

ALSO BY LAURA CARTER

Brits in Manhattan

The Law of Attraction

Two to Tango

Friends with Benefits

Always the Bridesmaid

Billionaires of London

Ruthless Love

Twisted Love

Tainted Love

Standalone Novels

Fake It 'til You Make It

Stuck in Paradise With You

Table for Three

Catch a Falling Star

In This Together

The Wild Card Series

A Rookie Mistake

Boldwood
EVER AFTER
xoxo

JOIN BOLDWOOD'S
**ROMANCE
COMMUNITY**
FOR SWEET AND
SPICY BOOK RECS
WITH ALL YOUR
FAVOURITE
TROPES!

SIGN UP TO OUR
NEWSLETTER

HTTPS://BIT.LY/BOLDWOODEVERAFTER

Boldwood

Boldwood Books is an award-winning fiction publishing company seeking out the best stories from around the world.

Find out more at www.boldwoodbooks.com

Join our reader community for brilliant books, competitions and offers!

Follow us
@BoldwoodBooks
@TheBoldBookClub

Sign up to our weekly deals newsletter

https://bit.ly/BoldwoodBNewsletter

www.ingramcontent.com/pod-product-compliance
Lightning Source LLC
Chambersburg PA
CBHW011759010726
47497CB00012B/3202